FINDING
the light

For all Content Inquiries, please visit my website:

Dedication

Find your people, build your fortress,

and if you find yourself at rock bottom,

let them help you up.

PROLOGUE

"Go, Travis!" Jeremy screams from the batter's box as I round third base and scramble for home.

I just hit my first home run ever and my heart feels like it's going to jump out of my chest. I slide into home base, but not because the ball is being thrown back, I slide because that's how baseball players do it on TV.

The dirt drags along my uniform and my elbow scrapes painfully through the gravel, but I don't care. I hit a home run! I stand up and jump up and down as everyone in the stands clap and cheer me on.

"Father!" I scream toward the seat he was sitting in when the game started. "Father!" Shielding my eyes from the sun, I turn toward the stands.

The spot he was sitting in earlier is now empty, and pity crosses Kevin's mom's eyes from the seat beside it. I don't know what I was expecting. It's been an entire year now, and he rarely stays for the full game.

"Don't worry, sport." Coach Halbert pats my back. "I recorded it. We'll show him later on."

"*Okay, Coach.*" *I nod and kick at the dirt with my shoe.*

"*I'm proud of you.*" *He rubs my back. "Your time was coming for a home run." It's nice to have someone pay attention to me, even if it isn't my father.*

Coach guides me over to the fence to line up with the rest of my team as Jeremy heads up to bat next. Coach records him too as he runs toward first base. He records all of us all the time. Even in the dressing room. He says it's good to review later and see what we can do differently and how we can become our very best. He's a great coach, and our team has gotten much better from his teachings.

We end up losing the game… again, but Coach says he's really proud of how far we've come and he's especially proud of me and my very first home run. I can't help but smile under the praise of an adult because that doesn't happen often.

My father is always busy with his business and rarely has time for me. At home, we have strict rules on how young boys conduct themselves, especially a future CEO like me. The rules are hard to follow and I always seem to break them, which makes my father very angry. So really, he's busy and angry all the time.

My mother is sad. She cries a lot. Once, I asked her why she cries all the time and she told me it's because she doesn't belong here with me and Father. She promised me, one day when I'm bigger, she'll leave and be gone forever. At first, that really scared me because I'd be alone with Father, but when I thought about it some more, I realized I'm always alone anyway, so it wouldn't make a difference.

"*My dad says I have to leave the team,*" *Kai tells us as he quickly changes back into his clothes.*

"*You didn't even shower yet,*" *I say to him, my nose crinkling in disgust. We're stinky after games and Coach says we always have to shower. No exceptions.*

"*My dad says I'm not allowed to shower here anymore, and this is my last game." His chin wobbles.*

"Why?"

"Because I told him Coach records us in the showers."

"So?" I scoff. "He does it so we can get better."

"I told him that!" Kai sighs. "But he got really angry."

"Your dad is acting like a weirdo," I tell him. It makes me sad he's leaving the team because Kevin and Kai are my best friends.

"I know." He rolls his eyes. "I'll see you at school tomorrow." He picks up his equipment bag and walks out of the changing room.

I hope we can still be best friends because Kai's mom makes the best spaghetti and meatballs I have ever had. That's why I always go to their house for dinner on Thursdays. Then Kevin's mom is just the best cook ever. She makes everything good, and I try to go to their house as much as I can.

I used to have another best friend named Vincent. He would bring the best lunches to school and share with me because my Nanny Sonja packs me veggies and fruit. Vincent used to have pudding and Twinkies. I really miss him since he moved away, but I still have Adri. She says we're like brother and sister since we don't have any. She's a girl though. I can't call her a sister because one day she's going to be my wife. I already called it, so none of the other boys at school can pick her.

"Let's get in the shower, sport," Coach says to me while his phone is recording us.

"Okay." I take off my uniform and grab my towel.

"I'll take you for some pizza after." He grins as his fat cheeks puff out and turn redder. "To celebrate that home run."

"Yay!" I always like pizza with Coach because we ride in his big truck

Chapter One

Coach Halbert's house burned down two days ago and the fire department says he was inside. Cause of fire? Falling asleep with a lit cigarette. Actual cause of fire? My best friend and pseudo-sister Ember. I don't have any confirmation of that though because she and my brother, Vin, are in Spain right now. They're chasing after a corrupt government official named Jennifer Talia and trying to bust her illegal adoption ring. It just screams an Ember hit.

I received a text from Ember two nights ago, short and to the point.

We need to talk.

That talk won't be happening soon because she'll be gone for the next two weeks and I'm here babysitting her twin brother, Emmett. Speaking of, said brother comes into the kitchen wearing only a pair of boxers, which is hanging dangerously low. A centimeter more and I'd be getting a cockful… eyeful. *Shit.*

"What's the plan?" he croaks out, still half asleep as he rubs while standing in front of me with his dick nearly out.

"Pardon?" I blink at him. It's too early for this shit.

"An explanation of how I came to be here in Whitsborough?" He lifts an eyebrow at me, his eyes finally fully opening. "What were you thinking?"

"Nothing." I turn away and sip on the coffee I poured for myself. "I thought we would stick to the story that Ember suggested. You came here looking for your birth mother and found Ember instead. You ended up staying, and that's it." I gulp down the hot liquid, letting it scorch a path from my mouth to my stomach, hoping it clears my head of any lingering images.

"Will it be enough?" I turn to find him pouring a coffee for himself, his biceps bunching and his abs flexing. "I want to spend a day outside of this house."

"Who cares?" I shrug. "Tell people to fuck off if they ask for more." My eyes slip over his face as he concentrates on the coffee pouring into the cup, then down over his body as he turns to face me.

"Oh, yeah?" He grins, catching my perusal. "What if your mother asks for more?" He brings the mug to his lips to take a tentative sip, his eyes dancing with mirth. Eyes identical to Ember's.

"Especially tell her to fuck off." I turn my back and head out of the kitchen, then back up to the spare bedroom Ember put me in. Right across from her annoying twin.

Today I need to go over to my house and check on my mother. She might've killed and buried Sonja in the three days I've been gone. Plus, I'm running out of clothing here since I only packed a backpack full. I'm still not completely sold on living here and living off of someone else's charity. A place with peace and quiet and a fridge full of beer is what I want.

I open my laptop and check my emails. Lately, the board of directors at my father's company has been up my ass. They want me to come to intern straight after high school, skip university, and fill my father's shoes as a ruthless piece of shit. It's not something I particularly want to do, or what I'm capable of doing. He was never a cheerful man, and I can only imagine his business reflects that.

My father's right-hand in the company, Gerald, has been pretty good at keeping me up to date with the inner workings of the board, their secret meetings, and especially all their plans to overthrow me.

The deep thumping bass of a hip-hop song makes its way across the hall and into my room. For the last three days, he's played his music all hours of the day and at varying degrees of loudness. Standing from the desk, I pull off my shirt, then untie my sweatpants. I'm going to take a shower and head out of this house for a bit.

"Uh… sorry… I knocked." Glancing up, I find Emmett standing in my open doorway, watching me as I undress.

"Guess I didn't hear it over the music," I retort, turning away from him and grabbing the last clean outfit off my bed.

"Oh… if it bothers you, I can turn it down." The concern in his voice has me pausing, not sure how I should react to it. No one is ever concerned about how I'm feeling.

"It doesn't matter. I'm heading out for a few hours. Play it as much as you like." I walk to my bathroom and peer over my shoulder at him. "Did you need something?"

"Oh! Yeah…" He scrubs his hand down over his face. "I wanted to know if you heard from your brother. Ember didn't check in with me last night."

"No, I haven't. I will call him after I shower." I head into the bathroom and stare back at him as I shut the door. He's still standing in my doorway, watching me with a scowl.

I step out of my room and Emmett is leaning against the wall by my door. He's dressed in a fitted white tee and a pair of baggy skater jeans with a chain hanging from the back left pocket.

He tugs his baseball hat low on his face, his features becoming bashful. "Can I come with you?"

"No." I walk toward the stairs, planning to ignore him until I'm out of the house. Ember said to watch him, but surely she didn't mean every hour of the day.

"It's just to your house, and you told me I could tell your mother to fuck off." I peer over my shoulder to find him grinning at me. His face is a duplicate of Ember's, especially that grin. It's so fucking freaky.

"It's not a good idea—"

"People will learn about me soon enough," he cuts me off with a pleading voice. "I start school next week."

He has a point and I hate the fact that they left me to be the one to deal with all of this. "Fine, let's go." I grab my car keys from the table beside the front door. "Stay in the car and don't get out the entire time we're there."

He eagerly nods and follows me outside to the driveway. A shot of guilt hits me in the stomach when I realize he's been trapped in the house for days. Even dogs need to be walked once a day at least.

As soon as we step out, he takes an exaggerated intake of air and throws his arms out at his sides. "I'm free." I roll my eyes and unlock the car doors with a beep. "Oh shit! You have the newest model Civic?"

"Yeah." I slide into the driver's seat.

He gets into the passenger side and whistles. "This is fully loaded. Did you add on the extra-large display too?"

"Yeah."

"Do you say anything else besides yeah?" I can feel the heat of his stare on the side of my face as I start the car, but I keep my eyes forward as we leave Ember's house behind.

I shrug and roll my eyes. "Yeah."

"Okay…" He turns his head and peers out the window.

Hopefully he just stays quiet and lets me think for a bit. I hate that I'm bringing him to a house that might be upside down right now, but I had no other choice. I didn't want him to feel like a prisoner in that house any longer. Turning on the music, "Who's with me" by USS fills the car, and I'm surprised when Emmett sings along, bumping his head with the beat. I've only heard hip-hop coming from his room.

"You're looking at me." He turns and grins at me. "I like all music. Don't act so surprised."

"Do you really want to leave New York and move here? Isn't that an enormous change for you?" I ask him. He seems sincere about Ember, but I wouldn't put it past him to be using her. It's instinctual to protect my best friend.

"Yeah, an enormous change, but I want to be where Ember is." He shrugs his shoulders as if it's nothing, but I can hear it clear in his tone. He loves Ember. Guilt rushes through me for thinking he could be anything but genuine.

A twinge of jealousy stirs in my stomach, and I immediately try to dispel it. Vin and I haven't had the best relationship, but for the past two weeks, we've both been putting forth the effort. Someday, I hope to have a brother like Emmett.

"I made out with Ember on her first day at Precious Blood Academy." I smirk, deciding to ruffle his feathers for putting me in this babysitting situation. If I said that to Vin, I'd be shoved out of the car into oncoming traffic.

"Really?" His nose crinkles, then he turns his head to gaze out of the window. Not the reaction I was looking for.

"Yeah." I decide to goad him a little more. "She's hot."

"You think my sister is hot?" He swings his head back around to look at me, his lips slowly curving into a smile.

"Yeah, but don't tell Vin or anything. He's irrational when it comes to her," I warn him, not wanting to face Vin's wrath. He's not acting the way I had hoped at all.

"So, you think I'm hot then?" My hands jerk on the wheel, swerving the car as I turn my head to look at him.

"What?" I glance at him and then back to the road, my heart pounding against my ribs with his accurate assumption.

"Well, we're identical. If you think she's hot, then you must think I'm hot." Another point for Emmett in this dangerous game we're playing.

"I think you're annoying," I huff out.

"So, I'm hot and annoying. I'll take it," he says while chuckling.

Thank God we pull onto my street because I was about to throw his ass out of my car, E's twin or not. The gate to my driveway is open, which can only mean my mother has been walking the streets again. Acid swirls in my stomach, but I tamp it down. Vin and Ember were right. I'm supposed to be her responsibility, not the other way around.

"You live here?" Emmett's voice fills with wonder as my house comes into view.

"This was never a home," I grumble. "Just a place to sleep and eat."

"I understand that all too well," he replies quietly, his voice coated with sadness. "I have a home now with Ember and so do you."

He's right. I have a home with Vin and Ember, and they are more my family than my mother ever was. I don't say another word as I park the Civic in front of a gigantic pile of clothes. This time, it appears to be mine. Not surprising at all.

"Stay here. I'll be out in a minute." My heart rushes up into my throat as I stare at my front porch, worrying about the hell I'm about to walk in on.

"Sure." He shrugs as he scrolls through his phone.

Stepping out of my car, I walk up to the front door and find it wide open. I stop inside the foyer as footsteps rush toward me.

"Mister Travis?" Sonja says as she rounds the corner, her face full of shock.

"Yeah," I answer with an exhale.

"I go out to grab those clothes." She holds up a few garbage bags.

"It's fine, I'll do it. I came to pick up more stuff anyway." I take the bags from her. "How has she been?"

"Oh, everything is fine here, Mister Travis." She waves me off. "You don't worry. Stay with your friends."

"It's Travis, Sonja,"—I shake my head as my eyes scan the place—"and things don't seem so fine." I gesture toward my clothes in the driveway.

"It does not matter. She just get little angry. You are in a much better place and with your brother, yes?" Her eyes glisten as she gives me an elated smile. Sonja has always tried to talk to me about Vin.

"I am at his girlfriend's house, but yes, Vincent comes by often." I tuck the garbage bags under my arm and gaze up toward the second level.

"That all that matter, you make good with your brother and continue school." Sonja tries to steer me away from the stairs, but I shrug off her hand.

Starting for the stairs, I head up to the second floor to check out the state of my room. I can only imagine she's trashed it in a drunken stupor. It wouldn't be the first time and I'd bet every cent I own that it won't be the last.

"She sleeping. Maybe you be quick and leave before she gets up," Sonja calls after me. She's the only one who witnessed what I went through as a child in this loveless home.

My room is a fucking mess. She even found the strength to flip over my extra thick, king-sized mattress. I walk around the room and gather some clothes she didn't manage to throw over my balcony and the baseball gear she left untouched in my closet. My balcony has some clothes strewn about it and a few of my books as well. I love my literature and all the classics, so seeing them like this sends a shot of anger through me. Picking up the books, I pack them inside a bag, then head back downstairs.

I find Emmett and Sonja in the driveway, picking up my clothes and packing them into more garbage bags. Suddenly, I'm hit with shame as Emmett converses with Sonja. Now he knows just how fucked-up living here was as he helps pick up the clothes my mother threw everywhere in a drunken rage.

I walk up to them and quickly stuff the last few items into one of my bags, then start throwing them all into the backseat of my car. Turning back, I find them both watching me with similar expressions of pity.

"Let's go," I say to Emmett before turning back to Sonja. "Call me if you need anything or if she gets out of hand." She nods and pats my back.

"Who have you got with you? Isn't he just gorgeous?" Her rough rasp floats from the front door and my heart goes into overdrive. This is what I was trying to avoid. "Is he your boyfriend? Your father always said you were a little queer."

"Get inside the house," I fume at her as I round to the driver's side of my car, "and sleep it off."

"Don't bother ever coming back here. You're a fucking disgrace. Your father is dead, so there's nothing left here for you," she sneers. I flip her the finger and slide into the driver's seat. Emmett is still staring her down with a look of disgust. "What are you looking at?" She turns on him. "You want to stick up for your boyfriend?"

Emmett has his back to me so I can't see his reaction, but whatever he's doing freaks her out enough that she hurries back inside the house. Sonja stares at him wide-eyed also and quickly follows behind my deranged mother. Then he opens the passenger door and gets into the seat, fastening his seat belt. Without a single word, he turns on the radio, shutting out any possibility of a conversation, to my relief. I don't even want to touch on the subject of her calling me a queer.

Emmett helps bring my bags up to my room when we get

back to Ember's house, then heads off into his own without uttering a single word to me. I should be good with this, but I'm not. My mind races with all the things he could be thinking about me right now, and I begin to wonder if he feels uncomfortable being in the house with me. Especially after what my mother said. His music turns on, a sign I won't be seeing him for a while. I fall across my bed and let my exhaustion come over me. I just need a few hours of sleep and then I'll tackle my mess of a life.

Emmett

I am in a state of rage right now, like liquid lava running through my body and heating my insides. When Ember told me about her rage and how it feels, I didn't understand it because I had never been that angry. But today, when Travis' mother looked at him like he was a piece of shit under her very expensive shoe, I almost lost it. Actually, I lost it briefly because I withdrew a knife from my waist and swung it around my finger. I wanted her to believe I wouldn't hesitate to put it through her eye if she continued. I bet she recognized something close to insanity in my eyes before she ran inside her house.

On the way home, shame was pouring off Travis in waves and it only made my anger worse. My vision was slipping into different shades of red and my breathing became short and quick. That's why, as soon as we were home, I made a beeline for my room and turned my music up loud. I can't face him right now because I don't want to make this situation worse for him. His mother is a waste of air and deserves to rot next to his father.

The shame Travis is suffering with would only increase if I stayed in his presence any longer. He would have mistaken my disgust as aimed at him, when really, it's for his mother. He's struggling internally and I don't know how to help him. Travis seems at war with himself, and I can bet it's because of his worthless parents.

I've become an expert in having a worthless parent. I was raised by a man—of my father's choosing—who thought I was useless too. He tried to make me into a hardened soldier at the tender age of ten by sinking a knife into the eye socket of someone who worked for The Rampage. After that, I was petrified of knives and couldn't even take the sight of one before I would lose it and scream until I passed out. He hated how soft I was and would beat me every chance he got in the name of toughening me up. All on the orders of my father, who was less than impressed with me as his son.

It's fucking hilarious. His daughter was the tough one, and she got away, leaving him with me, the fearful son. It's also funny she was the one he would've wanted to groom, but she tortured and killed him without mercy in the end. The sight of his body afterward is something I'll never forget.

When I first met Travis, I thought he was a pretty boy who regarded himself better than everyone else. Now that we've been forced together in this house alone, I see he rarely smiles and has yet to laugh. A genuine laugh, not a chuckle under his breath. He seemed stuck up, but fuck, I was so wrong.

The people who were supposed to be raising Travis abused him instead, and it's something I should have noticed from the beginning because I endured the same.

Until Ember showed up. She made me whole again, and I let go of all the hurt I had buried inside. I finally have a family who cares about me for me and not something they can use. I love Carm, but he doesn't have time to be a brother, and even though he loves me, he also treats me as a chess piece inside the Eastside Rampage.

My phone pings with an alert from the camera on the front porch. Ember made me download the app and learn to use it before she left. Adrianna is standing on the porch with a casserole dish in her hand, looking around nervously as she shifts from foot to foot. Blinking out of my thoughts, I scan the room and find it's darker now. I must have been seething in here for hours.

Getting up out of bed, I turn my music off to listen for any movement. When I don't hear anything, I open my door and look across the hall. Travis' bedroom door is slightly open, so I cross the hallway and peek inside. He's starfished on his bed and appears to be in a deep sleep. Closing his door completely, I let him rest and make my way downstairs to the front door.

I open it up and come face-to-face with the most beautiful brown eyes I have ever seen. They're like pools of chocolate with swirls of honey. "Hey!" she chirps. "I brought you something to eat."

Her eyes dart back and forth between mine and she gets nervous the longer I say nothing, my grin only growing.

"How'd you get here?" I ask and glance beyond her to the driveway. Adrianna doesn't drive.

"Oh, my neighbor dropped me off on their way to the airport." Her cheeks redden with embarrassment, and I like the way it enhances her olive skin tone.

"What if we weren't home?" I raise a brow, teasing her a little more.

"Then I would've left this on your front porch and walked home. It's only a twenty-minute walk." She holds out the dish and I give her a warm smile, liking the tentative one she gives back a little too much. How many times has she had to walk? Is it something she does regularly?

"Come in." I shake off the thought and open the door wider. "Thanks for the food. You didn't have to."

"I know." She shrugs as she steps inside, removing her shoes. "I wanted to come by and check up on you guys anyway. You haven't killed him, right?"

I choke on my laughter. She doesn't think it's possible I can though. That's what's funny. "No, I haven't killed him."

I follow her into the kitchen and finally take in what she's wearing. Adrianna is the complete opposite of Ember. She's a girly girl through and through. She wears these frilly sundresses in different shades of pink and her dark red hair has streaks of pink in it to match.

Today, she's wearing a jean skirt and a tight black tank top with a pink cardigan on top. Her hair is piled on top of her head, and she's stuck some cute little pink flowers throughout. Her long, tanned legs are shimmering in the light and her face is fresh and dewy. Adrianna is easily the most beautiful girl I have ever seen. It makes me want to ignore the feelings she and Travis share so I can make her mine, but I would be heading for a world of hurt when it all crashes down around me.

"How is he?" Worry lines her features as she gazes around the kitchen. It's clear she loves Travis, and it makes me wonder what happened between them.

"He's sleeping right now, but I haven't really talked to him today." I open my mouth to ask her if she knows how much of a cunt his mother is, but then decide not to. It's not my place to speak about his troubles at home.

"Ember texted and asked me to come by." She wants me to believe that's the only reason she's here, but I would bet every zero in my bank account that she was just waiting for the right excuse.

"Well, thanks." I nod to the dish she placed on the counter. "Did you want me to drop you back home?"

"No, I feel like walking today." She holds out her hand. "Give me your phone so I can give you my number. You can text me if you guys need anything."

I do as she says and hand her my phone. "Or you can just drop by unannounced like this whenever you want to check in. Excuse-free, of course."

Her cheeks bloom red again as she punches her number into my phone. "Just call me if you need anything." She turns on her heel and shuffles back toward the front door.

Leaning against the doorway of the kitchen, my eyes stay trained on her retreating form. Her ass isn't overly big, but just right, and her thighs are strong with her calves flexing as she steps into her shoes. Yes, Adrianna is every man's wet dream, and I can't do anything about it.

She peeks back at me over her shoulder and catches me checking her out. She raises her brow, but I just grin and wink at her. The blush that takes over her cheeks is breathtaking. "See ya," she rasps and steps out the door, shutting it behind her with a soft click.

"Don't eat any of that," Travis says from the top of the stairs, his sudden appearance making me stiff with surprise.

"Okay, man, it's all yours." His voice snaps me out of my thoughts as I swallow down the retort threatening to roll off my tongue before I head up the stairs.

"Adri is a terrible cook." He grabs my arm to stop me from walking by him. "Everything she cooks or bakes ends up tasting like burned fish."

My eyes flick down to where his hand is gripping my forearm, then back up at his face. "Thanks for the heads-up," I mutter, and he quickly releases my arm as if it's on fire.

"I'll get rid of it before it stinks out the kitchen," he replies as he moves around me and down the stairs. When he hits the bottom, I'm still watching him when his eyes finally meet mine. "The funeral for Coach Halbert is tomorrow. I should go, otherwise it'll seem suspicious. I don't want anyone reopening his case. He was my little league and high school baseball coach."

"Cool." I shrug, still watching him.

Travis has a perfectly symmetrical face, the type of face agencies look for in the next top model and fashion ads. He always has bed head, but it's sexy, like perfectly tousled and falling in the right spots on his forehead. His green eyes are intense against his golden skin.

"Did you hear me?" He brings me out of my scrutinizing, his perfectly arched brows coming together in confusion.

"No," I grunt, grabbing the banister to lean over a bit.

"Do you want to come with me? I think it'll be the perfect moment for you to *come out*." He uses air quotes for the last bit with a smirk on his face.

"Would it be perfect at some old pedophile's funeral?" I quirk a brow, the entire situation sounding absurd. It's also on brand for this family.

"Yeah," he replies. "But don't say that at the funeral. Only a few people know about it. Also, most of the town will be present and we can kill so many fucking birds with one stone. Plus, I'll text Adri with the details so she can back us up." He grabs his phone out of his pocket, making me wonder why he didn't just come downstairs while she was here. He's definitely avoiding her.

"Got it." I back up toward my room as his eyes flick back up to my face. "I'll just go dress in my brightest attire."

He chuckles and shakes his head as he makes his way into the kitchen to dump out Adrianna's concoction. I like the sound of his laugh, even if it's only a chuckle. I'll just work a little harder to get a full laugh out of him.

We arrive at a small chapel to find the parking lot and surrounding streets filled with cars. So, the pedophile was loved by this town. That's fucking weird. Travis' gaze meets mine as he chuckles again.

"Did you seriously dress in a yellow and red tracksuit?" He reaches out and pinches the fabric of my pants at the thigh, rubbing the material between his fingers.

"Yeah." I swallow down the urge to lock him in this car so he can feel all of me. "It's the brightest suit I own."

"People will stare at you more now." He shakes his head with a grin. He's secretly enjoying it and probably wishes he'd done the same instead of wearing the stuffy suit he has on.

"Let them." I shrug and get out of the car. A few groups of people are hanging around on the front lawn of the church and there is a line forming to go inside. Travis comes around the front of the car and nods for me to follow him. He leads us over to a group of older women and one of them is looking bored and a little sad. She's African American with short hair dyed a bright red. She's shorter with a slight stature. When she spots us walking toward her, her eyes grow wide as her mouth falls open. She must know Ember.

"Travis." She keeps her eyes on me. "Who is this?"

"Hi." I reach my hand out to her. "I'm Emmett."

"Emmett?" she asks as she tentatively takes my hand.

"This is Ember's twin," Travis explains, and the surrounding ladies gasp. I glance at each of them with a smile.

"Rebecca had twins?" the woman still holding my hand breathes out. "How?"

"I was adopted as a baby." Pulling my hand back, I slip them into my pockets. "I was looking for my birth mother when my adoptive parents passed away. I followed my lead to Whitsborough and found Ember instead."

"This is Sharla, Vin's mother," Travis introduces her, and I immediately see the resemblance.

"Oh, wow." She holds her hands to her mouth. "Does Ember know?"

"Yes," Travis answers. "She found out shortly before her vacation. She asked him to stay here and for me to keep an eye on him until she gets back."

"You remind me so much of Rebecca." Her eyes water as she lowers her hand. "You're identical to Ember, but different. More like Rebecca."

"Ember says the same." The other ladies walk away, and I can only hope they're small-town busybodies who will spread the word quickly. Saves us the work.

"Why were you adopted but Ember wasn't?" Sharla becomes confused as her shock slowly fades and skepticism clouds her eyes.

"Not sure." I hold out my hands. "I came looking for answers and instead brought us both more questions."

"Well, you're certainly where you belong." She puts her hand to my cheek, her features softening. "With your twin and your mother's friends." My heart swells to hear her say that. Whitsborough is where I belong.

"Thank you." I smile at her and follow behind Travis into the church.

Travis stops and starts talking to a group of guys all wearing Precious Blood baseball caps. This must be some of his teammates. A few of them have the toughened exterior Travis carries and they look like this is the last place they want to be. When Ember told me about her latest kill, she filled me in on how he was another pedophile and how he used to be Travis' baseball coach. She didn't have to tell me he abused Travis. That was something I just suspected, and it's apparent he wasn't the only one. If I had to guess, quite a few of these guys were taken advantage of at a young age by the monster my sister exterminated.

Travis claps them each on the back before standing back and running his hands through his hair. "When did you guys get back from camp?"

"Yesterday," one guy replies. "Then we heard about the fire."

While they discuss baseball camp, my eyes skim the small church, then land on Adrianna, who's sitting beside Vin's mother. She's wearing a black dress and her hair is pulled back into a bun at the base of her neck. She's toying with a string of pearls at her throat and her expression is sad as she leans in to whisper something to Sharla. By her expression, which seems genuine to me, I would guess she doesn't know about the coach and Travis either.

"Who's this?" one guy asks as I drag my eyes from Adri to find him looking me over.

"Shit," Travis says with an exhale. "My bad. This is Emmett Torres. He's Ember's twin brother."

"Wow. Now I see it." Another one nods.

"Emmett, these are a few guys from my baseball team." He points at the tallest guy of the bunch. He's slightly lanky and has a shit-eating grin on his face. "This is James."

"Hey, man." He nods and I return the gesture.

"This is Kevin." He points out a tall, broad, blond guy. His eyes hold a mountain of pain and barely settle on me at all. "And this is Jeremy." The last one is shorter and has been staring at his feet the whole time.

"Nice to meet you guys," I say to them.

"Emmett is coming to Precious Blood this year," Travis tells them.

"That's cool." James perks up. "Do you play baseball?"

"Nah, man." I scratch at my chin. "I can play basketball if I have to choose a sport."

"Our basketball team sucks," Jeremy mutters, his eyes skating over the room.

We all head into the packed church, and they have cordoned the front few pews off for the Precious Blood Academy's baseball team.

"You can come sit with us," Travis offers, but I can't sit close to the burned piece of shit in that casket.

"Nah." I gaze over my shoulder to the back of the room, then give him a smile. "You go ahead. I'll just chill back here."

Travis nods and gives me a lingering look before he backs away to sit with his teammates. When Ember asked me to take care of Travis while she was gone, my first thought was *hell no.* I wanted nothing to do with the smug shithead and I would've stuck to that if I didn't witness how much he's hurting. Was everyone else blinded to the suit of self-loathing he wore?

So here I am, standing inside a tiny church and listening to a priest talk about this kiddie fucker meeting God in the kingdom of Heaven just so I can keep an eye on Travis, making sure he knows I'm not going anywhere.

"Rebecca used to hate this guy." Sharla turns in her seat to speak to me. Adri glances over her shoulder and her cheeks bloom crimson before she spins back around. Fucking adorable.

"Why?" I ask as I take a few steps forward to stand behind Vin's mother.

"We went to school with him, and she just always hated him." Her brows lower in thought. "He was a bit of a weirdo." *You don't say?*

A ball of dread forms in my belly with her words. Did my mother know he was a sick, twisted piece of shit? How? Did he try anything on her or were his tastes always geared toward peewees?

"She'd be celebrating today." She nods. "Not mourning."

I snort softly. My mother sounds more and more like Ember. "She sounds like she was pretty great," I whisper back.

"She was," she says with awe. "Always a smart-ass and running her mouth." A nostalgic look seeps into her eyes as a small smile plays on her lips.

I smile back but don't respond. That sounds nothing like the mother Ember described to me and I can only imagine it's because our dad changed her so much. Or fear changed her. The thought cuts something deep inside me and I'm suddenly overwhelmed with grief. I wish I knew her. Even the quieter version Ember is always comparing me to. Maybe we are both like our mother and nothing like our abusive father. One can only hope, and I can't wait to tell Ember how, just maybe, she's more like our mother than she thought.

Thankfully, Sharla doesn't say much more, and the funeral mass ends without the casket igniting with the flames of Hell.

Adrianna

I've been asked no less than a hundred times who the new hot guy is, and each time my stomach churns with possessive jealousy. Emmett has a way of reaching inside of me and tugging on my damaged heart, slowly making it beat to a new rhythm. I'm pretty sure I'm falling for Ember's brother and I'm basically signing my death certificate. She'll rage when she finds out, but it'll only make it worse when I admit I also still want Travis.

Even worse still... it would be impossible to choose. Not that I truly have a choice. If I pick Emmett, I'll lose my very best friend, and Travis wants nothing to do with me anyway.

"It's eerie how much he resembles Ember, but also how much he takes after Rebecca," Sharla leans in to whisper to me as Emmett heads out of the church, his loud-colored clothing like a beacon in a sea of black.

"I'm still recovering from the shock of him showing up here in Whitsborough." While keeping to the story Ember created, I've been sprinkling in some truth as well. I *am* still shocked by his existence.

Sharla and I exit the church, the energy around us solemn as we head to her car. When she offered to give me a ride today, I jumped at the chance. I hate being chauffeured around, but I'm also fearful of getting my license. Me and coordination are not friends.

I miss Ember and our rides in Shelby, but most of all, I miss my best friend. She's been distant lately. Actually, since she was taken on the night of the play, she's become someone else. She loves me, that hasn't changed, but our trivial high school antics have ceased. I miss going to parties with her and dancing or taking shots and making fun of Marlana together.

"How are you and Travis?" Sharla asks, breaking through my thoughts as she pulls out of the church parking lot.

"I have no idea," I answer honestly. "He's been quiet. His hands are full with his mother and now his coach died in a horrific accident. I don't know how to tell him I'm here for him."

Sharla has always been a cool parent and easy to talk to. She's the mother figure I never really had.

"He's a man," she retorts. "You have to force him to open up. Now that he's staying over at Ember's, you have an excuse to see him." She gives me a wink as she pulls onto my street.

"Ember isn't even home, so I can't say I'm visiting her, and before you say bring something over to eat, I already did that." I fall back against the seat with a long exhale.

"Girl, you did not try to kill those boys with your cooking." Sharla gasps as she pulls into my driveway.

"I followed a recipe!" She stops the car at the end of my driveway and gives me a pointed look. "I mean, I think it turned out edible."

"Well, they looked fine today, so maybe you did something right." She snickers as I open the car door, looking toward my empty house. It's no secret that my cooking could use a little practice.

"Thanks for the ride, Sharla." I give her a smile over my shoulder as she waves.

I walk up to the front door as she's pulling out, my head turning to watch her slowly back away, leaving me to face yet another night alone in this monstrous house. Slipping the key in the lock, I open the door and step inside, greeted only by the warning beep of my security alarm.

CHAPTER TWO

Travis Then

My belly is super full as we sit in Coach's big truck in the empty parking lot of the school. He smokes a lot and I hate the smell of it, but when he opens the window, it's not as bad. When my mother smokes in the car, she never opens the window, and it's so hard to breathe.

"I am so proud of you, sport," Coach says. He has a weird scratchy voice, and it's probably from all the cigarettes he smokes.

"I can't wait to tell Father!" I exclaim, squirming in my seat as Coach chuckles.

"Guess what, sport?" The excitement in his voice has a smile stretching across my face. Maybe he has a gift for me. He usually has something special planned when we do a good job.

"What?" I ask as he takes my hand and holds it in his lap.

"You are my favorite boy." Then he presses my hand down onto a bulge in the front of his pants. "See? That means you will always be my favorite."

"What is it?" I ask as I pat the bump.

Coach's head tips back and he lets out a moan. I yank my hand back, afraid I hurt him and he won't want me to be his favorite anymore.

"No, no." He takes my hand again. "You didn't hurt me. That just felt really nice. Just like those massages I do for your shoulders after a game."

"Oh!" I nod. I can do that for Coach too. He always rubs my shoulders. So I rub the bulge in his pants and hope I'm making him feel better.

"My favorite always, Travis." He lifts his lap up to rub harder into my hand. "But you can't tell your father or mother about this. They would take you from me. Like Kai's dad did to him."

"I won't tell them anything." Shaking my head, I make the promise. "I never want to leave the team."

"Good boy," he groans and forces my hand down on him harder.

He rubs against my hand in quick jerks as I try my best to stay on top of the bulge. My hand feels funny from the roughness of his jeans scraping against it, but I don't want to stop making Coach relax because I want to stay his favorite forever.

"That's it, that's it," he moans and then stops moving as the bulge in his pants keeps jerking.

"Do you feel better, Coach?"

"Yes, sport. I feel so much better." I'm glad I did a good job. He deserves it for how hard he works to make sure we'll one day be a winning team.

"Remember,"—he pops the top of my nose with his finger, his skin stinking like smoke—"this has to be our secret, or you can't be my *favorite anymore."*

"Don't worry." I shake my head. "I won't tell anyone."

Coach starts the truck, then drives me back to my big house filled with silence and sadness. He pulls into my driveway and the gates are already open. Sonja is probably waiting for me with my favorite snack. Coach stops the truck in front of my front door, and Sonja is standing there waving at us.

"Remember our secret." Coach holds his finger to his mouth.

"Okay." I nod and hold my finger to my mouth as well.

He smiles widely before patting the top of my head. Coach really likes me. He's my favorite too. I get out of his big truck and run toward Sonja. I'm so excited to tell everyone about my very first home run today.

"Hello, Mister Travis," Sonja says as she wraps me up in a big hug. "How was baseball game?"

"I hit my first home run, Sonja!" I scream and jump up and down in her arms.

"Oh, my!" she exclaims. "That is wonderful! Come inside. I made warm milk for bed."

"But I need to tell Father!" I call out as I kick off my shoes and run for his office.

"Wait, Mister Travis!" Sonja calls after me, but I'm too quick and there's no way she can catch me. That's why I got a home run today, because I am a fast runner.

"Father!" I yell as I open his office door and run inside. "Father!"

I can tell by his face I made another big mistake. He's on a phone call and it's probably important, like all of his calls. He comes around the desk slowly, and I'm so scared that I can't make my feet move.

"Yes, we can complete that merger next week," he says into the phone as he stands in front of me.

He pulls back his lips and grits his teeth at me as he raises his hand to slap me hard across the face. I fall and hit my head on the carpet in his office, blood filling my mouth.

I forgot one of his most important rules: Do not enter his office when the door is shut.

43

Chapter Three

Travis

I haven't thought about how Coach started his grooming of me in a long time, if ever, and it makes me feel pity for what I endured as a child, but also shameful for not knowing any better at the time. His funeral must've triggered something in my subconscious that's causing me to dream about it. Tossing and turning, I try to make my brain shut off and fall back asleep, but it's fucking useless. I throw off my covers and bend down to grab my sweatpants off the floor. I might as well go downstairs and find something to eat.

Walking by Emmett's room, I pause just a few paces away to listen. No sound comes from inside though, so I guess he's sleeping. Continuing down the stairs, I head toward the kitchen when muted sounds coming from the den stop me in my tracks. I quietly creep toward the doorway and peer inside. Emmett is sitting on the couch in nothing but a pair of black silk boxers and he's playing some shooting game on the game console. I stand transfixed on his biceps bunching whenever he slams his thumb down on a button, or his abs tightening when he's intensely shooting someone on the screen.

"You're being creepy," he says after a few minutes, his eyes never leaving the screen.

"I didn't want to disturb you." I cross my arms over my chest as his fingers fly over the controller, his jaw flexing with concentration.

"Can't sleep?" he asks, finally breaking his eyes from the screen to focus on me, the intensity of his ocean blues making me suck in a breath.

"Nah, you?" I croak out, trying and failing to seem nonchalant.

"I actually haven't tried yet." He shrugs, then turns back to the TV. "I spoke to Ember earlier, and she said they're on Talia's trail. She also asked me if I was ready for school."

"Yeah, we should probably go school shopping tomorrow, seeing as school starts in a few days." I really should've thought of that. Honestly, I've never done it before. Sonja has always taken care of it.

"Sure." He nods as his game starts up again. He's two minutes in and gets killed, cursing colorfully at the screen.

"Alright,"—I shuffle from foot to foot nervously—"have a good night then." With the idea of grabbing food long forgotten, I turn to leave the room.

"Wait!" he calls out as I start to walk away. "Do you play?"

"Sometimes." I turn back toward him. "I doubt I'm any good."

"Who cares? It'll tire us out and we can sleep after."

"Okay." I head over to the couch and sit beside him as he hands me a controller. Then he leans forward and presses a button on the console, giving me a full view of the tattoo on his back. "I like the tattoo. It's really nice."

"Some nice things cover the most hideous," he grunts as he sits back.

Truer words have never been spoken.

We walk into the nearest office supply store beside Ember's house, and everyone stops to stare at us, or rather, they stare at Emmett. The words I once told Ember flood back to me.

"We don't have many new people here in Whitsborough, so you're a bit of a spectacle."

"Yeah, I've noticed," he says as he shoots his signature grin at whoever he catches looking at him. He's taking it a lot better than Ember did, that's for sure. I was worried about having to prepare our classmates for another snippy version of Ember.

Once we've grabbed everything we'll need for school, including some obscenely priced leather backpacks, we head to the checkout. When the total flashes on the register, I almost choke on my saliva. I never realized how much it costs for school supplies because Sonja always took care of it.

"I got it," Emmett states as he pulls out a black Amex card.

"You don't need to do that. I've got money," I retort as I pull out my wallet.

"I know, bro." He clasps my shoulder. "I've seen your house."

The cashier behind the counter snorts and accepts his card. "I knew your mother," she tells Emmett, the gossip having ripped through Whitsborough like wildfire.

"Oh, yeah?" He leans in, giving Carla a near heart attack with his flirtatious tone. The woman is the same age his mother would've been.

"Yes, you look like her." Her cheeks heat the same way Adri's does when Emmett pays her any attention, and I grit my teeth to stop from snapping at them both.

"I've been getting that a lot. Just wish I saw it for myself." His admission is filled with sadness and has my heart sinking into my stomach. Here I am, acting like a jealous fool when he's grieving for a mother he's never met.

"It's a damn shame what happened to you," Carla stresses, her hands on her chest.

"It wasn't all bad. I found Ember." Emmett straightens from the counter, putting space between him and Carla, letting me breathe easier.

"That's very true. Rebecca would be happy that you've both found your way here." She packs up all our bags before we bid her goodbye.

"Gosh, people here are so darn nice," Emmett says with a twang as we leave the store. "If only they didn't stare at me like I'm a zoo animal."

"They'll get over it." I shrug.

"Did they ever get over Ember?"

"Not really." I grin at him. "But in their defense, your sister started teaching a fighting class, and she has no intention of behaving."

"True." He slings his bags over his shoulder and pats his chest with his free hand. "I will have to redeem us on that good little girl quality."

We both chuckle and throw our bags into the trunk of the car. Then we sit inside my car and buckle up, but I don't pull out of the parking spot. I'm not really wanting to go back to E's just yet. Being cooped up in that house is starting to wear on me, and if I'm being honest, I'm enjoying spending some time with Emmett.

"Want to hit up that diner we went to before? With the amazing milkshakes and funnel cakes?" Emmett suggests, probably feeling more caged than I do.

"It's called The Route." I snicker as I start the car, relieved that Emmett wants to hang out with me a little longer as well.

"Sure, let's go to The Route."

When we pull up, a few students from Precious Blood are chilling around outside. It's a popular hangout for them, so there was a good chance we would probably run into some. Plus, it's good to have him acquainted with some students now instead of being bombarded by them all in a few days.

The collective gasps from girls filter around us as we walk toward the entrance, and I fight really hard not to roll my eyes. Emmett is an attractive guy. That's undeniable because fuck, look at his sister, but I also know his ego is going to grow huge here.

"I think I'm a celebrity." *See?*

"No." I shake my head and open the restaurant door. "You're fresh meat."

"Hey!" he yells out to a tenth grade girl. "Are you a shark?"

"No!" she squeals with a giggle. "Are you Ember's twin? Everyone is talking about you."

"Are they now?" he asks tauntingly while looking at me, a knowing smirk lining his mouth.

"Let's head inside and eat, you Kardashian," I mutter and

walk inside ahead of him. His full laugh hits the back of my head as I struggle to keep my own in check.

Our meal is peppered with interruptions from a few girls and stares from the guys. Everyone is beyond curious about Emmett, and I can just imagine what walking the halls of Precious Blood is actually going to be like. I'm the type who likes to keep my head down and make it through my day with minimal interactions. The most I ever did was chill with Ember during lunch and hang out with the team after school. I'm not a popular jock and I want to keep it that way, but seeing how much attention Emmett is getting already, that may be flushed down the drain.

"You're deep in thought," Emmett says later when I pull into Ember's driveway.

"Just thinking about how my days of just living under the radar are over."

"You're not a people person," Emmett muses, scratching at the growth on his chin. "I don't need you to babysit me at school. I can figure it all out."

The thought of not being around him all day leaves me feeling bereft, which is something I don't want to dwell on too long. "Nah, don't worry about it. It's senior year. I did pretty well until now."

"Plus, your brother is dating my sister, who's best friends with Adri, who's obviously fucking you. That's a circle you are not getting out of." He nudges me before jumping out of the car to grab our bags from the trunk.

"True." I shake my head as we make our way into the house. "Too fucking true."

"I'm going to nap some of this milkshake off," Emmett groans as he climbs the stairs.

"Cool." I shrug as I head to my bedroom. Might as well

respond to those emails I've been putting off. Gerald won't let my silence stretch for too much longer, that's for sure.

I'm not sure how much time goes by when low moans sound from Emmett's room. I'm not completely sure what the fuck he's doing, but I try to block it out as I attempt to form professional sentences in my email. The moans soon turn into shouts of anger and cries of pain, and before my brain can even process, my body is flying through his bedroom door and into his room. He's writhing around in his sheets as they cover his sweaty body and his face is twisted in pain as he swats at something above his head. He's clearly still very much asleep and reliving something terrible.

"Stop!" he screams. "No, please!" he cries out with a pained moan.

"Emmett?" I mumble as I place my hand on his back.

Raised bumps meet my palm and I discover more of them all over his back. His tattoo is covering severe scarring. I realize the moment he wakes up because his body completely stiffens and his breathing evens out. He has yet to open his eyes, so I give him time to compose himself.

"You okay?" I finally ask after a few minutes go by.

"Yeah." His bright, blue-green eyes flick up to meet mine, fear still lingering in their depths. "I'm okay."

My hand is still on his back as I run my fingertips over one particularly large scar. His body trembles before I realize what I'm doing. I pull my hand back and slide them both into my sweater pocket.

"Someone who was trusted to be my guardian gave those to me while my dad was in jail," he whispers. "A monster hired to groom a boy into a soldier."

"Carm?" I ask, shocked.

"No." He shakes his head and visibly swallows as he closes his eyes briefly. "Carm was young then. He's only five years older than me. We were raised by a man named Calen. Well, I was mostly because Carm was being groomed, along with Trent, from a young age to take over The Eastside Rampage. So most of the time, I was with Calen."

He curls into a fetal position on the bed and grabs a pillow to cuddle into. He seems so tortured and alone, both emotions I'm familiar with. I sit down on the edge of his mattress and place my hand on his thigh. I don't want him to be alone. We're his family now and I'm the only one present to prove it. His hand comes out and covers my own, making my heart take off inside my chest. Shock tears through me at my reaction to the touch of his skin, but I quickly tamp it down and breathe slowly.

"Calen was my dad's age, maybe older. He was tough and without kids of his own. He had very little compassion and an especially low tolerance for children, hence why my diabolical father chose him as a guardian. If I really try to figure it out, I'll have to face the fact that my father made it impossible to be found by my mother." His hand tightens around mine and I flip my hand over to link our fingers. His skin is just a shade or two darker than mine, the callouses on both of our palms scraping together. The weight of his hand is so different from the weight of a woman's, and it's not at all discomforting as I thought it would be given my past.

"My punishments were pretty extreme for a small child. Most of them included whips of some sort and those scars are the result from my running in the hallways or screaming too loud."

His story mirrors my own life so much that I gasp without meaning to. His thumb rubs circles into the side of my hand, and I try really hard not to let myself read too far into it.

"I'm so sorry," I murmur, our hands still linked.

"I am who I am today because of the abuse, so I've learned to accept it. Although my brain forgets sometimes and I have to live it all over again." He gives my hand a squeeze and then lets it go. "Thanks for checking in on me."

I stand from the bed and quickly start for the door. My heart is racing and the ghost of his touch still warms my hand.

"Oh, Travis?" I turn at the sound of his voice. "You can come talk to me whenever you're ready too."

I nod and hurry back into my bedroom, closing the door behind me.

Adrianna

My phone's screen illuminates the dark room as my thumb hovers over the send button, then I chicken out and throw the phone onto my bed. Travis rarely initiates conversations with me, and whenever I fold to my impulses and text him, I mainly get back one-word answers. There was a time when we were inseparable and talking to him was as easy as taking my next breath, but that's all ruined now. I want to blame him for everything, but that would be a lie.

When we had our falling out, it was more than just a little heartbreak for me. Travis *crushed* my heart, pulverized it, and I was left trying to mold it back together. The organ beating inside my chest has never quite been the same again, and yet, it still longs for him. It's embarrassing how often I think of him, or how many times I pull up his number on my phone to reread the texts we've sent each other over the last few months.

Ember has somehow worked her magic and reconnected us, but now we have to do the legwork to repair the damage. Neither of us seemed prepared to do so, and even though I make attempts, none of it has been effective. I'm afraid to take risks, to put my heart back on the line for a boy who has the power to obliterate me.

The vibration of my phone pulls me from my thoughts and my heart pounds inside my chest as I glance over at it. *Did I press send?* I scramble to pick it up and breathe a sigh of relief when I see Ember's name flashing on the screen.

"Hello?" I answer, a little breathless as my heart recovers from yet more abuse.

"Are you fucking Travis right now?" my best friend groans, instantly bringing a smile to my face.

"No." I snort

"Were you diddling yourself while you imagined fucking him? Because you're all breathy," she continues, dragging a laugh from the depths of my stomach.

"How's Spain?" I'm insanely jealous that Vin whisked her away on a surprise vacation. They're probably going on romantic dates in Spain while I'm here struggling to find the words to say to the man I love.

"It's nice. I'm ready to come home though. How are the boys?" Before she left, Ember asked me to check in on them periodically to make sure they weren't killing each other. I took it as a win that she was warming up to me being around Emmett without accusing me of soiling his pristine reputation.

"They seemed fine when I dropped off some food to them before," I mumble as her breath hitches in my ear, my fingers toying with the edge of my bedsheet.

"Adrianna Hinton! I asked you to make sure they didn't kill each other, not to kill them yourself." When I groan, she laughs, the husky sound bringing another smile to my face. "It's the first day of school tomorrow, right? Can you make sure Emmett stays clear of Marlana? I will seriously kill her if she so much as breathes on him." For some reason, I believe her.

"I'll keep an eye out, but I'm sure Travis has it covered." Her breath hits my ear as she releases it with a long exhale.

"Still not talking to him?" she whispers, making me wonder if she's near Vin. He's been adamant I have to push myself on Travis, but he doesn't understand what it's like to even be in the same room as the boy who ripped my heart apart.

"Not really. I'm scared," I admit as I twist my comforter with my fingers.

"You two really need to talk everything out," she huffs as a door opens and then the wind sounds against the speaker. She must've gone outside. "You're wasting the time you could have together. You don't understand how brief life is."

After Ember's mother died and then her aunt and uncle, she's been preaching about living for the moment and that family is everything. What she doesn't know is that I don't truly have a family, and every moment is as bleak as the last.

"Okay," I tell her, "I'll try."

"I love you," she says, not knowing what it means for me to hear those words. I've spent my entire life waiting for someone to feel that enough to say them.

"I love you too," I croak out and quickly hang up the phone before I embarrass myself.

After setting my alarm for the morning, I gather my blanket up under my chin and close my eyes, praying for a dreamless sleep.

Chapter Four

Precious Blood Academy is a massive, gothic-looking building. The brick structure stands three levels high and the large double oak doors in the front are intimidating as fuck. I'm standing beside Travis' car and watching as everyone heads into the place, looking identical in their uniforms.

Travis has his uniform on, but the button-up shirt is hanging loose around his pants and rolled up at the sleeves, the required tie hanging open around his neck, and the blazer thrown over his right shoulder. He lights a smoke and leans against the car.

"Nervous?" he asks me, his eyes soft as he scans my face.

"A bit," I admit. *A lot, actually.* This is all new to me, and the thought of being in that building surrounded by strangers is making me sweat a little, but I don't want to bring more attention to it.

"I should tell you the people to steer clear of," He exhales his drag. "You've probably heard of Marlana?"

"Yeah, my sister's nemesis, right? Failed sex tape distributor?"

"Yeah." He chuckles. "She'll be interested in you for sure."

"Oh, yeah?" His forearm flexes as he lifts the cigarette to his mouth and squints at me through the cloud of smoke. "Why's that?"

"Fuck off." He rolls his eyes and shakes his head. "I know what you're trying to do."

"Hey, guys." I glance behind me and over the top of Travis' car to find Adri walking toward us. Holy shit. Her legs with that kilt on? *Deadly.* How the fuck am I supposed to hide my boner in these thin dress pants?

"'Sup?" Travis replies, barely looking at her.

She comes around to stand in front of us. Her blouse has a couple buttons undone and a black lacy tank peeks out with her perfect tits sitting amply on top. "Thought I would introduce Emmett to a few people."

"Who? Jordan and Jake?" Travis quips, flicking his cigarette to the ground, his jaw tight with annoyance.

"And Cara!" she huffs as her hands land on her waist. "What? Were you going to force him to sit with you and all the jocks?"

"Guys!" I hold both my hands up as I try to diffuse the tension. "There's enough of me to go around." With a single wink toward Adri, I watch as her cheeks burn a bright red and her hands fall from her waist.

"We should also point out who you should stay away from." She glances at Travis, then back at me. "Unless you want your sister to place you in that mausoleum as soon as she gets back?"

"I'm sure I'll be fine. Lead the way, you two." I throw my arm out.

Following behind them, I smile as the distance they put between them gradually grows smaller. These two are drawn to each other, whether they admit it or not. A twinge of jealousy burns my stomach when I try to think of how I can fit into the equation.

Travis stops a few times to introduce me to his baseball friends and a few I recognize from the pedophile's funeral.

"You're a late transfer, so your schedule will be in the office with Anna," Travis explains.

"My locker is in M hall again," Adri states as she reads off a piece of paper.

"I'm in N this year, which is cool." Travis regards me with a shrug. "Closer to the baseball field."

I have no idea what they're talking about as I follow them to an administrative office. Inside, sitting behind a large desk, is a lady who reminds me of someone's grandmother. She seems sweet, jolly, and maybe bakes a lot of cakes and cookies.

"Welcome back, children!" she exclaims when she gazes up from her novel on the desk. "Travis, you seem well."

"Thanks, Anna." He grins at her. "This is Ember's twin, Emmett. I believe his schedule is here?"

"Oh, yes!" She finally takes her eyes off Travis to glance at me. "Holy geez, you certainly are twins."

"Yes, ma'am." I nod and beam at her.

Her mouth drops open and her eyes widen. Yep, still got it. The older ladies have always loved me. "Uh… right. Here's your schedule. I believe you have homeroom with Mrs. G." She blinks rapidly. "Also, your sister will be with you in that class, which will be nice."

"Me too," Adri pipes up and throws me a smile.

"Did you bring a lock for your locker?" Anna asks.

"Sure did." I throw her another megawatt smile and snicker when she flusters again.

Travis snorts and Adri chuckles softly under her breath.

"You're all set." Anna clasps her hands together. "I hope your senior year here at Precious Blood Academy is memorable."

"Thanks again, Anna." Travis opens the door for us to exit. "Poor woman may just pass out from her overheated hormones," he mutters as the door shuts behind us.

"Anna is sweet." Adri glances at me over her shoulder. "Emmett, I'll take you to your locker."

"Yeah," Travis agrees. "I should head to mine before the bell. Show me your schedule." He holds out his hand to me.

I hand him the piece of paper and gaze around at the other students as he reads it. No one is even trying to hide their gaping, and some are outright whispering to each other behind their hands.

"We have Chem together after homeroom and then Trig after lunch," Travis reads, looking up at me and following my gaze. "Don't mind them. They aren't used to circus freaks."

"Asshole," I retort, and we both chuckle.

"We have English together as the last period," Adri states. "One of us will be with you each period."

"See you in Chem," Travis says as he turns and walks away.

"See you," Adri mumbles with a roll of her eyes.

"Lockers?" I remind her, hoping to pull her out of her funk.

"Yeah." She pulls herself together and gives me a small smile as we walk toward the lockers. "What number are you?"

"296."

"Really?" she squeals, her beautiful eyes lighting with surprise as she bounces on the balls of her feet.

"Uh…" I raise a brow at her, my mouth curving into a smile. She doesn't know how gorgeous she is.

"That was your sister's locker last year. That's so fucking freaky." She continues to grin at me, her face glowing with warmth.

"That is weird." I twist my lips in thought. "Should you be swearing so much in a place called *Precious Blood*?"

Adri's head falls back and her hair touches her tailbone. Her plush, pink mouth spreads open as a full belly laugh spills out. Her skin is a perfect mocha color from the summer sun and her milk chocolate eyes dance with mirth. I take in every inch of perfection as though it'll be my last time.

"Who gives a fuck?" She continues to giggle.

"Maybe Jesus?" I mutter, still taking in how gorgeous she is.

"Let's go, you saint." She chuckles as she leads the way to our lockers. "I'm five down from you." Her big chocolate eyes meet mine over her shoulder.

"Sweet." I pull my bottom lip into my mouth and bite down. Her eyes follow the movement, her face turning a soft pink. So fucking delicious.

"This is your locker,"—she points to mine, then down the row a bit before giving me a smile—"and mine is right here."

I pull open the locker and start stuffing my bag inside. Movement to my left catches my eye and I stop what I'm doing. The next locker to my left is being opened by a pretty girl with purple hair. She's tall, maybe like 5'10", and her legs look like they stretch on forever. I stop my perusal at her feet and roll my eyes when I find six-inch heels. Scratch the tall. She's shorter than average but still has a sexy set of legs and her ass isn't too bad either.

"Are you done?" she sneers, and I peer up at her face with my signature grin. Her blue eyes widen as her pert mouth opens on a gasp. Her face is pretty enough, but why the fuck would she dye her hair this purple color? "You're Ember's twin." Her skin has gone a couple shades paler, and for this girl, it means nearly translucent.

"Yeah, my name is Emmett. Changed it from Ember's twin last week. Such a mouthful." I toss her a wide grin.

"You've met the skank of Precious Blood," Adri says from behind me, her tone nothing like the girl I know.

Cabbage Head closes her locker and averts her eyes as she scurries away down the hall. "Whoa, tiger, pull the claws in. This isn't a *Mean Girls* movie." I *tsk* at Adri as she continues to glare after Grape Jam until she disappears into the crowd.

"That was Marlana." She turns back and screws her nose up at me. "Didn't anyone tell you ahead of time about her purple as fuck hair?"

"I can't remember." I shrug. "The girl acts like a kicked puppy."

"She better stay out of our way this year or she'll be a dead one." The vitriol dripping from her tone leaves me momentarily shocked. This interaction with Marlana doesn't sound like Adrianna at all. My sister has somehow tarnished Adri without even telling her what she does in her spare time.

"Okay, tiger. Homeroom." I guide her away from the lockers

with a hand on her lower back, and my shock quickly fades when I notice how hot she is when she's angry. *Do not pop a boner, Emmett.*

During Religion class, it's obvious Mrs. G, our teacher, fucking loves me. Especially when I confessed to her how much I love to pray to Jesus every night before I sleep. I even closed the class today with a prayer for everyone to have a safe and productive first day. I could feel the Holy Spirit rising out of my body just for her. My father was a practicing Catholic, and Carm and I attended church every Sunday even while he was in jail. So I know my way around the Bible and I can certainly spout verses in my fucking sleep, which was a plus today in winning over one of my teachers.

"You are so fucking full of shit." Adri giggles while we leave the classroom, her shoulder hitting my arm as she slips through the doorway ahead of me.

"You're just jealous," I tease and side-eye her as we head down the hall.

"What'd I miss?" His deep voice slips around me, and I turn to find Travis leaning against the wall. He's undone a few buttons at the top of his shirt and his golden chest contrasts with the white material perfectly.

"My prayer for everyone's safekeeping on their first day of school." I widen my eyes innocently as he pushes off the wall and comes to stand with us.

"Must've soaked Mrs. G's panties." He snorts as he touches the cigarette he has tucked behind his ear.

"Fucking right." I hold my fist out to him as he crushes his knuckles to mine.

"Gross," Adri groans and rolls her eyes. "I'll see you douches at lunch." She turns on her cute little kitten heels and walks down the hall, her fine ass swinging in her kilt.

"Ready for Chem?" Travis breaks through my thoughts, making me blink the rest of the hall back into focus.

"No." I shake my head. "But maybe I can make it interesting by blowing something up at least once a week." I rub my hands together and wink at him.

After Chem is over, I'm ready for lunch. My brain is fucking hurting and I'm just realizing maybe my homeschooled life wasn't up to par. Thank God my sister is a straight-A student. She'll be using up her spare time tutoring me so we can both graduate together.

Travis and I both head to the cafeteria and find Adri standing in front of the doors. She's taken off the blazer, her blouse rolled up at the sleeves, and I can see a bit of a tattoo peeking out at the crease of her right arm. She also has on a pair of black, thick-framed glasses. I pray my brain doesn't alert my dick to how hot she is standing there.

"Hey!" she calls out with an enormous smile on her face. "How was Chem?"

"Shit," Travis grits out and moves past her into the room.

"Why the fuck is he so moody with me?" she huffs as her hands form fists, her eyes trailing after him.

"Not sure." I go with the honest route. "You should probably ask him."

"I don't care anymore." She shrugs her shoulders. *Liar*.

I hold my arm out for her, and she blushes as she slips her hand through it. The little spade tattoo on her hand, peeking out beside her thumb, is so fucking cute.

"What are we eating today?" I ask her.

"Your sister loves the grilled chicken salad here." Pain still lingers in her eyes from Travis' dismissal.

"And we both know my sister is a little crazy." I give her a wink, hoping to clear up that pain in her eyes. Obviously, she knows nothing. "I want something not intended to feed small herbivore animals."

She lets loose her full laugh, and I just bask in all its glory, happy I'm the one who keeps making her do that.

"I'm telling her you said that." She snickers and leads me to the line. "I like the burgers here and the crispy fries with gravy."

"Sounds pretty close to perfection." My mouth waters as my stomach grumbles.

After grabbing our lunches, I follow Adri to a table as we pass by Travis' table filled with jocks. As if sensing me, his head moves toward me, our eyes locking. He does a slow perusal from my feet to the top of my head, and I'd be fucking lying if I said I wasn't sporting a chub right now. When he comes back to my eyes, he gives me a quick nod and goes back to talking to his friends.

"He'll probably sit with Ember and Vin when they're back, but for now, we'll sit in my regular spot with a few of my friends. You'll like them. They really love Ember." She's rambling a little, sounding nervous as we walk across the lunchroom.

She leads me to a table with a few guys and one small, pixie-like girl. Her white-blonde hair is just a few shades lighter than her pale skin and she has big blue eyes, making her look like a literal fairy.

"That's Cara. Jordan has been in love with her forever. Just a warning," Adri whispers with a slight scowl on her face. It's fucking cute that she seems a little put off about me potentially liking another girl.

"Not my type." I shake my head as I stare into her eyes,

hoping she catches exactly what I've been into lately.

"Okay." She smiles a little and puts her tray on the table. "Guys, this is Ember's twin, Emmett. Emmett, this is Jordan,"—she points to a tall, built guy with a man bun—"that's Jake." He's a slighter build with a dark mop of curls on top of his head. He also has a skateboard propped up beside him. "And that's Cara."

"Hey." I wave to each. "Love the board, dude." I point it out to Jake.

"You skate?" He raises a brow, his face skeptical as he takes in my appearance.

"It's been a while but seeing that makes me want to." Enjoying a skate park in New York was impossible because of who my father was and the target that was always placed on my back, but I made do with what I could in the compound.

"We usually go to the skate park a few days a week," he mutters shyly.

"Oh, yeah?" I nod as I pop a fry in my mouth. "Maybe I will join you guys." My eyes flick from him to Jordan expectantly as I take a bite of my burger.

"Oh, fuck no." Jordan laughs. "I can't skate for shit. He's talking about Charlie and a few of the drama club guys."

"Bring your board tomorrow and I will introduce you to them," Jake offers with a little more confidence.

"Cool, man. I will." First day and I've already made potential plans with new friends. I didn't think it would be this easy.

"Didn't take you for a skater," Adri teases as I take another large bite of my burger.

"Why not?" Cara chimes in. "He rides a motorcycle and apparently sacrifices newborns for devil worship."

It takes all my strength not to spit out my chocolate milk. "What?!"

"Just what I've heard." She shrugs as she nonchalantly takes a bite out of her burger.

My eyes find Adri, who's bent over on the bench, laughing silently. "What the fuck did I miss?" I glance around the table while everyone laughs and snickers.

"That was all Ember. During the summer, we went to The Route and a couple of nosy students asked about her absence. That was her response." Adri giggles.

Of course this is all Ember. I should have known. "Obviously, we don't sacrifice newborns." I shake my head and look at each of them, plastering on my creepiest grin. "Just kittens."

Adri falls over again and this time her laugh is loud and full. "She said that too!"

"Done being a creep?" Travis says from behind me, and I instantly feel the warmth from his body penetrate mine.

"No!" I scoff. "I am what I am."

"Let's get to Trig, creep," he teases.

After dumping my tray, I follow behind Travis as he leads us to Trigonometry. His shoulders are always squared and tense, like he's on constant alert here, and the tension he exudes is thick. No wonder people had let him drift under the radar for so long. It wasn't because he didn't get noticed, because I can tell you, every guy and chick alike gives him a once-over when he passes. No, it's because the energy he throws out is standoffish and annoyed.

"Mr. Corelli is a bit of a prick. Just sit by me and I'll guide you through the shit. Don't ask him too many questions because he has no fucking patience," he informs me as we walk into the room.

"Noted."

He goes to the row in the far back and sits at a pair of desks, then slouches down immediately and throws his legs out wide. Fuck, Travis has no idea just how attractive he is and it's so fucking hot. I sit down beside him and my leg brushes against his, so I move it over only to have him move his wider until we're touching again. I turn to face him, but he's looking straight ahead with the same scowl he always has on his face, his jaw clenching as I harden in my pants.

I barely absorb anything in this class with my hard as fuck dick and Travis constantly brushing me with his knee. I just can't think straight. As soon as the bell rings, I exhale a sigh of relief and rest my head on my arms on the desk.

"You good?" he asks.

I look up at him and meet his eyes. "I'm fucking confused."

"You'll get it," he assures me as he packs up his bag. "I'll help you."

I don't just mean school; I mean him as well. Like what the fuck is going on with us? I don't say shit though. Instead, I gather my stuff into my bag. All the new textbooks are heavy, and I decide to make use of the ten minutes between classes to get to my locker for a drop-off.

"English is in this hall, just a few doors down," Travis says as he swings his bag over his shoulder.

"Thanks," I mutter as he leaves the classroom.

It takes about six minutes to find my way back to my locker, and standing at hers is Marlana. I've never been one who feels the need to bully or torment anyone unless I'm provoked, and looking at this girl makes me feel sorry for her. Did she fuck up? Fucking yes, she did, but I can only guess she was in love with Vin and was trying to keep her claws locked in tight when she felt him slipping. I want nothing to do with her because of the shit she pulled on my sister, but I don't want to partake in any bullying either. If she stays out of my way, I'll stay out of hers.

I open my locker beside her as her body tenses. She's afraid, and it's not a reaction I like. I don't want to have girls afraid of me, that's just not who I am, and I know my sister wouldn't force me into bullying this chick if I didn't want to. I'm not even completely convinced she would bully her either.

"So, how long do I have before the dream couple is back to make my life hell?" she sneers. So maybe not such a kicked puppy after all.

"Next week." After putting away my textbooks, I close my locker door and study her. She doesn't meet my eyes, but her face distorts with disgust. "Word of advice? Keep your head down and mind your own business."

"They don't scare me." She closes her locker door with a loud bang.

"That's your first mistake."

I turn around and start my trek back to where my English class is. I don't care to think too much about this Marlana chick. Honestly? It's just not my problem, and my sister is more than capable of dealing with her if she has to. I have my own fucking problems that need sorting out somehow. Like, who do I want? Travis or Adri? What if I want both? What the fuck am I going to do?

Adrianna

He strides across the field with his bag thrown over his shoulder and his wavy blond hair blowing in the breeze. His eyes are downcast as his steps pound into the earth with purpose. Travis Greene is the center of my world and doesn't even know it. He ripped me to shreds and continues to tear what's left of me apart every time we speak. The boy I wanted to love, to be with forever, has somehow turned into the man at the helm of my torture.

His head lifts and his eyes search the field, skimming over me on the bleachers, then flicking back immediately. If he notices I'm here, he doesn't really react as he continues toward the locker room, his head turning away to stare straight ahead. The chasm between us is wider than ever and I don't think we'll ever be able to seal it.

I stand from the bleachers and head back to the main building, my feet dragging even though I'm already late for class. It's worth it though just to see him, even if it rips me open a little more.

Approaching the classroom, I find Emmett rushing toward me, his face filled with panic and sweat dotting along his brow. "We're late!" he exclaims as he brushes by me into the room. The last ten minutes fade as a smile crawls along my mouth. Emmett has a way of chasing away the clouds overhead. My very own ray of sunshine.

English is his strong suit. He radiates confidence when he's discussing a book and the characters within it. Their flaws are scrutinized, and he knows exactly how they gained them. Does he have me figured out too? Does he see the lonely girl with a broken heart and a wounded spirit?

The bell rings, much to his dismay, and students rush from the room, throwing their books into their bags. "Wow. Today flew by," he mumbles as he slowly gathers his things.

"Yeah," I reply as I stand from my desk. His eyes are on me as

I zip up my bag, and I swallow down the nerves radiating throughout my stomach. My attraction to Ember's brother is dangerous, but it also confuses me. How is it possible he and Travis take up the same amount of space inside my heart?

"Do you need a ride home?" My heart stalls as I stare at him, my brows skating upward. "What?"

Travis drove them this morning. I saw them both get out of his car when my driver dropped me off. Two of Whitsborough's most beautiful guys in one small place together and now the entire school gets the privilege of being near them every day. My stomach twists with jealousy as I think of either of them dating another girl, and I adjust my bag onto my shoulder.

"I have a ride," I tell him as I try to plaster a smile on my face. "Thank you."

"With whom?" He stands and throws his bag over his shoulder, his brows falling together with irritation. Could he be thinking another guy is taking me home? I open my mouth to tell him my driver is waiting outside when he turns and heads to the doorway. "Whatever, Adri. You have a good night. I'll see you tomorrow."

Then he's gone, taking my light and leaving me alone with the dreary clouds once again.

My feet drag as I head out of the school and toward my driver, Klein, waiting in the parking lot. He's also the family's groundskeeper and the closest thing I've had to a parent, along with Vera, our cook. He pulls up to the front when he sees me pushing through the double doors and rolls down the passenger window of the Rolls Royce.

"Hello, Miss Adrianna. How was your day?" Klein's face is weathered with age, but it radiates with kindness whenever he sees me. I often wonder if he feels sorry for me, but I'm too afraid of his answer if I ask.

"It was okay." I shrug as I open the back door and throw my bag inside before climbing into the passenger seat.

"You must miss Ember," he assumes as I do up my seat belt. "You're stuck with me until she returns." His tone is playful as he winks at me.

"I don't mind that," I assure him as he pulls out of the lot. "But I do miss her."

Ember saved me when I had hit my lowest point. I had secluded myself entirely, wallowing in a depression so heavy that I feared I would be buried under it forever. Then she came along and pulled me out from under the weight of my life, embracing me like a sister. She doesn't know that I didn't have extended plans to stick around before she showed up.

"Vera made chicken Alfredo today," he says as we head toward the house. "She thought you looked sad this morning. We're worried with Ember being away that you're going back—"

"I'm not," I cut him off, making my tone firm. "I promise. It's just the beginning of school and summer is over."

"Did you see Travis today?" A hopeful lilt runs through his words, and it only makes my stomach twist more.

"Yes," I murmur and gaze out the window, hoping he'll leave it at that.

But this is Klein, and he's always had a soft spot for my ex-best friend. "He is doing well?" After Robert Greene died, Klein was worried about Travis, going as far as to bring them over meals cooked by Vera. He's always been drawn to sad creatures.

"I think so."

The rest of the drive back to the house is silent, leaving

me to the thoughts running through my mind. Where Travis once dominated my quiet, thought-filled moments, now Emmett is there with him. Green eyes paired with blue, and dark hair flowing into tousled dark blond. Both of them are seared into my mind, their features scarred there for an eternity.

Chapter Five

This week has been so weird. Adri and I are barely speaking and it's because of me. The sexual tension between her and Emmett is so potent, and I refuse to put myself in the line of fire over heartbreak. Not to mention the weird tension emanating between Emmett and me. I can't explain it, but it's as though my body demands I stay near him, and when I'm close enough, I need to touch him too. A discreet brush of our hands or legs, our eyes meeting whenever the other steps into the room, and the constant crackle of want surrounding us both. I often catch him staring, but I try to ignore it because I just don't know what it means. Yes, I have been with a few guys before, but the signs are different with him. This is E's brother, and there would be no turning back from that if I acted on my impulses and it all went south.

My phone rings on my bedside table and I pick it up, seeing E's name flashing back at me.

"Hey, E. You okay?" My heart thunders through my chest every time she calls or texts, and this time is no different.

"Hey." She sounds tired and slightly defeated. "We'll be home Sunday afternoon."

"Everything good?" I clear my throat, trying to alleviate the tight feeling of fear slipping through me. I wouldn't be able to bear it if something happened to her or my brother.

"We lost her," she whispers sadly. "Somehow she slipped through our fingers. She was right there, Trav. We had her. I don't know what happened."

"Fuck." I exhale and scrub my hand down my face. "Come home safely and we'll figure it out."

"Okay," she murmurs, and I hate the sound of dejection in her voice. "Your brother wants to talk to you."

"Okay." I let out the breath I've been holding in my chest, my body sinking into my mattress.

"I love you, Trav." Those three words never grow old, and I count my blessings that I have someone who means it when they say them.

"I love you too, E." I do. She's family, through and through, and my love for her is unconditional.

"Bro," Vin's deep rasp comes through the phone, "how's everything in Whitsborough?"

"Good, man." I shift on the bed as I readjust the phone at my ear. "Your mom is good. I checked on her a few days ago."

"Thanks. How's school?" He's asking mundane questions, trying to sound normal when I can hear the disappointment in his tone.

"Shit, nothing new there," I sneer, my disdain for the school evident in my tone.

"Marlana?" he questions with grit in his voice.

"Keeping her distance. Although she has a locker right beside Emmett."

"Of course she does," he growls, his heavy exhale coating my ear.

"You just worry about getting home safe."

"Yeah." He yawns loudly. "We'll see you Sunday."

"Okay, take care."

"You too." Then the line goes dead. I miss my brother and E, and I'm happy they're coming home, but I wish they had gotten their hands on Talia as well.

The sensation of being watched comes over me and I shut my eyes against the onslaught. When it doesn't let up, I turn my head to find him leaning in my doorway. His dark hair is wet and curling slightly at the ends and his lips appear pillow-soft against the harsh angles of his face.

"My sister?" Emmett inquires as he points to the phone still in my hand on my lap.

"Yeah." I swallow thickly as my eyes soak up every inch of him. Blinking out of my lust, I force myself to pay attention to him, pushing down my desire.

"Carm just called me too." He runs his hand through his hair. "They're coming home on Sunday."

"Yeah."

"How's Ember?" he asks. "We texted, but I can't read her tone over text."

"She sounds a bit defeated. Once she's here though, we'll

bring her back."

He nods and peers around my room. "What's there to do in Whitsborough on a Friday?"

"Uh…" I run my finger over my mouth and his eyes zero in on it, making me continue just to have his eyes on me. "There's always a house party somewhere. We also have one bar that'll serve us as long as we behave, but Fridays are karaoke nights."

"Done!" He turns around. "Get dressed, we're singing."

"Wait!" I sit up in bed as my heart pounds with anxiety. "I don't sing!"

We're riding in an Uber and on our way to General Grady's. This bar is run by a good friend of my father's, and as long as we don't cause a scene and have him busted for underage drinking, he's always looked the other way when us high schoolers come in. The high schoolers that do frequent here are Marlana, Shay, and their little group, and some drama club guys. Otherwise, everyone else just throws a party at their houses since parents aren't really present among our classmates.

"Ladies' night?" Emmett asks as he peers up at the neon sign above General Grady's.

"Oh, fuck no." I shake my head and lean toward the front to speak to the driver. "Turn this shit around."

"No!" Emmett opens the door and gets out. "What's ladies' night?"

I have no other choice but to follow him out of the Uber,

seeing as I'm his babysitter until his sister comes home. "Exactly what it says. A bunch of chicks screeching out songs while completely hammered."

"I'm in." He shrugs and walks up to the entrance. "Maybe we'll get you laid and you can ease up."

"Fuck you," I mutter and follow up behind him.

"What's up, Trav?" The bouncer at the front nods at me. "Word of warning, it's hella crazy inside right now. Some chick is having a bachelorette party too."

"Fuck me," I groan and tip my head back in exasperation. This night can't get any worse.

"That may actually happen tonight." He slaps me on the shoulder with a chuckle. "Head on in, guys."

"See?" Emmett says over his shoulder as we walk in. "He knows you need to get laid too."

We bypass the coat check and open the soundproofed inner doors. Suddenly, we're assaulted with the animalistic screeching of "Girls Just Want to Have Fun" by a drunk chick. Emmett stops abruptly, and I try to smother the laugh bubbling up from my chest. Thank God this is the first thing he's hearing, because he'll definitely want to leave now. His head turns as he glances at me over his shoulder, and my stomach sinks as a smirk grows on his mouth. *Fuck's sake, he's still into it.* I shake my head and continue to follow him inside.

The lights are off and a strobing disco ball hangs from the center ceiling, casting out prismatic light shards as it rotates. Neon lights flash up the walls in different colors all over the room and at the front is a large stage. It's currently holding three drunken and slurring women with mics, singing along to the words written across a TV screen.

I follow Emmett to the left toward a large bar that encompasses the entire wall. Currently, it's packed with mostly chicks waiting to be served. Tonight, they have five bartenders, looking stressed out from the overload of people asking for alcohol. I gaze to the right and sigh with relief when I find mostly guys occupying the tables, and some of them from school.

"Hey! Charlie is here!" Emmett hollers over the horrible music. "Let's grab beers and sit with them!" I shrug in response and he turns back to the bar to order us our drinks.

Charles is here with a few drama club guys and Jake. These guys are the skater crew and Emmett has been chilling with them a few times this week. He's also been bringing his skateboard to school and skating during lunch with them. It's good. I'm glad he's making his own group of friends. I can admit these are good guys, a lot better than some of the other drama guys—like Danny and company. He had the skate crew over once this week and we all chilled outside around the fire pit, drinking a few beers. I may have misjudged them for the past three years.

Emmett comes back with four beers, two in each hand. "We're double fisting all night!"

I roll my eyes and take two of the beers, then follow him over to Charles' table.

"Charlie!" Emmett yells, and the guys glance at us with surprise. Their shock turns to grins as they stand, bumping our fists or slapping our backs.

"Sit with us, man!" Charles shouts. "This shit is fucking hilarious!"

Emmett and I sit at the table next to them as another group of girls make their way up onto the stage. They're also looking pretty drunk as they stumble around and giggle at each other. Then the music for "Living on a Prayer" by Jon Bon Jovi floats through the sound system. All of us groan and roll our eyes. This means more girls screeching for sure. I finish the first two beers pretty fast and look to find Emmett is almost done with his second. I stand as a server walks by and motion for her to stop.

"Hey," I call over the screeching voices. "Can you keep this table stocked all night? I'll take care of the tab at the end of the night. You know I'm good for it." I smile for good measure.

She instantly blushes and nods as she runs off to the bar to load up her tray with beers. It's going to be one hell of a night. Might as well get perfectly drunk too.

A few songs later and all of us are pretty fucking wasted. A group of girls approach our tables, seduction oozing from their eyes. They're older, maybe mid to late twenties, and they're part of a bridal party, if their sashes or buttons mean anything.

The first bleach blonde with over-plumped lips sits on Emmett's lap and one of her brunette friends saunters over to me while the rest circle Charles and his crew.

"Our friend is getting married," the brunette slurs into my ear, spraying spit for good measure. Quickly I swipe at the moisture coating my ear, my body shuddering with disgust.

"I couldn't tell." I lift the beer to my mouth for a swig while keeping an eye on a smiling Emmett and his bimbo.

"You and your friend,"—she points to Emmett—"are the hottest guys here."

I smile and nod, staring at the handsy blonde and Emmett, who, by the way, is looking like he's in heaven right now. Irritation, red and hot, washes over me and it takes all my willpower not to go over there and drag her plastic-ass off him. I close my eyes and try to relax. This isn't normal for me, and I don't understand why I'm reacting like this.

"We came here to ask you two to do us a biiiiiig favor." She drags out the word as she runs a fingernail down the crotch of my jeans. *Wow, cougars are fucking ruthless.*

I grab her hand and pull it off my crotch. "I don't think we're interested in any favors like that."

"No!" She throws her head back, laughing. "We just want you guys to go up on stage and do a little karaoke striptease for our friend's last night of freedom."

"That's not happe—" I begin but stop as soon as Emmett stands up and turns to look at me. The gleam in his eyes says it all. This fucker agreed to us getting up on that stage and humiliating the fuck out of ourselves.

"Let's go, Greene!" he yells out over a horrendous rendition of Whitney Houston's "I Wanna Dance with Somebody."

I shake my head and down the rest of my beer. "You're fucking nuts!" I holler back.

"Don't make me do it alone." He grins at me mischievously. Fuck him. I don't know why I suddenly want to do this with him. Maybe because I'm fucking drunk off my ass.

"Fine," I growl and stand up, effectively knocking the brunette down onto her ass. She doesn't care as she laughs it off, and Emmett's body shakes as he tries to hold in his laughter. "Let's go now before I walk the fuck out of this place. You better have nice underwear on," I snarl at him, and he lifts his jeans out and away from his waist.

"Tighty-whities." He winks. *Great.*

We both jump up onto the stage and Emmett grabs the mic. "We had a special request tonight." He points down at the woman in a white dress with a veil on her head. "She wants to see me in my tighty-whities, and I really want to show them to her." He gyrates his hips and all the girls in the bar start screaming. I cover my face with my hand and try to convince myself to leave the fucker up here by himself. Would E kill me?

"Him too." He points back at me and the girls scream again. "You ready to see our undies?!"

Undies? What the fuck is he saying right now? He turns back to me and struts over. "Okay, we will have to do the song 'I'm Too Sexy' by Right Said Fred."

"Yeah… no." I shake my head adamantly.

"What? Really? Fine… 'Buttons' by The Pussycat Dolls." He snaps his fingers and two-steps.

"Again… fuck no." I'm not singing to a bunch of chicks to loosen up my fucking buttons. Has he lost his mind?

"Then which song?" He stomps his foot, clearly frustrated with me as his eyes narrow and his lips press into a straight line.

"Only *the* most popular stripper song of all time." I raise a brow at him, my lips slowly spreading into a devilish smirk. Tonight, I'm not Travis Greene, the tortured boy with a sordid past, I'm Travis Greene, the man who buries that past and dances on the earth. "'Pour Some Sugar on Me' by Def Leppard."

"Oh!" He points his finger in my face. "I know that one… kind of. You sing most of it, but I can do harmony."

"You wait till you hear this amazing voice." I grin at him teasingly. It feels so good to forget everything else and be here at this moment.

He runs and tells the DJ to play our song, and I wink at the bride-to-be in front of me. Yeah, I'm drunk, might as well have a fucking good time since I rarely do. Throwing my leather jacket to the side, I take in my appearance. I have on a white V-neck T-shirt and a loose pair of blue faded jeans. Thankfully, I remembered to throw on a belt, and a Gucci one at that. I'm fucking styling.

Emmett comes back and throws his leather jacket with mine. He's left with a tight, black tank and baggy, dark blue jeans. He also has a Gucci belt on but it has studs all along it. *That's kind of sexy*, I think to myself.

"You sexy pieces of shit!" Charles screams from our tables, his hand slapping the wooden top.

"Watch it or I'll come give you a lap dance after this!" Emmett screams back as he points at him. I'll kill him if he does that.

I start with rasping out the opening lyrics as the girls jump to their feet and start screaming again. Emmett is looking shocked, standing and watching me as the music starts.

Moving my hips, I walk to the front of the stage. He can stand there like a mannequin if he wants because I can do this all fucking day. This body is finally getting the attention it deserves. I drag my hand over my crotch, then up to the hem of my shirt, slowly lifting it and giving the ladies a peek of my abs.

"Take it off!" Charles and the guys yell and laugh from the table as I throw them a wink.

Finally, Emmett snaps out of his shock and rushes up beside me, just in time for me to start the first verse. As I'm singing, he's rolling his crotch in one of the girls' faces, and she's probably salivating. I can't help it as I chuckle over a few words. We harmonize on the bridge and both of us pull off our shirts. I doubt anyone can hear us singing over the girls screaming. We both somehow swing the shirts over our heads in perfect harmony and throw them to the side of the stage, looking like stripping is our usual side hustle.

We start on the chorus and Emmett winds his way down to the floor. He and E must have chilled with the same crowd. He's down on his knees and humping up into the air as he undoes his belt.

I undo mine as well, and the girl in the front—the plastic blonde—pulls her tit out of her shirt and gives it a squeeze while blowing me a kiss. Yeah, it does nothing for me as I roll my eyes away from the sight. I've never been into fake balloon titties.

Emmett rises to his feet, his jeans hanging dangerously low on his ass. He has his belt in his left hand and the mic in his right. Then the fucker snaps the belt out toward the girls like a fucking whip, each snap punctuated by a pump of his hips.

The second verse has us both stepping out of our shoes and pushing them aside, then we both unbutton and unzip our jeans. It almost appears choreographed. There's no way anyone is hearing us sing over the screaming girls, so we both ditch the mics and continue to work our jeans down our legs, putting extra attention on humping into random girls' faces.

We both kick our jeans to the side and dance in our fucking underwear. Thankfully, I have on a pair of black Armani boxer briefs that cup my dick and balls like a second skin. I glance over at Emmett and, sure enough, the fucker really has on a pair of tight, white Calvin Klein boxer briefs. They accentuate a bulge that has my breath locking in my throat, making it hard to swallow. Tearing my eyes away, I continue to move and hope no one notices my moment of weakness.

He jumps to center stage and grabs onto his dick through his underwear, sticking his tongue out while flipping the audience off with his other hand. I can't help it, the sexy shit has passed and I'm a laughing mess just watching him. Charles and the guys are still hooting and whistling at us, and Emmett keeps his finger in the air as he humps into his hand.

"He looks like Marky Mark!" the bride screams out. *Who the fuck is Marky Mark?*

Once the music stops, I pick up the clothes we've thrown to the side and Emmett comes up beside me to do the same. Then we make our way down the hallway toward the bathrooms, both of us still laughing our asses off in our fucking underwear.

"Guys," a voice sounds from our right. "Use the staff washroom. You're going to have girls swarming back here any second." I look up and find a familiar face.

"Thank you, James." I nod and we follow him to the staff bathroom.

"Lock it, just in case," he says and opens the door for us. "And thanks for the business tonight. If you guys want an extra gig, let me know." He shakes his head with a chuckle and walks out.

"He's the owner," I tell a confused and nearly naked Emmett. "One of my father's friends."

"I see," he murmurs, stepping into the bathroom behind me and locking the door.

I dump the pile of clothes in my arms onto the counter and lean both hands on it. My head is swimming, and I know I will have a fucking killer hangover tomorrow. Did I just strip on a fucking stage? I hang my head and groan. I'm going to regret this tomorrow.

His hot breath hits my shoulder, and I shut my eyes. Is this real or am I just imagining it? Then the brush of his fingertips runs along the waistband of my boxers along my lower back and a low moan escapes me. His fingers drift up my spine, increasing in pressure until he reaches my neck and grabs it. He tips my head up and forces me to peer into his ocean eyes through the mirror as he steps into me, his chest pressing into my back. His hard cock grinds against my ass and I groan.

"Tell me to stop right now if you don't want this," he husks out as his tongue hits my neck. He licks over my skin with his eyes still boring into mine. I remain silent, still watching him tasting my skin, and his mouth tips up into a sexy as fuck grin. "Good answer."

He opens his mouth and his white, perfectly straight teeth

bites into my flesh. The sound that escapes me sounds almost animalistic, and I press my ass back into his dick, grinding hard. I don't know what's come over me and it's confusing when my body reacts like this to him. I shouldn't want this. He's Ember's brother.

I turn around to tell him to stop. Maybe? I'm not sure, and I'll never know because as soon as I'm facing him, his mouth lands on mine, and we both open, letting our tongues fight out whatever conflicting emotions we have. One of his hands sinks into the hair at the back of my head, pulling me in tighter, and the other slips into the front of my underwear. My hands move, wrapping around his waist and down into his underwear to cup his firm ass. He flips the front of my underwear down and I break the kiss to stare at what his hand is doing to my rock-hard cock. He wraps his long fingers around me and drags his hand up to the wide mushroom tip, making me jerk into the movement.

"Fuck, you're huge," he moans as his thumb wipes the bead of pre-cum off the tip. Then he brings it to his mouth and sucks it clean, making my mouth dry out at the erotic sight.

I drag his underwear down to his thighs and free his cock, watching as it springs out, large and angry. Emmett's cock is shorter than mine, but he's thicker. I grab his hips and press our cocks together, and we both groan at the smooth velvet contact. His mouth is back on mine, and we devour each other as our cocks rub against our stomachs. I want to come all over him so badly, and it fucking consumes me. He sucks my tongue into his mouth as he grinds his cock into my belly.

The sudden urge to taste him and have his hot cum spill down my throat is overwhelming. I break the kiss and trail my lips down his neck and chest. I lick between his pecs before sucking one of his nipples into my mouth, swirling my tongue around it. His head tips back and his moan reverberates off the washroom walls. Then I make my way down his abs, licking and sucking until his cock hits my chin. Pulling my head back, I glance up at him, seeing nothing but potent lust in his eyes as his abs flex with his restraint.

His eyes are hooded with desire and his plump, juicy mouth tips up into that devious grin of his. "You don't have to do that—" he begins, but I cut him off as my tongue slides across the head of his cock, licking his pre-cum clean. He groans and thrusts past my lips and I close them around the tip slowly.

A sudden knock on the door has us flying apart and pulling up our underwear. "Yeah?" I call out, sounding every bit as shaken as I feel.

"We're closing up. You guys okay in there?" a girl calls out.

"Uh… yeah," Emmett replies as he pulls our clothes apart. "My friend here just puked up his beers."

"Ew." She giggles. "Hurry or you'll be locked in here tonight." Then her footsteps recede as the room falls quiet.

We dress in complete silence and avoid any eye contact. That knock was like a bucket of ice water over my inebriated state, and now I'm stone-cold sober.

After we're dressed, I stalk over to the bathroom door, unlock it, and swing it all the way open. I turn back and finally meet his eyes. They're just as closed off as mine and I'm glad for it because what happened here tonight? Whatever it was, I am nowhere close to being ready to deal with it.

Emmett

I lie in bed, staring at my ceiling. The morning sun blares through the room, but I don't feel like getting up to close the curtains. I can't stop thinking about last night. How his mouth felt on me, how he *tasted*. I want more, so much more, but I know that was it. Nothing more will come of it. The Travis I had on his knees and his mouth around my cock was gone in a snap. The ride home and the separating to our rooms after? Complete silence and no acknowledgment. I fucked up.

I fucked up bad.

Being drunk off my ass should be a pass, right? I don't do this shit. Ever. I've dated chicks my whole life, and yeah, sure, I've found certain guys attractive. Usually dark, brooding guys who look like they're ready to kill you or themselves. Very Travis-like. I never acted on it though. I held that in because I thought it was a phase.

Until last night.

Fuck me and my need to get out of the house, then drink enough to put down a horse. It's just as much his fucking fault too. The way he's been with me all week? Touching me, being around me constantly, and fucking rubbing my back after a nightmare. He's just as bad for sending mixed signals.

I pull myself out of bed and decide to shower away the stench of embarrassment and the brewery.

Once I'm satisfied I can face him without showing how fucking stupid I feel, I make my way downstairs. I hear him in the kitchen, shuffling around and opening cabinets. My breath gets lodged in my throat as I walk in. I'm not fucking ready.

Travis is bent over and looking for something under the sink, his back rippling and flexing, his biceps bunching, and the tattoos running down each arm make it impossible for me to rip my eyes away.

He senses me and stands up slowly to glance over his shoulder. Our eyes meet and some of the shame I'm feeling is reflected there. *Cool. He regrets it.* He says nothing, just throws me a nod and walks right on by me out of the kitchen. A few moments later, the front door opens and shuts.

My very hungover head falls back against my shoulders as I groan. I fucked up so badly. I should've fought the urge to touch him last night. He just looked so tortured leaning against the counter, his face painted in pain. I don't know what he was thinking about and before I could stop myself, the skin of his back was running beneath my fingertips. That was all it took for every bit of willpower to leave my system, especially when he did nothing to stop it and almost everything for it to continue.

I turn around and leave the kitchen. I need a day. I'm going to lock myself in my room and just wallow. Then I promise I'll pick myself up and forget every-fucking-thing.

The sounds of a heated argument filter through my sleep and I open my eyes when Adri's voice rings clear. So, after the shit we did last night and how he acted this morning, he goes running to her right after? I can see what he's trying to do. Either he's trying to prove he's straight or he's attempting to make me jealous. Both options have him hoping for a reaction. Where he's fucked this up? I don't get jealous of Adri because I want her too. Just as much as I want him.

Rolling out of bed, I decide to give the bastard what he wants… my attention. At the top of the stairs, I gaze down to find them standing in the foyer. Adri is fucking delectable in a leather crop top and shorts, her hair up in a messy bun of curls on her head, and her tanned skin a shimmering bronze. It's as though Travis senses me because he glances up, a grin pulling on his lips when he sees me leaning on the railing. Adri follows his gaze and her eyes find mine.

"Oh, hey, Emmett." She gives a nervous little wave as her cheeks light up in a blush while she peruses my naked chest. *So fucking adorable.* I run my gaze from the tips of her pointy heels to the top of her head.

"'Sup?" I grin and nod my head at her. Travis stiffens beside her, his grin falling into a frown. If he was looking for a different reaction, then he'll be sorry. I'm done hiding what I want.

"Do you have IG?" she asks.

"Yeah." I lift a brow.

"Do you follow anyone at school?"

"A few people." I shrug. "Why?"

"Go check it," she says, tucking her arms under her chest, making her tits bounce. I lick my lips and leave my gaze there, making it painfully obvious what I'm looking at. She lowers her arms, and her blush magnifies into red splotches on her face, but her eyes peer right inside me and all I see there is lust. Baby girl wants me too. I chuckle and turn around to grab my phone out of my room.

Then I walk back out with my phone in my hand. "What exactly am I looking for?"

"Oh, you'll see," she snarls, making my eyes flick to her anger-filled face.

Gazing back down at my phone, I click on Charles' stories and an instant grin lights my face when I see a video of me and

Travis on stage. "Yo! He fucking recorded this shit?" I laugh.

"Are you kidding me?" Adri yells. "There are videos of you two naked all over social media!"

"We were fucking hot!" I whistle. "We kept our underwear on," I try to reason with her.

"Told you it wasn't a big deal." Travis' deep voice washes over me. Fuck him. I wonder if she would think what happened after was a big deal.

"Not a big deal?!" she screeches. "You guys stripped in front of old fucking ladies!"

"They weren't that old." I roll my eyes. "Are you feeling jealous?" I ask her with a wink.

"No!" she huffs, her eyes avoiding mine as her cheeks bloom red with her lie.

"Well, if you change your mind, I can rectify that with a private show."

Her blush comes back full force, and I chuckle. Travis grabs the top of her arm and pulls her toward the kitchen. "Let's go."

Her eyes flick up and meet mine. "See ya later, sweetheart," I say with a wink, then laugh when I hear Travis' exhale of breath.

I hope he's not using Adri to get at me because that's just not fair to her. If he wants her and me as well, then that's different. He's struggling, and I know right now he is in major denial and there's nothing I can do about it.

I head back into my room and lie on the bed again, continuing the Netflix show I was watching before I fell asleep earlier. The show is about high school kids in Spain and since I speak fluent Spanish,

I'd rather watch it without English dubbing. One group has a female who fucks with two males and sometimes they all fuck together. It's intriguing and I can't help but think if that's possible. One guy in this group is straight, but the other is definitely bi, so it's a struggle there too.

But what if both guys are bi and the girl wants them both?

Chapter Six

Adri is pissed at us for stripping last night, and I'm pissed at us for stripping last night and getting carried away afterward. Emmett hasn't spoken one word to me, and I want to curl up and die of embarrassment. His fucking cock was in my mouth, and if we weren't interrupted, I don't know how far that would've actually gone. There's no point in denying that I'm attracted to him, but... I'm also in love with Adrianna Hinton and have been since elementary school. I just haven't been able to tell her, because if I do, I'll also have to admit that she isn't enough. I would never be completely content.

I'm messed up and I'm fucking selfish. One day, I'll figure out what it is I can live with and just exist. That's all I'm expecting for my life anyway. To just exist.

"I can't believe you don't see how bad this is." Adri is still berating me as we stand in the middle of E's kitchen. "Your father's business partners could see this video and pull contracts."

"I don't care about any of that shit." I shrug my shoulders. "My father's company can burn to the ground for all I care."

"What?" she breathes out. "Travis, this was your father's legacy to you." She rubs at her temples, confusion clouding her features. It's not her fault I never opened up to her and told her just how messed up my family was.

"What do you know about my father, Adri?" I take a step toward her, my heart pounding inside my chest as I push us into foreign territory. We've never discussed this before, and for some reason, I need her to know the man my father was to better understand me. "You think he built that empire just for me? Maybe for my mother too? To sustain us in the future?"

"Well, y–yeah," she stutters and takes a step back. I'm not angry with her, not at all, but the dam I've constructed is cracking and I can't stop it.

"My father was fucking evil," I grit out between my teeth, taking another step closer. "He hated me and hated my mother. That business was his escape from us."

"No…" She shakes her head as her eyes fill with tears.

"Yes," I grid out. "So maybe I do hope every investor he's ever worked hard for sees that shit and deems *my* business not worthy any longer, and just maybe that shit will self-destruct. A final *fuck you* to the man who ruined my whole life." My chest heaves with my confession, each breath I suck in scorching its way through my lungs.

"Ruined… how?" Her voice is strangled as she reaches a hand toward me, her eyes filled with fear. Fear of learning the truth. Fear of finding out I wasn't the spoiled playboy she's always thought I was.

I shake my head and turn away from her to open the fridge and grab a Gatorade. I could never tell her everything that's happened to me. The thought of shattering the image she has of me and my family is the only thing stopping me. The guilt I'd force on her would be devastating, and I wouldn't be able to live with myself. She saw my father the same way most of this town did; an upstanding citizen who gave plenty to charities and built wings on hospitals and schools. He had buildings made for the homeless and he loved to volunteer the entire family on Thanksgiving at the local soup kitchen. Robert Greene gave a lot to Whitsborough, but he also took what he considered his. He was ruthless and, as much as the townsfolk loved his contributions, they never warmed up to him as a neighbor.

"I k–know he w–wasn't the nicest man," Adri stutters as I gulp down the Gatorade. "But I didn't know… I had no idea—"

"I know, Adri," I cut her off and put her out of her misery. "Just don't assume the same things that were important to him are important to me as well."

"Okay," she reluctantly accepts. She wants to say more, to press me for information, but it would mean breaking through the wall I've built, and she knows the aftermath could destroy us both. "I actually wanted to talk to you."

"About?" I throw the empty Gatorade bottle in the recycling bin and lean against the counter. Her brown eyes are filled with apprehension as she takes a step toward me, her cheeks flushed.

"Us," she whispers, and when I don't reply, she carries on. "I just don't know what's going on with us. Earlier in the year, when we thought I was… you know…" She waves her hand and swallows thickly at the mention of our pregnancy scare. "You were different, more attentive, and it seemed you actually wanted to give this a shot, to be together. But after, you just froze up, and since I wasn't carrying your child, you just tossed me aside."

"I have never tossed you aside." I'm failing her. Articulating my feelings is difficult when so much needs to remain hidden away. The thought of picking apart my love for her and the emptiness inside me is just too overwhelming. "I just can't give you what you want, Adri. I'm not ready."

"You don't even know what I want," she persists as a tear runs down her cheek and she angrily brushes it away. I make her do that too often. Cry. It kills me every time she sheds a tear for me.

"Tell me," I say as I take a step into her. It's wrong to force her to admit how she feels when I can't. I'm selfish, but hearing that someone cares about me is like having a cold gulp of water when you're nearly dead from thirst.

"Fuck!" she groans, slipping her fingers into the bun on top of her head. "I want us back to what we were before that fucking party in grade nine." That's so far from what she wants. So far from what I want.

"You sure about that?" I ask, taking another step closer, bringing our chests flush. Just like always, the magnetic pull between us wins, and I need to feel her love. To feel that I have a chance at happiness, even if it is fleeting.

"Yes," she breathes out, her eyes searching mine.

"Then we couldn't do this." I run my fingers along her cheek and lean in until our mouths are an inch apart. "We couldn't even think of this." I press my lips to hers and she gasps, opening her mouth beneath mine, and just like every other time I've felt Adri's soft plump lips, it's never enough. My tongue slides into her mouth and my hands grab her face to bring her in closer. Her tongue tangles with mine as a longing groan escapes her.

Then I pull away from her mouth and stare into her eyes. "Tell me you wish we had never done that and more."

"As good as that is, I'm losing you regardless." She drops her head to my chest, every fracture of her heart reflected in her words. "At least back then you were mine."

Pulling back now would be best for her. Letting her go once and for all would be torture, but it would mean a future for her. I have nothing worth holding onto and she'll realize it eventually. None of that matters though because I could never fully let her go. She was made for me. Our souls were woven from the same thread, her life doomed before it even started. "I have a lot going on, Adri. A lot of shit I need to work through. I'm not ready to plan the rest of my life, because that's what you would be. The rest of my life."

She looks up at me, her chocolate eyes widening and glistening with tears. "I don't get it."

"You're mine, Adri." I press her hand against my chest, feeling my heartbeat against my palm in a quick staccato. "This has always belonged to you. You just deserve so much more."

She throws her arms around my neck and jumps up to wrap her legs around my waist, catching me off guard. My hands automatically go to her ass and I squeeze it in handfuls, my body giving in to her as it always does. "Show me how much I'm yours," she says into my ear, effectively shutting down every negative thought in my brain.

"Done," I murmur against her cheek before carrying her upstairs and into my room, kicking the door shut.

Her legs release from around my waist and she slides herself down my body until her feet hit the floor. She begins to take off her clothes as I stand and watch, my eyes soaking in every inch of skin she exposes. Adri thinks I've been in many girls' beds, that I've been able to watch another get naked and lose myself in their touch, but it's so far from the truth. Adrianna is the only girl I've longed for, and no other will ever meet her standard. She owns that part of me.

"You're beautiful," I breathe out as I take her in. Her bronze skin radiates with warmth, the goose bumps along its surface begging for my touch.

"I need you to get naked, Trav," she whimpers as she reaches out to grab the hem of my shirt. "It's been too long."

She doesn't know what she's asking for because I've been worked up since last night and no amount of jerking off has helped. I'm in a constant state of arousal and now I'm needing to sink into Adri's wet warmth to rid myself of the agony.

I pick her up and throw her on my bed, her squeal loud as she bounces on the mattress. Her head lands close to the bottom end as her hair escapes the bun and cascades toward the floor. When her eyes meet mine, they darken with a sultry look as her teeth sink into her plush bottom lip. She slowly spreads her legs wide and runs one hand down her stomach and into her folds while the other hand works hard on a nipple. A groan escapes me while I fist my hands at the sudden urge to come, hoping to stave it off long enough to thoroughly enjoy her.

Her fingers sink deep into her pussy as she pumps them in and out, her wetness gathering in her hand. I quickly undress and climb onto the bed at her feet, dragging my nose along her leg. The smell of her arousal hits my nostrils and my mouth waters with anticipation. She smells like sweet musk, just so uniquely Adri. I bring myself directly in front of her glistening pussy and grin when she tries to bring herself closer, instinctively telling me where she wants me to be. I lightly blow some air onto her slit and quickly dart my tongue out to lick her clit. Her back arches off the bed and she moans so loud, I'm sure Emmett heard it. I'm also sure he's heard quite a bit already, considering his music is off for once. I want him to hear it. He needs to know what Adri means to me, what she will always mean to me.

Opening her legs farther with my hands, I dive in like her pussy is my last fucking meal. Like I'm fucking dying of thirst in the Sahara. I thoroughly lick every fucking inch from her asshole to her clit, leaving nothing untouched. As soon as I sink two fingers into her, she comes around them, her pussy clenching and her scream loud.

I run my mouth up her pelvic bone and over her stomach, wiping off the juices smeared along my lips and chin, then suck a nipple into my mouth. Right now, she's a mumbling, writhing mess, and I can't help but toy with her a little longer. I know what she wants, and it's my cock deep inside her, trying to punch a hole through her cervix, but I'm not done yet. I want her teetering on the edge of anger and so worked up and pissed off because that's when our sex is the hottest.

While I continue to toy with her nipples, I push my cock against her clit, pumping my hips every so often to get her worked up without a release. After a few minutes, her moans become growls of frustration and she grabs a handful of my hair, pulling my head up in front of her face.

"Put your cock in my fucking pussy, asshole, or I will kill you." There she is.

"Yes, ma'am." I grin as I grab her right leg and push it up over my shoulder.

Then I line my cock up to her entrance and slam it in just how she likes it, rough and unyielding. Adri gasps and tips her head back over the edge of my mattress as I continue to push my way inside her. The sound she makes each time I'm fully seated inside her will always be ingrained in my brain. She's wet—so fucking soaked—her juices dripping down my balls. I pull out to the tip and gaze down to where we're connected. My cock is covered with her arousal, and when I slide back in, the sound her pussy makes drives me almost to blow my load.

"Harder, Travis," she pants. "Really fuck me." She reaches up to grab her tits, her hands massaging their fullness as her hips thrust to meet mine.

She asked for it.

The sounds of her moans and her wet pussy spurs me on, making me quicken my pace. I need her to come again, but I'm nearing my own release and can't control it as it takes over.

Each time I pound into her, I grind into her clit with my pelvic bone, praying she reaches her climax when I do. As she grows louder and her moans turn into shouts and curses, my door opens, and Emmett is standing there in the doorway, just watching us. Adri sees him, but she's already in the middle of her orgasm, unable to stop or really care. He's watching me though, not her. Not the bounce of her tits each time I pound into her, not her plush open mouth or flush cheeks. No, he's watching me, and fuck if it doesn't make me grow harder. He lifts his arms up and leans them on the top of my doorway, making his shirt rise and showing his Adonis belt, still keeping his eyes on mine.

I grab Adri's hips and prop her up as I rise onto my knees. Her quick intake of breath tells me she's noticed us watching each other, but I don't care—I can't care right now.

With our eyes still locked, I fuck her punishingly, and I can't help it as I make myself believe it's him. He licks his lips and pulls the bottom one into his mouth, biting down as he zones in on where I'm connected to Adri. That's all it takes before I'm coming so hard and intensely inside her as she comes again with my name screaming from her lips.

I don't break eye contact as I pull out of her—still hard—and get up from the bed. He hasn't moved, and I don't bother to cover myself as I walk by him to my bathroom, my cock glistening with Adri's juices.

"Emmett!" she squeals, breaking our stare off. "What the fuck?"

I glance back at her as she's wrapping herself up in my sheet, and then I look at Emmett to find him watching me again. "My bad," he mutters, his eyes dark with lust. Then he turns around and walks back across the hall.

"Why did we let him watch?" she whispers as she watches him leave, her knuckles white as she grips the sheet.

"Don't act like you didn't like it."

With a click, I shut the bathroom door behind me. A part of me should feel shameful, but instead, I'm turned on, like I haven't just blown my load inside Adri. I'm content, but not fully satisfied. The overwhelming need to go into his room, grab him, and finish what we started last night has me nearly storming from my bathroom. The urge to find out what he feels like has my fingers wrapping around the edge of the counter, my nails scraping into the wood beneath. I wrap one hand around my dick and pump slowly, closing my eyes while imagining his plump lips wrapped around me. His cheeks are hollowed as he sucks me deep into his throat, and I can't help the groan that escapes me, my cock still so fucking hard. I imagine shoving my cock so far down his throat as he gags, and I spill myself while he swallows around me. Once I've come again all over the bathroom floor, I peer up at myself in the mirror, finding agony reflected back at me.

Will I ever be able to have them both?

Emmett

The click of Travis' bathroom door shutting behind him sounds as I'm walking into my room. The rustle of fabric follows behind me and I turn to find Adri—wrapped in a sheet—hurrying across the hall to my room.

"Emmett!" she whispers harshly. "Why did you stand there and watch us?" Her cheeks are flushed from her many releases—I heard them all—and from the embarrassment of being watched.

"I heard you screaming and was just checking to see if you were okay." I throw my hands up and say the first excuse that comes to mind. "What if you were injured?" My eyes narrow on hers as a smile grows along my lips.

"Obviously, you saw I wasn't! Why did you stay there and continue to watch?" Her eyes are saucers as they flick between mine, her pulse evident through the thin skin of her throat.

"Because I liked what I saw." I shrug and slowly scan my eyes down her body. "Admit it… you liked it too."

"Oh my God!" she growls out with exasperation. "What is with you two?" She clutches onto the sheet, but the thin material does nothing to hide the tightening of her nipples beneath. She did like it.

"Answer me." I step into her sheet-covered body and grab onto her waist. "Did you like it too?" My mouth is so close to hers and her eyes darken quickly as the scent of them combined assaults my senses.

"I…" she trails off as she watches my mouth descend toward hers. I can't help it. The need to taste her, and maybe him *on* her, is driving me crazy. "Yeah," she groans just before I slam my mouth onto hers.

Her lips open instantly against mine and my tongue slides in. My hand runs down her hip and finds the slit in the sheet as I push inside to feel the skin of her inner thigh. Her body trembles as she moans into my mouth, kissing me harder. My hand continues its ascent to the apex of her thighs until I brush the evidence of what she just did with Travis as it slowly runs down. Smearing my finger through it, I continue upward into her folds.

Her pussy is drenched with his cum and her rapidly increasing arousal. When I push my finger inside, all I feel is their cum running down my hand. Fuck, I want my cock inside there so badly.

The feeling of being watched cascades over me, but I continue my assault on her mouth and her pussy, the sucking noises getting louder as the mixture between her legs soaks my hand. He hasn't made a noise, but I can hear the rapid intake of his breath as he watches.

Finally, I pull away from her mouth and stare into his face. He's not angry. No, not at all. He's exactly like he was last night when his mouth was wrapped around my cock. I pump my finger inside her again and slowly pull it out. She has her head resting against my chest and has yet to realize we have an audience.

"What is happening right now?" she asks, lifting her head up to look at me. When she notices I'm looking over her shoulder, she spins around, finding Travis standing there in a pair of sweatpants and his hands in his pockets. "Fuck!" she screams as she stiffens.

He slowly tears his stare off my face and back to her, a grin forming over his lips. "Not quite, but it sounded like it could've been if I hadn't interrupted." Then his eyes are back on me, his brow notching upward.

Adri turns to glance at me as well, the nervous tension radiating off her. I swing my eyes to hers and wink before sticking the finger full of both her and Travis into my mouth. Their combined taste has my eyes rolling back into my head and I moan softly. "You both taste divine together," I say once my tongue has sucked off every bit.

"Holy fuck," Adri whispers as her eyes nearly bug out of her face. Yeah, it won't take much convincing to win her over. He, on the other hand, will be the challenge.

"Glad you enjoy it," he retorts as he turns back into his room, and Adri runs quickly behind him.

"Travis, wait!" she yells, her voice becoming shrill. He stops and stares at her as I lean against my doorframe, not bothering to hide. I'm listening in on this conversation. "I don't know… I went there to ask him…. Fuck!" she screams again in frustration. "I've told you I love you and you have yet to say it back to me. You just string me along with empty promises, even though I told you I wanted to be with you. I'm not enough for you!"

"Adri,"—he raises a brow at her—"stop freaking out. I'm not mad." From my perch at the doorway to my room, I can also see how not mad he is. It gives me hope that just maybe I can convince them to do something unconventional with me.

"That's just it!" she shrills while stomping her foot. "You should be mad!" I can't blame her for the turmoil she's feeling because she doesn't know about Travis' predicament. In her eyes, he should be mad that she seemingly just cheated… right after fucking him.

He just shrugs and walks to her clothes all over the room, slowly picking each piece up. "You like him, right?" he questions her, his voice even and detached.

"I… guess so." She looks back at me with sorrow in her eyes. It makes my heart sink into my stomach, but I can't do anything about it. He has to explain himself to her, try to make her understand what it is he desires.

"Then be happy, Adri. Do what makes you happy, and if

it's Emmett, by all means, fuck him." He throws her clothes on the bed, his actions and words effectively pushing her away. That's his intention. He wants to avoid confronting his own feelings by shutting Adri out.

"What?" she asks with an exhale, her back straightening. "What the fuck does that mean?"

"It means I can't give you what you're looking for,"—he points over at me—"but maybe he can."

I cross my arms over my chest and raise my brow at him, his cowardice shining through. What is it she's looking for? A relationship? Someone to love her? I can guess why he feels like he can't give it to her, and I think it's because he doesn't just want her, he wants me too. It's exactly how I'm feeling because I want them both and I'm not afraid to admit that.

Adri stormed out of here about an hour ago, after Travis refused to continue the conversation. Even though I tried to stop her and talk to her about what we did, she was too worked up to listen. I don't blame her because I'm still not sure why I took it so far. I just wanted them to see that this thing between us—between all three of us—is real. It feels real, and it feels like it could work. But how do I explain that to them?

Travis has been locked up tight in his room and avoiding the situation. It makes me nervous as I try to piece together what he's feeling. He told Adri he was fine with it all, but that can't be completely accurate. He loves her but feels like he doesn't deserve her. I can see that.

I get up off my bed because I am not spending my Saturday night moping in my room. Walking right across the hall, I bang on his bedroom door but am met with silence. Of course he doesn't answer me. So I do it again, louder.

"Fuck!" he bellows, his pained voice echoing through the door. "What?"

"Let me in." I rest my head on the slab, my heated skin soaking in the chilled surface. "We need to talk." I stay there for a few minutes as he rustles around inside. Just when I'm about to knock again, he swings his door open, revealing his tousled hair and tension-filled shoulders.

"What is it?" he asks, his jaw tight and his eyes filled with irritation.

"We need to talk and we need to do it before Ember gets home. If we continue to act like this,"—I wave a hand between us—"she'll figure it all out."

"What's there to figure out?" He raises a brow at me with a scowl tugging on his full mouth.

I step into him, bringing us chest to chest as he sucks in a breath, his chest heaving at my nearness. Travis is about an inch shorter than me, so we look each other in the eyes. "The fact that you were ready to swallow my dick last night and then got off on me watching you fuck Adri." My tone is infused with exasperation as I push him to realize what's happening between the three of us.

"She couldn't know all that." He rolls his eyes with exasperation.

"No." I shake my head. "You're right, she couldn't. Not until she threatens me within an inch of my life—and we both know she's capable—to tell her why we are so motherfucking awkward."

"Fine," he huffs out, holding his door open wider. "Let's talk it out."

I walk into his room and sit on his bed. "A few questions first," I say as he closes the door. "Are you into guys and girls?"

"I guess." He shrugs and leans against his door, his arms crossing over his chest. It's a defensive move, his way of protecting the secrets threatening to tear his chest apart. "To be honest with you, I've only ever been with two girls, with Adri being the only one consensual."

"What?" I stare at him with wide eyes. I couldn't have heard that right. "You raped a girl?"

"No." He shakes his head and drops his arms from his chest, looking a little shocked that he told me so much as he sits on the bed beside me. "I was forced to fuck a girl. It's a long story, but she was willing."

"Fuck." I scan him over as it really hits me. Travis has had a fucked-up life. "Guys?"

"I've been with a few guys." He swallows, his throat working as he nods. "Most consensual."

"Coach?" I whisper, fearful of the answer.

"Not consensual." The words ricochet around the room until they find their target in my heart, ripping rage from the pit of my stomach. I grip the blanket beneath my hands and take a deep breath, knowing my loss of control will only make this moment harder for him.

"Right," I croak out as I take another breath. "You need to talk to Adri about this. She doesn't know what you're feeling and she's internalizing it, thinking she's not enough for you."

"I know." His mouth hardens into a scowl as he stares down at his hands in his lap. "How do I even talk about it?"

Lifting my shirt over my head, I turn so my back is facing him. "The scars you see under my tattoo were caused by cat-o'-nine-tails. It started when I was twelve until I was fifteen. The hooked metal tips would dig into my skin and rip it off, creating the most agonizing pain I've ever felt to this day. Calen was a disturbed man, but what was more disturbing was the fact that my father sanctioned it. Told him to beat the shit out of his young son." I turn back to face him, finding his face a mask of pain as he drops his hands to the bed. "Then I grew too big for him to overpower, and I killed the piece of shit."

"That's fucked," he says hoarsely, his fingers twitching as though he wants to reach out and touch me but is restraining himself. "Why this tattoo to cover it?"

"Because the little boy represents the death of my childhood innocence." I clear the emotion out of my throat as I shake my head with a chuckle. "And when my asshole father got out of jail, he congratulated me on killing his closest man, telling me that's what my training was for." My eyes flick to meet his. "It's not nearly everything I have been through, but it's some. That's how you begin, with something small."

"Why are you trying to fix things between me and Adri?" His eyebrow raises as he blinks back the tears flooding his eyes. "Don't you want her?"

"Do you read manga?" I ask as I put my shirt back on.

"No." His brows come together at the weird turn of our conversation.

"Okay." I put my finger up when he opens his mouth to speak. "Let me finish. I have a few series of manga and one of them is about a group of friends. There's three of them, two guys and a girl, best friends through school. In their final year in high school, the girl catches feelings for both guys and instead of them fighting, they decide to all be together."

"What the fuck?" His nose crinkles in confusion. The movement almost has me leaning forward to kiss them away.

"I know," I explain as I run a hand over my face. "It's not a societal norm, but it happens. I believe we're meant to love multiple people in our lifetimes. I don't believe in soul mates, or rather, I think they're really rare. With my sister and your brother, I believe they are soul mates," I ramble as his brows lift higher on his face. "We can love more than one person."

"So, you want us to both date Adri?" he asks, still looking slightly confused.

"Yes, and no." I lean into him, noting every shade of green in his eyes. "I want the three of us to date each other."

"What?" The surprise in his voice has me reaching out to brush a lock of hair off his forehead, hoping my touch can soothe him.

"It's obvious I want you too. I know you've been through some shit and trusting me is not coming easy to you, but I want you." I look him in the eyes as my hand falls away.

"This is weird," he whispers, and my heart soars because it's not a no. "How would we explain any of that to our friends and family?"

"We don't have to explain shit to anybody until we're ready. Not a moment before then." I don't have a single doubt that Ember and Vin will accept us. They love us unconditionally and both of them only want what's best for us, what makes us happy.

"So you're bi like me?" he asks, his voice low with curiosity.

"I guess so?" I shrug. Sexuality is something I just let be, never forcing myself to fit any mold. "I like what I like and never paid much attention to male or female, just how I feel, and I feel a lot for both you and Adri." I stand up and walk toward his door, knowing he'll need the space to work it all out. "Think about it." I open his bedroom door and say, "Nobody's rushing you."

Adrianna

It's taken me twenty minutes to walk home and my anxiety has only increased with each step. What is wrong with me? How could I fuck Travis and then let Emmett touch me like that after? I've been grasping at remnants of mine and Travis' past, trying desperately to hold on to him, and my actions today have ruined it all. He'll never forgive me. Everything I've accused him of over the past few years is now slapping me in the face. I'm the one who jumped from one guy to another, and I've never been so ashamed of my actions.

Everything would be so easy if I could blame it on my confusion, but that's not good enough. My need to be loved, to be with someone, is making me irrational. Self-loathing bubbles up inside of me as I punch in the code at the gate, waiting for the sound of the hinges as they open. My feet drag as I walk up my driveway, my heart becoming like lead inside my chest. How does one recognize love when they've never really been shown it?

No. I won't let my despicable actions today be explained away by my upbringing. I still make my own decisions, and I made them today. There's no denying I love Travis. I always have and I always will, but I'm falling for Emmett too. This would be the moment I'd want to call my best friend and beg her to help me figure it all out, but she'd kill me for pulling Emmett into this love triangle.

Ember is going to kill me when she gets home, especially because she warned me about this.

Opening my front door, I'm greeted with silence. It's the third Saturday of the month and that means the staff has the day off. I kick off my shoes and head toward the kitchen, knowing I'll find food ready to be reheated in the fridge. I grab the containers filled with pasta and pull off the lids to pop them into the microwave as my eyes flick to the calendar on the wall. My parents have been gone for three weeks now and not once have they called to check up on me. Sometimes I think they would rather pretend I didn't exist, but then their pride gets in the way and the family name must carry on.

There is no one colder than my parents. After learning about Travis' dad today, I was taken aback by just how similar we feel toward our parents; the people meant to love and care for us. This entire time, I thought I was the only one neglected, but I was wrong. Maybe that was one reason we were so drawn to one another. Our pain was one and the same.

The beep of the microwave pulls me out of my melancholy thoughts, and I take out the container, heading to the large table to eat by myself. Robert Greene was always a presence here in Whitsborough with his donations and charitable works, but I couldn't say I knew him personally. He was often busy and rarely around when I would visit Travis at his house. I thought he was a successful businessman, someone who had to work hard for his family, and that meant being away. Clearly, I didn't know everything.

How much of Travis' life did I assume? How many holes did I fill with my own explanations?

I stuff a forkful of chicken Alfredo into my mouth as I grab my cell phone out of my sweater pocket. No missed calls and no messages. Not that I expected there to be any. My thumb hovers over my message icon before I press it, intending to torture myself over Travis' texts, but instead, I land on Ember's. The love she has found with Vin makes me grow green with envy. I'm happy for her but I want the same. I begin to type out a long message to her, detailing my broken home, my heartbreak over Travis, and the feelings I'm having for her brother. Once I feel lighter, I delete it all and retype an appropriate one.

Me: Hey! How's Spain?

Turning back to my container of pasta, I don't expect a quick response and I'm shocked when my phone pings with a message.

Ember: Coming home tomorrow.

My head snaps to the calendar as my brows fall together. They're supposed to be staying another week.

Me: Is everything okay?

Ember: Yeah. Just miss you guys and home.

My heart sinks when I think about her time there and how it was meant to give her some space from the grief here in Whitsborough, but maybe she doesn't need space. She needs the people who love her.

Me: Can't wait to see you.

She sends me a heart emoji and I shove away the container of pasta, my stomach too knotted to continue eating. Maybe with Ember coming back, I can shove aside whatever feelings are growing for Emmett and concentrate on her. She's had too much loss in such a short amount of time. I can only imagine how hard it is to be loved by your parents and then lose them soon after. It's more painful to lose something you've experienced than it is to yearn for something you've never had.

CHAPTER SEVEN

Travis Then

"I'm going to need you to stick around after practice, sport," Coach tells me as I'm helping to carry out the bats.

"Okay, Coach." I nod.

Lately, after each game, Coach has me staying to massage his sore muscles. I don't mind helping because he works really hard at making our team great, and last week we won our first game!

I'm still Coach's favorite boy too. It makes me so happy because after my father hit me in his office, I refused to talk to him and that's been almost a month now. Coach says I'm right and I shouldn't talk to my father because he's mean. I'll just talk to Coach about everything from now on. He asked me if I had a girlfriend and I said no, but soon that will change. I will have Adrianna. She has to start out as my girlfriend first, then she can be my wife. Coach thought that was funny and told me one day he will show me how to do all the things to make my wife happy.

I told him he should also teach my father because my mother is always crying. Coach says I should just stay away from my parents and be with him as much as possible. He says they aren't good parents, and he can teach me things they can't anyway. Coach is my favorite person ever!

After practice, I have to help Coach clean up. That means I have to stay later with him. I call Nanny Sonja and tell her not to send our driver, Pete. Nanny Sonja does not like me staying late for practice, but she knows my father is mean to me and my mother is always telling me she hates me. So she would rather I be here.

After my shower and putting away all the equipment, we go to Coach's truck. This is where he likes me to massage him, and then he takes me to Dairy Queen afterward. Fudge sundaes are my favorite! Coach lights up a cigarette and then rotates his neck. I already know that means he's feeling sore, so I kneel up on the seat and rub the back of his neck. Coach has a big neck compared to mine, and it has lots of fat too.

"Thanks, sport. Today I am so sore," he groans.

"It's no big deal, Coach. You work super hard," I tell him as my fingers dig through the fat on his neck.

"You're a good boy." He pats my leg and continues to smoke his cigarette. When he's done, he flicks the butt out the window and unbuckles his belt. Coach has an enormous belly, and he says he hates the way his belt digs into it. "I need a closer massage today, sport," Coach rumbles as he opens the top button on his jeans. "Through the jeans just doesn't cut it anymore."

"Okay..." My heart pounds really hard and I feel like my stomach is full of swirls and maybe I might puke.

"My underwear will stay on, okay?" He peers into my face, his glassy eyes growing darker as he licks his lips. "The jeans just make it hurt more after."

I guess that makes sense. Coach lifts his butt and slides the jeans down to hang around his knees. He's wearing white briefs, like the ones I usually wear, but the front of his is different. His weenie—that's what my Nanny Sonja calls it—is bigger and poking out. He sees me looking at it and gives me a smile.

"It's like yours, but bigger. This is what yours will look like one

day. See? I am already teaching you things for when you get bigger." I nod, because he is. My father has never shown me his weenie, so how would I know what it's going to be like when I get bigger? "Next time I will show you more, but right now I need that massage."

I slowly reach out my hand and place it on top of Coach's underwear. His weenie inside jerks into my palm and I gasp, pulling back. Coach reaches out and grabs my hand to place it back on his underwear. Using his hand, he wraps my fingers around his weenie. It's big. My entire hand doesn't even fit around it. He then makes me move up and down, guiding me. It feels weird, but it's not a big deal. It's not like it hurts me or anything. I look up into Coach's face and find his eyes closed and his mouth hanging open.

"Squeeze harder, sport," he says, his voice sounding all weird and whispery.

I do what he asks and clamp my hand as hard as I can around him and keep moving it up and down. After a few minutes, Coach's head falls back against the car seat, then he lets out the same noise he usually does at the end of his massage, but this time it's louder and longer.

"Coach," I whisper to him. "Did I do it right? Are you okay?"

"Yeah, sport." He smiles over at me, his yellow teeth showing through. "You did that perfectly."

Chapter Eight

Travis

Lying here thinking about my life and how the downward spiral started is not helping me figure shit out. Just the thought of telling anyone the details of what happened to me makes me physically ill. The most I have ever told anyone was to Vin and Ember and even then they had minimal details.

I get up out of bed and head out of my room as Emmett's music rushes at me, making me exhale with relief because I'm not ready to talk to him just yet. He wants to be with me and Adri, a threesome, not a couple. Fuck, it even sounds weird. What would Adri even think of that? Maybe it's something she would like, considering she went to him right after I had just finished fucking her. I know Adri loves me, but it's clear she has a connection to him. So do I, if I'm being honest. How would we explain it to Ember? She is the one person who really intimidates the fuck out of me, and here I am messing around and trying to figure out how to be in a threesome with her *twin brother*.

Yeah, I'm going to have to change my name and go on the run.

Entering the den, I walk over to the large double doors leading to the backyard to look out at the landscaping. This house is breathtaking, and Ember's aunt and uncle really made it into a home. It feels lived in and it has that feeling of love radiating inside its walls. I enjoy being here, but I need to get to my house and see what the fuck my mother has been up to. It's been over a week since I have been over there and I'm a little worried about Sonja.

"Can't sleep?" His voice sends goose bumps across my skin as my spine tingles with his nearness.

"No." I shake my head. "Can't shut my mind down."

"Yeah, I think I sprung too much on you. I was selfish and was only thinking of myself." I turn toward him. He's leaning against the wall just inside the den, his hair mussed like he's been running his fingers through it and his face is drawn. "You have a lot of shit to deal with, Travis, before you enter any relationship."

"I may never be over the shit that happened to me," I whisper, my heart sinking with the realization. Maybe I'll be forever broken.

"No, you probably won't. I can only speak from experience, but it will probably stay with you forever. That doesn't mean it owns you," he grits out as his face fills with anger. Fuck, when he's mad like this, I can't help but see Ember.

"No, it doesn't own me, but it fucks with my head, and I feel like I don't deserve good things," I reveal, my voice cracking with the confession.

"Yeah." He nods and runs his hands through his hair. "I get that. I'm going to step back and not bombard you about our complicated situation anymore. Again, I'm sorry and I'm here for you, as a friend, until you are ready to face this together."

"Friends?" I ask, because I need the reassurance he's not going anywhere. I need him to still be here… with me.

"Best friends." He grins, the sight taking my breath away. There was a time when I thought Ember was irresistible, her personality, her appearance. She was the complete package, but Emmett? He takes the fucking cake.

"Okay." I swallow thickly and smile. "I should probably tell Adri the same. It's hard to stay away from her, especially considering our past."

"She's like a magnet, I know." He smiles sadly, his eyes shining with understanding.

"I think you guys should continue to see each other." It's out of my mouth before I can stop it, and even though I've suggested it, I haven't really had the chance to mull it over. What would it be like to see them together? Will I always long to be a part of them?

"No." He shakes his head vehemently. "It's all or nothing for me." My heart soars when I hear that, and I can't even put into words how happy I am. It proves to me he wants me, and he wants this with Adri. It solidifies my decision. I trust him. I trust them both to accept me with open arms if I ever come to terms with my demons.

"I think you need to. When I am ready to take this"—I wave between us—"to the next level, I will need you and her to be where she and I are." I want them to experience love, to nurture their feelings so we might all be on the same page one day.

His brows come together in concentration. "I don't know…"

"I do," I press, hoping he can hear the sincerity in my voice. "We need to all agree when we make that decision or else there's no way it will work. I still can't see it actually working, but I'm willing to try for the sake of how we're feeling."

"We can decide here all we want, but it will be up to her. So first, we will talk to her… together, and then figure out the next step, yeah?" He pushes off the wall and stalks toward me, his abs flexing with each step. He doesn't know what he does to me, how much he affects me when we're alone, and he's looking at me like I'm everything he desires.

"Yeah." My heart speeds up inside my chest, banging against my rib cage as he stops to stand in front of me, so close that the heat of his bare chest hits mine. "Okay."

"We should probably try to sleep because Ember will be through here tomorrow like a hurricane." His words are hoarse as his eyes flick from my eyes to my mouth, the intensity in their turquoise depths making me take a small step back.

"Fuck." I scrub my hand down my face to avoid his stare. I've never been this nervous, this unsure. "True."

Emmett gives me one more lingering look before turning around to head upstairs. I follow behind him, my regret growing with each step. Would he have kissed me if I didn't make the moment awkward? He stops and stands in front of his doorway as I run my eyes over his body. Even in pajama pants, Emmett exudes confidence. He's sexy as fuck, and he knows it.

"Stop looking at me like that." He points a finger at my face, his eyes flashing with heat. "Or else I will forget every single thing I agreed to downstairs."

"Sorry." I grin at him sheepishly. "I'll try my best to not check you out."

He reaches out his hand and fists it into the front of my shirt, dragging me into his body. He smells like his bodywash, musky and male. I look him in the eyes, keeping my smirk firmly on my face, then I lift a brow. His mouth crushes into mine, and I am opening my lips quickly just to taste him. I really need to taste him. His tongue slides into my mouth, making my cock harden. He kisses me slowly, almost like he's savoring me. It feels like a goodbye and I fucking hate that. I push my fingers into his hair and growl into his mouth, wanting to replace that feeling with something more.

His other hand that's not curled into my T-shirt grabs my waist, bringing me in closer. The movement presses my erection into his and he moans at the contact. Eventually, he releases my mouth and brings his lips to my ear.

"This is to be continued." Then he pushes me back a step and smiles. "It's not over." He turns and walks into his bedroom, his hair mussed up even more from my fingers. "Night."

"Night," I repeat as my fingers tentatively touch the swollen flesh of my lips, then I turn to walk into my room.

"Mama's home!" E calls out from the foyer the next afternoon. My heart pounds and I can't get myself out of my room quick enough to see her. She's only been gone two weeks, but I've fucking missed her. She has the type of strength that seeps into everyone around her, and things have felt out of control since she's been gone.

I hurry down the stairs and find her ocean eyes staring up at me, full of mischief. Finally, I reach her and lift her into my arms, turning a full circle as I breathe in her scent. She's back, and I didn't realize just how much I needed her here. "Hey." Her hands grab my face once I let her down. "You all right?" Her eyes take on this fire like she's ready to kill anyone that fucks with me and I don't for a second doubt that she would.

"Just missed you." I smile at her and kiss her forehead.

"'Sup, bro?" Vin comes in with their bags, a pair of aviator glasses covering his eyes. They both got a bit of Spanish sun as their skin radiates a few shades darker than when they left. Vin lifts his glasses up onto his head and that's when I noticed he's cut his hair shorter into a buzz cut and all his curls are shaved off.

I grab his outstretched hand and drag him in for a hug. "Missed you guys."

"Yeah." He claps me on the back. "I missed you guys too. It's good to be home." I never thought I would be experiencing this with him. I'm a part of my brother's home and it settles a piece of my broken heart.

"Is that my oh-so-very-good-looking *identical* twin sister?" My heart goes into overdrive when I hear his voice. I take a deep breath and force myself to school my features. I need to make sure we appear the same as we were before they left. So I roll my eyes and glare up at him standing at the top of the stairs.

Yeah, I wish I hadn't done that.

He has no fucking shirt on, again, and his abs start flexing as he reaches his hand up to run his fingers through his messy bedhead.

"Hey." Ember grins up at him and he matches hers with one of his own. "You'll probably get a call from Carm soon. Don't believe everything he says. I did not almost kill him ten times."

Emmett throws back his head and laughs, and I swallow down the lump in my throat at the sound before discreetly reaching down to adjust my growing hard-on.

"Just eight times." Vin chuckles as he wraps his arm around her neck and drags her in to kiss her temple.

"He's going to express how worried he is about my sanity and wants you to come home." She waves her hand like it's no big deal.

"Meh." Emmett shrugs and joins us all in the foyer. "I'm more concerned with what you found while in Spain."

"Yeah." I tear my eyes away from the man who's quickly becoming my obsession. "What's happening?"

"I need wine for this conversation," Ember huffs as she walks into the kitchen, her mahogany hair swaying against her back. She's in a pair of short jean shorts, her attire still clutching to the warmth of Spain even though she's back in chilly Whitsborough.

"She's been thoroughly fermenting since the first day we stepped on Spanish soil," Vin whispers loudly, his tone filled with teasing. He's nothing like the brother I knew last year, and Ember is the reason he's changed, making me that much more grateful for her and hoping it stays this way.

"Fuck you, I heard that!" she calls back from the kitchen.

"Hope I get in trouble." He winks at me and chuckles as he heads into the kitchen. What they have is what I want, being unconditionally in love.

"We'll get it." Emmett places a hand on my shoulder.

"Did I say that out loud?" I ask him as my eyes round.

"Nah." He shakes his head with a smile. "I'm just getting great at reading you." Then he slaps my ass and walks into the kitchen. My heart races at the nearness of his sister and my brother, but my heart warms with the sentiment.

I walk in behind him as Vin leans against the island while Ember sits on a stool with a very large and very full glass of wine. "How bad was it?"

"I almost had her,"—she gulps down a few mouthfuls—"twice."

"Are we going to drop you off for AA in the mornings before school?" Emmett teases as he points to her glass.

"Maybe." She grins at him.

"Jennifer is a slippery bitch," Vin chimes in. "She's also so fucking corrupt it's insane. She's been taking orphans out of New

York foster care and giving them to families in Spain at a cost."

"That's just fucked-up." I shake my head. Knowing my father was in business with her isn't surprising. None of this is.

"Not to mention, she may very well be the cause of those children becoming orphans in the first place," Ember grinds out. "Her trail went cold about four days ago. Carm is on it to figure out where she went. I'm expecting some sort of retaliation from her for Carlos, so as soon as I lost her, I knew I needed to get back here to you guys."

Carlos was the son of Jennifer Talia. He had captured Vin and me to torture info about Ember out of us, but he failed and was killed by Carm.

"What's the next step?" I ask her as I fall into a chair at the table.

"We chill for a bit and try to act like everything is normal." She nods as she refills her glass.

"Try being the operative word," Emmett murmurs as he takes her glass and drinks some wine.

Emmett

"How's school been?" Ember asks a few hours later as she comes into my room. "Do you like it?"

"Actually, it's hard as fuck and I am going to need you to tutor me. Other than that, it's good. It's fun." I cross my arms behind my head as she heads toward me.

"Who are you chilling with besides Travis?" She lies beside me on the bed, crossing her legs at the ankles. I want to say something about these shorts she's wearing and them being a bit too revealing, but I'm sure she wouldn't think twice about kicking my ass.

"Adrianna has been nice. She's in most of my classes, and I met Charles and Jake. We skateboard a lot." I kick at her foot and knock it over, making her growl with irritation.

"That's good. Those are good people." She turns her head toward me, her eyes filled with questions. "Have you met Marlana?"

"Yeah." I nod and shrug my shoulders. "I don't think you will have problems with her this year. She seems scared as hell."

"Don't underestimate her." She shakes her head, a sneer playing around her mouth.

"My locker is right beside hers."

"No!" Amusement dances in her eyes as she grins from ear to ear.

"Yeah, and it's your locker from last year." I nudge her with my elbow as she gasps.

"No way!" she squeals, the sound reminding me of Adri.

"Why do you look like you want to puke? Is it the squealing?"

"No." I chuckle and turn my body to face her. "I'm fine."

"Did you talk to Carm?" She waggles her eyebrows impishly.

"Yeah, he called." I narrow my eyes and scratch at the hair on my chin. "You seriously kicked him out of the car in the middle of nowhere and made him find his way back to the hotel?"

"He annoyed the fuck out of me that day." She shrugs.

It's hard to keep the grin off my face as I say, "Then you waited in his hotel room with your skull makeup on and dressed in black?"

"He was keeping information from me. I needed him to know I was serious." She shrugs again. "He finally confessed to setting up that guy to jump you."

"Yeah, I figured." I snicker at her, already having figured that out. I know my brother and his tactics well. "Did you really shove him in a pen with a horny bull?"

"That was purely a coincidence! I didn't know that thing was ready to mate!" She widens her eyes, feigning innocence. "Besides, he deserved that."

"And then screaming at a *PolicHa* to save you when you were both walking back to the hotel? He was arrested!"

"And I went and bailed him out. They had to drop the charges once I insisted I forgot my meds that day." She flutters her eyelashes.

I can't hold it in any longer and burst out laughing. She joins in soon after and we turn into a hysterical heap on the bed.

"How much does he hate me?" She giggles.

"Actually, I think he might miss you already. He has a job for you next weekend."

"Really? Why didn't he call me himself?" She pouts.

"Probably because he doesn't want you to know he misses you." I chuckle.

"Pussy." She rolls her eyes. "What's the job?"

"A fight… to the death." Her eyebrows shoot up as she stares at me.

"Who is it?"

"Someone working for one of the Heads. I think he was high in the ranks. He was plotting a hit on him," I reveal as she chews the inside of her cheek in thought.

"Which Head?" she finally asks, like that answer depends on if she will do it or not.

"Wade."

"Pass." She scoffs. "I'll help the fucker plot his death."

"Seriously?" I look at her with my eyes wide.

"Ugh." She rolls off the bed and stands next to it, her hands on her hips. "I probably shouldn't, right? Like, that's bad for business?"

"Yeah." I laugh at her expression. "Terrible. Besides, Wade's not that bad."

"He's a cunt," she retorts as she's walking out of my room. "Call your brother and tell him I miss him too."

"He's your brother too!" I yell out to her.

"Yeah, yeah," she mutters from the hallway.

God, it feels so good to have her back. As much as she is the embodiment of darkness, my sister really brings light to the gloom that hangs over us. A walking fucking contradiction. Travis may be worried about telling her about our situation, but I know Ember. She won't disappoint me. He may have known her longer, but she and I will always have a connection that trumps anybody else's. She might not get it and she may not think it would work, but she would never judge us for how we feel.

Travis' trepidation reminds me of how I used to be. Back when Calen enjoyed taking a whip to my back, I was beyond traumatized. I soiled myself every time I heard anything crack. I could barely sleep, and eating was so fucking difficult when I wanted to puke constantly. He loved how he instilled a fear so deep inside me and relished in my fucking responses. When I look at Travis, I can see fear still lingering inside of him deep down. Every time he is near me, it's like he's tortured by his feelings after constantly being told they are wrong. Having an attraction to males after being abused by one for so long is damaging. I took back my courage and killed the man who tortured me. That was my therapy. Travis doesn't have that option, and even if my sister had saved his coach's life for him, I don't think he'd ever have it in him to kill. So my therapy wouldn't be his, but Travis needs something to give him back his courage and his sexuality.

My phone lights up on the bed with a text.

Adrianna: Hey, it's me, Adri.

Me: Yeah, I figured when I saw your name.

Adrianna: Don't be an ass.

Adrianna: Travis won't answer my texts…

Adrianna: He hates me.

Me: No, he doesn't.

Me: He's just going through it.

Adrianna: And I fucked it up more.

Me: No, u didn't.

Me: We should talk.

Adrianna: What we did was wrong, Emmett.

Me: You really feel that way?

Adrianna: Yeah.

Adrianna: I shouldn't have done that to him.

Me: Meet me right now.

Adrianna: Emmett…

Me: I'll come to u… parents home?

Adrianna: No, they are in Spain.

That's a coincidence, being that Ember was just there.

Me: I'll come by.

Adrianna: I don't think that's a good idea.

Me: Don't worry.

Me: I'll tell Travis.

Adrianna: Is there something going on that I should know about?

Me: Yeah, that's why I'm coming over.

I don't read her reply as I get out of bed and head across the hall to talk to Travis. If he really wants this to work, I need his full support and we have to have complete transparency. I knock on his door and hear him call out to come in.

"Hey, Adri is texting me. Are you not answering her?" He's sitting on his bed with his laptop open in front of him, the screen illuminating his face.

"No, my phone is downstairs in the kitchen. I forgot to bring it up with me," he replies as he turns to give me a concerned look. "Is everything okay?"

"I was just about to head over there and talk to her. She's pretty upset about what happened and I thought I would tell her my idea. You're still on board for this plan, right?" My stomach twists with anxiety as I chew my bottom lip. I really don't want him to change his mind.

"Yeah, I am." He nods, his face shining with sincerity. He's been different since my sister came home. "Don't put the moves on her too soon."

"Probably won't happen, seeing as I'm a virgin." I shrug nonchalantly. I remain stoic on the outside, but I'm writhing with fear on the inside.

"What?" He sits up in bed, shock evident in his eyes. "With girls?"

"No, just a virgin all around." I scratch my head as he continues to stare at me. "I was homeschooled and didn't get out much. What do you expect?"

"But you seem so..."—he waves his hand at me—"experienced."

"I'm really not. I just know what I like and how I like it."

"Fuck," he mutters as he adjusts his cock in his sweats. "I'm so hard right now."

I swallow down the groan threatening to spill from my mouth and take a deep breath. "Oh, knock it off." I turn and walk out of his room, deciding to put distance between us before I force him into this situation right now. "Text Adri and let her know you know I'm heading there."

"Good luck!" he calls after me with a chuckle.

Asshole.

It's been a while since I've had my baby between my legs. The Ducati purrs as I pull into Adri's driveway. Fucking sexy-ass bike. I missed her. All week I had been riding with Travis because I liked being in the same vehicle as him, but this week, I'm taking her to school.

Adri opens her front door and stands there with her arms crossed over her chest. Her hair is in a high ponytail and her face is void of makeup. Her face is puffy like she's been crying a lot, and it makes me feel like a piece of shit. I get off the bike and remove my helmet as she stands up straighter, watching me closely.

I walk up to her, but she doesn't move to let me in. I raise my eyebrow, and she raises hers to match mine.

"Travis texted me and told me you were coming to explain some shit," she says, her voice sounding hoarse.

"You okay?" I reach out and run my finger along her cheek, needing to touch her.

"No, I'm not." A tear runs down and onto my finger. "I fucked everything up."

I gather her into my arms and kiss the top of her head, smelling her strawberry-scented hair. "Nah, baby, you didn't. Let me in so I can talk to you."

"Just talking, Emmett." She turns and leads me into her house. "I'm already in trouble because of you."

"That wasn't just me, baby girl. You did that too." My eyes fall to her ass, the silk of her pajama pants hiding nothing.

"Yeah, well, let's not get into any more trouble," she snaps from over her shoulder.

"We won't." She guides me into her kitchen, which is all dark colors and stainless steel appliances, and picks up a half-drunk bottle of wine. "I'll be taking you to meetings along with Ember," I quip as a smile comes over my face.

"She texted me she was back, but I can't stomach talking to her right now." Her bottom lip quivers.

"Don't ignore her for too long. It'll just rile the beast." I sit in a chair at the table as she sits across from me, her hands wrapped around the wine bottle and her eyes glassy from its effects.

"I'll call her later. What are you here for?"

"You have feelings for me, right?" Her brows crinkle as she lifts the wine bottle to her mouth. "Okay, let's try this again. I have feelings for you, Adrianna."

She swallows a gulp of wine, then pulls the bottle away from her mouth. "Okay…" Her plump mouth turns down into a frown.

"I would like the chance to take you out to see where this

can go."

"But Travis…"

"He knows and says we have his blessing." Her face crumbles with despair and she falls forward, her head landing on her crossed arms on the table. "Hey." I get up and lean across to run my hand over her hair. "Adri?"

"So he and I are over then." She lifts her head as more tears run down her cheeks.

"No." I scrub my hand over my face. How the fuck am I going to do this? I decide to conjure Ember and do it her way. "We both want you, but right now, Travis is not in the right headspace to have a relationship, and I want to take care of you. Then later, when he's good and ready to tell you everything, maybe we can both have you."

Her mouth drops open and her eyes are the size of fucking dinner plates. "What the actual fuck, Emmett?" she shrieks as she sits up straight in her chair.

"Uh… too direct?" I raise both hands as my heart races with the fear of pushing her too far.

"What? Like my very own harem of guys? Do I just keep adding to it?" She gulps down the wine, then runs her arm along her mouth. I shouldn't find that as sexy as I do, but I think anything Adri does has the power to bring me to my knees. "Don't you see how that shows how little you guys care?" Her tone is filled with pain as hurt skates over her features.

"No one else. Just me and Travis." My eyes roam over her face, soaking in every beautiful feature. "We both care about you… a lot. He and I have come to an understanding. Now think about it… do you have feelings for both of us?"

"Yes," she whispers, her hand reaching for the bottle again, but I grab it before she touches the glass, her eyes shooting daggers at me as I take her hand in mine.

"Good." I rub my thumb along her smooth skin as her eyes flick down to our clasped hands. "So while Travis is getting himself together, I will woo you."

"Woo?" She glances back up, her brow raising.

"Yeah. Taking you out and dating you. Give us a chance to get to know each other to see if we even work."

"God, this all sounds so fucking crazy," she mutters, her fingers tightening around mine.

"It does, but it can work if we want it to." There's nothing I want more than for her to agree and to give this crazy idea of mine a chance.

"And you two are just good with sharing a girl?" Her eyes are filled with skepticism as she raises her brow.

"Yeah." She doesn't need to know she will have to share us too. I'll wait until Travis is ready before I let her in on that bit.

"I need to think about this." She releases my hand and rests her head on her arms once more.

"Okay." I get it. It's a lot to take in. The last thing I ever want for her is to think we don't care enough. I want her to always feel like she's cared for. Getting up from my chair, I place my hand on her hair and push the bottle of wine back toward her. "I'll let myself out. I'll see you at school tomorrow."

"Hey, Emmett?" she calls out as I reach the kitchen doorway. "Tell Travis he needs to call me before I take this any further!"

"Yes, ma'am." I nod before blowing her a kiss, watching as

the blush forms on her cheeks, then chuckle as I head for her front door.

Adrianna

Pushing the bottle away from me, I stand on drunken legs as disgust rolls through me. It's not even dinnertime yet and I'm drunk off my ass. I'm becoming my mother. Whenever life becomes too hard, I reach for alcohol and let it consume me, erasing whatever pressure I'm feeling at that moment. I was sure I had lost Travis for good after the stunt I pulled with Emmett, but after hearing the *plan* they have for the three of us, I'm left even more confused. It will never work. Or it will work perfectly because Travis can't seem to bring himself to care enough about whoever else has their hands on me. A fact I don't want to face. Why would they think this is a good idea? Two men dating the same girl? What do they get out of it? Nothing makes sense and I can't determine if that's because I'm too drunk to understand it or if they're hiding something from me.

Give us a chance to get to know each other to see if we even work. What does that mean? Get to know each other? Do they want to become brother husbands? From what I've gathered over the last few weeks, Travis and Emmett can barely stand each other, let alone share a girlfriend. Except... there was that one time at the bar when they liked each other enough to strip together.

I stagger to the kitchen counter as my stomach rolls before retching into the sink, saliva pooling in my mouth as the room spins. Grabbing my phone from the marble surface, I swallow back the urge to vomit, not wanting to waste a two-hundred-dollar bottle of wine. I swipe open the screen to find my text conversation with Emmett, then quickly close it, not wanting to reread my most vulnerable moment, and open Ember's instead. It's been nearly three hours since she sent me a text saying she's home and I have yet to reply. What do I say to her? How can I have a conversation with her and push aside everything that's happened? She's bound to ask me about Travis, she always does, and I wouldn't know what to say. But I can't ignore her forever because Emmett is right. It'll only piss her off, and I have to face her at school tomorrow anyway.

My feet drag like lead across the wooden floors as I head toward the stairs, my heart trapped up inside my throat as I try to think of what to message Ember. The house is completely still, the silence mocking me as I climb the stairs. I've always longed for a family, brothers and sisters to bicker with and parents who give a fuck about their children. That's why when Travis revealed he wasn't close with his father, it shocked me. For a second, I was envious of him, even having one to know enough to hate. I don't hate my parents, but I don't exactly love them either. How could I? They're never here. I push open my bedroom door and stumble to the bed, my stomach hitting the mattress with a bounce and sending another wave of nausea through me.

My text conversation with Ember glares at me in my darkened room, the light of the screen and the alcohol sitting in my stomach making me squint as I stare at her words. I begin to type out an apology for falling for her brother, the one thing she warned me off doing, then let out a long exhale as I quickly delete it. When I tell her, I'll be brave enough to do it to her face. Consequences be damned. My fingers move over the screen with a simple reply, hoping she doesn't read too much into my text.

Me: I can't wait to see you. I missed you.

It takes a few minutes, but she reads it and then those three dots appear, sending my heart into overdrive. It's better that she didn't call instead.

Embs: I'll be there in the morning to pick you up.

She knows. My face goes numb as the wine I drank earlier

threatens to make its way back up. She fucking knows. My body feels heavy with guilt and fear as I stare at those words, reading between the lines. I'm dead. When those three dots appear again, I nearly shut off my phone and throw it on the floor.

Embs: I missed you too.

That's a good thing, right? She doesn't want to kick my ass if she misses me. I roll onto my back on the bed and lock my phone, watching the ceiling spin circles over my head. I'm treading on thin ice, and if push came to shove, would I choose my best friend over my heart?

Chapter Nine

Travis

"Hey." A soft knock lands on my door and my eyes flick up to find Ember in the doorway. She's freshly showered, her hair damp around her shoulders, and she's wearing a black tracksuit. She has a smile on her mouth, but it doesn't quite meet her eyes.

"Hey." I smile back at her. "Come in."

She comes into the room and sits at the bottom of my bed, her shoulders hunched forward and her head hanging against her chest. "I need to talk to you about something." She exhales a heavy breath as my heart slams into my rib cage and my mouth dries out.

Fuck, did Emmett say something? Am I getting kicked out right now? "Okay." My voice sounds worried with tension.

"It's about what I found at your coach's house." Her eyes meet mine. "I need complete honesty, Trav." The coach she killed for me. My best friend who loves me, more than any of my family members combined, gave me my revenge for a childhood of misery.

"E, I am always honest with you." I raise a brow as my words come out a little breathless with trepidation, daring her to tell me otherwise. Ember knows more about me than anyone else. I wouldn't lie to her.

"Okay." She nods and turns to face me. "Before I killed him, he was throwing just about everyone in this town under the bus to save his ass."

"Obviously, he wanted to live." I shake my head in disgust as I imagine my spineless coach begging for his life. "What was he saying?"

"He was telling me about a large group of criminals here in Whitsborough, and the shit they're doing is not petty." Being the son of an evil man who practically owned this town, none of this comes as a surprise. What is surprising is how Coach knew about any of it.

"Really? Did you actually believe him? He knew he was about to die." It's more likely he tried to say just about anything, bargaining for his life and grasping at straws.

"He gave me proof, Trav." Her voice remains calm as she stares at me, waiting for something, but I have nothing to give her.

"Okay, what is it?" I don't know what proof she got, but whatever it is has her looking at me like I have two heads. She reaches into her sweater pocket and shows me a USB. I instantly recognize it as a brand my father used and it sends chills down my spine.

"This is what he gave me. It has a lot of information on here and a lot of it is fucking disturbing." It doesn't matter how deep we buried the asshole, his life here in Whitsborough will forever haunt me.

"That came from my father," I tell her. She asked for honesty and that's exactly what she's getting.

"Yeah, he told me that. He had also added to it over the years," she adds, which explains why she was looking at me for answers. She thinks I know exactly what my father was up to while he was alive.

As if she doesn't know that I was the son he dreamed of killing every time I walked into the room.

"What's on there?"

"You don't know?" She raises her eyebrows with surprise.

"No." I shake my head. "Should I?"

"I'm going to go grab my laptop. I'll be right back." She gets up and leaves the room, and I can't help the feeling that comes over me. My body flashes hot and my stomach churns. What the fuck could be on there? And why does it feel like she's questioning me? "Okay." She comes back in, snapping me out of my panic as I suck in a breath. "I'm warning you, some of this shit isn't pretty. Also, I found other stuff in that fucker's office we will have to go through together, but first this."

I just nod because right now I can't seem to find my voice to speak. She loads up the laptop and inserts the USB. It takes a few minutes, but the window finally pops up with a list of files.

"Let's start with this one." She clicks on a file and a list of names comes up. "These are a group of men who are into the same shit Coach Halbert was."

"What?" I gasp and lean forward. "Who?"

She turns the laptop so I can read them myself. Some big names are on this list and a few of them I know very well since they were at my house and in meetings with my father regularly. The ones that stick out the most? Andrew Cox: elementary school principal, Wilson McKay: local fire chief, and Joseph Watkins: local district judge. These three men were in my house at least once a week before my father died. The rest of the list I either only know in passing or not at all.

"I know those three." I point out the three I recognize to her. "They spent a lot of time at my house with my father."

"I figured." She nods. She closes the list and clicks open the next file. "Here is a list of cops who could be paid to look the other way or even assist in cover-ups... for the right price."

I lean over and scan through the list and see police chief Bill Moore on there. It makes a lot of fucking sense. No wonder Coach Halbert was so fucking brazen in the shit he did and these other people too. If some of the highest officials were turning their cheeks, then who was there to fucking protect the helpless?

"I paid him off to *convince* the fire chief that Halbert set that fire with his cigarette." She finger quotes *convinced*. "It was really easy."

The sick feeling in my stomach magnifies as I think about all the children that needed help at the hands of these sick fuckers and didn't receive it. She clicks over to the next file, which is named 'Babies.' When it opens, there are about ten couples on that list, but I only recognize one and I feel my heart racing.

"Georgina and Abe Hinton," I read out loud.

"Is that…?"

"Yeah." I nod as blood rushes through my ears. "That's Adrianna's parents. What does this file mean? What's 'Babies?'"

"I have no idea about this one," she murmurs, her eyes scanning the screen as she loses herself in thought.

"We have to figure it out," I stress to her as my head begins to pound. "Adri... she needs to know if her parents are a part of some sick ploy involving kids."

"We will." She places her hand on my arm and gives it a reassuring squeeze. "We have a complete list to work with here."

"Ember, why would you think I knew about any of this?" I

question her, my mouth drying out with the assumption that Ember thinks I'd be in business with my father.

"Because of this last file." She clicks open the last file and I feel like I've lost all feeling in my face and my mouth is suddenly parched. It's a photo of my father, his evil smirk lining his lips and his eyes hooded with arrogance. Next to it is a long list of names.

'The Whitsborough Rapist.'

Something jogs in my memory, dancing around the edges, but I just can't get a good grasp on it.

"Trav?" I hear Ember's voice, but she sounds so far away.

Today is my thirteenth birthday, and I celebrated it with Coach and my baseball teammates. We had a game this afternoon and we won. It just added to the happiness of my birthday. I also have a plan to meet up with Adrianna after and go get some milkshakes at The Route.

The locker room is deathly quiet because I'm the last one here and I always help Coach clear up our equipment. I strip out of my filthy uniform—I slid into home base three times today—and wrap my towel around my waist. Coach has given us more space in the locker room because of the guys complaining about privacy. I know he can be a bit much, but they just don't understand it like I do. Coach has selected me as his confidant and tells me everything about how he's training us to become our very best. He really wants us all to become something and maybe make it out of this town, but I will never get to leave. I'll just take over my father's position and business when I come of age. Whitsborough is my prison forever and my mother and father are the jail keepers.

I turn on the hot water for the shower and step inside the steam. My muscles hurt in my arms and shoulders, but it's a good hurt. It reminds me I can always hurt more, especially at the hands of my father. Lathering up, I wash away the dirt remnants on my body, watching as the grit runs down into the drain.

He's here. I can always sense when he's watching me. I say nothing because at least he no longer records me. As messed up as it sounds, I know he does it because he cares about me. If it weren't for Coach, there would be a lot of shit I just wouldn't know about myself. Things about my changing body that would've worried me if I didn't have him to ask about it. I'm not stupid. Some of the shit we do is wrong, but I'm loved in a way I have never been and I don't want to lose that. I don't care about touching him. It means nothing to me, and in doing so, I keep the only person who has truly cared about my well-being in my life.

I step out of the shower, and sure enough, I spot him across the locker room, standing beside my locker with his dick in his hand. I know what he wants, and I can get it done in under two minutes now because I have learned every little thing this man likes.

"Gotta be quick today. I have somewhere to be," I say as I drop my towel and reach into the locker for my clothes.

He places a hand on my arm to stop me, and I turn toward him, regarding him with mild irritation. "Somewhere to be?" He's still stroking his dick as his face contorts with a sneer.

"Yeah, I'm having milkshakes with Adri."

"Like a date?" His head cocks to the side.

"Maybe." I shrug. I hope so.

"Have you kissed her yet?" He smiles at me.

"No." I shake my head. "Not yet." I really want to though and I plan on doing it today.

"Has your father told you anything about what a woman likes or what to expect?" he asks me. My heart kicks into overdrive, and I suddenly become nervous. I don't know any of that. What if Adri expects certain things and I just don't know how to do it?

"No." I swallow down the shame of my ignorance. "Expect what things?"

"I'll show you." He shrugs.

"Sure." I mirror his shrug. Someone needs to show me. Plus, how bad can it be?

"Rest your head back against the locker and imagine I am Adrianna," he pants, his arousal clear in his tone.

Sure, sounds easy enough. I do as he says and lean my head back. I imagine Adrianna and her long brown hair that waves slightly toward the ends, her tanned, golden skin, and the deep brown of her pretty eyes. She's grown a lot this year and the top of her head has finally reached my shoulders.

I stiffen as soon as I feel his hand reach and touch my lower stomach. "Shh," he soothes, making me relax and imagine it's Adri's soft fingers and not Coach's rough ones. His hand gradually glides lower and touches my dick. My eyes fly open and I try to move away from him. He hasn't done this before. I only have to touch him and not the other way around.

"Uh, Coach?"

"Do you want to learn or not?" he prods with his hand still pressed against my privates. I do want to learn, so I rest back against the locker and imagine Adri and her soft pink smile, her one dimple that comes out when she smiles on her left cheek, and her wet tongue as it licks my dick.

Whoa!

I steal a glance and see Coach licking me and sucking me into his mouth. This is what girls like to do? Holy shit, that feels really good. I've touched myself this year with my hands and that feels good, but this? Oh my God, this is amazing. I bring up Adri in my mind and imagine it's her, and she's loving having me in her mouth. With that thought, I finish quickly.

When I open my eyes again, Coach is jerking off his dick in his hand and moaning. I'm feeling too relaxed to move, so I let him watch me as he does it. Finally, when he finishes, I turn around and get dressed.

"Did you like that, sport?"

I nod because I can't really find the words about how I'm feeling. Yeah, it felt good, but that was only because I imagined Adri was doing it. Now, when I see Coach doing it, my stomach tightens up and I feel a wash of shame filling my body. Nobody can ever find out this shit happens because I know it's wrong and I may lose Adrianna forever.

"Needless to say," he mutters as he gets up and fixes his clothes, then lights a cigarette. "This stays between us."

"Yeah."

"I have a lot of shit on your father, Travis," he puffs out, smoke encircling our heads. "Wouldn't want that to get leaked to the press, would we?"

"Like what?" I turn to glare at him as I pull my shirt on.

"Real bad things, sport." He shakes his head with a pitiful expression on his face. "You know the things you and I do?" I nod. "You know, if you told me you didn't want to, I would just leave your life, right?" I nod again. I don't want Coach to leave my life. "Well, your father does that to girls and women, but they don't like it. They cry and scream, and he forces them to do it."

My face screws up into confusion. "What?" That makes little sense. My father is not the type of man to be that cruel. Is he? He is mean to me and Mother, sure, but… I close my eyes and deep inside I know he can be that cruel. Besides, why would Coach ever lie to me? He has only ever told me the truth.

"Your father is a dangerous man." He nods at me as my face falls with the realization. "And I am always protecting you."

"Yeah, well, you don't have to threaten me with him." Slamming my locker shut, I pull my baseball bag over my shoulder. "I'm not going to say shit, and I don't want to hear this again." Storming by him, I leave the locker room and him behind. I don't care what my father does as long as he leaves me alone.

"Travis!" I pull back out of my memory and look Ember in the eyes, my face crumbling and my breath hitching in my chest.

"Yeah," I finally force the word from my mouth. "Coach had mentioned some shit on my thirteenth birthday. I don't know if I just didn't believe it or if I didn't care. I just wanted nothing to do with my father."

She nods with relief and runs her hand down my cheek. "You were young—"

"No." I shake my head and look away, cutting her off. "I understood what Coach told me and I knew there was a possibility he was doing it. My father was cruel and hated us."

"Doesn't matter, Travis," she growls and forces me to meet her eyes. "What could you have done anyway?"

"Gone to the police!" She drops her hand and releases a long sigh.

"Oh, yeah?" She turns the laptop toward me and points at the list of dirty cops and the chief himself. "Like these? The ones that were under your father's pay? Then he'd find out and kill you, or worse."

"There's always worse," I mutter as my chin hits my chest.

"Yeah," she agrees. "There is."

"I think my mother knew about it too," I whisper and look back up to find surprise in her eyes as they begin to water. Talking about this brings back a lot of repressed memories. "The day I found out about my father from Coach, I went home after hanging out with Adri so I could have a talk with my mother. As much as she hated having me around, I still loved her and wanted nothing to happen to her."

"Of course." Ember wipes a tear from her cheek.

"I had a plan too. I would run her a bath that evening because that's when she'd be the most tired after an entire day of crying and screaming. A few years later, I learned my mother was bipolar and my father would refuse her the medication she needed." Shaking my head, I release a sarcastic chuckle. "I didn't know that then though. I just thought she hated being in that house with us. Anyway, I drew her a bath and brought her up a bottle of wine from downstairs. I poured her a glass and set it in front of her and then I asked her if it was true." I scrub my hand down my face. "She laughed at me. Fucking laughed! Then she slapped me so hard I saw stars. She grabbed my face, pressing my cheeks together, and said, *'One day, you will bring them to him too.'* That's how I knew she was involved." I take a deep breath. "I was always fearful of my parents, but after that, I was downright petrified. So I minded my business and stayed out of their way."

"As a kid, you did the right thing." She runs her fingers through my hair, then drags me in for a hug. "Now we can do a few things differently." When she pulls away, my stomach flips at the grin lighting her face. It's the one I like to refer to as her murder face.

"Like what? You already killed my father."

"B[illegible]ople need to be taught a lesson, and I need to add another name to this list." She pulls up the list with my father's name and adds my mother's beside it. "I think it's time we paid your mother a visit."

While we're driving in E's car to my house, my stomach is a swirl of nerves and nausea. Ember is radiating some intense anger, the potency so thick I can almost taste it. When she's like this, it's easy to imagine her taking down grown men like they're nothing.

"Look through these." She throws an envelope onto my lap. "I found them in Halbert's office."

I open the brown envelope and pull out a stack of photos. Slowly, I go through them. I recognize most of the baseball team as we got older in various stages of dress. There are quite a few of me and Kevin, probably about the same amount, and I see the pain so similar to mine in his eyes. I'll have to talk to him next week at school. Coach also took pictures of some girls that ran on the track team. I knew he had shit like this and I'm sure he had videos as well, but Ember probably burned them down with the house.

"The photos get older the farther you get into it," she mutters as her fingers tighten on the wheel. "Back to when he was in high school."

She's right. There are some with Coach as a teenager in a baseball uniform and standing next to a bunch of jocks. One of which really boils my blood, my father. I don't recognize too many others, but I see Adri's dad there too. Then a few photos later, a few girls sit out on the track and appear to be drinking water. I recognize Debby and Sharla, but the third isn't familiar.

"My mother," Ember says quietly as her eyes flick from the photo in my hand then back to the road.

I should've known that because even though the photo is blurry and old, I can still see the scowl on her face, much like Ember's and Emmett's.

"Why did he have these?" I ask, pushing the photos back into the envelope and placing them in the glove compartment.

"Because I think he also farmed girls for your father."

"What?" I stare at her, my body stiffening with shock.

"Yeah." She nods. "I read that list your coach made of your father's known victims. My mother, along with Sharla, are on that list."

"Sharla?" I question. "But they were together and had Vin. That doesn't make sense." I shake my head.

"You're right, it doesn't, but that's why I told Vin everything and he's going to figure out how to talk to her about it." Vin, I didn't even think about how this would affect him. He probably didn't see it as much of a surprise, considering the man treated him and his mother like dirt.

After I learned about my mother and father the summer going into my eighth-grade year, Vin came back. He arrived in Whitsborough with a vengeance and was out to get me at every corner. He made sure I found out he was my half brother too that year. The beatings I took from him and the way his face looked while he did it reminded me of my father. The look in his green eyes—an exact match to our father—and the set of his jaw as he punched me repeatedly whenever he felt like it was too much like our father. I took it every time though because I felt like I deserved the punishment for the shit I knew was going on and didn't stop.

We pull into my driveway and again the gates are fucking open. Ember looks at me with her brow raised and I just shrug. I really don't know what's been going on here since I left. Sonja hasn't called, so I've just assumed she's been dealing with it. The familiar weight of guilt settles over me and I realize I should've just called her myself.

"Seems empty," Ember says as she puts the car in park. "The lights are all off."

"She likes the dark and quiet when she's severely hungover," I remark through clenched teeth as the memory of my mother sends anger through me.

"Well, let's go turn on all the lights and ask her some questions really loudly." Ember smirks at me and gets out of the car.

I lead her up to the house and use the number pad on the front door to open it. The light blinks red, letting me know I used the incorrect code. I try to punch it in again, but the same red light comes on.

"She changed the code," I mutter with disbelief and kick at the door.

"Hmm." E looks around and then up. "Think you could climb to that?" She points to my room's balcony.

"That'll be a last resort. Let's check the back doors first." Stepping down from the porch, I gaze back over my shoulder once more to eye the front door. My mother really locked out her only child. How heartless can she be? It shouldn't surprise me the depths she'll go to show her hatred, but I'm hurt each time regardless.

Leading Ember around to the back of the house and into our backyard, I point up at the various cameras and glance back at her. "I don't think they're on."

"And your pool is pretty fucking gross too," she remarks, her voice filled with disgust. The pool is a dark green color, and the pumps aren't even on.

When I turn the knob of the back door, it swings open. "I was hoping she would forget this in her drunken state." I shrug.

"Hey, wait," she says as I walk inside. "You realize what will happen here tonight, right?"

"Yeah." I nod, because I do. My mother's last hours on this Earth are winding down fast and the thought of killing anyone has my veins filling with ice. Even if she does deserve it.

"Okay." She motions for me to continue through the house. Ember hasn't had the grand tour, not counting when she broke in and killed my father.

The kitchen is a filthy mess of dishes and old rotting food everywhere. My mother left the fridge door open, and the smell of sour milk hit us, making both of us retch out loud.

"Holy fuck," E hisses into her sleeve. "What the hell happened here?"

Now I'm worried. Not about my mother, but about Sonja. She would've definitely cleaned this up if she were here. Did she finally see that this family wasn't worth her time? No, I can't see her just getting up and leaving. She would call me first.

"Dude, how long has it been since you were home?" E asks around a gag.

"Like a week? I brought Emmett with me, and my mother asked if he was my boyfriend and called me a queer." I glance at her out of the side of my eye, waiting for her reaction.

She gives me a confused look as one of her perfectly arched brows quirks upward. "What? Were you two making out or something?"

I snap my head back and glare at her. "No!"

"I'm just playing." She laughs, then gags and groans into her sleeve from the rancid smell.

"Jesus Christ." I breathe through my heart palpitations her question has caused and lead her into the foyer, then to the stairs.

There are two empty bottles of vodka on the stairs and what appears to be a few spots of blood. It's not a lot, just a few spots, but I feel my blood pressure soar and my heartbeat is thumping in my ears. We get to the top of the stairs and find my bedroom door with an enormous hole in it and there's some blood around it. That's probably where those spots of blood came from. She must've attempted to punch a hole through it.

Heading a little farther down the hall, I stop in front of my parents' room. The bedroom door is shut. "This is her room," I say to Ember and turn the knob. "It's locked."

"Kick it in," Ember coaxes. "If she's already dead, then that makes our job easier."

"True." I should probably have a bit more tact when talking about my mother, but she's never earned that from me.

I kick in the door, and it flies open to hit the wall behind it. Wood splinters fly up and land around our feet as we make our way into her bedroom.

"Wha…?" my mother mumbles as she tries to sit up in bed. There's a puddle of vomit beside her and it's fresh, unlike the one on the floor which has long dried up.

"Hello, Mrs. Greene!" E singsongs into the room, and the sound of her voice sends chills down my spine. "Gosh! You sure made a mess this last week, huh?"

"Who are you…?" My mother slowly sits up as her head sways back and forth.

"Mother," I growl as I stalk toward the bed. "What the fuck happened here?"

Her face immediately morphs into one of pure hatred. "You!" She points at me and then, to my surprise, tries to spit at me, her saliva landing far to the left of me. "I told you to never come back here. There's nothing for you here."

"Have you lost your fucking mind?" I yell into her face.

"You don't belong here," she snarls back.

"This is my fucking house! The deed says so."

"Fucking Robert!" she screams as she pulls her hair, and I take a step back from her. "He did this to punish me. He left everything to his worthless son."

"Now, now… Christina, is it?" Ember sits at Mother's feet at the edge of the bed. As crazy as my mother is acting right now, E looks as calm as a peach. It's such a contrast to my anxious insides, and I try to pull some of her calm energy around me.

"Who the fuck are you?" Mother snaps back at her, her spine hunched and her blonde hair matted to her head.

"I'm Ember Craven." She focuses on my mother, a small smile on her face.

"Craven?" She straightens at the name as her body begins to shake with suppressed rage. Something I know well enough.

"That's right." Ember nods emphatically, her lips tipping upward.

"Like Rebecca Craven?" My mother screws up her face in disgust. "The one my husband fantasized about." The urge to vomit next to my mother's dried pile with her admission is overwhelming as I breathe in through my nose and out through my mouth.

I watch as E's hands fist into the comforter on the bed, the only thing betraying her calm exterior. "Did he now? That was my mother."

"Whatever." My mother shakes her head and lies back on the bed, deciding the conversation is over, but she doesn't know Ember very well.

"It's time to get up," Ember says as she stands and walks to my mother's side of the bed. "Now." Then she grabs my mother's arm, hauling her up and out of the bed. Fuck, she's strong.

"Hey!" Mother struggles, but she is no match for E with how drunk she still is. Ember throws her down onto the armchair in the corner and grabs her chin.

"We're going to play a game," she growls into my mother's face. "I'll ask you questions, and for each one you don't answer, or you lie, I will cut into your face." She brings out a large hunting knife from her sweater pocket and presses it into my mother's cheek.

My mother becomes deathly still, her spine straight, and peers up into Ember's face, nodding slightly. Finally, she's beginning to understand just who is standing in front of her. It's not some regular teenager here to stand up for her son.

"Good." E sits on the end of the bed across from her, laying the knife on top of her thighs. The sharp blade shines in the darkened room, save for the little light left streaming in through the window. "First question: Was Robert Greene the Whitsborough Rapist from the early 2000s up to a few years ago?" She doesn't hold back, nothing sugarcoated and directly to the point.

My mother nods as her gaze quickly comes to land on me, then narrows. She thinks I told E this. She must remember when I asked her about it. I stay quiet and wait for Ember to continue.

"How many of those girls did you bring back for him?" She snaps her fingers in my mother's face to draw back her attention.

My mother regards Ember, her lips turning down into a frown, and her eyes take on an angry gleam before she purses her lips. If she's calling E out on her bluff, she's fucking dumber than I ever thought.

"Tsk, tsk! Mrs. Greene! We're only on the second question and you already broke the rules?" E giggles. I have never heard her like this and it's creeping me out, making me stagger back a few paces. "To be honest, I was hoping you would, and just my luck, it happened quicker than I could even anticipate." She chuckles and pats my mother's cheek.

"Fuck you," my mother growls menacingly.

"Wrong answer," Ember grits through her teeth as her hand clasps my mother's jaw. She then takes her knife and carves it down my mother's cheek while she struggles, making her scream as the blood drips off her chin.

I stand completely transfixed and suddenly feel numb, like I'm floating outside of my body and watching this from another dimension. My mother is about to die at the hands of my best friend, and I can't be bothered to care about it.

Ember releases my mother's chin and shoves her back into the chair, making her back bounce off the cushion.

"Answer the question, or I get back to carving," E threatens while she twirls her knife in her hand.

My mother has her hand up to her cheek as she shakes. "Most of them," she mewls out as the blood runs from her wound between her fingers.

"Bad girl, Christina." Ember shakes her head and looks back at me. I nod once to let her know I'm fine and she turns back to my mother. "Did he rape Sharla?"

"I don't know." She shakes her head and Ember brings up her knife. "I swear! I really don't know."

"So, what you're telling me right now is you are a useless sack of shit and I should just kill you?"

My mother's eyes narrow and a small smirk ghosts her lips. "Robert raped your mother though. He told me all about it. He and Halbert took turns while the other held her down."

Oh fuck, this is bad. E immediately stiffens, and my mouth goes dry. My father and Coach actually did shit like that? And Ember's mother really was their victim? My hand comes up and I cover the gasp that escapes my mouth.

Ember quickly pulls herself together and shakes her head. "I wish I knew all this the night I came to kill him because I would've tortured him instead of offering him an easy way out."

"What?!" Mother shrieks as she looks from me to Ember. Her eyes fill with rage as her hand drops to wrap around the arms of the chair, leaving bloodstains on the fabric.

"That's right, Christina." Ember nods. "I came into your house in the middle of the night and forced dear Robert to slice open his wrists with this very knife. Isn't it like fate or something that each of your blood has kissed its blade?"

"You bitch!" My mother remains seated in the chair only because she fears what Ember can do with that knife. Otherwise, I have no doubt she would've already attacked.

E throws her head back and laughs. "I wish I would've taken you that night too."

"Do you hear this?" My mother turns her attention to me, her eyes narrowing with hatred. "Why are you just standing there? She killed your father."

"Yeah." I tip my head to the side and stare at her, the numbing void encasing my heart. "I know."

"You know?" Her eyes widen as her mouth falls open with shock. Then the rage seeps back in, along with the hatred I find so fucking familiar. "You really were a waste of our time. We should've killed you the second we knew you existed."

"Wow." I chuckle and shake my head. "You would've aborted me?"

"No." She giggles manically. "We should've killed your mother."

"What?" I screw my face up in confusion. "Are you that drunk?"

"Your mother!" she screams at the top of her lungs as she leans forward in the chair, seemingly forgetting Ember and her knife. "As soon as we found out she was pregnant, we should've pushed her down the stairs."

"My mother?" I question as my head spins and my racing heart creates fissures in the numb encasing.

"I can't have children," she sneers at me. "Not that I ever wanted them, but your father found a favorite and continuously raped her. Of course she was bound to get knocked up. Then, instead of killing her, he decided he wanted to keep you as an heir. The other son he fathered could never run the business because he was black." The venom spewing out of her is making me sick.

"You're not my mother." Everything makes sense. Her hateful, dismissive, and cold behavior toward me my whole life. It all fucking makes sense.

"You're so fucking stupid," she snarls. "Just like her."

Ember gets up and walks into my parents' closet as I keep an eye on the woman I always thought was my mother.

"Who is she?" I demand, my tone falling flat as I try to process everything.

"Who cares!" she screams as spit flies out of her mouth. "She's a nobody!"

"Christina," E says with a warning in her voice. She steps out of the closet with one of my father's belts in her hands and she's looping it through the buckle. "Tell him who his mother is."

"Or what?" She chuckles. "You'll spank me with that belt?"

"No." Ember leisurely walks up to her and slaps the belt over my mother's head and around her neck. "Tell him," she grids out as she tightens the belt around her neck.

Mother's eyes widen and she grips her fingers into the belt, trying to pull it off her neck, but E is too strong.

"So—" She coughs and claws harder. "Son—"

"Who!" I scream.

"Sonja!!!"

CHAPTER TEN

Emmett

I get home and find the house empty. I search everywhere, but both Ember and Travis have gone out. First, I call Ember's cell and it goes straight to voicemail. This isn't strange because she hates her phone. Next, I try Travis' and his rings but ends up going to voicemail too. If they're together, I know they're safe, but a niggling thought of something being wrong keeps worming through my mind. Where the fuck are they? I head into the kitchen and make myself something to eat. I haven't eaten since Ember came home and stirred everything up.

After I've made my food and eaten it, they still aren't home and haven't even called me back. Worry is seeping in, and I decide to call Vin. After a few rings, he picks up.

"Sup?"

"Hey, man. Do you know where Ember and Travis are?" I toy with the sleeve of my sweater as sweat begins to collect along the nape of my neck.

"They aren't home?" he asks, concern filtering through the phone.

"No, and I tried to call their cell phones. No answer."

"How long ago did you call?" I can hear rustling on the other end, sounding like he's getting dressed.

"An hour? Somewhere around there."

"I spoke to Em earlier, but I had to come home and talk to my mom about something," he explains as a door shuts on his end of the call.

"It's all good. I'm sure they're fine." Worrying my lip between my teeth, I'm not completely sure if I believe it.

"I'll call Em now, and if I don't get an answer, I'll head over to you, okay?" Wind hits my ear as he steps outside, the sound of the alarm on the Hummer disengaging.

"Nah, man. Your mom hasn't seen you in a while. Chill there, I'll figure it out."

"I'll see you soon."

I roll my eyes and grin when he hangs up. Vin is completely twisted up by my sister and I love him for it. I clean up the kitchen and try both Ember's and Travis' cells again… no answer. It's late and I can't seem to shake this feeling that something bad is happening. It's probably because something bad is always happening to us. I'm not seriously worried because I know both Ember and Travis can take care of themselves. I'm more worried about what they are actually doing.

The front door opens, and Vin yells out, "Emmett!"

"Kitchen!"

He comes in and raises a brow. "You find out anything?"

"Nah." I shake my head. "I just tried both cells again and no answer."

"Okay." He nods as he slips a gun out of the back of his pants, then pulls out the mag and checks the ammo. "I think I might know where they are. Get your knives and let's bounce."

"Is it Talia?" I ask as I scramble after him, steeling myself for any situation we may face.

"I don't think so, but it's always good to be prepared." He stands by the front door, tucking the gun back into his pants. "Hurry."

I run up the stairs and grab my knife band from my closet. After strapping it around my waist, I grab a black bandana to tie around my head. It matches the one Vin has on and this way we'll look like some badass mercenaries. I smirk in the mirror as I tighten it on my head, then I jog back downstairs.

"Let's go," I say as I walk past him and outside. He closes up the house and we both get into his Hummer. "Talk," I demand as he pulls out. "What the fuck am I missing here?"

"When Ember killed Travis' baseball coach, he outed some people in this town." His jaw tightens with his admission as his fingers grip the wheel.

"What people?" Whitsborough isn't as idyllic as it seems.

"Sick fucking people doing sick shit to kids." My stomach drops as I take in what he's saying. A pedophile ring in a small town in fucking Canada of all places.

"Fuck," I breathe out.

"Yeah." His jaw tics. "My father was at the top of that list as the serial rapist of Whitsborough for like ten-plus years.

"Are you fucking shitting me?" I exclaim, my words bouncing around the confined space.

"Not even a little. This coach fucker even had a list of his victims. My mom and yours are on it." His voice softens as he breaks the news about our mothers, and even though I never knew the woman, my heart breaks for what she endured.

"Your mom?" I swallow down the lump in my throat. Bringing up my mother is too hard. It'll be something I'll speak to Ember about later because being vulnerable with her will be easier.

"Yeah." He nods as he stops at a stop sign and scrubs a hand down his face. I take in his appearance while he groans into his hand. He seems exhausted, and rightfully so. They came back from Spain and landed in a pile of shit. "I'm trying to figure out how to ask her about it without blowing this list out of the water. Ember wants to make her way through it and pick off all the fucking pervs."

"Of course she does." It's exactly what I would want to do too, and I'll help her do it if she asks me.

"I'm thinking she went to one of two places. Either Travis' to speak to his mother or Adri's."

My heart kicks into overdrive as my eyes widen. "Why Adri?"

"Shit." He glances over at me, then back to the road. "No, man, not like that. Adri was never raped or anything. Just her parents came up on another list."

"What list?" My fists are curled tightly in my lap as my heart pounds in my ears, the sound only heightening my fear. I've never been afraid of much, but the thought of these people, my new family, being in danger has brought out the new emotion.

"We're not sure what it means. I think Ember will want to ask her about it." He gives me another sidelong glance, his mouth set in a grim line.

"They're not at Adri's," I mutter as I exhale a sigh. "I just came from her house."

He's looking at me from the side of his eye. "Her house? Does Travis know about this?"

"He knows." I don't get into it any further because even though Vin is like a brother to me, he's loyal to Ember and we're just not ready to speak to her about the situation yet.

"All right," he says, sounding very unsure.

We pull up onto Travis' street—I recognize it from the first time I was here—and Vin speeds up, burning his tires as he turns into Travis' driveway.

"There's Em's car," he states as he slams on the brakes and jumps out of the Hummer.

I'm right behind him as we hurry to the front door, finding it locked. Banging on the door, I yell out for Ember and Travis. Finally, after a few minutes, the door unlocks and slowly swings inward. Travis' pale face greets us, and I reach in to pull him into my arms. Vin is watching us, but I don't give a fuck right now. Travis needs me. His head lands on my shoulder and he lets out a shuddering breath.

"Bro," Vin starts, "what's going on?"

Travis lifts his head off my shoulder and regards Vin. "Upstairs." He turns and breaks my hold on him to lead the way. Vin glances over at me with his brow raised and I shrug my shoulders. I don't know what the fuck we'll be walking into right now. We follow him into a bedroom and the first thing that hits me is the smell of piss and vomit. The scent is magnified by the room's stale and humid air. I cover my nose and mouth with the sleeve of my sweater as Travis sits on the bed.

"Where's Em, bro?" Vin asks him, placing his hand on Travis' shoulder.

"I'm in here!" she yells from behind a closed door.

Vin and I open the door and hear a thump behind it. Ember is standing at the sink washing blood off her hands and knife.

"Babe?" Vin says cautiously as he approaches her. "What's going on?"

"Close the door." She points to it and goes back to washing her hands.

Vin grabs the edge of the door and swings it shut. Another thumping sound causes us to turn toward it. I just barely hold in my scream as Travis' mom swings with a belt around her neck and one notch hanging from an industrial-looking robe hanger attached to the top of the door. Her eyes are the size of dinner plates and looking at me through the broken capillaries, and her mouth hangs open, her tongue lolling out of the side of it. She also has a nasty-looking cut running down her cheek.

"She helped him," Ember mutters as she finishes drying her hands.

"Helped him?" I whisper, still too shocked to look away from the woman still slightly swinging from a belt in her own washroom.

"Travis' mom captured and lured girls for Robert to rape." She wipes down the faucet and sink with a towel, then reaches out and wipes down the door handle too.

"Oh, fuck." I turn and use my sleeve to open the door. "I need to speak to Travis."

Walking back into the bedroom, I find Travis is missing and my heart slams up into my throat. If I were him, I wouldn't want to be considering the scene in the bathroom. Vin comes out to grab the stool from Travis' mother's vanity and brings it back to the bathroom, likely masking this as a suicide. I leave the room and stand at the top of the stairs. I don't see him anywhere on the first floor, so I open doors one by one. After opening a few closets and a bathroom, I come to a door with a hole in it. Opening it, I find Travis out on the balcony, smoking a cigarette, and my chest deflates with relief. I head toward him and lean on the railing beside him to stare out at the surrounding landscape.

"She wasn't even my mother," he whispers as he flicks his butt out onto the driveway.

"What?" I snap my head to him, slightly confused.

"I was the result of a repeated rape on one of the house staff. They kept me since Christina couldn't have children. You know… as an heir to this fucked-up legacy." He holds out his arms to encompass the house around him.

I don't know what to say as overwhelming sadness pours through me for him. To learn your father was a rapist and the woman you thought was your mother, but wasn't, was helping him is just too much.

"Who was it?" I ask tentatively, worried about setting him off. How much more can one person take?

"Sonja." He bows his head. "I can't find her anywhere."

"She's not here?" I inquire, and he shakes his head. "We'll find her." Now that I think of it, Travis has similar features to Sonja.

"I want to get out of here." He turns around and I do the same, willing to follow him into the pits of Hell if that's what he needs.

Vin is leaning against his doorframe and gives him a grim look. "Let's go for a drive."

Travis nods and ambles over to his brother as Vin wraps his arm around his shoulders, leading him out of the room and down the stairs. The front door opens and shuts, and I turn back around on the balcony to watch them both get into the Hummer and drive away. Vin will take care of him. He needs his brother right now, and I'm cool with that.

"Let's get the fuck out of this den of evil," Ember growls from behind me.

"Yeah, okay." I follow her numbly out and into her car. "Any camera footage?" I slump into the seat as my stomach sours at the thought of what happened in the last few hours.

"Nope. She had everything turned off." Cool as a cucumber, she throws the car in reverse and shrugs her shoulders.

"That's weird," I hum as my eyes scan over the front of the house, its darkened windows making it look abandoned. I guess, in a way it is.

"Worked out for us." She pulls out of the driveway and onto the street without a backward glance.

"I'm really worried about Travis. Was it necessary to do that in front of him?" She stops at a stop sign and looks at me, then rolls her eyes.

"Yeah, it needed to be done. Besides, if he weren't there, he wouldn't have learned who his actual mother was." She raises her brows at me and then looks back to the road. "Thing is, Emmett, our lives aren't fucking fairy tales. It's never going to be. He needs to see what it is we all do. Then he can decide to stick around or not."

"You're right," I admit, because she is, but Travis has never had a fairy tale life. In fact, his was worse than anything we endured.

"He's been handed a shitty stick in life," she quips, almost like she's reading my mind. "But I'm hoping he can see through all of us how to grab that shitty life by the horns and make it his bitch. Not the other way around."

"Truth."

We get home to find it empty. No Travis and no Vin. I'm guessing Vin is doing the brother thing and showing Travis he still has family. I hope he realizes he has all of us for the rest of his life, unconditionally, if that's what he wants.

"You and I need to have a chat," Ember says as she follows me into my room. "Carm and I had a discussion in Spain, and he let me know a few things about you."

"Like?" I raise my brow at her as I remove my belt and place it back in the closet.

"Calen?" she snarls through gritted teeth, her hands landing on her hips. "The fact that our father made sure his son was beaten occasionally by a madman?"

"Occasionally?" I snort and pull the bandana off my head, throwing it on top of my dresser. "Ember, my life wasn't a fairy tale either, but I grabbed that bitch by the horns and killed it in cold blood."

"He told me you killed him." She nods, her hands dropping with an exhale. "With your knives."

"Seemed fitting." I shrug. I'm calm about it now, but it's taken years to overcome the trauma I dealt with. "He made me fear them for most of my childhood."

"How?" she asks as she sits on my bed. Sitting beside her, I settle in for a story I hate recounting, but something I want her to know about.

"Whenever the beatings would happen, I would end up being

holed up in my room for a couple of days, unable to lie on my back." I gaze into Ember's blazing eyes. "We had a cook. His name was Angelo. He would come to my room and apply a homemade salve to the wounds on my back and legs. Then he would sit with me until I finally fell asleep. Someone eventually told Calen, and he pulled me into his office. I remember sitting on the chair as he berated me for being weak. Then they dragged in a gagged and bound Angelo."

"This asshole is lucky he's dead," Ember growls as her body stiffens with anger and her fists clench in her lap.

"Calen forced him to kneel in front of me while I sat on the chair. He then went on with his speech about how soft I was, and people could see my weaknesses and felt sorry for me, like Angelo did." I close my eyes and take a breath, opening them to find Ember's slowly welling with tears. "He then got up out of his seat and stood behind Angelo. He drew out a large knife and stuck it through the back of his head and it came straight through his eye. The blood sprayed all over my face and I immediately started screaming. I remember little after that, but I remember being kept in my room in the dark for days. I had nightmares that repeated each time I closed my eyes, and I was petrified of anything sharp for a long time."

"How did you get over it?" Ember reaches over and grabs my hand, our fingers interlocking. Her strength bleeds into me through our clasped hands and it gives me the courage to continue.

"Carm and Trent. When they found out about Calen, Carm wanted to kill him, but it was Trent who said it should be me to do it. Then Trent trained me with knives. It was hard at first because I was so scared, but I slowly got over it. I took the beatings from Calen, knowing soon I would kill him, and eventually I did, with a knife through the eye, thrown from across the room." Her eyes widen with glee as a tear slips down her cheek and her hand tightens around mine.

"That's a happily ever after if I ever heard one." She snickers, releasing my hand to wipe the tear from her cheek as we both laugh.

"Trent continued to train me, but I surpassed him quickly. I just continued on my own, honing my skills and perfecting them." It sounds easy enough, but there were days when holding a knife would have me spiraling into a well of dark memories.

"I'm proud of you."

"Thanks, Ember." I smile at her. "Means a lot coming from you. Any idea where Travis and Vin are?"

"Vin texted me to say they were fine and he'd bring him back later. Vin will help him." She places a hand on my shoulder. "Get some sleep. We have school tomorrow."

"Yes, Mom."

Travis

I don't know where Vin is driving us, and I don't care. I just witnessed the woman I believed to be my mother die while clutching at the belt around her neck. Her eyes had slowly widened in their sockets as the tiny blood vessels burst open. Her tongue grew puffy and fell out of her opened mouth, and the only thought that ran through my mind was she should have died with my father. Both of them were evil incarnate, and I won the lucky draw on being their son.

"What are you thinking about?" Vin's voice breaks through my thoughts.

"Did we really enact justice?" I turn to look at him, finding his profile solemn as he drives. "Wouldn't it have been better if they just rotted in jail?"

"I thought like that too for a while. When I found out Em killed our father, I was thinking it wasn't enough. But now? I wish they had suffered more. But, bro,"—he darts a glance at me—"our system here in Whitsborough is not just."

He's right, they would've paid their way out. If they even got that far to begin with. "I guess. Where are we going?"

"To my house."

"What?" I glance out the window in shock. "Why?"

"Ember showed you the list of our father's victims?" Turning back to him, I find his eyes on me as he stops in the middle of the road. Thankfully, it's late evening, so no one is out.

"Yeah." I swallow down the guilt resurfacing. "I didn't read them though."

"My mother's name was on that list, so was Ember's mother." He says it gently, knowing they were victims of our father, the one who I spent my early childhood trying to make him love me.

"I know about E's mom," I croak out, my throat dry. "Mother dearest taunted her with the details."

"Fuck," he grunts as he grips the steering wheel tighter and continues to drive toward his house.

"It's hard not to feel somehow responsible," I admit in a small voice, my chest feeling heavy with sadness. "I really don't want to face your mom with the knowledge of what my father could've done to her."

"Our father," he corrects me, "and you had nothing to do with it. We are family and always will be. I want you to get to know her and maybe help me out with this. I tried to talk to her earlier and I just couldn't bring it up."

"Okay." I'll do it for him because he's been my rock when everything else has crumbled, even though the added guilt could bury me alive.

We pull into a driveway, and I take in Vin's house up ahead. It's smaller than mine and E's but still a good size. The lawns are well-manicured and the outside of the house looks clean. I was here once for the pool party he had, the night I slept with Adri for the first time. He puts the Hummer in park and I follow him up to the front door.

"Ma!" he yells out once we are inside. This is Vin's way of greeting everyone, I noticed.

"In the back!" she screams from their backyard. As soon as I hear her voice, my heart begins to pound and my palms grow damp. Vin's hand lands on my shoulder as he gives it a squeeze, reminding me he's here with me.

We head out through the kitchen and into the enclosed pool area. She's lying on a lawn chair and sipping what appears to be a margarita. "Hello, Ms. Germaine."

"Oh!" She startles and sits up. "Travis, how are you, honey?" Just the concern lighting her eyes has emotion welling up inside of me. She should hate me, despise me, for the shit my family has caused her.

"I'm okay." I shrug my shoulders and swallow down the urge to turn and run.

"It's nice to see you two together." She looks between Vin and me, a small smile curving along her lips.

"We want to talk to you, Ma," Vin says and sits in a chair beside her.

I really don't want to do this. I'm scared as hell she'll hate me and order Vin to have nothing to do with me. Then I will have no family. None sharing the same blood, that is. I understand it has to be worked out sooner rather than later and I can't not help him when he helps me every time I need him.

"About?" She looks between us again as I take a seat beside Vin.

"Robert." His eyes flick to mine, then back to her as he wrings his hands hanging between his knees.

"Greene?" She gets a slightly worried look in her eyes as they flick over me again. I get it. I'm the son of the monster, and she doesn't want to say anything in my presence.

"Yes," he pushes as he leans forward in his chair.

"What about him?" She stares at me and then back at Vin. I squirm in my seat from her scrutiny, knowing what's coming next and yet helpless to the guilt consuming me.

"I can't tell you how I found out this information, but do you trust me?" he beseeches her.

"Yes," she says so softly as her teeth bite into her bottom lip.

"Were you raped by Robert?" My body tenses with his direct questioning as her eyes widen, landing on me again. I want to apologize, to beg her for forgiveness, but I can't find the words that would suffice.

"What?" she whispers, her voice slightly trembling as she gazes back at her son. She sits up straighter in her seat, placing her drink on the pool deck. I don't miss the way her hand shakes when she brings it back to her lap.

"Were you?" he pushes, enunciating each word.

"Oh, God." She covers her face with her hands as the first tear falls from my eye and skims over my cheek. Despair, pure and potent, floods me and my body begins to tremble with the strain of trying to keep it all contained.

"Maybe I should…" I start to get up when I feel Vin's hand on my arm.

"No." He pushes me back down. "You're our family."

"He's right, Travis." Sharla regards me, her eyes swimming with tears. "You are our family. The first time I had… relations with Robert was at a party. It was actually Halbert's house and his parents were away. That night, Rebecca and I got pretty intoxicated, and I can't really remember much." Pain etches through her features as she sinks into the memory, her mouth turning down into a frown as her words are spoken through agony.

"Was Rebecca with Ray at this point?" Vin sounds calm, but

his tense shoulders and whitened knuckles speak a different story.

"She had just met him the week before. He was friends with Robert's older brother. They weren't at this party since it was a younger crowd. At that point, I hadn't really seen how possessive Ray could be with her. They were still young in their relationship." She reaches down to grab her drink and takes a sip, closing her eyes as she recounts what she can remember. "Honestly, I've always been really confused about that night. I had never blacked out before, but that night I did. I'd drank more on different occasions, and I've questioned a few times if maybe they had slipped me something. Despite blacking out, I can recall fragments of the night. After dancing with Rebecca, I remember everything turning black. The next thing I remember is being over someone's shoulder, but I was too heavy to move or talk. Then I remember very little after, except for blurred faces over mine. I was a virgin." Her mouth twitches as she opens her eyes and takes a deep breath. "I woke up the next morning with a soreness between my legs and some blood. I knew what had happened, and when I questioned Robert, he told me I'd begged for it."

Vin has his eyes closed, his breathing erratic. "You believed him?" he snaps with anger.

"Yes." She runs the hand not holding her drink over her face. "I was already in love with him at that point."

"Where was Rebecca during all of this?" I cut in.

"I'm not sure. Whenever I brought it up, she would quickly say she passed out and didn't recall much." She shakes her head, then takes another sip from her glass. "She woke up in the back of Halbert's pickup truck, she told me."

I wonder if maybe the same thing happened to Rebecca that night as well. "Did she act any different afterward?" I press, hoping to get the entire story once and for all.

"Why?" She frowns as her eyes flick over my face.

"She was also a part of the information I received," Vin answers for me as he falls back into his seat with a sigh, his eyes scanning the starry night above our heads.

"No!" she says on an exhale while covering her mouth, tears escaping her eyes.

"Could it have been that night as well?" I prod, fearing I already know the answer.

"Yes." She drinks the rest of her drink and sets the glass back on the deck. "She acted strange after. Rebecca didn't speak to Halbert again and she just about hated the entire group of them. She tolerated Robert for my sake, but she rarely spoke to him."

"She may have remembered more than you," I murmur, speaking my thoughts out loud.

"Rebecca left with Ray not too long after that." Her voice hitches as she presses a hand to her chest, piecing things together.

"Why wouldn't she tell you?" Vin turns his head from the sky toward his mother.

"Probably because I was so in love and she was worried I wouldn't believe her. To be honest, I'm not really sure if I would've," she admits as tears continue to roll down her cheeks. She brushes them away as she shakes her head with shame. A look I know all too well.

"Thank you for telling us, Ms. Germaine." And before I can stop myself, I blurt out, "I'm so sorry. So, so sorry. I know it changes very little and means nothing coming from his son, but I truly am sorry."

"Oh, baby." She gets up out of her chair to crouch in front of me, reaching her hand out and putting it on my cheek. "Call me Sharla, heck, call me Ma, but no one in this family calls me Ms. Germaine." Her hand curls around my neck as she drags me forward into a hug, the feel of her arms soothing a bit of the pain inside me.

"Thank you," I mumble as I try to hide the quake in my voice, wrapping my arms around her.

"Why don't you stay here for a bit?" she suggests when she pulls back and stands. "Get out of that house."

"Thank you for the offer, Ms.… Sharla, but I've been staying with Ember the last few weeks. My mother hasn't been well." I might as well lay the groundwork for her suicide.

"Yeah," Vin adds. "She kicked him out of the house. Threw his clothes all over the driveway."

"What?" Sharla shakes her head as shock gathers in her eyes. It must be unfathomable for her to imagine a mother doing such things to her child. "That's terrible."

"She's been grieving hard for him." I roll my eyes and spit out each word. "Ember has been kind enough to let me stay there."

"Well, my house is open to you too." She runs her hand over my hair. "There are decisions I regret in my lifetime, but none as much as I regret taking my anger out on you. I should've pushed you two to see each other sooner, to be the brothers you both deserved. I'm sorry." My insides quake at her kindness as I struggle to accept her offer. It would be nice to fill the void Christina could never fill.

"After everything I've learned here tonight, I completely understand your decision. Keeping Vin away from Robert was the best choice, and I'd endure everything again if it meant the same outcome." Their life wasn't an easy one because of how my father treated them, but they were far out of the monster's clutches.

"I should get Travis back. It's getting late." Vin stands and I do too, coming face-to-face with Sharla.

"Yes, you have school tomorrow." She pulls me in for another hug, her hand rubbing circles into my back. "You're loved, Travis. Thank you for never giving up on him."

I hug her back and force myself to keep my feelings in control. I've never had people care this much before.

As soon as we get home, Vin walks up the stairs and into Ember's room before shutting the door. I'm glad we somehow overcame our past to become the brothers we were meant to be. I need to give thanks where it's due, and it's because of Ember, the girl who revels in another's blood and loves to use her fists to make a point. She's violent, turbulent, and I'm convinced an angel sent straight from the hottest depths of hell. But she loves so fucking hard, and once she's decided she loves you, there is no end to what she will do for you. I'm so happy she deemed me one of those people, even if I feel like I don't deserve it.

Turning away from their closed door and mumbling voices— he's probably telling her everything we learned from his mother—I step into my room and softly close the door behind me.

"Can we make a new rule?" My head snaps up at his voice and I find Emmett lying across my bed in only a pair of black boxers. "Can you text me when you don't come home?"

"Uh…" I'm still shocked to find him in my bed… nearly naked.

"You never had to do that before, right? I get it." He slides his hands up and behind his head, his muscles flexing. "You have people who care about you now. Some more than others."

"Okay," I whisper, finding my voice at last. My feet are glued to the spot as shock still radiates through me.

"Wonderful talk." He gets up from the bed and stalks toward me. Then his hands come out and his fingers sink into the hair at the back of my head, dragging me forward and into a crushing hug. "I care about you... a lot." He then kisses the side of my head and releases me from his hold. "Good night," he says as he opens my door and makes his way across the hall toward his room.

"Good night," I mutter to his retreating back.

"Oh." He turns and smirks. "Call Adri, please. She needs to hear from you."

"Okay." I continue to watch him as he steps into his room. He closes his bedroom door and instantly, the cold, slithering tendrils of loneliness curl themselves around my heart. It's not a new feeling. I just wish it would stop making an appearance. Both of the people who made me feel that constantly are now dead, thanks to Ember. So shouldn't this feeling die with them?

Lying on my bed, I pull out my cell phone. I have a few missed calls and texts from both Adri and Emmett, and even a missed call from Vin. Seeing that makes those cold tendrils shrink back in fear enough for me to focus on other things. Having people who care about me means I'm no longer alone and I'm trying to learn how to accept it. I press on Adri's name and listen to the ringing until she finally picks up.

"Travis?" Her voice sounds sad and hoarse, like she's been crying all day.

"Hey."

"What's going on? Emmett was here earlier." She's hesitant, her words slightly mumbled as rustling sounds from her end of the call. She's most likely in bed.

"I know, babe. He told me what he was going to talk to you about."

"And what? You're okay with all of this?" she asks incredulously, her voice rising.

"Yeah, I trust him. It's completely up to you, but I want you to trust us too. I want you to try it, because right now I'm so fucking lost and I can't give you what you deserve."

"Let me help you," she begs as her words shake, sounding so close to tears.

"I will. I promise as soon as I am ready."

"And do you trust me, Travis?" She sniffles. "Do you trust that I love you?"

"Yes, I do, Adrianna." I take a deep breath as her words warm a part of me that has long been frozen in doubt. "I love you too."

She whimpers in response. "I've always wanted to hear you say that."

"I've always felt it, probably since preschool, even though you were so fucking mean to me." I snort as memories of a young Adrianna full of attitude flits through my mind.

She giggles, and I join in. Her giggling tapers off as she takes a deep breath and asks, "You really want me to date Emmett?"

"Yeah, I do. I promise to fill you in on everything, but I need to see if what you two have could be anything like what we already have."

"It's so strange, Trav." She exhales in my ear, the sound filled with confusion.

"Yeah, it's different. But you'll see, it'll make sense. Just try this out for me?"

"Okay," she agrees softly. "I'm going to sleep. School's tomorrow."

"Do you have a ride?"

"Yeah, I texted Ember. She's going to pick me up."

"That's good." I smile. "I'll see you tomorrow."

"Okay… Trav?"

"Hmmm?"

"Tell me again." Her voice becomes low and sultry, and my cock hardens in my boxers.

"I love you," I say and mean it.

"Me too." Then she hangs up the phone.

Chapter Eleven

The ping of an incoming message startles me out of staring into a full glass of orange juice, my hand nearly knocking it over as I reach for my phone. After texting with Emmett a bit last night, I told him it was best if I told Ember we decided to date on the way to school today. Keeping secrets from her isn't a good idea, besides, she's my best friend, she deserves to know what's going on. Regardless of if I disappear on the drive there.

I run my sweaty palm over my uniform skirt as I swipe the screen open with my other hand, exhaling a long, shaky breath.

Embs: Come out, come out, wherever you are!

Well, if that's not ominous.

Grabbing my backpack from the floor at my feet, I swing it over my shoulder and head toward the front door. With one last look over my shoulder at the empty house, I release a breath and hope I'll be back after school to see Klein and the rest of the staff. The house is too quiet without them, and I am too lonely. I should be used to it by now, the lonely nights and endless days when I don't have school, but it never gets any easier. Having Ember move here changed all that and it only makes me more fearful about losing her.

Is being with Emmett worth it?

The answer is complicated because even though Ember's presence in Whitsborough brought me my first taste of family, her brother is slowly healing my heart. A heart Travis pulverized years ago. I don't hold any resentment toward him, we were young and it's becoming clearer now that he was troubled. My love for him is still there, only now it's making room for the love I have growing for Emmett. Confusion rips through me again as I step out of the house and shut the door behind me. How will this work between the three of us?

An incessant honking pulls me from my thoughts and I look up to find Ember sitting in her sexy red Mustang, her hair full and wavy around her head and her signature large sunglasses covering her face. I really hope she had time to grab her coffee, it may be the fine line that stops her from beating me to a pulp. Taking a deep breath, I walk toward her, keeping my gaze on my feet. When I open the passenger door and throw my bag on the floor, I find her staring at me over the rim of her glasses.

"Hey, bestie," she coos, her voice sugary and her smile sweet. Does she sound too sweet? Maybe it's because we've never been apart for this long. Except the time she was taken from the school parking lot.

"Hey." I swallow thickly and slide into the passenger seat. "I'm glad you're back." My voice is hoarse as I shut the door and avoid eye contact. Yanking on the seat belt, I clip it in and look straight ahead, feeling her eyes on the side of my face. Does she already know? Did she corner Emmett and force it out of him?

"You're acting weird," she states as she puts the car in reverse and backs out of my driveway. "What happened while I was gone? Is it Travis?"

"I got drunk last night and feel like shit this morning." I wave her off and turn to look out of the passenger window. Suppressing the urge to turn to her and spill everything is overwhelming. I don't just mean about her brother, I mean *everything*. How lonely I am, how I crave family and that's why I show up on her doorstep whenever it becomes too much to ignore, and how petrified I am about losing it all.

She hums in response and I turn to look at her as she moves the sunglasses to the top of her head, sounding as though she doesn't quite believe me, and it only increases my anxiety.

"Tell me about Spain." Turning in my seat, I face her as she turns off my street and heads toward Precious Blood Academy.

Her eyes flick from the road to me then back again as a smile curves along her mouth. "It was uneventful." She shrugs as she stops at a red light, then looks at me. "Tell me what's going on. I know you're hiding something." That's the only problem with becoming family, they can read you like an open book. Still, I wouldn't trade it for anything in the world, even if today is my last day.

"Promise not to maim me?" I whisper as she scoffs, easing the car through the green light. "There is something I want to talk to you about."

"Out with it, Hinton," she growls as my heart beats into my ears and my palms grow damp.

"While you were away, Emmett and I grew a little closer. Nothing has happened yet, but I wanted to let you know that we've decided to start dating. Travis knows about it and he's fine with it. Actually, he's given us his blessing." The words rush out of my mouth as I wipe my hands on my kilt and my head begins to throb with anxiety. Her face is hard as stone, her mouth set in a stern line as her eyes remain on the road. She's never looked this serious with me. "Ember?" My voice breaks with her silence and her eyes stay averted as we turn onto the dirt road leading toward the school.

Then she smiles eerily and begins to hum to the tune of "Bodies," making my heart slam up into my throat. My mouth opens and shuts in surprise as I try to find the words to say to her. It feels like everything is crashing down around me and I'm losing the only family I've ever known. My vision distorts as Ember's head swirls through the tears collecting in my eyes, and when I finally find my voice and begin to speak, her hand lands on my knee and she gives it a pat while continuing to hum.

Closing my mouth, I breathe in deeply through my nose and try to calm my pounding heart and rolling stomach. It's as close as I'll get to acceptance right now, and I just thank god she hasn't thrown me out of the car and made me walk. She pulls into her usual parking spot and turns off the car, her eyes finally meeting mine as she stops humming. I don't know what to say to make it better, and she gives me a strained smile before getting out of the car.

Vin and Travis are waiting next to Vin's Hummer, and both give us large grins as we stride toward them. I let loose the breath I've been holding and brush my hair from my shoulder, praying Emmett doesn't end up on the wrong side of Ember's wrath when he gets here.

Emmett

I pull up to the school parking lot and rev my engine a little, seeking some attention on this fine Monday morning. It works because everyone looks my way, even my sister who has her arms crossed over her chest and a look on her face that could scare Satan himself. Adri mentioned she was going to tell Ember about us dating this morning on the drive to school. Thankfully, I see she's in one piece, but Ember looks ready to spill blood. Most probably mine because I could never see her harming her best friend. I know she warned Adri before about liking me, but she really doesn't know the whole story, so I can't fault her for her anger. She doesn't need to know shit though until the three of us are ready to fill her in.

I also caught the attention of a small group of girls by the entrance doors. Purple-headed Marlana being one of them. They all start chatting amongst themselves and stealing admiring glances my way, except Marlana. She just stands there watching, her face a mask of boredom and making me feel slightly creeped out.

I remove my helmet and clip it onto my backpack—this thing is too expensive to leave out here—and then I amble my way over to my sister and the others. Travis is there with a small smirk on his face, already knowing the shit-kicking I'm going to receive. It's all worth it though because what I found with Adri and Travis is a once-in-a-lifetime thing. "Good morning, family!" I throw my arms out.

My sister is quick to throw her fist out and hit me in the chest, making me bend over as the air expels from my lungs with a *whoosh*. "We'll have a chat later, understand?" she asks through her teeth.

As soon as I get my breath back, I look at her and nod. "Understood." I swallow thickly at the look on her face.

"Good," she sneers, and we follow her toward the school.

"Pussy." Vin snickers and shoulder bumps me, his voice filled with humor.

"I don't want her to maim my face. It's pretty." I side eye him, finding his eyes bright with mirth.

"I sure love this face," he says as he grabs my cheeks in one hand, smashing my lips together, and then smacks a loud, wet kiss on my cheek.

When he releases me, I smear my hand down the wetness and screw up my face. "Gross, asshole."

He just throws his head back and laughs as he catches up to my sister and wraps his arm around her neck. They walk ahead while Travis and I follow with a nervous-looking Adrianna in the middle.

"You okay?" I whisper to her as she shrugs her deflated shoulders.

"Your sister is scary." She shudders.

"Did she threaten you?" I stop and look at her, readying to go to war if Ember said anything that would interfere with what we're building. I love my sister but she doesn't have a say in who I can and can't date.

"No." She looks over at Ember and Vin as they open the double doors. "She smiled at me and then hummed the tune to "Bodies" the rest of the way here."

I can't help it as I laugh out loud, because my sister is a fucking sadist and I know exactly why she hummed that song. She's imagining kicking the shit out of me. "I'll handle her."

"I don't want to fuck up my friendship with her. She's already warned me away from you," Adrianna moans as she steals a glance at Travis. His head is bent downward as he walks beside us, his shoulders drawn as he thinks to himself. His demeanor is warranted for what he's been through lately, and I begin to wonder if he'd ever be able to accept my comfort. I want to be there for him.

"I'll handle her," I repeat before throwing my arm around her. Travis finally lifts his head and looks from my arm around her shoulders to my face, and then he smiles. Not a trace of jealousy on his features. It's a good start.

In homeroom, I'm sitting between Adri and Ember, one tossing me nervous glances and the other shooting me murderous looks. When Mrs. G calls on me to end the class with a prayer—like she did all last week—I stand up and thank God for my beautiful sister and the unconditional love she gives me, no matter what I do. Don't think that softened her though. Oh no, I just made her incensed, and I'd be lying if I said I wasn't scared. It wouldn't take much for her to drag me into a janitor's closet and force me to drink bleach.

I practically fly out of class and away from Ember, leaving Adri to hopefully soften her a little. Girls have a way of calming each other down, it's why they take bathroom breaks together. I've got it all figured out. I get to Chem and see Travis has switched our partners and is now sitting at my table. "You said you needed help." He shrugs, looking sheepish.

"Yeah." I nod and swallow down the sudden onslaught of emotion. Not many people have offered me help in my life. "I really do. Can you create something to make my sister love me again?' I blink my eyes at him innocently and point at the Bunsen burner in front of him.

He full-out laughs and my breath gets lodged in my throat. He looks so fucking sexy, and I just want to make him do it again and again. When he stops, he looks just as surprised as I do. "Your sister loves you." He clears his throat, trying to regain his composure. "She just doesn't get this yet," he explains, waving his hand between us.

Chem goes by smoothly, and I can't believe I actually

understood something today. It's fucking amazing. We pack up our shit and quietly make our way to the cafeteria. I'm nervous about seeing Ember at lunch. I need to be using this time to convince Adri I care about her, but Ember is making that difficult. We walk into the lunchroom and I spot Ember and Adri sitting with Jake, Jordan, Cara, and Charles. Travis clasps me on the shoulder and nods toward his group and table. He wants to sit with them as he always does, so I give him a smile before starting toward Adri. Time to amp up the pressure. I need Ember to get used to the idea of her and me.

I stand behind Adri and watch as she stiffens. It's as if she can sense me even before she sees me, which I take as a good sign. I bend down to wrap my arms around her neck and kiss her cheek. "Hey," I whisper in her ear.

"Hi," she whispers back, sending a nervous glance in Ember's direction. She's either acting obtuse or purposely ignoring us.

I stand up and sit between her and my sister, leaning over to kiss Ember's cheek with a loud smack, then grab a piece of grilled chicken off her plate. At first, she looks completely murderous, but then I grin at her and she rolls her eyes, focusing back on her plate.

"You're brave," Adri hisses as she eats her fries. I steal one of those too. Why get my own when I can just eat everyone else's? They never finish their lunches anyway.

"I actually just shit myself," I continue to whisper, and she giggles.

"Bro, are we skating today?" Jake asks, breaking the awkward tension between the three of us, and I look up at him. His eyes swim with humor as he looks at me and Adri.

"I rode my bike today. I couldn't bring my board. Tomorrow?" I reach for another fry as he bites into his burger.

"Yeah, man, that's cool," Charles chimes in.

"Or maybe we can all head over to the local bar and strip?" Ember tosses in as she stuffs some green leaves into her mouth.

"Ew, no thanks. You're my sister. Take Vin." I pretend to shudder and everyone at the table laughs, including my stone-cold sister.

"I can't believe you two did that," Ember mutters, giving me a stern look as she chews. Her eyes blaze with irritation as I shrink closer to Adri.

"Travis got talent though," I say around a mouthful of Adri's burger, trying to diffuse her wrath.

"It's true." Charles nods, and we all laugh again, my sister's chuckle making me breathe a sigh of relief.

"Where's Vin?" I ask as I look around the table, finally noticing his absence.

"Sitting with the drama folks. No peasants allowed." Cara throws in her one-liner, making me snort. "Ember is the only one that will sit with her fans."

"Thank you." Ember mock bows. "Thank you."

I have yet to see Ember act and I'm hoping she gets another lead role this year. I heard she did amazing last year. When the bell rings, I groan and lay my head on Adri's shoulder. "Don't make me go to Trig," I whine.

"I'll be with you." Ember grins sadistically before yanking on my ear. "Let's go."

"Ow!" I bellow and hear the table snickering behind us as Ember drags me out of the cafeteria.

"You have some serious explaining to do." She releases me

with a shove, forcing me to stumble a few paces.

"I promise no kittens were harmed in the time you were gone." I hold up my hands as she narrows her eyes at me. "Just trust that the three of us know what we're doing." Dropping my hands, I stop walking and give her an earnest look. She stops a few feet in front of me and exhales a breath.

"Both of you want to date Adri at the same time?" Her brow raises skeptically as she places her hands on her hips.

"Something like that." Her eyes narrow again, and I hold up my hand. "Let us sort it out and then we'll talk to you, okay?"

"Fine," she grinds out, then stomps off in front of me.

"That looked dangerous," Travis muses, walking up beside me with a small smirk on his mouth.

"Can I sleep in your room tonight? I'm scared she'll kill me in my sleep." I steeple my hands and give him my best puppy dog eyes.

"Sure…" he drawls out. "No clothes rule though." Then he winks and walks ahead.

"Did you just flirt with me?" I whisper loudly behind him and watch as his shoulders shake with suppressed laughter. "Goddamn…"

Travis

When Trig is over and my cheeks are hurting from holding in laughter while listening to Ember and Emmett's bantering, I get ready and head to the gym for baseball. Entering the locker room and heading toward my locker, I find Kevin sitting on a bench tying his shoelaces.

"Kev," I call out to him. "Can we talk after this?" He lifts his head to look at me, his eyes empty of emotion. I've never really paid attention to it, but now that I think about it, it's been a long time since I've seen depth in his eyes.

"Sure." He shrugs and goes back to tightening the laces on his shoes.

It's time for us to have a discussion about Coach and what I suspect happened to him. Maybe if he knows what went down with me, he'll want to open up. As soon as I told Vin and Ember what happened, it was like a weight lifted off my shoulders. For once, people who actually cared knew what happened to me and wanted to help. Ember killed Coach, but that was her way of helping. I want to be able to help Kevin and whoever else that sick fuck touched.

I've decided that tonight I will go to 'check' on my mother and call the police when I find her body. I really don't want her rotting stench sticking to the insides of that house any longer than necessary. Then I plan on demolishing the entire thing to the ground. Maybe I will rebuild in a few years, raise a family and be content for once. One can only hope.

I've received no answer after calling Sonja's cell phone once last night and again this morning. What the fuck did my mother do to make her not want to talk to us? She's put up with a lot of abuse at the hands of those monsters for years and now I know it was so she could be near me, her son. I'm worried. I can't think of anything more terrible than what she's already been through to make her up and leave, but there's always worse, and I know that for sure. When I asked my mother, Christina, where she was, she just kept repeating, 'She left.' I've had a bad feeling about it ever since.

"Travis." Coach Wheeler sticks his head in the locker room. "Almost ready?"

"Sorry, Coach." I tie up my shoes. "I'll be right out."

Coach Wheeler nods and closes the locker room door. He's an excellent coach, keeps his hands and dick to himself, which is a plus these days, but he just doesn't have the hunger to see us as champions. The drive for that has to come from us. Coach Halbert wanted championships and accolades, but Coach Wheeler just wants to make sure we have fun. Big difference. Most of the team has been conditioned to go hard and win everything we can. I hate to say it, but that was because of Halbert. The newer guys on the junior team just fuck around and find baseball as an easy last period.

Today's practice was pretty good, we focused on a lot of infield and outfield drills, but I am a fucking mess. My concentration has been on Sonja, on my mother's corpse, and the ramifications I may face because of it all. I play infield, but I like to run both drills just because. The outfielders need fast burst stamina and it's something I always lacked in. I still push through though.

After showering, I find Kev sitting on the bench in front of my locker. His legs are spread and his arms are resting on his knees. "I have a feeling I know what you want to talk about," he mutters, his tone solemn and his eyes averted.

"Yeah?" Sitting beside him, I lean back against the lockers and release a loud sigh.

"Coach Halbert?" He looks up at me and I nod. "Yeah, I figured." His eyes flick back to the floor at his feet, still void and emotionless, as he begins to wring his hands, the knuckles turning white with tension.

"I found some shit at his house," I say, and his head snaps up, his eyes widening on mine as his jaw tics with frustration.

"What shit?" He scratches his fingers through the growing goatee on his chin as his nostrils flare with an intake of air. "Videos?"

"Pictures," I correct him, and immediately wonder what the fucking perv had on tapes.

"Oh." He drops his head again. "Of what?" His jaw remains tight as he shakes out his hands, releasing the tension.

"Nothing really crazy, just that there were a lot of you… and me." Revealing to him my situation with Coach is much easier now that I've already spoken about it to others.

He looks back up into my face and nods. "I thought so." His voice is soft, barely a whisper as he shakes his head, his eyes flicking to the lockers across the room. It's hard to admit what happened, even if he's speaking to someone who endured the same thing. "He abused me since elementary school. I think he fucking followed me to this school." I sit up straighter, my hand itching to rest on his shoulder. I refrain from touching him though, knowing exactly what these memories are capable of. Touches become twisted realities and it's hard to differentiate them from what we had done to us in the past. "It started in the seventh grade for me," he starts quietly, his hands back to wringing in his lap. "By grade nine, he had taken it all from me and kept me quiet by threatening to expose my parents' sham marriage." He looks at me, his eyes filled with fear and tears. "My father is gay, but they stay married to hide that."

"Fuck," I mutter. "He was just plain evil." My hands curl into fists as I remember just how good Coach was at idle threats. To us children, it was terrifying.

"Jeremy too, man. I think he may have had it the worst. Coach dated his mom for a few years in elementary school." Kevin hits his fist into his open palm, his anger radiating around us.

My stomach sinks at that thought, and I mentally run through all the interactions I can remember between Coach and Jeremy. I realize Kevin is fucking right. I'll need to speak to him next.

"He changed a lot in grade nine." Dropping my head, I rub my fingers against my temple as the throbbing begins to increase. I should've known they were in the same boat as me, should've tried to help them sooner.

"Didn't we all?" Kevin stands up and places his hand on my shoulder, forcing me to look up at him. His eyes are filled with gratitude as he squeezes me, a small smile appearing on his mouth. "Thanks for this. When you have that talk with Jeremy, let me know. We can do it together."

"Okay." I nod and swallow back the lump forming in my throat as Kevin heads to the door. Guilt is a hard emotion to conquer and I have it in spades.

"Oh, and, Travis?" Kevin turns back as he opens the locker room door. "Whatever you did to make him leave this school? It saved us, thank you."

I nod once more as he leaves the locker room, my eyes burning with tears. When I confronted Coach during the summer before eleventh grade, I thought I was the only one he was abusing. I knew he recorded and took pictures of others, but I really thought I was the only one who was physically touched. Hearing from Kevin about him and Jeremy really hits home. This town is fucking infested, and it may be time to join ranks with Ember to exterminate them all for good.

"Did you want us to come with you?" E asks, her voice serene as she smiles at me.

We're all gathered in her family room, and we just finished

filling in a shell-shocked Adrianna on the recent turn of events. It was my idea to bring her into the fold slowly, starting with my family and what they were. I left out the part where Ember killed Christina and my father, because when the time is right, Ember can tell her exactly what it is she does.

"I think it's better I just go over there alone and maybe call you guys once I find her." I clear my throat with the sudden onset of fear, making my voice shaky. "That way, we won't be seen coming all at once. That would be suspicious."

"So, you found your mother dead a few days ago and didn't call it in?" Adri scrunches her nose up in confusion as she looks from Ember to me.

"When she admitted about my father raping Sonja and impregnating her, then stealing her infant to raise as their own, I was fucking pissed." Her eyes widen and her mouth falls open with my confession, and maybe the fear seeping through her eyes is aimed at me. "So when I came back that day to talk to Sonja, I found Christina hanging in the bathroom. I was still fucking pissed, and yes, I left her there." I shrug as I try my best to maintain my composure, but it's only making me look like more of a psychopath. Hopefully her love for me doesn't change because of it.

"I get it," she whispers, pulling on the end of her ponytail. I'm not sure if she really does, but it proves that her love for me is unconditional.

"Come here," Emmett says as he pulls her down onto his lap and kisses her cheek. I'm glad he's here to comfort her because I don't have the strength in me right now.

E looks at them and then directly at me. When she scrutinizes my face and finds whatever it is she was looking for, she sends me a rare, sweet smile. "How about I go with you?" Ember suggests. "That's not unbelievable."

"Fine." I give in because I know she won't relent otherwise, and a small part of me is relieved I won't have to face it alone.

Pulling into my driveway, I put my car in park and look over at Ember. "Ready?" I release a breath as nerves swarm my stomach, sending waves of nausea through me.

"Hell yeah." She grins, her ease settling my anxiety a little as I soak in some of her strength. "I'm hoping Chief Moore himself comes so I can watch him squirm."

"Let's go." I open the car door and stand, my knees shaking slightly as my heart races in my chest. We head to the front door, and Ember's hand lands on my back, her support making me stand a little taller. I'm glad she insisted on being here with me. I open the door and we step inside, bracing ourselves for the chaos we're about to unleash.

The smell of rotting food and sour milk has made its way to the front foyer. It's nauseating, and I quickly cover my nose and mouth with the sleeve of my hoodie. Ember though, waltzes through like it's fresh as a flower. "Still smells like utter shit in here." She nods as she looks back at me. I can't help it as I laugh, the sound just exploding out of me. "You okay?" She grins.

"I think I'm going to be okay." Dropping my sleeve from my mouth, I walk up to her. "Because of you." Then I wrap my arms around her and hold her for a few minutes. She lets me as her hand rubs circles into my back.

"I don't know if I'm helping you, Travis, but I know I can't let anyone else hurt you. I'll always do what I can to make sure you're safe." Her words are muffled against my chest as my chin drops and my nose lands in her hair.

Then I kiss the top of her head before releasing her. "Thank you."

We head up the stairs with E close behind me, and when we get to the second floor, she looks over to my bedroom door and the hole in it. "There's blood there," she states, her tone filled with concern.

"Yeah." Stopping beside her, I reach out to touch it but she pushes my hand away. Right, prints. "I think she tried to put her fist through it."

"No." Ember shakes her head. "The indent is too big. It looks like the top of a head." I stare at the door, transfixed by the indent, which indeed looks like the top of a head. Like maybe someone was rammed into that door. The sudden urge to actually punch a hole beside it overwhelms me. Why didn't I see that? I need to find Sonja because I have a feeling it's her head that hit my door and it was my mother who did it. "Everything is still dead in here!" Ember calls out from my parents' bedroom, and I finally peel my eyes off the door to realize I'm standing here by myself.

Pulling out my cell phone, I dial 911 and meet E in the bedroom as the cloying scent of decay hits me. I quickly relay to the operator in a shaky, terrified voice that I found my mother dead. She tells me not to touch the body and that she's sending over police and an ambulance. We sit on the bed and wait, Ember tapping her foot while I try to tamp down the overwhelming anxiety. When the cops and ambulance arrive a few minutes later, we watch as they pull her down from the door and lay her stiff, cold body onto a gurney. Dropping my face into my hands, I hope I'm playing the part of a grieving son convincingly.

"She took a nice cut to the face," one cop observes, and my heartbeat picks up. I look over at E, but she's as cool as a cucumber.

"Look," another says. "She has blood under her nails. She probably did it to herself."

"Travis Greene?" The first cop looks at me with questions in his eyes, then continues when I give him a nod. "The chief is on his way here to ask you a few questions."

"Okay." The tremor in my voice isn't fake, and it earns me a few pitying looks from the officers.

"Sorry about your mom," the other cop adds, sympathy coating his words. I must look like a sad little orphan, but I'm not. If anything, I'm relieved to be free of my monstrous parents. I just don't want Ember and I to go to jail for said freedom.

"Thanks, man," I mumble as Ember reaches for my hand, linking her fingers through mine and giving them a squeeze.

As they wheel her out of the room, my eyes stay trained on the stark white sheet covering her. My anxiety boils over as I stand and begin to pace with Ember's stare like hot lasers on my face. The chief is going to squeeze the most information out of me and be very suspicious since both of my parents offed themselves within a year. The two people most unlikely to do so, and he would know since they knew each other so damn well.

"You okay?" Ember asks, her tone filled with concern.

"Yeah, just stay in the room when he gets here." My hands are coated in moisture as I drag them along my pants, trying desperately to get my breathing under control.

"You bet." She grins like this is the most fun she's had all day. Fuck, maybe it is… it's E after all.

A few moments later, Chief Moore's voice fills the bedroom. "Ah, Travis. We keep meeting under these horrible circumstances."

"Hello, sir." I turn and nod at him, forcing myself to relax as tears coat my vision.

"And Miss Craven as well." He looks around me toward Ember, his eyes shining with curiosity as a knowing grin grows along his mouth.

"Maybe we should speak downstairs in the family room," I suggest as I start for the bedroom door.

"Sure." He smiles and waves his arm out. "Lead the way. You'll join us too, Miss Craven." His demand has my heart sinking into my stomach. He knows what we did.

I lead them to the family room, and Ember sits to my left while Chief Moore sits across from us. He crosses his left foot and rests it on top of his right knee, then leans back with a weird smirk on his face. His demeanor is too nice, too understanding, and it's ringing alarm bells in my head. "Tell me what happened."

"I came home to check in on Mother. Her grief over Father was terrible, and she had upped her drinking and prescription intake because of it. I tried to stay and help her and contacted many facilities in search of programs, but she made me feel bad for 'getting rid of her,' that's how she put it. Then a few weeks ago, she threw all my clothes off the second-floor balcony and told me to move out. She destroyed my room and threatened to kill me in my sleep if I stayed." I bow my head in my hands and hold back on the tears, the shakiness of my voice making it all sound believable. "I left. I did what she asked me to do, but look how it turned out."

"I spoke to the neighbors while the paramedics removed your mother and they corroborated your story about the clothing, and you seemed to be away while your mother was roaming the streets the past few weeks. Did you know she did that?" He flips open a notebook and begins writing, the motion of his pen snagging my eye.

"Yes." I swallow thickly.

"You already spoke to the neighbors?" E cuts in as she leans forward, her chin resting in her hand.

"Of course." His eyes flick up as he smiles at her. "This is not just an open-and-shut case. I now have two people in the same household who have killed themselves in less than a year."

"Such horrible circumstances," she says mockingly while nodding.

"Listen, Travis," he starts, his eyes moving slowly from Ember to me. "There's a lot of suspicion here because your father and mother were two of the richest people in Whitsborough, and now, as their sole heir, you inherit that money. It goes without saying, while you became emancipated this past summer..." He flips through his pocketbook and stops on a page. "Here it is... Based on your mother's inability to properly parent you, this makes it look even worse." I can feel Ember's eyes boring into the side of my head. I didn't tell anyone about my emancipation, especially because she was going through a hard time and Vin was consumed with her recovery. It needed to be done and I hadn't thought of the consequences at the time.

"So, let me get this straight,"—Ember straightens, her hands linking in her lap—"because Travis' father decided in a moment of weakness to kill himself, which drives his wife insane, then to protect himself, Travis gets emancipated but still looks after his mother until she threatens his life, then because she's weak and decides she would rather be with her husband than to raise her only son, Travis is at fault?" She's playing his game of being passive-aggressive as her tone remains neutral, but her body is stiff with suppressed rage. Everything she says is accurate, and I wait for the chief's reaction with bated breath.

"No, no." He raises his hands in a defensive posture. "I'm not stating fault. I'm investigating." It's hard to tell if he's actually wary of Ember or if he's playing her game. He looks at me as he drops his hands before quirking a brow, my body strung so tight I swear it'll snap at any moment. "You understand, right, sport?" That name coming from his mouth has me instantly freezing up, and I lose all train of thought.

But E—knowing what that name means—flies off the couch and grabs the chief by his throat, his eyes flashing with anger, but he doesn't fight her as he remains still. Never entice a predator and don't provoke a dangerous person. Cop shit 101. "If you ever call him that again, I will take your gun, shove it up your fat asshole, and pull the motherfucking trigger. Test me, see if I won't do it." My eyes skate toward the front of the house, listening for anyone coming and going from upstairs, but thankfully they remain in my parents' bedroom.

His hands come up again and he has all the right to look uneasy right now, especially knowing exactly what Ember did to Coach while he slept peacefully at night. "Okay, Miss Craven," he speaks soothingly. "Didn't know I couldn't say that. I will remember not to repeat it." She releases his throat with a shove and both his hands come up to rub at the skin. He doesn't take his eyes off her until she is sitting once again beside me. "I think I got enough from you today, Travis." He flicks his eyes to Ember as he visibly swallows. "I will see myself out. Miss Craven." He nods at each of us, then disappears out the front door.

"I'm going to make his death long and painful," she vows, her tone filled with ire as she cracks each of her knuckles.

"You're going to kill the chief?" Surprise races through me as I begin to panic, my heart still in overdrive from her outburst a few moments ago.

"Most likely," she hums, her tone changing as she looks at me. "Once I work through the list, but there's no timeline right now." She speaks like it's any other day and this is her job. I don't think I'll ever get used to this side of Ember's life. "Let's clean this place up." She pulls out her phone and calls everyone over. We're going to need them.

While Adri and Emmett tackle the kitchen, Ember and Vin take my parents' room, and I decide to sort out my bedroom. It's still a mess from the beating it took from my mother. I start by tidying all the shoes and clothes strewn across the room and flip my mattress back into its proper place. Laying underneath is the book *The Three Musketeers* by Alexandre Dumas. This was the book Sonja had given to me as a child. It's strange that it's tucked under the mattress with no other books. I pick it up and sit on the bed. Sonja gave it to me, unbeknownst to my parents. She had made me promise not to tell them and would read me a bit of it every night. She gave me my love of reading through this book. I throw it behind me on the bed as a reminder to grab it before I leave the room, then start picking up the clothes and sheets and straightening up my desk. I have to find out where Sonja went, and I need to tell her that I know she's my mother.

"Hey." I turn at the sound and find Adri standing in my bedroom doorway.

"Hi." I smile at her as she pushes her hair back from her face.

"We're mostly done with the kitchen." She shuffles her feet, looking slightly nervous.

"Come here," I tell her as I hold out my hand. Her head quickly pops up, and she looks around to see if anyone is listening or watching. "Just come here," I say again, not really caring if we're caught in this moment. I just need her.

Her movements are slow and unsure, and it makes me feel bad about how much I have confused her in the last year. She stops in front of me and looks up through her thick, black lashes. Adri is gorgeous and the one and only female who could make my heart pound and my body heat. I run my fingers down her cheek and she leans her face into my hand. Today, she smells of flowers and her strawberry shampoo. My other hand slips into her hair as I bring her flush into me. I told Emmett I would back off until they formed a bond, but there's something about Adri that makes it hard to stay away. I did it for three years and it just about killed me.

She wraps her arms around my neck, and I slowly lower my mouth and press it to hers. It was only meant to be a sweet kiss, but the moment her mouth is against mine, all thought escapes me, and I open my mouth to lick her sweet lips. As soon as she gasps, I'm inside her mouth, feeling and tasting what I know belongs to me. I deepen it further and suck on her tongue, pressing my cock into her soft stomach.

Forcing myself to pull away, I rest my head on top of hers. If I continue this, I'll have her naked and under me on the bed in no time. Opening my eyes, I find Emmett sitting on my bed, his legs stretched wide and leaning back on his hands. "Don't stop now." He grins. "It was just getting good." Adri gasps and spins around to look at him. Emmett rises from the bed and walks toward her, pressing his chest into hers. Then he slowly forces her to step back into me, her back against my chest and her firm ass pressed into my cock. "Now,"—he lowers his head, his voice filled with desire—"my turn."

He tips her chin up and licks her lips before he crushes his mouth to hers. I can't help it, a moan escapes me, and I slide my hands up Adri's sides toward her breasts. Emmett brings himself in closer, and I feel the second he presses his cock into her because her ass thrusts against mine.

When they pull apart, Emmett looks into my face, and what he sees there makes him smile. There isn't one ounce of jealousy, just raw lust and wanting. I want to strip Adri down and watch Emmett take her, then maybe I can take him. Adri bends her head back and looks up at me. "This is what you guys want?" she moans as Emmett continues to suck and kiss on her neck.

"Close," I murmur with a small smile. "How are you feeling?"

"Like I want to be fucked," she confesses, her cheeks heating. "By both of you." Emmett's head comes up, his eyes filled with surprise, and he looks from her to me. "At the same time," she finishes, and both Emmett and I groan.

"That's a start," he growls while he presses another sweet kiss to her mouth.

"We should probably continue this another time," I huff with annoyance because I really don't want it to stop. "I don't want to answer a million questions from my brother and your sister."

"True," Emmett agrees and steps back. His sweatpants don't

do a single thing to hide what I know he's packing in there, and I almost reach out to drag him back in.

Adri remains pressed against me, and I give her a quick kiss to the temple. "I'm almost done in here, then I need to do a quick sweep of the backyard and pool house."

"Hey!" Emmett exclaims and flops onto my bed. "I love this book." He picks up the book Sonja gave me and flips through it.

"Yeah." I smile at his excitement. "I've had it since I was a kid."

"Travis loves to read," Adri adds and brushes her hand along my chest hesitantly. Her touch sends sparks through me, making my heart race.

"Really?" Emmett looks up from the book with surprise, a grin shining brightly from his face. "Ember is making me a library for all my books. You should check it out."

"I will," I promise as Adri sits on the bed beside him.

"What's this?" He holds up a folded piece of paper, his brows crinkled together.

"I don't know." I shake my head and take the paper from him. "Where did you get it from?"

"It fell out of the back of the book." He continues to flip through it, looking for anything else as my fingers tremble.

I open the letter and find Sonja's perfect cursive writing on the page. It's new because the blue ink looks fresh. "It's from Sonja," I whisper.

"Adri and I will head out to the backyard." Emmett puts his hand on my shoulder. "When you're done, meet us there."

I nod as they leave the room, their hushed voices floating back to me. I want to read this, but I'm afraid to fucking see what she has to say. It explains why the book was tucked neatly under the flipped over mattress. She knew I would find it and eventually find her letter as well. I sit down on the bed and let out a heavy exhale. This is going to be hard to get through. I can feel it.

Dear Travis,

I named you that. It was after my papa. This book I give you when you a little boy was from my papa. He loved this book and I bring with me to America to help me remember him. I hope you take good care of it. He died when I was very young. You will be wondering why the nanny named you and I have finally decided to give you all the truth.

Sonja always had a European accent, and her English was fine but not perfect. I smile as I read the words, because I can almost hear her voice in my head.

My family is in Ukraine. My mama is there and also I have three other sisters. When Papa died, we became very poor, and Mama never have to work before, and my sisters were younger than me. So I decide to come to America to make the money and send home to my family. Many girls from my country do this and they enjoy the learning a new language and to experience different countries. I was lucky because my mama speak some English and she teach me already.

When I get here, I find ads for nanny and for teacher. I love children so much and I decide to try for nanny. It is a funny thing because my first place I call was to your father. He tell me his wife is pregnant and will have baby in a few months. They needed help because he was so busy. I was excited! I love newborns, so I come to this house, and I have an interview. When I meet them, I think they are so young. Younger than me! And your father he seem not so nice, but your mother was sweet. She have a belly and I even feel the baby kick inside.

Christina was pregnant. Did she fucking lie to me about Sonja? I rub my hand down my forehead and try to hold off the headache that's threatening to spill out.

I get this job, and I am so happy because the pay is so good. I have enough to send to Mama and I can also save. Those early days were nice for me. Your mother just sleep a lot and your father was always away at school or business. I mostly read to learn my English better, and I cleaned to prepare house for baby.

Then one bad day, Christina was in swimming pool, and she fall asleep. But not a regular sleep, the one you get from drinking so much alcohol. I find the bottle of her favorite vodka by the pool. I did not know she drink like this, and I did not know she have the mental problems. I find out later that she was always sad because she leave college and her family to live here and have baby. Your father was building a business and still in college. Nobody tell me. She look like she was dead, and I jump in the pool to bring her out. I cannot swim very well, and it take me a long time.

I bring her out and her face look blue, so I press her chest and give the breath to her and finally she bring up so much water. I cannot believe her lungs have that much. I run inside to call the ambulance and they take her to hospital. It was so bad. The doctor say the baby was not alive for at least one week inside her belly. This make her insides bad, and she can no longer have child.

I was scared. For sure, I need a new job. But Mr. Greene surprise me and ask me to stay. Christina need my help and I could stay with her when he is gone. I was happy and I try my best to help her, but she was impossible. She drink so much, and I worry about her.

Mr. Greene become angry a lot to her, and they fight. He also become mean and not so nice to me too. He would hit Christina and he did things to me I do not wish to say. But you came from that bad thing, Travis. You are my son. I carry you for nine months and I give birth to you here in this house. I could not be allowed at the hospital because Christina make everyone believe you were hers. They take you from me, but Christina was not kind to you. Mr. Greene, he tell me to raise you and I can name you, but I must tell you Christina is your mother.

I watch as a drop of water hits the page and spreads out quickly, distorting the ink. I reach up and touch a hand to my cheek, and I'm surprised when I pull back and see tears. My whole life, I thought they hated me. I thought I was cursed with parents who wanted very little to do with me.

I am sorry I did not tell you sooner. Mr. Greene threatened to cut off my pay and my family in Ukraine. They need that money to survive. When he died I had a plan to tell you, but you were so sad, and I did not know how to do it.

You have a bad childhood. I know this. So many people treat you badly. I tried my best to protect you, but even I could not do it properly. Please forgive me, my son.

I love you,

Sonja Koltyk

P.S. I am from a small village in Ukraine called Iza and I hope one day I can bring you there to meet your baba (that mean Grandmother)

I need to find Sonja.

She wouldn't leave to go back to her country because she needs this job for her family—my family. I need to find her and make sure she knows I appreciate every wonderful moment she gave me as a child. If it wasn't for her, I don't think I would've continued to live past my fourteenth year. Tucking the letter into my back pocket, I cross the hall into my parents' room. E and Vin are no longer in here, but everything looks like it's back in order. The bed has been stripped of vomit and whatever else, and the vomit on the carpet looks slightly better, but I'll need to bring in a professional cleaning company for sure. I walk into the bathroom and my gaze immediately locks on the back of the door. It's bare, obviously, but E went a step further and even removed the robe hook as well.

I exit the bedroom and head downstairs, then out into the backyard. Everyone is walking around picking up lawn chairs and cushions that were thrown about or the wind tossed them around.

"Bro!" Vin calls out as he holds up our patio umbrella. "Where's the base for this?"

"Base?" I raise an eyebrow. "You mean the like eighty-pound weight that's filled with sand?"

"I guess so." He shrugs.

"Should be out here." I do a full circle, looking at the ground as I turn. "Did it break off?"

"No, the bottom is fine," he answers as he turns the umbrella upside down and inspects the pole.

I walk over to the shed where we keep our pool things and the patio furniture. The base is large, and I should see it right away, but it isn't in here either. "I don't know," I say with confusion. "Bring the umbrella in here so it doesn't get damaged until I find it."

We load up all the patio furniture into the shed, and I go to stand in front of the nasty, dark green pool.

"How deep is your pool?" Vin asks as he comes to stand beside me, his arm brushing mine.

"Ten feet," I mutter as I let out a breath. This is going to be a pain to clean.

"Nice, like mine."

"Are we gonna clean it out?" Adri stands on my other side, her nose scrunched in disgust.

"Nah." I shake my head. "I'll come over another day and drain it. It needs to be cleaned before it's refilled. I'll get professionals to deal with that."

Everyone follows me out of the house, and I lock it up. We all get back to our cars and Ember hops into mine with me. I pull out of the driveway, closing the gate behind me.

"So, what now?" I gaze at her as we approach a stop sign.

"Now,"—she looks at me and grins—"we get to work." I swallow down the trepidation at her expression before giving her a nod.

Chapter Twelve

Emmett

I drove our aunt and uncle's Mercedes to pick up Adri when we all helped Travis at his house. Now, as I'm driving her home, all I can think about is her mouth on Travis and him grinding into her. It's on repeat, and the tent I'm making in my pants for the second time today is borderline embarrassing. Just those few minutes of the three of us together gave me a teasing taste of what my life could be like forever. I've never wanted something more in my entire existence.

"Ember's classes are starting this coming Sunday. Are you going to join?" she asks, breaking through my continuous fantasy.

"Yeah, I already signed up." I flick my eyes to her with a wink.

"I also heard her say she was fighting in New York this weekend. Does she do classes there too?" The tip of her head and the genuine curiosity in her eyes has my stomach tightening and my throat swelling with shock. Ember wasn't careful with what she was saying earlier at the house. Maybe she was talking to Vin or Travis while Adri was walking by. How the fuck do I explain this one?

"Uh, yeah. Ember fights sometimes in New York," I hedge as I clear my throat, hoping she lets it go.

"Like legit fights or classes?" No such luck.

I pull into her driveway and turn to look at her. "I like your house." I try to distract her from her question. "I meant to tell you that the other day."

"Oh." She looks up at it with a shrug. "My mother came from old money. My grandfather was a founder here in Whitsborough along with Travis' grandfather, and yours too. My parents inherited my grandfather's money but hate living here. So they travel the world and check in whenever." Her voice is small as her eyes stay trained on the house in front of us, her solemn tone telling me it's a bigger deal than she's letting on.

"I'm sorry," I mutter, because that's no life for a kid, practically living alone.

"I'm used to it," she breathes out, but I can tell it hurts her, no matter how hard she's trying to cover it up. "They started leaving for a week at a time when I turned thirteen. I had a cook and a driver, and they figured I didn't need them. Which I guess I didn't. Then the trips grew longer, and I now see my cook and driver as family. Well, my driver also couples as a groundskeeper. They're nice people." Finally, her brown eyes meet mine, and in those depths, I find loneliness and longing.

"You can always come to Ember's." I reach out and run my knuckles along her cheek, giving her a mischievous grin to break the tension. "You can sleep with me."

She laughs and nudges me with her shoulder. "Yeah, right. It's your house too, ya know? They were your family too." Family means something to Adri, and it breaks my heart she didn't really get to experience one. That all changes now because we've become the family she's always deserved.

"I know." My hand drops from her face as I bite the inside of my cheek. "It's just taking me a while to wrap my head around it all. I came from having just Carm to all of you. It's a change." This family is new to me too, and I'm glad I'm experiencing it with her.

"I get it," she exhales in a huff. "I always felt like they had me because they needed an heir to take over the money and upkeep everything belonging to our family." The urge to sic Ember on her family is overwhelming. How could they bring a child into this world only to serve a purpose? I shouldn't be surprised because each one of us has a similar story.

"So you take over that shit and you make your own family. Doesn't need to be blood-related to be family." I hold my hand to my chest as my heart beats wildly with anger. Schooling my features, I try my damnedest to hide it, not wanting to upset her further.

"You're right. You guys are my family."

"I'm honored, Adri," I croak out, my eyes burning with her admission.

Her eyes shine with love as she gazes at me, her lips curling upward into a sweet smile. Then she leans over slightly as her eyes fall shut. Fuck, she is utterly breathtaking. I lean into her and press my mouth to hers. Her guttural moan sends me into a near frenzy as I attack her mouth with my tongue. "Come inside," she whispers as she pulls her mouth off mine.

"I haven't even taken you out properly yet," I argue, wanting to do this right. She doesn't know just how much she means to me and I'm willing to take all the time in the world to show her.

"Do you want me?" Her eyes widen slightly as her bottom lip is sucked into her mouth, her vulnerability emanating from her face.

I grab her hand and place it over my hard and throbbing cock. "What do you think?"

"Then come inside." Her hand rubs me through my sweats and my dick jumps in her hand.

Sure, I've made out with girls before and I've been given head, but I have yet to experience my dick in a warm vagina. I don't know why I waited. Despite what I told Travis, there were many opportunities. I guess I was waiting for this feeling, being so overwhelmed and anxious all at once. To be in love with the person I decide to give that part of myself to. Adri is that girl.

So what am I waiting for?

"You sure?" I lean in and brush my lips against her mouth, unable to deny myself any longer.

"Yes." She nods and moves back to get out of the car. "Now."

I follow close behind her as we walk up the driveway, then stand to the side as she fumbles with her keys. Her hands are shaking, and I would find it so fucking endearing if mine weren't doing the same in my pants pockets. We finally get in the house, and I close the door behind me, then turn as Adri launches herself up and into my arms. My hands land on her short-clad ass, my fingers gripping the skin on her thighs.

"Tell me where to go," I murmur around her lips on my mouth.

She drops from my arms and grabs my hand to lead me to a staircase. At the top, we turn right, and she opens the first door. Her room is enormous with large bay windows and a gleaming marble floor. Scattered around the room are various types of fur skin carpets.

"Are those real?" I point to a large gray one, wolf head still attached.

"Yeah." She snickers. "My parents collect them. This used to be in their bedroom, but I took it over at the start of high school."

I look over at a large fireplace and nearly scream when I see the gigantic black bear fur rug. Adri notices my startled expression and giggles.

"That one is my favorite. It's the most comfortable." She grabs my hand and leads me over to it. "Especially on naked skin."

"Huh." I swallow down my revulsion at the thought of rolling on something that was once alive. "Sounds… amazing."

Adri lifts her shirt up and over her head, revealing a black and lacy bra that clearly shows her nipples. The hard points are a soft dusty rose color, begging for my watering mouth. Next, she undoes her shorts, slowly pushing them down her legs to step out and kick them aside. The initial repulsion of lying on the bearskin rug is quickly forgotten as she stands in front of me—on this fucking bearskin rug—in a lacy bra and panty set.

"Your turn," she says expectantly, her voice husky with want.

"Uh…" I glance down at the black fur around my feet, the apprehension slipping back in.

"I'll help." She drops to her knees and starts untying my sweats. I didn't bother with underwear today since I was in a rush to get to Travis' house. She slides the waistband down and my hard cock pops out, almost hitting her on the forehead. "Holy shit," she breathes out, her eyes widening.

Her small hand circles around me as she slowly pumps up and down. Everything around me fades to the background, taking away all my hesitation. All I see and feel is Adri. When her breath coasts over my cock, I look down and watch as her tongue comes out to quickly lick the drop of pre-cum off the tip. I can't hold in the moan that escapes me as my hips jerk forward of their own accord.

"Sorry," I mumble. "I'm kind of new to this."

"To having your dick sucked?" She grins as her mouth opens and she sucks me inside.

The feel of her warm, wet mouth has me on the brink of exploding. The slight scrape of her teeth as she draws me in farther feels like fucking heaven. When she has most of me inside her mouth and her throat, she hums and swallows, constricting around me. My hands find the top of her head before I push in a little more, her gag startling me and I pull myself all the way out.

"Shit!" I tip her head back with my hand under her chin. "I'm so sorry."

"You really are new to this." She raises an eyebrow as questions swim in her eyes.

"I've watched porn, but the whole gagging part doesn't look comfortable," I confess, suddenly feeling overwhelmingly inexperienced.

"It's not comfortable, but it's not horrible." She places both hands on my thighs as she looks up into my face. "Are you a virgin?" There's no judgment in her eyes, just complete sincerity as her fingers grip a little tighter into my flesh.

"That obvious?" I run my hand down my face and exhale the breath I'm holding.

"More surprising." She chuckles as she rubs my thighs reassuringly. "You're so fucking hot."

"I didn't want it to be with just anyone," I explain, hoping she sees exactly what I'm feeling.

"I'm honored. Are you giving it to me?" She stands up, her chest heaving with each breath. "Or are we just fooling around?"

"I want you to have it." I lift off my shirt and throw it onto the pile of discarded clothing. "You already own my heart."

"What?" Her eyes widen.

"You heard me." I reach forward and pull her into me, my hands slipping behind her to undo the clasp of her bra. My nerves abandon me as Adri looks at me with complete want in her eyes. I slowly draw the straps down her arms and pull the bra off her body, her full breasts tempting me as I lean down to take a nipple into my mouth. Her gasp and moan drives me on, and I bite down while I grab her other breast in my hand.

"Oh God, Emmett." Her husky words have my cock jerking, seeking her warmth as I kiss my way down her stomach. Getting on my knees in front of her, I hook my fingers into the straps of her g-string to pull it off, then I kiss her lower stomach and lift her leg by the knee to drape it over my shoulder, her glistening pussy meeting my eyes and I groan with how much she wants me. Grabbing her ass cheeks in my hands, I pull her in against my lips. Her scent taunts me as I slowly lick her clit and gently suck it into my mouth.

Adri's hands slide into my hair as she presses herself against me harder to ride my face. I slide my tongue as deep as I can inside her and let her continue her grinding. Her juices slip down my tongue and over my chin, driving me crazy with how turned on she is right now.

"I need to feel you inside me," she groans and slowly pulls back.

Completely forgetting about the bearskin rug, I lie on my back as her feet move to straddle each side of me, and I watch as she runs her fingers through her folds. As she plays with herself, I grab my cock and begin pumping it, imagining myself deep inside her wet heat. Dropping to her knees, she hovers her wet pussy over my cock. My eyes stay transfixed on it as she positions herself over my throbbing cock and begins to slowly lower herself down. The feeling is the best damn thing I have ever felt, like a tight, wet sleeve caressing me and sucking me in. Once she's completely seated, she lightly rocks her hips forward, and I moan as her walls clamp around me, her head falling back as she rocks again on a loud gasp.

"You're so fucking big," she whispers, the tendons in her

neck straining with each word.

I can't speak. I'm so wrapped up in the velvet feel of her insides as she raises herself up on her knees and slams back down onto my cock. She does that a few more times, taking me on a ride I will never forget. I set a rhythm, using my hands on her hips to guide her as I pump up into her, praying I can last just a little longer. Her walls clamp down hard as the sounds coming from her grow loud and fervent.

"I'm coming," she gasps and grinds herself onto me.

Her pussy becomes almost unbearably tight, and I have a hard time thrusting into her as she screams my name, her walls continuing to squeeze around my cock. Her wetness seeps down and runs over my balls, and the pressure I'm holding back rushes through me, making me realize too late that we're not using a condom. "Adri, I'm coming," I pant and try to stave it off with shallow thrusts. "No condom."

"It's okay, I'm on the pill," she says as she moves quicker. Before she even finishes her sentence, I'm coming so hard I see fucking stars. Her body falls forward on top of mine as she licks a line up the column of my throat. I'm still firmly lodged inside her, still just as hard as when we started.

"Holy fuck," she groans and undulates her hips again. "Are you sure you came?"

"Yeah," I moan as she squeezes around me.

Her mouth presses against my ear. "I love you too. I'm about to show you how much."

I close the front door and then alarm it again. It's late because Adri and I decided four rounds were finally enough. I'm tired and my cock feels so sore, but it's a good sore.

"Everything okay?" Ember calls from the family room, surprising me that she's still awake.

I walk over and smile when I find her sitting there playing the shooting game I usually play. She's wearing Vin's hoodie and her hair is piled on top of her head, her face fresh and makeup free. "Yeah. All good."

"You're sure Travis is okay with this?" She lifts her brow in my direction, her eyes scanning over me like she can see exactly what I've been up to for the last few hours.

"With what?" I ask innocently as I languidly lean against the wall, my muscles like jelly.

"I know a freshly fucked look when I see it." She chuckles, her eyes rolling.

"I promise he's okay," I reassure her without getting too detailed. "Although you may have to talk to Adri about New York. She overheard you talking about fighting there."

"Shit." Her eyes widen as she bites her bottom lip. If Adri is going to be coming around often, and she will, Ember will either have to fill her in or be a little more careful about the things she discusses out in the open.

"Yeah." I nod as she leans back on the floor, dropping my controller to her lap.

"Maybe it's time to bring her into the fold," she mutters as she rubs her fingers along her forehead. It's not an easy decision, especially if she decides to tell Adri about everything she does and why. It could result in Adri not wanting to be a part of it, or even knowing about it, and we could lose her. There's no way I would let that happen, I'd find a way for us to remain together.

"It's a death fight though." I push off the wall and sit beside her on the floor. "Maybe it would be better to show her a regular fight first."

"Adri is tough." She nods, seemingly trying to convince herself. "Let's bring her this weekend. Eventually, she's going to need to know. It looks like she's becoming serious to you." Her voice softens as she shrugs her shoulders.

"She is, but I don't want to scare her off." My words are filled with fear because my mind still reverts back to the young boy who lost anything he loved. It's hard to rewire that insecurity.

"Adri is family. She's not going anywhere." She sounds so sure and I can only hope she's right. I don't want Adri drawing back and away from us, but mostly, I don't want her to pull away from me. Ember is right though. If we plan on keeping Adri around—and we do—then she has to know everything. We'll have to show her slowly because dumping all of it on her at once could cause permanent damage.

"Okay," I give in and stand up. "I'm heading to bed."

Ember gives me a small smile, her eyes scanning over me again as she releases a breath. "I'm happy for you. Good night." Her acceptance is both shocking and a relief, and I don't dare question it for fear of her remembering she was against it previously.

I lean down and kiss the top of her head, then head out of the room. When I get to the top of the stairs, I find Travis' bedroom door open a crack. I can't explain why my heart picks up or the sudden feeling of nervousness that comes over me. Maybe it's because I know I have to tell him about what just happened between me and Adri, and this would be the ultimate test. I don't want to lose him either, and I'm afraid he would finally break and tell me to fuck off.

I open his door further and see him lying on his bed, rereading the letter I found in the book in his room. "Hey," he says, startling me out of my thoughts.

"Hey. Did you get a hold of her?" I point to the letter as his eyes drift from me and back to the page, his mouth turning downward.

"No." He shakes his head as his voice trembles. "Her phone goes straight to voicemail. I think I have to report her missing."

"I'll come with you." I step into the room and brace my hand on the door handle, my heart sinking with his forlorn expression.

"Thanks," he murmurs, placing the note on the bed beside him before turning to look at me. His eyes scan over me, similarly to how Ember's did a few minutes ago, and I shift nervously on the spot. "You're coming home late. Is everything good?"

Ah shit, here we go. "I slept with Adri," I blurt out, my hand tightening around the handle on his door, readying myself for something.

"Really?" His eyes widen in surprise. "How was it?"

His reaction catches me off guard as I straighten, my heart still hammering through my chest. "That's it?"

"We knew it would come to this, right? This is what we wanted." He sounds so levelheaded about it, and his expression is filled with sincerity, making me feel stupid for worrying.

"Yeah." I nod slowly, letting his acceptance sink in as the tension in my body fades.

"So?" He grins, his eyebrows raising.

"I love her," I answer seriously, the relief I'm feeling letting the words flow. "She said it back too."

"Really?" He sits up with a bright smile on his face. "You both deserve this."

"You do too." I take a few more steps closer to him, needing to be near enough to convince him.

He smiles at me sadly as my heart breaks. I want him to feel like he deserves it, to feel loved, and I want to be someone who does that for him because I fucking love him too. He and I are nowhere near ready to say that to each other yet, but it warms me to know I'm feeling it. It's very possible to love more than one person at a time. This is my proof.

"I need sleep if I'm going to function at school tomorrow." I yawn into my hand as he settles back into his bed, his eyes flicking to the piece of paper at his side.

"Okay, good night," he murmurs, his voice sounding distant.

I don't know what makes me move toward him, but before I can process my actions, I'm leaning over him on the bed and pressing my mouth firmly to his. "Good night," I whisper when I pull away.

His hand fists my shirt, pulling me forward to completely ravish my mouth. His tongue demands entrance, and I open my lips, relenting to him. He tastes so fucking good, and when I'm close to Travis or Adri like this, I finally feel like I'm home. Then he pulls away with a grin. "Your scent is mixed with hers. It's so fucking good." He licks his lips to drive his statement home.

I stand up and throw him a smirk. "It'll be even better when the three of ours are mixed."

His eyes darken with lust and all I want to do is slide inside those sheets with him. I force myself to back away and turn to leave his room, taking one final look back before closing his door to find him gazing sadly at the letter in his hands.

When I get into my room, I almost shit my pants… literally. There, sitting on my bed, is Ember, and just a few seconds ago across the hall, with the door open, I had my tongue down Travis' throat. There's no way she missed that exchange. I stop dead in my tracks as my heart threatens to jump out of my chest. I don't know why I'm so scared, but I am. I'm not ready, and I know Travis isn't ready to explain this thing we have either.

"Just wondering if you want to ride with me tomorrow morning?" she asks as she leans back on my bed with no expression on her face betraying whether or not she saw anything. This is Ember though. She could lie her way out of the most advanced technology the FBI possesses.

"Sure." I shrug while feigning nonchalance. "I want to board with the guys at lunch anyway."

"Cool." She stands up from the bed and walks over to me, clasping my shoulder. "Good night." Then she leaves the room. "Night, Travis," she singsongs before continuing toward her room.

Fuck, I think I just had a heart attack.

Adrianna

Stepping out from the shower, I swipe my hand across the mirror, wiping away the moisture and finding a light in my eyes that I haven't seen in a long time. A light Emmett has gifted me, one of many gifts he's given me.

My body still throbs in places, a reminder of what we did not too long ago, and that's also a gift. He's healing the wounds in my heart left from my first love, and with it, bringing Travis and me back together. He truly doesn't realize how perfect he is.

But maybe Travis does.

Travis knows how lonely my life has been, how much I craved to be loved, and even though the pressure to give me that was too much for him, he found a way for me to experience it, even if it's with someone else for a little while.

Only until he figures it all out.

I don't know what he means by that, what it is he has to figure out, but I've learned my lesson in trying to force him to tell me. It only pushes him away and he seals himself up back inside his shell made of steel. I don't want to be shut out again, and if it means practicing a little patience, I'll gladly do that for him.

After tonight, I'm letting fate take over. I won't question what the three of us mean, how we'll work, or what the end result will be. I'll let Travis work through his feelings and I'll be right here the moment he needs me. Until then, I'll let myself fall in love with Emmett, I'll nurture my relationships with Ember and Vin, and open myself up to finally having the family I deserve.

The years of pitying myself are over. I can't force my parents to love and treat me like their child, and I need to stop punishing myself for that. Their inability to love me isn't my fault. Emmett, Ember, Vin, and Travis have shown me I am someone worthy of love, and it's time I realize it too.

The injuries in my heart are finally healing, those wounds becoming nothing more than scars. I can learn to forgive, but those faint lines of past agony will never be forgotten.

I blow-dry my hair and get dressed for bed, the empty house creaking around me as I walk around my room. I've grown accustomed to the sounds and they've turned into a source of comfort over the years, although it wasn't always like that. Those noises terrified me as a child, and unlike most of my friends, I didn't have parents whose room I could run into when I feared the monster in the closet would eat me.

Now I have Ember who would stand up to any monster for me, using her fists to punish anyone who dared to threaten me, and I have Vin to stand behind if ever I feel like the storms of life could knock me down. But most of all, I have both Emmett and Travis to stand on either side of me, supporting me if I ever feel too weak to walk on my own.

My family.

It's those thoughts that warm me as I crawl between my cold sheets and the walls of my empty house crowd around me. I smile as I picture them all and snuggle into my pillow, closing my eyes in anticipation of a new day. Another day with them.

Travis Then

Coach is in my father's office, and I can't really hear what they're saying through the door. The hushed sound of their voices permeates through, and I can tell it's not a good topic. Suddenly, I hear footsteps coming toward the door, so I duck into the adjoining den.

"I just don't think he needs to be forced into a situation like that," Coach says to my father, his voice sounding filled with irritation. "His time is wrapped up in baseball."

"I doubt that's all he's wrapped up in." The sneer in my father's voice is evident, his statement making my heart pound through my rib cage. "He's fourteen years old. He needs to be a man. We were long men by his age."

"It was different back then. We didn't have anything to work toward. Travis has talent. He can be in the major league," Coach insists, his belief in me warming my chest.

My father lets out a full belly laugh. "Travis will take over the family business. That's the only reason I had him."

Wow. How sweet of him to reveal just how much he loves me. Not that it surprises me. I've heard this plenty over the years, the only difference being he usually says it to me, not to anyone outside of the family.

"Let me talk to him and I will see what I can do," Coach attempts to persuade him one more time. For what? I don't know.

"Why are you so invested in my son, Halbert?" Father asks curiously. I feel like the floor drops from beneath my feet. Could my father have an idea what Coach and I do together?

"I'm his coach." There's a slight hitch in his voice, and I can guarantee my father heard it too. "I am invested in all my boys."

"I'm sure you are." Father's dry chuckle fills my ears like a roaring white noise. "Keep that investment away from my kid, Halbert."

Coach exhales as they move to the front door, and I take this chance to escape the den and move quickly upstairs to my room.

"Mister Travis." Sonja's heavily accented voice greets me as she exits my parents' bedroom. "Everything is okay?"

"Yes, Sonja." I smile at her even though my stomach is churning with anxiety. This woman is the only one in this big house who cares about me. "I was just going to get ready for bed."

"Okay, you sleep well." She pats my cheek and disappears down the hallway.

I'm just finishing getting into bed when my bedroom door opens. My father's looming figure darkens the doorway, and I am instantly on alert. He rarely comes into my room.

"Son," he snaps, his tolerance low from just being in my presence. "Tomorrow you will be home before eight. I have a meeting you will sit in on."

"Okay," I answer with a small nod.

"Do not be late," he warns. "Your mother leaves for her spa weekend, and I would rather not waste the peace of her being gone."

Again, his loving attitude is charming.

"Okay," I repeat.

He pivots on his heel and exits my room. I don't know if this fear of my father will ever go away.

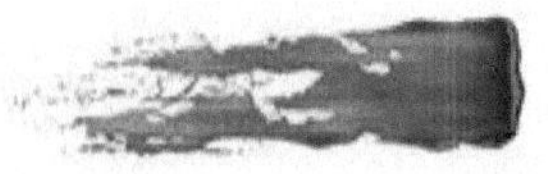

"Coach!" I yell out to him, knowing he's somewhere lurking in this locker room while I shower. "I can't stay late today! I need to get home for a meeting with my father!"

I turn off the water and wrap the towel around my lean waist. I've noticed my body changing a bit this year, becoming leaner and my muscles more noticeable. Within six months, I've shot up a foot. Even though I've been getting a lot of attention from girls at school, Adrianna is still the only one I want. I just don't know how to tell her yet.

Three of my closest friends have lost their virginity already and they've made fun of me for still having mine. I plan on losing it to Adri though. She's going to be my wife, so it only makes sense.

"What kind of meeting?" Coach's worried face appears next to my locker.

"Not sure." I shrug as I reach in and grab my deodorant. "He didn't say."

"Maybe you should skip it." He places his hand on my lower back as I swipe the deodorant under each armpit.

"Are you dense?" Throwing the deodorant back in my locker, I turn to look him in the eyes. "He would beat me to within an inch of my life and enjoy it." His face is looking older than usual as stress deepens the lines around his eyes and his frown cuts deep into his cheeks.

"I just don't want you to go there right now," he stresses as he wrings his hands.

"Is there something you know that I don't, Coach?" My body tenses as his frown grows and my heart sinks into my stomach.

"Just be careful," he mutters and walks away with his head down.

Lately, I've been questioning the feelings I used to have for Coach. I was a young child, starved for attention, and he took advantage of that, but deep inside, I still have this attachment to him. Something that keeps me coming back because then I can feel what it's like to have someone who loves me.

Precious Blood Academy is not too far from my house so I decide to walk home instead of calling the driver. It's about a fifteen-minute walk and I take this time to think through the things I need to do in my life. Foremost, I need to get my father off my back. So if I act like I'm interested in the business and attend these meetings, he'll ease up. Secondly, I need to sort out this shit with Coach. I need to put an end to our particular meetings because I know they are sordid and wrong. Last but certainly not least, I need to let Adri know how I feel. Being around her every day and not kissing or touching her is driving me crazy.

The large, wrought iron gates of our estate looms in front of me. The large Sphinx statues standing at each corner have a devilish grin on their faces. If I really look at them, the faces resemble my father's.

He's so warped in the head.

Opening the gate with the code, I walk up the large, winding driveway. Our house is the biggest on this street. My father always talks about how his father was a founder of Whitsborough and our status ultimately comes from him. I really couldn't care less. If he was just as messed up as my father, then I don't care to know about who he was.

The front door opens in front of me, and Sonja is hoisting her large purse up onto her shoulder.

"Where are you going?" I ask her, startling her as she spins to look at me with wide eyes.

"Oh! Hello, Mister Travis. Mister Greene ask me to go pick out new bedroom set for your mother. A surprise for when she get back from the spa." She grins with excitement, her cheeks flushed with the prospect of being out of the house. I don't blame her. Her excitement only makes me that much more anxious. My father is clearing out the house. But why? I smile at her

and nod as I brush by her and into the house. "Mister Travis?" she calls out from behind me. Looking over my shoulder, I raise a brow at her. "I will be in Toronto. You need anything?"

"No, thank you," I mutter and drop my stuff beside the front door.

"Your father have guest in the office for a meeting. Do not disturb him, yes?" she asks.

"I need to be in that meeting." I look toward the office door. "Did you see who it was?"

"Yes." She nods, her brows coming together in thought. "It is woman. She look like businesswoman."

"Oh, okay." I don't know why I feel a hundred times better. I was worried about being in there with my father and another man. I walk to the office door and lightly knock. "Father?" Turning slightly around, I watch as Sonja closes the front door behind her, and a sense of foreboding comes over me.

"Yes, son. Come in!" he calls out, his voice scarily sweet. He's never sounded like that before. Tentatively, I open the door and look around before I step inside. There certainly is a woman in here and she's sitting on a chair across from my father's desk. She looks like a businesswoman in a skirt suit, but her skirt is a little short. "Son,"—he points to the lady sitting in the chair—"this is Tonya. She's here for the meeting with you."

"With me?" I ask, swallowing thickly as the woman gives me a thorough scan with her eyes, her mouth tipping upward. "You mean with us?"

"No." A menacing grin comes over his face as his hands flatten on the desk, and a ringing sounds in my ears as I shake my head. "Just you. I will observe."

Tonya gives me a smile as her gaze roams over me from head to foot again. "You're right, Robby, he is growing nicely."

"I want you to give him the same treatment you give me. Or rather, let him do what I do to you. Understand?" He's looking at me the entire time he talks to her, his eyes shining with evil.

"Oh, yes." She licks her lips and bites down on the bottom one. This time, I really take a good look at her.

She's about 5'5 and pretty skinny. Her thighs don't touch, even as she's sitting down. She has huge boobs inside of her suit jacket because they are nearly spilling out and over. She has overly bleached hair that's nearly white against her black eyebrows and her skin is an unnatural orange color. If I were to guess her age, I'd put her aging face at nearly forty.

She stands up and removes the jacket. When she's finished unbuttoning it, she lets it drop to the floor, and that's when I realize she doesn't have anything else on underneath. I gasp and look at my father. What the hell is happening here?

"Look at those tits, boy," he says, his words like razor-edged blades, each one slicing through my ears. "Get over there and grab them."

When I don't move, Tonya comes to me and grabs my hands to place on her boobs. They are hard and way too bouncy to be real, not that I have anything to compare them to. I screw up my face and try to remove my hands.

"Do as he says," she whispers quietly, her eyes widening. It's clear Tonya is afraid of the man behind the desk as well. "Let's enjoy this."

I look at my father's face and watch as his eyes become dark and narrow at me. If I don't do this, I can expect the beating of a lifetime. "What do you want me to do?" My voice shakes with fear as I try to swallow it down.

"I want you to slam her down over my desk and fuck her roughly from behind." My breath gets lodged in my throat and my mouth is suddenly dry. He's asking me to have sex with an older woman I don't know? And in front of him? "Did you hear me, boy?" His sneer is firmly in place as disgust for me emanates from every feature. "Fuck that whore. Now."

"Whore?" I look at her again and am hit with the sudden realization. She's a prostitute and one who knows my father intimately.

She drops her skirt to the floor, revealing she has no underwear on either. Her private area is shaved completely, the skin looking a little raised and bumpy. I've seen pictures of girls naked in magazines the guys bring to the locker room, so I know what different vaginas look like. Some with hair and some without.

She drops to her knees in front of me and undoes the button on my jeans. "Wait," I mumble, and she looks up at me.

"Don't make it worse for yourself," she whispers and gives me a pointed look, her eyes filled with a fearful pleading. Before I can collect my thoughts, she has my jeans and boxers down around my ankles and my limp dick in her hands. My hands curl at my sides instead of pushing her away because I'm so damn scared of my father.

She looks back at my dad with a chuckle. "Not what I was expecting."

"Of course. He's my son, after all."

She licks the head of my dick, and the fucker betrays me by instantly growing hard. I get it feels good, but I don't want to do this. My body shakes and I feel like I'm about to throw up. I feel ill as she sucks me into her mouth and down her throat. She moans like this is the most amazing thing she's ever done and that just increases my displeasure. I make the mistake of locking eyes with my father who discovers my discomfort immediately. His face turns red and his eyes become like a storm.

"Tonya, get over here." He stands and points at the edge of his desk. She does what he says, and he roughly shoves her down. Her head smacks against the desk and she moans loudly. "See? She likes it rough. Get over here." I don't move, and the trembling in my body increases. I shake my head as he lifts her head off the desk, only to slam it down again. This time, she cries out in pain. "Get over here or I will kill her in front of you, then force you to fuck her dead body." She whimpers, clearly sensing the truth in his words.

Walking slowly and removing the jeans and boxers from around my ankles, I stand behind her. I can see she's shaking now too and bet she regrets ever agreeing to do this. At least I hope she does.

"See this nice wet pussy?" he asks as the fingers of his other hand roughly spreads her open. It looks like a wet alien. "You are going to stick your dick in here and fuck her rough."

I really don't want to do this, and he can see it in my eyes. His hand tightens in her hair and she cries out in pain again. I nod and he immediately loosens his hold. I stand close behind her and he uses both hands to spread open her butt cheeks.

"Two holes here," he says. "You can fuck whichever one you want. The asshole is tight as fuck, but the pussy hole is nice and wet. You pick."

My dick becomes hard again while I look at her pussy, and shame rolls through me tenfold. I want to throw up all over her back. My hand shakes as I grab onto the traitor, and I fumble a bit behind her.

"Line it up," he encourages. "Then just slam it in. That's how you like it. Right, Tonya?"

"Mm-hmm," she moans as the head of my dick touches her pussy. It's warm and slightly wet.

"Slam. It. In," he grits through his teeth.

I prepare to do as he says and grab her hips to keep my balance. Then I ram myself deep inside her. It feels good, but it's not erasing the nausea rolling through me. Her moaning becomes loud, and my father continues to hold her head down while watching me pump into her. It's gross and so fucking uncomfortable.

I continue to roughly slam my dick into her, and when I feel the tingles of my release, my father shoves me back. I stumble and come on the floor at her feet. As I'm staring down at my dick, sticky with her stuff, and then my cum on the floor, I begin to cry.

I didn't want to do this. He took the choice from me, and now I won't be able to lose it to Adri like I planned. My crying becomes sobs as I feel the sting of my father's slap across my cheek.

"Get the fuck out!" he yells, his face red with fury and his eyes bulging from his skull. "I make a man out of you and you cry about it?"

"I d–didn't... w–want... to d–do... it," I get out between sobs.

"Are you a little queer?" he sneers into my face, spit flying from his mouth to land on my cheeks.

"No!" I stagger back a few steps, ensuring I'm out of range of his fists.

"Get out!" he screams and turns to undo his belt. Tonya hasn't moved from the desk, and I can only guess this was a two-for-one deal. Picking up my jeans and boxers, I run out of the office, leaving the sounds of Tonya's pleasure behind me.

Chapter Thirteen

The rest of the week goes by with little drama. Jeremy has been away all week, so I haven't had the chance to speak with him. Hopefully, I can get it done next week. I also reported Sonja's disappearance to a fat, lazy cop who asked the most ridiculous questions. He promised me he'd look into it, but I have my doubts the department will put in any effort. I called her cell phone another twenty times this week with the same response: voicemail.

It's Friday evening and we're preparing to tell Adri about Ember's extracurricular activities. Tomorrow morning we're driving to New York, and much to my disapproval, Ember thinks it's time Adri knows the truth, starting with this. Emmett is currently on his way to pick her up, and from his constant good mood all week, I'm guessing they have been pretty active. I'm happy for them and I'm especially happy for Adri. She deserves it.

"I really don't know if this is something Adri should know about, let alone watch." My stress levels have soared since Ember informed me of her decision to gradually bring Adri into the fold.

"Bro, it's gonna happen eventually. She's a part of our family," Vin stresses from his spot beside Ember on the couch.

"I just don't think she's made for this type of life." Adri is sweet and soft, with not one single ounce of violence in her body.

"Adrianna is tougher than what you're giving her credit for," Ember retorts, crossing her arms over her chest.

"I've known her since pre-K." I raise a brow, irritation climbing inside of me. "I think I would know her better than anyone."

"You sure about that?" Ember questions as she leans forward. "You were MIA for a few important life-developing years."

It's a low blow but an honest one. Fuck, I can only hope she's right because the Adri I knew before could never handle watching her friend beat someone to death, or plan a hit, or handle a boyfriend who was sexually assaulted most of his life. I fucking hope E's right.

The front door opens and voices drift into where we're sitting in the family room. Emmett is laughing and Adri is huffing at whatever silly thing he said. I feel bad because her perfect little bubble is about to burst.

"Don't look so fucking worried," Ember says, her arms dropping from her chest and her eyes softening. "Trust me."

"I do." The words are said with very little thought because it's the honest truth.

"Hey, guys." Adri comes in and heads straight for where I'm sitting on the other couch across from Ember and Vin. Standing up, I pull her into my arms and press my lips to her temple, inhaling her sweet scent. "Everything okay?" I want Ember and Vin to get used to seeing the three of us being affectionate with each other.

"Yeah." I release her and sit back down on the couch. "Ember wants to have a meeting."

"Oh." Her brows come together as she sits right beside me,

Emmett taking the seat next to her. "Okay."

Ember looks between the three of us as a crease appears between her brows. I'm pretty sure she's starting to catch on to what's developing between the three of us. I actually hope she figures it out before we have to sit her down and blow her fucking mind.

Ember leans forward and rests her elbows on her knees. "Remember when I told you last year I fought in illegal matches while I lived in New York?" she asks Adri.

"Yes." A grin appears on Adri's face as she chuckles softly. "I asked you if you took a pound of flesh for your mob boss."

Ember laughs. "Yeah. Well, you were close to being right."

"Get the fuck out. I forgot to make you elaborate back then." Adri leans forward too, her words breathless. "You used to kill people for the gang?"

"I didn't kill, no." Ember shakes her head. "Just roughed them up, maybe broke a few bones."

"Damn right, you did," Adri says, hitting her fist into her hand. "Are you back to doing that again? Is that why I heard you say something about a planned fight in New York?"

"Kind of. You know Carm…" Ember waits for Adri's nod. "He runs the gang in New York."

"Okay…" she drawls, her head tipping to the side.

"My father ran it before him," Ember continues, gauging Adri's reaction.

Adri's huff has me turning my full attention to her. "You already told me this. He was murdered."

"Yes." Ember narrows her gaze, then finally drops the first bomb. "By me."

The room falls silent as Adri stiffens, her head slowly turning to look at me, her eyes wide with shock. My mouth tightens into a grim line as I give her a small nod. "Why?" Adri asks, turning back to Ember. The word is barely a whisper as a tremor of emotion skates through it.

"He kidnapped me the night of the play, forced me to fight in a ring, and I found out he killed my mother." Ember's eyes shine with tears as her throat works on a swallow. Her mother's death still haunts her and even though she knows the circumstances of it now, she still blames herself in a way.

"How did you do it?" Adri's voice is hoarse and she clears her throat.

"I tortured then shot him." Ember lays it all out there, leaving the air in the room thick with tension. Adri's body is strung so tight that I fear any quick movement will snap her in half. I run my hand along her back as Emmett brushes a tendril of her hair behind her ear.

Adri looks at each of us in the room and then faces Ember once more. "Judging by everyone else's lack of surprise, I guess I'm the last to know." The pulse in her neck flutters quickly, betraying her shock as the room falls quiet again.

No one speaks and the silence around us is like a fog, making it hard to breathe. What will she think of all of us? Is this the nail in the coffin that pushes her away for good?

"Yeah, it's not something to be taken lightly," Emmett mutters. "Ember had her reasons, and it's a lot to take in, but we think you can handle it." His hand rubs her back, and I exhale the air from my lungs when she doesn't push him away.

"You don't say?" Adri says sarcastically, facing Emmett before looking once more at Ember. "How did you get away with it?"

"I never confessed to it," Ember clarifies. "It helped that the piece of shit actually kidnapped me and Carm corroborated that story. Not to mention, most of the cops in New York are on his payroll, so they were easily swayed to believe my version of events and declare me not a person of interest." Ember clasps her hands together between her knees, her intense stare aimed on Adri's face.

"That was why you were so different when you came back," Adri murmurs to herself. "You found out he killed your mother, then he had your best friend killed, and you snapped. Jesus, Ember, you should've told me. I would've understood." It's clear she's feeling hurt as her voice drops low.

"I didn't know either," I cut in as Adri turns to face me. "I was as much in the dark as you were at that time."

"But clearly you were told before me." Her head drops as she looks at the floor, waves of sadness pouring from her. "Don't leave me out of these things if you really want me to be a part of this family." Despair rings through every one of her words and my heart breaks with them.

"I'm sorry," Ember tells her. "I didn't want you to be afraid of me."

"I'm tougher than that," Adri retorts, echoing what Ember told me earlier. Ember's eyes meet mine and she tosses me a wink. My eyes burn as I hold in the eye roll, not wanting to be immature.

"I'm glad to hear that." Ember nods and that murderous grin lights up her face. "I have a fight lined up this weekend in New York, but they're a little different than what you're probably expecting."

"Like bloodier?" Adri's voice drops, the husky tenor making my cock jerk to attention. Is she excited about that?

"Deadlier," Ember states, her eyes rounding on Adri as my

girl tips her head to the side with confusion. "To the death, actually."

"To the fucking death?" Adri screeches, her spine straightening as her shrill words echo around the room. "Why?"

"Because I'm hired to do so," Ember explains, her voice soft as she shrugs a shoulder. "It sounds barbaric, but I only kill people who truly deserve it."

Adri sits back and crosses her arms over her chest, inhaling a deep breath. "Tell me everything. From the beginning this time."

A few hours later, Adri knows almost everything. Almost… Ember hasn't told her about anything pertaining to me except the fact that she killed our father because he was terrible to Vin when he was a child. She hasn't told her about killing my mother or anything regarding Coach and my father being the Whitsborough rapist. I guess she's leaving that decision to me.

"Wow," she mutters, her face a mask of nonchalance. "My best friend is an assassin for hire." She bites her bottom lip as she contemplates everything, the silence around us deafening.

"Are you okay?" I ask her after a few minutes, my hand rubbing circles on her thigh.

"Yeah," she slowly responds and looks back up at Ember, a wide smile growing over her mouth. "I fucking knew you were badass."

We all collectively relax, the tension in the room breaking with her acceptance.

"Did you want to come with us this weekend?" Ember offers, her eyes alight with excitement. "I would feel better if you did. I don't want you here in Whitsborough alone."

"Because of this Talia woman, right?" Adri looks at each of

us, her eyes shining with trepidation.

"Yeah." I link my hands with hers as I explain, "She's dangerous, and we haven't really figured out what her motive is."

"I want to come and see you fight," Adri declares as she locks her gaze on E. "I want to see how you kill them."

Both Emmett and I snap our heads toward our girl, shock lining both of our features.

"Wow," I breathe out, my mind scrambling to process as her statement leaves me speechless.

"What?" Adri looks at me, her brows crinkling together in the center with scrutiny.

"You've changed from the girl I remember," I confess as her hands slip out of mine.

"Maybe it's time you faced that." Her face hardens with a strength I never knew she possessed.

I swallow thickly as my eyes flick between hers. "You're right." I brush my fingers along her cheek, swooping a tendril of her hair behind her ear. "Maybe it's time we got to know each other again."

"I'd like that." She smiles, her eyes shining with appreciation.

"As touching as this is,"—Vin stands up and stretches his arms over his head—"I need to fuck my girl and get some sleep. Be up at five."

Asshole has me smirking as E giggles, following Vin out of the room. She turns back at the doorway and gives us all a look. "Don't do anything I wouldn't do, kids." Then she's gone with a wink.

"I think she's basically given us permission to kill just about anyone that looks at us wrong." Adri snorts, and both Emmett and I laugh.

"Did you want to stay here tonight, or do you want me to drop you back at home?" Emmett asks her while twirling a piece of her maroon-dyed hair around his finger.

"I should go home and pack a bag. I didn't think I'd be going to New York." She wiggles in her seat as she beams at us.

"I think now that you know the entire story," I begin, "maybe you should start staying here instead of being alone in that house."

"I'm not alone," she protests. "I have Klein and Vera." Her voice drops a little, the words losing their tenor as she looks from me to Emmett.

"The driver and the cook?" I clarify, my heart breaking at the fact that Adri has lived her life perpetually alone.

"They are my family. What would they do if I'm not there?" Her brow rises as her eyes narrow on me.

"Oh, I dunno," Emmett starts, his voice laced with sarcasm. "Go on vacation?" He knows how to read a room and his gift of breaking up tense moments will come in handy to smooth over the rough edges of mine and Adri's relationship.

"We'll discuss it more in New York." Pushing up from the couch, I stretch and look down at the two of them. Emmett has his arm around her shoulders, his fingers brushing along her neck.

"Yeah, sure. Along with discussing what you two have planned for this"—she waves her hand around between us—"situation."

My heart begins to pound as sweat collects along my neck. I'm not ready to bare myself completely because I haven't worked through my feelings yet. "We'll get there." I head out of the room and call out behind me, "Good night." I'm still finding the light on the shitstorm that was and is my life. Opening up to another person about my traumas and inadequacies only makes me feel nauseous.

About twenty minutes later, the front door opens and shuts, signaling their departure. As happy as I am that they're meshing and finding love in one another, I long to be a part of it. I'm not holding back to be difficult, I just know this is my second and final chance to get it right. Adrianna was always in my periphery, even when I wanted nothing more than to curl up inside myself and die. She was there. Yes, I let her go, but I had my reasons.

That night, long ago, after my father set up the 'meeting' with his regular prostitute, I was at the lowest I had ever been, but I had promised to go to Danny's party with Adri. I knew Vin wouldn't be there because his mother had put him to work at the restaurant on Friday nights and my night would be clear to spend it with Adri.

After the situation inside my father's office though, I was in no mood to be in public and I should've listened to my intuition, but I was overcome with stress, sadness, and a soul-wrenching hatred. My father had a temper that could bring down an entire army. I wanted him dead, and I could only hope I would grow the balls to do it one day.

I remember chugging half a bottle of expensive bourbon from my father's study and then walking to Adri's house with the other half in my hand. By the time I had reached her house, I was severely intoxicated. Adri could tell I was drinking, but she wasn't aware of just how much. I remember her looking me up and down as I stood on her front porch, her brown eyes more expressive than any other time.

She was home alone again. Her parents had made it a regular occurrence since the beginning of the school year, only popping in once a month for a week to make sure she was okay.

Fucking chumps.

She didn't say much to me as we walked to Danny's, just frequent glances out of the side of her eye. I knew she could sense something was wrong. We were just that close. What Adri didn't know was the extent of how bad my home life was, how brutal my father was, and how much my mother hated being there.

Most of the night was a blur, but I remembered the main points. Being intoxicated finally made my balls drop, and I started a kiss with Adrianna. When she reciprocated, I was happy. I know a lot of the night was making out with her, but I vaguely remember Stacey showing up. I don't know how she got my attention, but I could tell by her face it was important.

Stacey was a grade eleven student at Precious Blood Academy, and her mom was dating Coach Halbert. I remember being in the bathroom, and when I came out, Stacey grabbed my hand and dragged me into a bedroom. She had clearly been crying, and I remember feeling slightly nauseous from the copious amounts of alcohol I had consumed. The events are fuzzy in my memories, but Stacey basically told me Coach raped her and when she tried to tell her mother, she called her a slut. To be fair, there were rumors Stacey was free with her body. She said she found pictures in Coach's desk of all the guys on the team, some of us in the shower, but mostly they were of me in different stages of undress.

By the time I came out of the room, Adri was long gone. It wouldn't be until Monday at school that I would find out the extent of the damage. When I opened my locker, I found a doodle Adri made of the two of us. We were on the seesaw—one of our favorite places to chill—and on the back she'd written a note.

I will hate you forever, Travis.

Emmett

"Have you been to New York before?" I ask Adri as I pull into the garage at Vin and Ember's condo.

"No." She gazes out the passenger window, watching the parked cars as we drive by. "I guess there won't be much sightseeing."

"It may feel like Ember is being overprotective, but trust me, Talia is not to be fucked with." I pull the Mercedes into the visitors' parking spot and hop out quickly to stretch my legs. "I'll take you to a bomb-ass restaurant though." I wink at her.

"Okay." She smiles and her gorgeous brown eyes melt my fucking heart.

We grab our bags out of the trunk and walk to the elevator. To get to the penthouse, we have to punch in a code. "The top floor of this building has two separate penthouses, and it's fucking huge," I describe to her with a grin.

"I can't wait to see it." Her voice sounds excited but sketched with worry, her smile no longer really meeting her eyes.

"You okay?" Pulling her to face toward me with my fingers under her chin, I stare into her eyes as they begin to water.

"I'm scared about Ember's fight," she whispers softly, her lips trembling as she tries to hold in her emotions. "Don't tell anyone else. I don't want them to worry about me while she's fighting."

"I won't say anything," I assure her, my fingers slipping along her cheek as she closes her eyes with a shudder. "Why are you scared?"

Her eyes open as she stares up at me, the fear shining so

bright that it makes my stomach flip. "I haven't seen her fight yet and anything with the description 'to the death' should be worrisome."

"Yeah, I know what you mean. The first time I saw her fight, I was worried about her. Especially seeing her put up against a large man. But you'll see, Ember is quick. She's so fucking fast, and you'll notice she has her whole fight mapped out before it even starts, all while considering everything her opponent might do. Let go of the worry and enjoy it. It's like watching that Picante guy paint a picture," I reassure her.

"Picasso?" She tips her head as a genuine smile begins to form on her mouth.

"Him too." I nod as I lean in to kiss her forehead, her chuckle reverberating around the elevator and easing my worry.

I take her hand when we reach the floor and guide her down the hallway to the door. Ember, Vin, and Travis are already here, having left together a few hours earlier than us. I knock on their door, and after a few moments, it opens to reveal Travis with a backdrop of New York behind him. I'm a little awestruck as the streaks of blond in his hair seem brighter, highlighting the tawny color. His green eyes sparkle as his smile curves along his plump lips. He hasn't shaved in a few days, and I really like the light brown stubble on his chin and cheeks.

Adri goes to him and falls into his arms while he looks at me, affection for us both radiating from his eyes. "How was the drive?" he asks me, Adri still nestled in his arms.

"Emmett drove the entire way here without a break. We stopped maybe twice to use the bathroom. He should probably rest before tonight." Adri pops her head up and glares at me.

"Nah!" I walk by them, placing my hand on Travis' shoulder. "But if the hosts of this place want to get me a beer, I wouldn't complain!" I call out.

"Get it yourself, asshole," Vin retorts as he rounds the corner with a grin on his face.

We bump our fists before he slings an arm over my shoulder. "I dropped your sister off with Carm. Felt like he was missing her with how much he was blowing up her phone. Something about her needing to warm up before tonight."

"Yeah, after the shit-show in Spain, it seems he's grown fond of her. He's constantly asking me if she's okay." I snort, knowing our brother has fallen under Ember's spell. Even with the warning I gave him, he didn't stand a chance. He put up a good fight though, I'll give him that.

"Yeah, I can't believe he can look at her and not want to kill her after that."

"Should we be worried she's there alone?" I crinkle my brows. I love Carm, but the way he thinks and conducts himself can be unorthodox.

"I was a little worried at first." Vin chuckles as he drops his arm from my shoulders to scrub his hand over his face. "But you should've seen his face when she got out of the Hummer."

"He came up to get her?" I ask, slightly astonished.

"Yeah." Vin nods, his eyes wide with shock as well. "He tried to look annoyed, but as soon as she was close to him, his eyes were all soft and he pulled her in for a hug. It was obvious he missed the shit out of her."

"Wow." I rub my fingers across my mouth as I smile. "That is crazy."

"Maybe he just needed a sister to soften him up." Vin heads to the fridge in the large open-concept kitchen as I follow him, and Adri and Travis lean on the counter.

"Ember?" I raise a brow at him. "Soften him up?" Adri giggles as Travis presses a kiss to her temple. Vin catches the movement but thankfully doesn't say anything to draw attention to it.

"Especially Ember." He winks as he pops the caps off a few beers and hands them to each of us.

He's probably right. Carm needed a tough sister he wouldn't have to protect but still feel protective of. Again, I'm struck with a familiar sadness. Too bad we didn't all grow up together.

"What time do we have to be there?" Adri asks from under Travis' arm as she takes a sip of her beer.

If Vin has questions about the three of us, he doesn't show it. "Ten. Before that, they have regular fights."

"Oh?" Adri raises a brow. "Regular? Like you-don't-have-to-kill-each-other-if-you-don't-want-to fights?"

"Yeah, those." Vin leans a hand on the counter as he grins at Adri. "You guys eat?"

"Yeah, we grabbed burgers on the way here." I take a drink from my bottle as Travis does the same, our eyes meeting briefly. He's looking more relaxed being away from Whitsborough and the stress we left behind.

"You're not worried about Ember in these fights?" Adri asks Vin, her eyes back to being filled with anxiety.

"I always fucking worry about her. I feel like it's my new state of normal." Vin swallows half his beer in one go. "But Ember doesn't need anyone to protect her or worry about her. She needs people who will stand beside her and support her when she needs it. She's the toughest person I know. Trust me, Adri, after tonight, the way you see Ember will be shattered. In a good way."

"Aren't you worried?" Adri looks up into Travis' face. He hasn't seen her fight either.

"A bit," he admits. "But it's E. She has a lot of power packed in that body. I've also seen her single-handedly take out two large gangsters with just a set of brass knuckles."

"Oh, yeah!" Vin snaps his fingers. "I fell in love that day." He scrubs at his chin, and we all laugh.

"You also saw her fight that dude in her defense class," Travis reminds Adri, his chin resting on top of her head.

"Yeah, but she was bleeding," Adri says quietly, her voice trembling a little.

"I'm going to head over to the compound," Vin announces as he finishes his beer and places the bottle on the counter. "I want to make sure she's warming up properly." His sadistic smirk has Travis snorting.

"I don't think your idea of warming up is the same as hers," he retorts.

"Says who?" Vin winks and grabs his leather jacket from the hook by the door. "Make sure you guys lock up properly when you leave."

As soon as he steps out the air around the three of us becomes charged with energy, none of us daring to say anything. I swallow the rest of my beer down, needing to distract myself from the awkward moment when Adri clears her throat.

"Do I get a taste of what the three of us will be like before I really decide if I want this?"

Adrianna

Travis spits his mouthful of beer across the kitchen as Emmett curses and rushes to the sink to grab a dish towel to clean it up.

"Uh…" Travis clears his throat and places the beer bottle on the counter, his cheeks turning pink under my scrutiny as Emmett wipes the beer off the floor.

"How will this work if you can't even handle me asking a question?" I place my hands on my hips as Emmett comes up behind me, his arms slipping around my waist. I'm tired of us all walking on eggshells about our situation.

"She's right," he murmurs as his face presses into my neck.

"About us having a threesome?" Travis tries to sound aghast, but the heat in his eyes says anything but.

"How else would I be with both of you?" I whisper as Emmett's lips skim along the sensitive skin of my neck, making me suck in a breath.

"Yeah, Travis," Emmett husks as his tongue flicks against my earlobe. "There's only one way to figure this out."

His hands glide over my stomach, his fingers dipping into the waistband of my leggings as I tip my head back and moan.

"Fuck," Travis hisses as he steps closer, the heat of his body washing over me. "Take off her shirt," he demands.

My head snaps up as my eyes widen on him, his words shocking me at how easily he folded. Emmett hooks his fingers along the hem of my shirt and slowly lifts it over my head, revealing my white lace bra. Travis' finger begins to circle my nipple through the material as my chest heaves with anticipation.

Emmett unclasps my bra and drags the straps down my arms, baring my breasts and puckered nipples. "So soft, Travis," he murmurs as his hands cup them, bringing my tits together to entice the man in front of me. "Taste them."

Travis' eyes meet mine, the pupils dilated, and his jaw tics with the effort to hold himself together. I lift a hand to brush along that tense muscle, then slip my fingers into his hair to bring his head forward. I want him to have a taste.

His control snaps, and with a snarl, his hands are on my hips and his lips around a nipple. The warm, wet feel of his mouth drags a guttural groan from my throat as his teeth clamp around my sensitive flesh.

"Fuck yes," Emmett growls as his hands travel down to my pants, bypassing Travis' as they skim up to my breasts. So many hands, so many sensations. Emmett grips my pants and panties, then hauls them down to my feet, forcing me to step out of my shoes as he kicks them all aside. "Naked and ready for us."

Travis slowly raises his head from my chest, his eyes lifting to meet mine before they leisurely scan my body. Then his fingers dig into my ribs as he groans, the sound raspy and deep. "Delicious."

"You want the first taste?" Emmett asks Travis as he crowds back in behind me, his cock pressing into my ass from inside his jeans. My heart begins to pound as Travis' eyes flick back to mine, the heat radiating from them making my core clench.

"Yeah." The word comes out strangled as he bends at the knees and lifts me into his arms, my legs wrapping around his waist and his hands gripping my ass cheeks. "Lead us to a bedroom."

Emmett heeds his demand and moves in front of us just as Travis' lips land on mine and his tongue snakes into my mouth. My arms wind around his shoulders and my hands grip the hair on the back of his head.

The next thing I know, I'm being tossed on a bed as two hot guys stand before me, both undoing their pants, making my mouth water as my pussy grows wet.

"Look at her," Emmett breathes out as he kicks his pants aside. "Look how wet she is for us."

Both of them are standing there, completely naked, hard, and thick. Travis has a look of desperate hunger on his face as Emmett smirks, his expression reminding me of a cat that got the cream. Travis crawls on the bed at the same time Emmett falls beside me, his mouth finding a nipple as Travis spreads my legs.

It all feels like too much but at the same time not enough. Travis' nose brushes along my inner thigh, breathing me in deeply as Emmett flicks his tongue against my nipple.

As soon as Travis' tongue meets my center, Emmett leans up to capture my moan with his mouth, swallowing my pleasure as his fingers toy with my breast. My back arches off the bed as Travis slips two fingers deep inside me, knowing exactly how to work my body as Emmett continues to explore, breaking the kiss to watch Travis devour me.

"You like him eating your pussy while I watch?" he asks, his fingers slipping into Travis' hair, shoving him deeper between my legs.

"Fuck!" I hiss as Travis looks up, his eyes flashing with mischief. "Yes."

Emmett's hand caresses Travis' cheek as he continues to work my clit, driving my arousal to the highest peak, my core tensing. Is this how it will be? So intense it's fucking painful?

Travis pulls away as his fingers pump into me, his thumb working my clit and his face glistening with my juices. Emmett runs his forefinger along his chin and gathers my wetness, then turns to look at me while he sucks it off with a groan, the both of them making me shatter into a million pieces with their tag-teaming. I scream toward the ceiling, the hoarse pitch of my voice ripping through my vocal cords and bouncing off the walls.

Falling back to the bed, I take in a deep breath as the bed shifts, and I lift my head to see Travis kneeling between my legs, his hand soaked from my release pumping over his cock. Emmett moans while he watches him, his own hand doing the same as my pussy clenches, ready to take them both if that's what they wanted.

"Turn over," Travis demands, and I obey, my stomach hitting the soft sheet. "Get on all fours so I can feed this pussy my cock while you suck our boy."

Our boy.

My eyes meet Emmett's as he gets on his knees with a grin, his smile lazy. Opening my mouth, I invite him to fuck my throat as Travis eases into me, the stretch making me gasp. Emmett's cock drags along my tongue as Travis bottoms out, my senses in overdrive as my brain scrambles to keep up with what's happening.

Emmett thrusts into my mouth at the same time Travis slams into me, driving me forward and opening my throat for Emmett's cock. I gag around his length and he tips his head back on a groan, the sight making me clench around Travis who curses loudly.

Cresting again, my body tenses as another orgasm rolls through me, and Travis' grip on my hips tighten. "I'm going to fucking come," he grits out, his voice a deep timber and filled with ecstasy. I moan around Emmett as Travis fills my pussy, the warm spurts of his cum dragging out my release. A few pumps later, Emmett is coating my tongue with his cum, his face filled with love as he watches me take every drop with relish.

"Let me taste that," Travis says as he pulls out of me and pulls me up, forcing me to release Emmett's cock. Then he ravages my mouth, his tongue cleaning out any bit of Emmett's essence left behind.

It's filthy, depraved, and so perfectly us.

285

Chapter Fourteen

We get to the compound a few hours before the fight starts, all three of us lax and sated. Adri was getting anxious and wanted to see Ember before the fight, so there was barely time for us to recover after our bedroom session. We all get out of the Mercedes, and as soon as I lift my head, I find Trent standing by the entrance. I haven't seen him in almost a year because he was off on some mission in Mexico for Carm.

He looks good, healthy, and a little more jacked than before. His jet-black hair and matching black eyes always made him look demonic, but Trent has a fucking heart of gold for anyone he cares about.

"Pequeco!" he yells out, *little one*, a nickname from when I was a kid. "Get over here!"

I do as he says, and he crushes me in a huge bear hug. "I missed you, dude," I tell him, my voice cracking with emotion.

Vin comes out of the warehouse, his head tipping to the side as he takes in me and Trent. It's clear by the look he's lasering into Trent's back that he hasn't been introduced yet.

"Me too." Trent pulls back and pats my cheek. "Now, introduce me to everyone."

Trent is Mexican and his parents used to work for my father until they were gunned down in a retaliation attack. They were alone at their house, and luckily, Trent was with Carm at the time.

"Guys." I motion Vin over, then look over my shoulder to Travis and Adri standing by the car, watching our exchange. "Come meet someone very important to me."

They walk over and I make all the introductions, Trent nodding until he meets eyes with Vin. "Vin, huh? I heard about you from Carm. You really do look like a pit bull." He nods and grabs Vin's bicep. Trent knows no boundaries, and he never has to worry because he's quick on the draw when need be.

"Pit bull, huh?" Vin raises a brow, not caring in the least of what Trent is doing. "I'll have to work with Carm on his adjectives."

We all burst out laughing, and Trent has a megawatt smile. "I also heard you're all good people and that's all I care about. Emmett deserves good people."

"He's family." Vin nods, and Travis nods as well.

"Come inside." He motions for us to follow him in. "I've been watching your sister through the two-way mirror as she took out your brother multiple times in the last hour. Is she real? I keep wanting to ask if she's a robot or something, but I'm afraid she'll kill me."

"Ember has some pent-up aggression for Carm, so she may be a little rougher on him." I chuckle as I imagine our brother taking her brute force as punishment.

"Who doesn't?" Trent winks at me as he closes the large garage door to the compound, then presses the button for the elevator. "She has a technique I haven't seen before."

"She's good." We step into the elevator, and Adri curls into Travis' side, her eyes wide as she takes in everything.

"She's really fast. Something you both were gifted with." He's referring to my knife throwing.

"Yeah." I shake my head with a snicker. "She's something to see when she's in action."

"Carm will be sore after this, but I could see he wasn't allowing anyone else to spar with her. He's become very fond of her as well." We step out of the elevator and the scent of the underground compound hits me full in the face. The best part of moving in with Ember is the fresh air.

My eyes flick to Adri as she gazes around our concrete palace, her teeth chewing into her bottom lip. The sight brings me back to what the three of us did not too long ago, and I have to focus on breathing to avoid growing hard in front of my family.

"Yeah, he has. Even if Ember is giving him a hard time," Vin cuts in, a smirk lining his lips. He would know, having witnessed their antics in Spain.

"It's not hard to see how much he regards her," Trent muses. "Carm filled me in on how she used to run for us?" His eyes land on mine. "And now she's become one of the Heads?"

"Yeah. We obviously didn't know who she was to us. Raph of course didn't reveal it until the night he kidnapped her." It still angers me to know my father kept so much from me. "She's as smart as she is dangerous and she'll make a good addition to the Head Corp."

"She sounds like your father." He sounds pensive, his voice low. "Should I worry?"

I get it. My father was unhinged and maniacal, and yes, Ember is a lot like him, but what she has that he lacked is heart.

"Are you comparing Ember to her father?" Vin snaps, his eyes flashing with ire as Travis reaches out to touch his arm. "Her psychotic father who murdered her mother in cold blood? The man who forced her to kill?"

I hold my hand up between Vin and Trent, knowing that Vin is protective of my sister, but also understanding that Trent doesn't know her like we do.

"Yes, she is a lot like him. Scarily so, but she loves hard. I want to say there's a balance, but I'd be lying. She's violent, volatile, and yes, downright murderous. She likes to kill those who deserve it and she has no regrets." Vin's growl vibrates against my hand as he steps in closer, and I'd guess I'm seconds away from being murdered myself. "Killing doesn't bother her and she actually feels better after she's done it, very much like him. But…" My hand taps on Vin's chest as I turn to look into his raging eyes and continue, "She's also like our mother, from what I've heard. She loves who deserves it, and she would do just about anything for those people, even if it were to kill her. She doesn't think twice, and her heart just continues to grow as she allows more people in." Vin's eyes soften as I turn back to look at Trent. "So to answer your question, no, you don't have to worry about her and I'm sure you'll love her in no time."

"I get it." Trent looks at each of us before his eyes land back on me. "Twins. You are both meant to be each other's balance. It's amazing."

"Yeah, they are." Vin chimes in, his voice still gruff with lingering irritation. "There's been a good change in Em since she discovered Emmett."

"Good." Trent smiles widely. "Now let's go see this girl kick Carm's ass."

We all enter the gym and find Carm on one side of the mat, clutching his ribs, and Ember on the other side, drinking a bottle of water.

"One more time," he says to her through gritted teeth, sweat dripping from his hair.

"You sure, old man?" She snickers and drops her bottle of water back to the floor. She's sweaty too, but not as out of breath as Carm.

Carm stretches his arms above his head and breathes out his pain, then his face drops, and the mask I always see him in when dealing with anyone outside of the family is firmly in place. He nods at her once and Ember cracks her neck to the side.

"Last one," she states and walks onto the center mat. Carm flies at her without warning as Ember's eyes widen a fraction, then a grin curves over her mouth. I suddenly feel afraid for Carm.

When he reaches her, Ember drops her shoulders slightly and maneuvers her body so that she lifts and throws him over her shoulder, using his own momentum. As soon as his back hits the mat, she's on top of him with her hand wrapped around his throat. He flips her over and swats her hand away, but doesn't pay attention to her other hand as it comes up and punches him right in the spot he was favoring earlier.

"Fucking brutal." Trent chuckles, his arms crossing over his chest as he shakes his head. "I can't wait to see her tonight."

"She's beautiful," Adri agrees, her face filled with awe.

"She's a fucking machine!" Carm calls out, correcting us. "I'm done, sis." He stands from the mat, accepting Ember's offered hand with a groan.

"I'm going to hit the showers and get dressed." She walks over to us and grabs the front of Vin's shirt to drag him along with her. "You can wash my back."

"That's me." He rolls his eyes as a smirk slowly spreads across his mouth. "Professional back washer."

We watch them leave and then Trent turns back to the three of us. He's grown older since he's been gone, and I know a lot of it is due to dealing with the cartel. His parents were part of a cartel, and Trent took over their position when they were killed. He's our liaison and has to do quality checks on everything we get from them, so he spends more time there. Yes, the Eastside Rampage deals with drugs, whores, and just about anything that will make us money, like Ember and her fights. Tonight may be about Wade and some piece of shit out to get him, but for Carm, it's admission and betting.

I've always ignored drugs and prostitution when I think of the Eastside, but I can't do that anymore. The money sitting in my account, the 'inheritance' I have, came from those very things. I would like to clean it up and create legitimate businesses, but Carm has always brushed it aside. We are a district and part of The Head Corporation. We can never change.

"How's the training?" Trent asks me, breaking me out of my thoughts and bringing me back to the present. Adri's head turns to look at us with his question, curiosity clear in her eyes.

"I haven't done much these past few months." I run my finger across my mouth. "It's been a fucking whirlwind. Finding Ember, chasing down Talia, and then attending a real school."

"Let's go toss some shit and shoot some bullets." He looks over at Adri and smiles. "Are you his girlfriend?"

"Yeah." She lifts her chin, readying to defend what we have. My heart swells at the same rapid pace as my cock.

"Come see what your boy was made for." He chuckles and leaves the gym.

I turn to look for Travis and find him talking quietly with Carm, and whatever he says makes my older brother laugh in a rare show of cheerfulness. A pang of jealousy hits me, and I'm stunned. I don't want him talking to and enjoying my brother. Travis is fucking mine.

"Trav!" I call out, my tone a little harsher than I mean for it to be. "Let's go."

"Where?" he inquires and raises his brow in a show of defiance.

We both have dominating personalities, I may be a bit more obvious with it, but Travis is understated with his. Right now, I can imagine us clashing, and even though the thought of us butting heads turns me on, it's also pissing me off.

"Shooting range." I jerk my head for him to follow us as a smirk creeps over his mouth.

"I need to see how much my little brother has suffered since he left me." Carm smiles and makes his way over to us, holding onto his sore ribs.

"Sure." Travis shrugs and follows close behind.

He's getting punished later for this.

We get to the shooting range, and I pull out the M4 Carbine. I pop in a full magazine, then head over to the handguns to pick a Walther PPK pistol. This is the same gun Ember used to kill my father. Little did she know at the time, her twin favors this gun and imagined killing their father with it many times.

"Sexy little thing," Trent coos as he nudges his shoulder into mine.

"She's still my main bitch." Pressing my lips to the barrel, I kiss it soundly.

"This the one that blasted a hole into your father's head?" Trent quips with a snicker.

"The same." I look at the piece in my hand lovingly, the gleam from the metal making me smile. Carm has kept her nice and clean.

We head out to the range, and I pick the first lane as I always have. Except this time I have more of an audience instead of just Carm and Trent. Not that it bothers me, because that bullseye is about to become my bitch.

"Did you bring your knives?" Trent asks, and I lift my shirt to show him the waistband I always wear. "Sweet. Let's fuck up some targets."

Trent steps into the aisle next to mine and we set up our targets in the farthest setting. Pulling out my M4, I bring it in close to my shoulder and nearly purr with contentment. This paper target is about to be decimated.

"You know," Trent talks to Adri and Travis. "I trained this kid from a young age. The sounds of guns firing used to make him piss his pants."

I snort and let loose my magazine, watching as I create a beautiful blooming flower over the heart of my target.

"Shit." Trent whistles as our targets fly back toward us. "You fucking beat me on that one, kid." We both set our rifles aside and switch out fresh targets. "I'll fuck you up with the pistols though."

He wishes. He's been gone for a while and doesn't know how I filled my lonely hours with training. Trust me, there were many hours. The target flies back out to the farthest position, and I hold the sight with my right eye as I close the left. Then I release eight bullets into its brain and call it back to me.

"Honestly?" Trent growls. "This is you after you live a life of schoolgirls and cushion?"

"Fuck you." I laugh. "This is me on the regular, bro."

"Let's see you dance with those knives," he counters, giving me a shit-eating grin.

"Fine." I shrug. If I'm being honest, knives are my best skill. Guns come as a close second.

We put our guns back into the armory, and my eyes flick over my shoulder to find Travis speaking quietly with Carm. He's really fucking testing me tonight. I'm not sure what I'm so pissed off about. Carm is straight. I've seen him with girls. It's just seeing Travis finally look comfortable, at ease with someone, and having a laugh to top it off. All things he rarely does.

Adri comes up and runs her hand along my back. "That was so good," she coos. It's as if she can sense the frustration climbing inside of me and her touch is the balm that soothes it.

"Thank you, babe." Leaning in, I press my lips to her forehead, then we follow behind Trent to another door across the hall.

They filled this room with dummies in unique positions throughout the space. Some are even mechanical and move out of certain spots. I have been training here for years, so I know all of them. Trent turns the switch, making the motors start and the dummies move. I throw off my shirt and palm two of my knives, feeling the grin hitting my face and a sense of complete calm washing over me.

I'm about to fuck these fake bitches up.

Travis

Emmett is throwing his knives at an alarming speed, each one sinking deep into the mannequins dressed in different clothing. Trent is chasing him around the room, trying to keep up and failing. I'm amazed by how many knives are sticking out of these things' heads. I know Emmett has skills, I was there when he threw a knife into the back of the guard's head, but this is something else entirely. He is a weapon. The way he shot those guns and is now throwing the knives shows he was trained to be a weapon for the Eastside Rampage.

"We had always hoped he would want to work for us," Carm says from beside me, reading my thoughts. "But he wasn't cut out for it. Emmett isn't a killer by nature, regardless of what you're seeing today. Every person he's killed will weigh on him forever."

"I would say that's a good thing." My eyes meet Carm's, their dark depths brimming with malice. His face is guarded, and to a regular person, they would see a mysterious man with a charming facade, but I know that emotion running deep in his irises, resentment.

"Sure." Carm shrugs, his eyes flicking away to look at Emmett again. "Not in this business though. It's why I let him go be with his sister."

"Ember though," I continue, feeling those dark orbs lasering in on the side of my face. "She's perfect, right?" It's clear Carm is feeling trapped in his position and possibly losing his hold on the people around him. It must've been a low blow to have Emmett move to another country.

"No." Shock hits me at his answer and I turn to look at him. Carm shakes his head as a smile comes over his face. "Fuck no. She can't be controlled. Sure, she loves to kill. She gets that high, but she will never follow orders. When she used to work for us, before we even knew who she was, she did her own thing and agreed only to the jobs she wanted. She was so good that we didn't fight her on it. No one in this world could tell her what to do." There's admiration in his tone, and when he looks back at me, I can see pride shining in his eyes.

He's right. E will always walk her own path and every decision she makes is with her family in mind. I would never fault her for her way of thinking, but I'm worried about her need to kill and fight. How potent is her bloodlust and will that ever be under control?

"I better get ready for the fight. First one starts in ten minutes." He clasps my shoulder, then I watch as he leaves the room.

There's something that's bothering me about Carm.

Yes, to everyone, he looks like a doting big brother to both E and Emmett, but I can sense something lurking under the surface. I paid close attention to him as he watched Emmett shoot, and his face wasn't one of pride. It looked like he was pissed. As soon as he saw me watching, he schooled his features into bored indifference. I could be wrong. Maybe he feels like the burden of this gang is resting solely on his shoulders and his brother and sister get to live normal lives. Mind you, I'm using the term normal loosely.

"Like what you see?" Emmett sneers from behind me, having crept up without me noticing.

"Excuse me?" Spinning around, I come face-to-face with a seething man, his nostrils flared and his eyes filled with anger. His body is tense as he stares at me, his arms crossed over his chest.

"You've been watching and talking to my brother this whole time."

"And?" I press, enjoying the way his temper flares as my cock jerks to life.

"You want him." He nods, dropping his arms from his chest while blowing his breath from his mouth in a rush.

I can't help it, I let out a hearty laugh and slap him on the shoulder. It catches the attention of Adri and Trent, and they stop their conversation to watch us.

"We'll talk later," he grits out before walking out of the room.

"What was that about?" Adri asks as we watch Trent follow Emmett, who peers back at us over his shoulder curiously.

"Emmett wanted to know what I was saying to Carm." Telling her that Emmett is acting like a jealous fool will only lead her down the path of questioning why. It's not that we're hiding our feelings for each other from her, it's more like we don't know where this is going yet.

"Is Carm up to something?" Her eyes widen as she looks around the room, really taking in the training facility.

"I don't know." I lead us out of the room, and we meet Emmett and Trent in the hallway. When I see my brother coming down the hall, I sigh in relief. He'll provide a buffer between Emmett and his rage.

"Em is taping up her hands right now. You guys ready to head to the ring?" Vin looks from Emmett to me and Adri..

"Yeah," I answer quickly, wanting to get away from Emmett's intense stare. As much as I like pushing him, I wouldn't want to do it too far. "Let's go."

"I have to walk Ember out," Emmett tells me, his eyes still hard and his jaw tense. "I'll see you guys after."

I nod and guide Adri into my side. I can only imagine the type of crowd that frequents these things, and it's not somewhere I want

Adri to be alone. We follow Vin into an elevator and it takes us down two floors. When we step out, two guards nod at Vin and step aside.

"We got money on Blur tonight," one guard says to Vin, his face filled with excitement. The atmosphere down here is completely different and the air is tinged with feral energy.

"Fucking smart." Vin holds out his fist for the guy to bump.

It's a little disconcerting how comfortable Vin is becoming with the gang life here. I know when he went to Toronto he said he was caught up in a rough crowd, but I never got to hear the complete story. I need to ask him about it and make sure he's not falling into the allure of violence. I will always have my brother's back, even if I have to drag him back out myself.

"We'll sit up here near the front." Vin nods at ten open seats in the front row. "If she makes it bloody, you may get sprayed. You okay with that, Adri?" He smirks at her.

"I would be so lucky." She flutters her eyes at him, making his eyebrows rise with surprise.

I can't help it. I let out a snort at the look on Vin's face. He was expecting a squeamish girl who's scared for her friend, and instead, Adri is excited to see E kick some ass. I'm just as surprised as he is.

In the next twenty minutes, the place fills up and chants for Blur circles the ring. I keep watching Vin because I can see his nerves plain as day on his face.

"Bro,"—I lean over Adri and tap his arm—"what's up?"

"I'm good." He waves me off as his leg bounces at a rapid pace. "I always get like this. It'll go away once she starts to fuck shit up."

"Do we know anything about the guy she's fighting?" It's a question I should've asked Carm, and now that I'm here in front of a fucking cage, it springs to mind. Who the fuck will she be up against? Ember is a force in her own right, but she's not infallible.

"Yeah. Carm says he's one of Wade's top guys. Well-trained in combat."

He has a right to be nervous.

The lights dim and a bright white light shines overhead, cutting off our conversation. When it begins to strobe, everyone cheers. A man dressed in an impeccable suit walks up beside a guy with his head covered in a black shroud with Trent on the other side as he drags him forward. They open the cage and toss the guy in, closing the door behind them. Then they make their way over to us and sit on Vin's other side.

"Everyone,"—Trent leans over to look at each of us—"this is Wade." He points to the suit.

We each nod to him and turn to watch as the guy in the cage roars out at the crowd. He's ripped the shroud off his head, and Adri gasps at the sight of him.

"He's huge." Her voice trembles as the man in the cage flexes his muscles, his face red with rage. "Will she—"

"Yes," Vin cuts her off. "She always does."

The lights cut out then, and the area fills with the roars of the angry asshole in the cage. The sound of "Bodies" by Drowning Pool plays over the speakers and the crowd fucking loses it. The light comes back on, strobing to the beat of the song.

"Tonight, we have your favorite fighter! She's here and she's not fucking around!" the MC says over the mic. "Everyone, give a hand for your girl, the decimator… Blur!!!"

The screaming pitch hits an all-time high and Adri covers her ears to protect herself from the assault. We see E coming down the center aisle. Her dark hair is braided back and she's dressed in all black. Flanking her are both Emmett and Carm. They each have a knowing smirk on their faces. E's face though, is calm and her eyes are void of emotion. This is what she looked like when she got back after the kidnapping. It makes my blood spike with fear because each time she turns herself over to the darkness, there's more of a chance of losing her to it forever.

"She looks so tough," Adri breathes out, not having seen her friend this disconnected before.

"She is tough," Vin corrects, his eyes never leaving her form.

E pops up into the cage and throws her sweater off into the corner. Then she flexes her taped hands and cracks her neck from side to side. She looks so small compared to the muscled asshole in there with her. I can hear him from here, taunting her and calling her names. She remains unfazed though as she slowly paces back and forth.

Emmett and Carm approach us and sit on my other side. Emmett leans over into my ear. "This guy is fucking brutal. I'm worried."

I twist my head and look at him as concern floods me. "Can she drop out?"

"No." He solemnly shakes his head. "She would never be hired for another job again."

"So what?" I shrug and nervously look back at E.

"This is her job now as a Head. Besides, she won't hear anything about dropping a fight. She's confident she can beat him." He bites his bottom lip as he watches his sister with apprehension, his anxiety bleeding over into me.

"Then we just have to trust her," I whisper, knowing he can't hear me.

"It's a special night again tonight, guys!" the MC calls out over the mic. "We have another... fight to the death!!!" The crowd's roar only intensifies the gnawing feeling in my stomach.

I lean over and look at Vin. His gaze is steady on E and it looks like he's mouthing something. Fuck, is he praying? I sweat, and the complete unease I'm feeling makes me want to rush through that cage door and sweep her out of here.

The bell sounds and the fucking beast of a man rushes at Ember. My heart stalls and my breath gets trapped in my chest as a slight smirk hits her mouth. His large right fist flies out, aimed for her face, and she quickly—so fucking quickly—leans back, her spine parallel with the mat before popping back up, lifting her leg and kicking him in the stomach. He flinches slightly and staggers back a few steps, but he's undeterred. He comes back at her, swinging around and kicking out his leg in a roundhouse kick. Again, Ember leans back as she dodges his foot, then pushes herself through his legs and comes up behind him, only to give him a hard swat on the ass.

"What the fuck is she doing?" I snarl. The crowd is eating it up and laughing at her antics. "She's only making him angrier."

"It'll also tire him out. His anger will only make him sloppy!" Carm yells to me over the noise.

Adri has been in a state of hands over mouth since this began, her eyes filling with unshed tears. She's worried, and fuck, so am I.

I turn back just in time to see E throw out her fist and hit the guy in the throat. His hands come up to grip it and she uses the distraction to pummel his stomach with her fists. The last hit is against his ribs, and he roars out in pain. Looks like she might have cracked one. Finally, she's dealing out some damage, and the sight begins to ease my anxiety.

The guy staggers back and hits the cage, but Ember is right up on him, hauling herself up, climbing the cage, and kneeing the guy repeatedly in the stomach and ribs. He gets a hold of her waist and throws her off, and I watch with bated breath as her back hits the mat with a loud *thud* as she skids to the other side.

My breath is lodged in my throat until she flips herself back up to her feet and turns to throw us a wink. At this moment, I both love and hate her fiercely.

The guy isn't so fast anymore, but it doesn't look like he's any closer to giving up. He thunders toward her, his feet making loud noises with each step. E stands completely still until he is practically on her and then she quickly sidesteps and punches him twice in his left ear. The hits are hard. I could hear the crack of each one, and he tosses his head and screams. I watch as blood runs out of his ear, and E stares at it, her breathing increasing as a look of pure lust comes across her face.

"This is it," Emmett says beside me, his hands rubbing together. "This is where she fucks shit up."

I fucking hope so because I don't know how much more of this I can watch.

Ember swings her arm out and blocks his punch, then delivers one of her own straight into his nose as the blood spurts out and sprays across her face. Instead of being disgusted, she looks almost euphoric. She's delivering punch after punch to his face until he sways on the spot and drops to his knees. Finally, it looks like this match is ending and it couldn't be soon enough.

Ember stops and takes a deep breath, tipping her head to the ceiling as if enjoying the blood coating her skin and clothes, breathing in the scent and committing it to memory. I'm sitting here, nervously anticipating the ending. How will she do it? All that keeps flashing through my brain is how she killed my mother with ease and it somewhat soothes my anxiety further. She can handle it.

The crowd gasps and I spin my sights onto the guy, watching as he holds out a knife, pointed directly at Ember's stomach. Before it fully registers in my brain, Vin is on his feet, and both Carm and Emmett are lightning fast, running toward the cage door.

"How the fuck did he get in there with that?!" Vin screams out.

My eyes flick over to the suit-covered Wade and find his face has a slight smile. He walked the guy out here and could have very well given him that knife. Looking back to the cage, I watch as E holds her hand out, halting her brothers from entering. They both stop and look at each other, contemplating whether they should heed her demand or storm in there anyway. After a few seconds, they stay rooted to their spots and watch her closely. She slowly backs away from the guy still on his knees as he sways there on the spot, and his arm holding the knife shakes as his head lolls from side to side. His face is a mess of bright red blood, and his left eye is completely swollen shut and purple. His nose is bent at a weird angle and his bottom lip has several splits.

"Let it be!" she yells out, her eyes never leaving her opponent. "I enjoy the challenge."

I want to kill her.

When she gets her ass out of that cage, I will fucking kill her myself. The anger I feel is indescribable. The only thing I'm comprehending is wanting to kill him and her for putting me through the stress of this fifteen-minute fight.

The guy gets to his feet and tries to steady himself against the edge of the cage. He looks nearly defeated, but his one good eye holds an anger that looks like it could burn through us all. I rise out of my seat and make my way over to the cage. My feet move of their own will and my eyes stay trained on the one person who has shown me love, the very first to prove it's unconditional. My fingers curl and lock around the linked wire and I narrow my sights on her form.

She's slightly bent, watching this guy and his erratic hold on the knife. My heart is literally in his hands. If he in any way injures her, I will be forever broken watching from the outside.

He lunges forward, holding the knife straight out and aimed for her stomach. Time slows, and I count the seconds between each of my heartbeats. He quickly slashes out and catches her on her upper stomach, cutting through the fabric as blood sprays out in a perfect arch. She twists around, her hands holding onto the wound, and stumbles away to the other side of the ring. Horror coils inside of me as the blood pools around her fingers.

He doesn't let up, going at her again. My attention is trained on her form, how her feet move slightly and her body curves away from the pointed edge. This time, he misses her by mere centimeters. She reaches out and grabs the wrist holding the knife and slams her knee into his elbow. The crack is loud and cuts through the silence that has descended inside this ring. The knife hits the mat and bounces twice out of reach.

She still has a hold on his wrist and twists it over and above her head. It lands behind his back, and he bows in pain. Then she yanks down, and I wince as his shoulder is pulled out of its socket. There's a gaping hole in her shirt and blood is running fast. I'm scared, and before anything can register, Emmett's arms come around my shoulders as I'm screaming in complete fear for my family inside a locked cage, fighting for her life. His hand closes over my mouth and he presses his mouth to my ear.

"Don't scream," he soothes, his voice trembling with his own terror. "She can do this."

I vaguely hear Vin bellowing just a few feet down from me as he bangs his fists against the cage. The fact that he isn't running in there to get her is a testament to how much he respects her. She'd be pissed if he interfered. If I'm feeling like this, how the fuck is he surviving?

I step back from Emmett and pull my eyes off the mat to

look at Ember. Her eyes are on me, and she gives me a slight nod before her hands hit the mat in a handstand. Then, quick as shit, she wraps her legs around his neck and hoists herself up on top of his shoulders. He drops under her weight to his knees as her chest rises and falls under strained, painful breaths. She wraps her left arm around his head and nods once more toward me, then slams the fucker's very own knife into the side of his head. She jumps back as his body hits the floor, still and unmoving.

The place erupts into hushed chants for Blur and it's like everyone knows something terrible happened here tonight. That guy should never have had that knife and now there's the problem of finding out how he got it.

She's staggering slightly as she walks to the cage door, her hand clasped to her stomach. Carm and Vin rush to the other side to let her out as she bends to pick up her sweater and holds it to her wound. They help her out of the cage and try to lead her back up the main aisle, but she's refusing. Her head is turned, and her gaze is locked with mine. She shoves Carm off and starts stumbling toward me. Vin rushes to her and picks her up bridal style, and briskly walks her over. As soon as she's there in front of me, breathing and smiling through her blood-soaked face, a sob escapes me.

"Shh." Her bloody fingertips touch my cheek, her eyes filled with pain. "I'm okay."

Then her face becomes hard as her eyes move from mine and stare over my shoulder. She motions for Vin to let her down and he does with a pained expression on his face.

"Tall, dark, and cunty!" Ember calls out, and I turn to see who she's talking to.

"Blur!" Suit bellows, his smile large and devious. "Another victory."

"Looks like the guy who tried to off you was given the means to off me." Her voice drops a few levels as she walks to stand directly in front of him. The fucker doesn't even have the decency to stand as he remains lounged in his seat. "I'm sure the both of us will figure this out, no?"

"Of course." He nods, his throat working on a swallow as the smile falls from his face while his eyes land on her sweater clutched to her stomach.

She bends down and winces as she presses her blood-soaked face and mouth against his cheek. When she pulls back, that side of his face is coated in blood. "Thank you."

She stares at him a little longer before turning back to Vin. He picks her up and whisks her away with Carm, Trent, and Emmett close behind, Carm barking out orders and telling someone to get the doctor.

"Oh God." A moan sounds from behind me and I turn to find Adri still sitting in her seat, but her golden complexion is pure white and she's shaking uncontrollably.

I rush to her side and take her hands in mine, her ice-cold skin shocking me. Her eyes don't move from the cage as she stares transfixed at the body that's still lying on the mat. Adri is in shock. I slowly pick her up into my arms as I follow the path the others took.

I find a hallway and Trent pacing the width of it up ahead. When he sees us approaching, he groans.

"Fuck, I'm sorry, man. I shouldn't have left you there." His hand comes out to rest on Adri's forehead. "She okay?"

"I think she's in shock. Is there a quiet room we could go to?"

"Yeah." He turns and leads us a few doors over.

It opens up into what looks to be a large bedroom and has an adjoining bathroom. The king-size bed looks clean with fresh linens.

I lay her down gently, brushing the hair from her forehead.

"Thank you," I say as I turn and look at him. His face is drawn with worry as his eyes remain wide with shock.

"The rest are right across the hall with Ember. The doctor is there now. I'll let them know you guys are here." Then he shuts the door, sealing us inside.

"Is she going to be okay?" Adri asks, finally looking at me. Her voice is so small inside the room, the tone fragile. Her eyes are filled with fear as I sit on the bed beside her and take her hand.

"Of course. It's Ember." I infuse my answer with confidence I'm not really feeling, not wanting her to worry more than she already is.

"When that guy slashed her with the knife, I couldn't breathe." Tears start rolling down her cheeks. "I never want to see that again." Her body begins to tremble as my own tears well up in my eyes.

"You won't have to," I assure her. This is what I wanted to avoid, and even though I understand Ember's reasoning for telling Adri everything, I don't think she needed to watch this fight.

"When can we see her?" Her voice becomes clearer as she leans up on her elbows, her cheeks still wet with tears.

"As soon as the doctor is done."

The door opens and I stand as Emmett comes in and closes the door behind him. His hands are a reddish-brown color from dried blood and his face has a few streaks on it. He looks tired and the slump of his shoulders gives him a defeated look.

"She's okay," he croaks out. "Nothing important was hit, but the cut is deep and she needs stitches." His face falls then, like he's depleted all his strength to remain strong.

I don't think about my actions or worry about what Adri will think. I just cross the room and wrap him up in my arms. He wraps his arms around my waist and grips me tightly while burying his face into my neck, his chest heaving with each heartbreaking sob.

311

Chapter Fifteen

Time stood still as I watched that motherfucker slice open my twin sister. Her blood ran in quick pulses and her face was covered in shock. When they say your life flashes before your eyes before you die, the same can be said when you feel like you're losing your twin. Every moment of importance with her flashed like a slideshow in front of my closed eyelids. The only thing snapping me out of it was Travis' anguished cries.

With my face buried in his neck, his scent helps to calm my turbulent insides. All I keep seeing is blood. So much blood.

"Emmett?" Adri's small voice penetrates my thoughts, and I lift my head from Travis' shoulder.

She's standing a foot away from us, her hands wringing together and her pale face swollen and tear-soaked. I pull her in, and she nestles between us, my head resting on top of hers as I peer at Travis. He stands still behind her, his arms wrapping around her and touching mine as his sad gaze meets mine. The green of his eyes is vivid against the unshed tears pooling in them.

"When can we see her?" Adri's muffled voice asks, her hands gripping into the fabric of my shirt.

"The doctor had to give her a sedative because she wasn't really cooperating. She should be up in a few hours," I answer, my body suddenly heavy with exhaustion.

"Let's lie down for a bit. Maybe get some sleep while she's resting," Travis suggests.

I barely make it to the bed before I fall onto the mattress, and I'm asleep before my head hits the pillow.

"See?" Vin's hushed voice seeps into my sleepy brain. "They're fine and all cozied up… the three of them."

"Thank you," Ember whispers. "I just wanted to make sure."

I open my eyes and look up at Vin holding my sister in his arms and the both of them staring down at me. I feel someone stir behind me and turn my head slowly to see Adri pressed up to my back and Travis pressed up to hers. I guess we do look real cozy. I slowly sit up and yawn.

"How are you feeling?" I ask her as I scrub my hand over my face.

"A little sore and groggy," she replies with a small smile. "I'm okay."

"Are you able to leave?" Being in this compound is only adding anxiety to my stress. Every memory weighs heavy on my shoulders the longer I'm here. I miss Whitsborough, my home. "Did you want to get home?"

"I should be fine. I'll just lie across the backseat of Hummy." Her gaze turns to Vin, her face softening with affection as my heart squeezes. I'm so thankful she's okay.

"Ugh." Vin rolls his eyes in exasperation. "You need to come up with another name." He's trying to act strong, but there's exhaustion etched all over his face, like he hasn't slept for fear of something happening to my sister while she was resting.

"Okay, let's get out of here. I want to go home." I stretch and reach over to hit Travis on the shoulder. "Wake up."

His green eyes open and focus on my face, the smile ghosting his lips is meant for just me and he has yet to realize we have an audience.

I angle my head in their direction. "Ember wants to head home."

When he finally looks up and sees them, the small smile leaves and his eyes widen. "E!" He jumps up out of bed, waking up Adri. "Is it okay for you to leave? Are you okay?" His fear bleeds into every frantic question.

"Are *you* okay?" she asks him, worry lining her features.

"Me?" His mouth opens in shock as he presses a hand to his chest.

"Yeah. I never wanted you to see that. It was supposed to be an easy in and out fight," she explains as remorse floods her tone. "I'm so sorry."

"I'm just glad you're mostly okay." He grimaces as he looks at her bandaged stomach, little spots of blood seeping through.

"I've had worse. It'll be good in a few weeks." Vin huffs as she looks up at him, her eyes filled with sadness, making his own soften.

"Okay." He nods as he dips his head forward to kiss her forehead. "Let's go home."

Travis hitches a ride with me and Adri on the way back, and after eight straight hours of driving, we're finally back home in Whitsborough. I exhale a sigh of relief as the gates open, my body losing the tension it's been harboring as our home appears up ahead. We dropped Adri off first, and just like every other time, her parents weren't there, but the cook and groundskeeper greeted her like family.

"What's up with Adri's parents?" I ask Travis as we pull up in front of our garage.

"I haven't had much interaction with them but it's clear they never wanted children. They're kind of like hippies. They just travel around the world and live off the money Georgina's parents made."

"Georgina?"

"Adri's mother." Travis' face screws up in disgust. "I've heard some stories about her arrogance because her mother and father were the richest founders here. They practically built this town and funded the school as well."

"How did Adri turn out so different?" I muse as Travis scratches the growth on his chin.

"Probably because they didn't raise her." Travis chuckles as I park the car and we both get out to head inside. The house is empty because Vin and Ember are about a half hour behind us, having left after us because Ember wanted to speak to Carm. "Want to make some food before they get back? I know I'm hungry, and Vin can always eat." Travis heads to the kitchen. If this keeps him busy and wipes the anxiety off his face, I'll help him cook a fucking feast.

"Yeah."

We're deep in the middle of stirring a pot of spaghetti and meatballs when Ember and Vin come home. Ember is walking on her own, which I expected because that girl just can't relax, and Vin is carrying their bags.

"You guys hungry?" I ask as I approach my sister and pick her up into my arms.

"Emmett…" She sighs in exasperation. "I can walk!"

"I can piss sitting down too, but I'd rather stand." I shrug as I carry her into the kitchen.

"That makes zero sense, you idiot." She grins up at me as I kiss her temple.

"I can always eat," Vin states, and it pulls a chuckle from me.

"Travis knew you'd say that." Vin winks at me as I set Ember in a chair.

"Smells delicious in here, bro!" Vin hollers at Travis as he enters the kitchen.

"Let's hope it tastes as good." Travis nods and heads over to kiss Ember's cheek. "How are you feeling?"

"Hungry." She smiles sheepishly.

We're all sitting at the table quietly eating when I broach the subject of the knife. "How are we finding out about what happened during that fight?"

"Carm says he's on it," Ember states around a mouthful of pasta. "He's questioning Wade."

"Good for him. What are we doing though?"

"You want to go against your brother?" Vin raises his brow before taking a sip of his water.

"Not against, but I think we should do something too." I look around the table to find all of them watching me with guarded expressions.

"He's right," Travis says, breaking the awkward silence while he puts his fork down. "Carm seems nice, but maybe his workload is high."

There's something he's not saying, I can tell by the way he avoids my eyes. What exactly did he talk to my brother about? Maybe what I thought was flirting was something else entirely, and it makes me wary of Travis' feelings toward my brother.

"Okay. We should have a look into Wade and Trent since those were the two who walked him out," Ember replies as she twirls some pasta on her fork, her eyes on her plate. "Trent is adamant the guy was held in a room for three hours before the fight. The only people in there were Wade, himself, and a guard."

"I can never see Trent doing that." I drop my fork to the plate with a *clang* as everyone turns their sights on me. "He's been loyal to our family since before I was born."

"Not to me," Ember states, her eyes flashing as her jaw tenses. She feels betrayed by whoever gave that knife to her opponent, and so do I, but it wasn't Trent. "He just met me."

"But he knew you worked for us before. You were always one of us in some way," I argue.

"Regardless," Vin interjects, "we need to look into all three, but if I were to wage a bet, my money is on Wade."

"Let's think about the motives," Travis suggests as he brings his napkin up to wipe his mouth, his body relaxed while mine is strung tight. "Wade is a fellow Head member, which means he worked in some capacity with my father. Does he know you killed Robert Greene?"

"Yeah." Ember shifts in her seat. "I told them all I did."

"Maybe they were close?" Travis puts forward, his fingers drumming on the table. "This could've been his revenge?"

"That's an excellent theory," Ember agrees, but her tone is cautious. She's dancing around something and it's only winding me up tighter. Could she truly believe it's Trent?

"Carm." Travis glances at me in apology before he continues, "You messed up his flow by sneaking in as a Head. You interrupted his life and stole his younger brother away. He's now solely responsible for a large… organization."

"Whoa." My hands slap against the wooden table, the sound echoing around the kitchen as anger burns hot throughout my chest. "You've been thinking about this."

"I'm just being objective." His words are soaked with sincerity but his eyes shine with pity. He doesn't trust Carm.

"Carm loves Ember."

"He's barely known her a year," he stresses. "In that span, he kidnapped her, killed her best friend, and hasn't really provided much in the way of help with Talia."

"Hold on." I stand, letting my napkin fall to the floor as my body trembles with my suppressed anger. "I've barely known her a year and I love her. Are we really thinking it's Carm?"

"No, fool." Ember tosses her napkin at me. "We are

considering all angles."

"Carm wasn't even near the room," I protest as my hands fist at my sides. "He was training with you and then we stayed with you until the fight."

Travis clears his throat, his green eyes bright with apprehension. "But Carm could get Trent—"

"Stop!" I cut off Travis, my outburst ringing around our heads. "It's not Carm!"

"I agree." Ember reaches over with a hiss, her hand landing on my arm. "Carm wouldn't do that, nor do I think Trent would. I always figured it was Wade. I just didn't see his motive. We should look into his background." Anger clouds everything, and her soothing touch does nothing to quell it.

"I'm not hungry anymore." Shrugging off her hand, I bring my plate to the sink before making my way out of the kitchen. "Good night!" I call over my shoulder.

My behavior may be childish, but I can't believe Travis would actually imply that my brother, the man who took care of me, would ever do something like that to my twin sister. It's better if I just keep to myself tonight and cool the fuck down. Hearing all their *theories* is getting me worked up.

Once I close my bedroom door, I turn to find my room a mess. My school uniform and books are tossed all over the fucking place, reminding me that I need to study for a Chem test this Monday and I have a paper due for English. So the rest of my weekend will be trying to get caught up. When I was being homeschooled, I was sent monthly packages of workbooks that met the required curriculum of my grade. As long as I completed them and sent them back on time, I passed. Being in an actual school and learning a lot more than I'm used to is stressing me the fuck out, on top of everything else.

A few hours later, I hear bedroom doors open and shut,

breaking me out of my studying as I realize I can barely keep my eyes open. After everything that happened with Ember and the long drive home, I need to get some sleep. I try to listen for anything from Travis' room across the hall, but it sounds completely still. Is he in there thinking about me? I wonder if he's trying to figure out how to talk to me or maybe apologize for his accusations earlier.

He better be.

Adrianna

"Your parents will be home next week," Klein states as he scoops up the last bit of Vera's apple pie from his plate. Vera made us a feast today before she left to go home.

"Oh?" My heart begins to pound inside my chest as my stomach tightens with anxiety. It doesn't help that I've been stressed out for the last few days, but having them come home means I'll be walking on eggshells until they leave again. It's been like this for as long as I can remember.

"Your father said he has a few meetings to attend to. Your mother asked how you were doing. I decided to leave out the bit about your trip to New York." He looks at me pointedly as my cheeks heat.

"I'm sorry I didn't tell you. It was a last-minute shopping trip with Ember." My lie tastes like ash on my tongue, but there's no way I could ever tell him the truth.

"Let's make sure to postpone any more surprise trips until they leave again, okay?" He rises from the table and takes his plate with him to the sink. "I need to head home. Will you be okay?" He turns to look at me as I plaster a wide smile on my face.

"Of course." Whatever he sees beyond my false facade has his shoulders dropping and his mouth turning downward.

"Sometimes I think you should move into that big house your friend has with Travis and the rest of your friends." He exhales a long breath as his hands move to his waist. "Your parents should be ashamed of themselves."

"Why don't they want to be around me?" The question is out of my mouth before I can stop it, and I bite my bottom lip as his tortured eyes meet mine. It's the first time I've ever voiced my trauma to Klein.

"It's nothing to do with you as much as it's Whitsborough in general." Klein comes back to the table and sits across from me, his eyes shining with sympathy. "In their quest to not become their parents, they grew into something much worse."

"As soon as I turn eighteen, I'm moving out," I reveal as I raise my chin, hoping he doesn't see the effort it takes to keep it from trembling. "I will always keep in touch with you and Vera though."

"As long as you know it won't change who you are and what you will one day own." He stands from the table and places a hand on my shoulder. "Don't run from being a Hinton like they did. Take the name and everything it represents and change it. You'll have that power one day. Break the cycle."

He squeezes my shoulder before heading toward the front door, the sound of it opening and closing echoing around the empty house. As much as my parents despise being in Whitsborough, it'll be nice for this empty house to have people inside it. My father will most likely spend his time in the study, but the sound of his decanter and the muted voices of his phone calls adds life to the place. My mother will walk the gardens and chastise Klein for not adding to her rose bushes, or Vera for not putting enough salt in her casseroles, but the activity will chase away the loneliness inside these walls for a little while.

Rising from the table, I bring my plate to the sink and look around the empty kitchen. The sunset shoots reds and oranges through the large patio door, the colors cascading across the marble floors. Everything looks so sterile and cold, even with the warm rays of the setting sun washing across them. My heart tugs inside my chest as the image of Ember's house flits through my mind. I wish I could just walk out of this place with a packed bag and never look back as I cross the gates of Ember's estate.

As soon as I think about it, Klein's words filter through my mind. *"Don't run from being a Hinton like they did."* Steeling my spine, I swallow down the urge to run from it all, suppressing what's literally embedded in my genes and standing my ground. This will all be mine one day and I've been through hell to earn it. What's a few more months of being lonely? I'll be an adult Hinton soon, and once I've gained everything I'm owed, I will create a life with Emmett and Travis. Whatever that will be.

I turn off the lights and let the darkness shroud me as my thoughts wander. Emotions were high the last two days, but there was something between Emmett and Travis. At the time, I chalked it up to all of us being distraught over Ember's brush with death, but now I can't seem to get it out of my head. The way Emmett came into the room and fell into Travis' arms, the comfortable hold and the familiarity of it.

Do Travis and Emmett have feelings for each other too?

What does that mean for me?

I head toward my bedroom, turning off the lights as I go, the darkness feeling like an old friend. My only friend right now. My mind rewinds back to our childhood, our adolescence, and finally, our young adult life, and never have I questioned Travis' sexuality. He's always been with women, and even though he spends time with his baseball teammates, I've never witnessed him holding them like he did Emmett.

I fall onto my bed, my arms spread wide as I picture it again. Their bodies were pressed together, not even an inch of space separated them. Travis' hand was at the nape of Emmett's neck, his fingers splaying in his hair, and his other hand was wrapped around his waist, rubbing circles into his back as Emmett's face pressed into his neck. So intimate, so fucking familiar.

Heat begins to coil in my core as I picture Emmett grabbing onto the shirt at Travis' back, his fingers gripping the material and his knuckles turning white with tension. It's wrong of me to be so turned on by a traumatic moment, but it wasn't what happened that has my pussy clenching, it's how intimate my boyfriends are.

Maybe this is how the three of us would work. Not just each of them dating me, but all of us dating each other.

Travis Then

This whole week has been a nightmare. Adrianna is completely ignoring me, acting like I don't exist, and it hurts because she's the only one that has ever given a damn about me. So having her cut me out like this is killing me, especially not knowing why. On top of that, my father is acting so fucking strange. He's been giving me weird looks and grins like an evil mastermind whenever I'm called into his office. He has something planned, and after the last 'meeting,' I'm scared.

It's Saturday, and that means baseball practice. I run into the kitchen and find my mother sitting at the table, her bottle of vodka already open in front of her. She turns at my running footsteps as a sneer comes over her face.

"The only time you look happy is when you get to play balls with a bunch of boys." Her laugh is downright evil. "Are you a queer?"

"No!" I yell at her before grabbing an apple. Maybe I should tell her how her husband and I shared a prostitute while she was away. Ew, that sounds nasty. . . never mind.

Usually before practice, I eat oatmeal or cereal, but I don't see Sonja anywhere and I don't want to be in this kitchen any longer than I have to with this woman. I run out of the kitchen and hear her nasty cackle behind me. I don't know why I was cursed to be in this screwed-up family.

With my baseball bag on my shoulder, I walk out of the house and head toward Precious Blood Academy. We've always had our practices there, even before we actually attended as students. It has the best and biggest baseball field. Adrianna's grandfather made sure of it when he had it commissioned because he was a huge baseball fan. The thought of Adri makes my stomach twist. I don't know what I did to piss her off. Was it because we made out? Did she feel like I ruined our friendship? I don't want to lose her completely, but I don't know if I can ever just be her friend.

"Travis!" Kevin calls out as I step onto the field ten minutes later. "Hurry, we have to do burpees!"

"Kay!"

I rush into the locker room and quickly change into my uniform. Thankfully, Sonja washed it for me. She even placed my favorite protein bar and a milkshake inside my bag. Sometimes, I wished she were my mother and not the evil hag I was cursed with.

Running back out to the diamond, I find Kevin talking to the others. He hates warmups, and burpees even more. It's probably because he's scrawny.

"Hey, Travis," Kevin whispers as I approach them. "Jeremy isn't here today."

"Why not?" I ask as I scan the field.

"Coach says he's sick." Silence falls over us as Kevin kicks at the grass, the rest of us watching the motion.

This past summer, Jeremy came down with mono and he still forced himself to come and watch, even if he couldn't take part. How sick is he?

After practice is done, I help Coach put all the equipment away and watch as everyone leaves until it's just me and him. I trudge back to the locker room and find Coach standing near my locker. After what Stacey told me, I'm having a hard time looking him in the eyes.

"What's going on, sport?" His hoarse voice grates on my nerves, his nearness making me feel sick to my stomach.

"I can't stay late anymore," I tell him as I open my locker door. "You should find someone else to help you put stuff away."

"Is this because of your father?" When I give him a confused look and shake my head, he continues, "That's too bad." He scrubs his hand *against his double chin. "I liked having you as my favorite boy."*

"Not anymore, Coach." I give him what I think is my sternest look, then head to the showers.

Turning on the tap, I let the water run as I pull off my clothes, my stomach filled with knots. I know it won't be this easy to get rid of him, he'll have something up his sleeve. The warm water hits the top of my head and I let it slide down over my face. Suddenly, I'm pushed against the tiled wall, my head hitting it with a thud. Coach presses in behind me, holding me there with strength I didn't know he possessed, and I'm too stunned to do anything about it.

"Thing is, Travis…" His breath fans my ear. "I've been plenty patient with you, but that ends here today."

He kicks my legs apart and steps between them. He's naked as well, and I suddenly feel as sick as I did with that woman in my father's office.

"Don't, Coach," I try to reason with him as I struggle in his hold. "Please. I will stay. I will help you." My fight barely budges him as his weight crashes against me, forcing me to stop as my body soaks in the cold surface of the tiled wall.

"Too late," he growls into my ear. I try to fight him off, but he just presses my head into the tile harder and I whimper as the pain radiates down to the base of my neck. "Stop fighting and I'll ease up," he says a little breathlessly. Coach is not in good shape, but he is a lot bigger than me.

I nod slightly and let the fight leave my body. What's the point anyway? The more I fight the bad things in my life, the more they screw me over. He spreads me, and I let my mind carry me to another place. Away from the piercing pain and the pink water swirling down into the drain.

Chapter Sixteen

Travis

Monday mornings feel like weekly torture. I hate having to drag myself out of bed and go to a place I can't fucking stand. It's not so bad now that Adri is back in my life, but that building holds a lot of terrible memories.

After avoiding Emmett last night, hoping he would calm down enough to see I wasn't attacking his brother, I ended up passing out early. Do I think calm would do that to Ember? I'm not sure. To be honest, I don't know him. Is it possible? Yeah, it is, but Wade is a bigger possibility. Emmett has also steered clear of me, going as far as to take his bike to school this morning.

Adri texted me as I was stepping into the shower, asking if I could pick her up since Emmett wanted to take his bike. He must be pissed if he couldn't even come tell me himself.

After picking up Adri and just barely getting us to school on time, I run into homeroom and nearly crash into Vin's chest. He raises a single brow over his green eyes and takes a step back.

"What's up, bro?" he questions as his hand lands on my shoulder.

"Sorry, just running late." I walk around him and set my bag down on my desk.

"Mr. Gamry is late anyway." He follows me and nods at the clock. "Trouble in paradise?" He has a shit-eating smirk on his face as he sits at the desk beside mine.

"No." I shake my head and fall into my chair. "Everything with Adri is good."

"I meant with Emmett."

My head snaps around so fast that I fear I've just given myself whiplash as I struggle to keep my face neutral. "Uh… what?"

"You think I don't see shit?" He grins as he leans on the desk, placing his chin in his hand. "You two are always giving each other eyes."

"We do not give eyes." I roll my eyes as my heart begins to pound. If Vin knows, then Ember does too.

"Yeah, you do." He points at my face. "Is that why you're sharing Adri?"

"Shh!!!" I lean over and smack his shoulder as I look around us for listening ears. "What's wrong with you?"

"Nothing. Who cares what anyone thinks?" Vin gives me a confused look.

"I do," I mutter as I slouch down in my chair. "Besides, it's not like that."

"I know you and Adri love each other, and I also know Adri is dating Emmett. Is that not going to be difficult?" he presses, not at all holding back.

"Dude, stop," I moan, dropping my head to the desk. "Don't tell E about your wild ideas."

"Oh! I get it." He snaps his fingers and then laughs. "You're scared about what Ember will do."

The teacher thankfully comes in at that moment and forces my big-mouthed brother to shut up. I can't believe he figured that out, and it makes me nervous when I try to think about who else has figured it out. If Ember knew, she would've told Vin, right?

An hour later, the bell rings, ending homeroom, and I breathe out with relief.

"We'll talk at lunch." He looks over with a smirk.

Yeah, I'm not avoiding him today.

Thankfully, the day moves by quickly and I make it out of lunch without falling prey to Vin's incessant questioning. It's unnerving how much the fucker actually picked up on. I need to learn to never judge how much someone is paying attention by how quiet they are.

I grabbed all of E's work from Trig and noticed how Emmett barely looked at me all period—just like during Chemistry. I'll just stick to the plan and talk to him when we're at home. There's no need to make a scene here at school where more people can deduce our relationship.

Once I arrive at the locker room for last period, I find Jeremy is back. Kevin sees me and gives me a brief nod before motioning his head in Jeremy's direction. I nod back and continue changing for practice. When most have cleared out, it leaves me, Jeremy, Kevin, and a few stragglers.

"Hey, Jer," I call out to him.

"'Sup?" He turns from where he's seated on the bench, tying his shoes.

"Can I have a word with you after practice?" His eyes widen before flicking quickly between Kevin and me, and his brows come together in thought as he drops his eyes back to his shoes.

"Sure." His voice sounds hesitant as he studies his laces, making my stomach twist with nerves.

The moment is interrupted when Coach Wheeler sticks his head in the locker room and yells at us to move it. Practice is the same as it always is, and I become more and more bored with this sport. I'm an excellent baseball player, but it's not something I want to continue with beyond high school. I would like to become an author or write screenplays. That shit is interesting. Plus, the thought of taking over a business that belonged to the man I hated makes me feel so fucking worthless.

After baseball, we all take our showers. Jer, Kev, and I slowly get ready, waiting for everyone else to clear out. This conversation absolutely cannot be overheard. As soon as the place clears out, both Kevin and I look at Jeremy.

"What's up?" His voice wavers a bit as he shrugs on his pants, his shoulders tense.

"Last night I was randomly thinking about the time you missed baseball practice for two weeks. Remember in grade nine?"

Kevin's brows come together as he thinks about what I just said, and Jeremy's hands slowly curl into fists. The air in the locker room grows thick with tension and I find it hard to draw in a breath. I wish we didn't have to have this conversation at all.

"Yeah, I remember," Jeremy finally answers as his shoulders slightly fall.

"What happened?" I ask him as we all remain seated.

"Yeah." Kevin's head pops up, his face filled with realization. "You were there even when you had a fever from Mono."

Jeremy runs his hand down his face, then shakes it out. "I could barely walk, let alone sit on a fucking bench," he answers quietly, his face turning red.

Yeah, I know that feeling all too well. I also had a week off after what Coach did to me in the locker room shower.

"The first time?" My voice is soft, filled with sympathy as Jeremy's jaw tightens.

"Yeah," he whispers, the break in his voice making my stomach push up into my throat.

"That Saturday you missed practice was my first time too," I reveal as my heart crashes through my chest.

Kevin slumps down to sit on the bench and exhales loudly. "Mine was the summer before."

We're all quiet as we think about the actions one man did to us all. The silence is like a heavy blanket, wrapping us closer together.

"I don't want anyone to know," Jeremy stresses as he looks at each of us, fear flashing in his eyes. "I'm just glad the fucker is dead."

"We just want to make sure you're okay and to let you know we're here for you," Kevin reassures him, his hands held out in front of him.

"Okay." Jeremy nods and gets up to grab his bag. "Me too."

Then he leaves the locker room as we silently grab our bags from the bench. Kevin clasps me on the shoulder and throws me a nod before he ducks out of the room. I feel less alone knowing I have people I can talk to about this and they know exactly how I'm feeling.

When I get home, I find Emmett's bike parked in the driveway. Losing him over something we can easily work out would be a shame, but I'm used to people leaving me. Pressing my thumb to the finger scanner outside the front door, I hear the click of the lock. Once I'm inside, I head up to E's room to drop off her Trig assignments. I open her door and find her and Emmett lying on the bed, looking at her laptop. Two identical faces look up at me, one with a smile and the other a scowl.

"I got your Trig," I say as I drop my bag to the floor at the foot of her bed.

"Thanks." She pats the bed beside her, her face looking a little perplexed. "Can I ask you something?"

"Sure." I sit down beside her and look at what's on her screen, avoiding Emmett's intense stare on the side of my face. It's the list with Adri's parents on it.

"Do you think it's time to bring Adri into this? Or, at the very least, ask her what she may know about her parents?" It warms me that E is asking my opinion before acting on her ideas. It means she's trusting me to give her sound advice.

"I think we should start off small and maybe ask her about why her parents are on that list." I scratch my chin. "She's still recovering from the shock of your fight."

"Right," she murmurs as she bites the inside of her cheek. "That's true."

"I'm going to go over there and get her." Emmett stands up and stretches, his shirt inching up to reveal his firm abs and Adonis belt.

He catches me staring and throws me a small grin. I don't look away, and instead, feel myself smiling back.

"Bring pizza back too," E demands.

"What?" Emmett looks at her incredulously. "I don't wanna go anywhere else."

"I need pizza to recover, fool." E snickers as she watches him stomp out of the room. "Sucka," she adds as she drops her voice, giving me a devious smirk.

I can't help it as I burst out laughing. Their antics and how they feed off each other is so natural, like they've been raised together their entire lives.

"I heard that!" he screams from the foyer, which sends us both into another fit of giggles.

She clutches her stomach and groans. "Ugh, this shit is annoying."

"Sorry!" I cover my mouth with my hand as worry floods through me. When she's in such high spirits, it's hard to remember she has stitches across her stomach.

"No, don't be." She smiles at me. "I love when you laugh."

Truth be told, before E moved to Whitsborough and after Adri and I fell out, I rarely laughed. I had no reason to be a cheerful person, and I hadn't been in a really long time, if ever, before Ember.

"You stopped smoking," E remarks quietly as she lays back on the bed, her hand absently rubbing over her stomach.

"Yeah. Someone told me they can kill you." She gives me one of her brilliant smiles, the sight taking my breath away. She has no idea just how much her coming into my life saved me.

"True enough." She pats my cheek, then looks back at the laptop screen. "Any ideas on what this list means?"

"No, I really can't imagine. I can't see Adri's parents having anything to do with babies. They didn't even want her." My eyes scan over the list as Georgina and Abe Hinton glare out from the screen.

"Harsh."

"It's true. As soon as they could get the fuck out without raising her, they did." My eyes flick from the screen to Ember as I shrug a shoulder.

"Do you think they gave a baby to Talia?" Her eyes widen with the realization as my heart begins to pound. "What if they had another child unplanned and didn't want it?"

"That's a possibility." I fall back on the pillow as my eyes stare up at the ceiling. If Adri's parents had another child, another burden as they would see it, they would keep it a secret and then quietly give it away. With how absent they've been in Adri's life, there's no doubt in my mind that they would do something like that.

Sitting back up, I look over the rest of the list but it's people I don't know, and they certainly don't live in Whitsborough, but they could have at one point.

"These people aren't in Whitsborough." I point at the list.

"Could it also be surrounding areas, like Toronto as well?" Her finger hits her mouth. "Your dad was the Head for Toronto, it's possible he could've helped them."

"Yeah, you're right. It could very well be people who live around there."

About an hour later, the front door opens and the sounds of Emmett and Adri coming up the stairs filters through.

"Ember!" Emmett yells out. "Your boyfriend is a bitch. He won't let me pretend I didn't buy the pizza!"

"Watch your mouth, little man," Vin sneers from the landing outside of the room. "I'll put you over my damn knee."

"Now, now, big guy," Emmett purrs, his voice hitting me low in the stomach, my cock thickening at the sound. "Don't make promises you can't keep."

"Is it weird I'm slightly turned on?" E whispers to me, and I fall back in another fit of laughter.

Vin comes into the room and crawls up the bed to squeeze himself between E and me. He tucks an arm under each of our heads and brings us into him. "I love my family," he says with contentment, making my chest warm.

"What took you so long?" E whines. "I texted you to come over here when Emmett left to get Adri."

"It's my mom." He pulls his bottom lip into his mouth as he releases us. "She's been really sad since we had that talk with her." He looks at me.

"Really?" I sit up as concern runs through me. "Is she okay?"

"I think she'll be fine, but reliving her past has put her in a funk."

"Understandably." E rubs at her stomach as her face pinches with the pain she's suppressing. Before I can comment on it, Adri's voice sounds.

"Hey, guys." She sticks her head in the room. "Another meeting?" I don't miss the fear lingering in her eyes, or the way they flick to Ember's stomach with worry.

"I promise it won't be as traumatizing as the last one." E winks at her.

Adri relaxes and comes into the room to sit at my feet, then her knee begins to bounce as she looks from me to Ember.

"What's up?" I ask her.

"I'm hoping I don't hear anything about having to kill someone else because I just need some time to process the last one," she whispers, almost like she doesn't want to admit just how affected she was.

"It's not," E reassures her.

Emmett struts into the room with three boxes of pizzas and a stack of plates. "If this shit tips, you are all getting up and doing the cleaning with me." He points at E. "Especially you."

"Bring me food. Now, fool," she grumbles as she slowly sits up.

After making sure E is fed, and Emmett's done with his grumbling, we all wait as E opens the laptop once more.

"Adri,"—she motions her over—"come look at this list. I believe your parents are on it."

Adri's face scrunches in confusion and she goes to sit beside E. The confusion on her face only worsens when she looks over the list.

"Those are my parents," she confirms. "But why is the list titled 'Babies?'"

"We're not exactly sure," I answer her. "We just have theories."

"You and your theories," Emmett groans, folding his arms across his chest.

"I'm sorry about the whole Carm thing. I was just trying to

see things at all angles. I should've considered your feelings," I admit to him, and his face softens.

"Wait!" Adri exclaims as she moves closer to the screen, breaking us out of our moment. "I also know this couple. Sandra and Leon Telis."

"Who are they?" Ember presses as my heart races.

"Sandra is a distant cousin to my mother." Her mouth puckers up in thought. "What is the theory?" She looks at me.

"Well, we know your parents didn't really want kids," I begin. "Could they have had another child by accident and given it away?"

"Impossible." She shakes her head and opens her mouth to continue.

"Wait, hear me out." I hold up my hand and cut her off. "Think it through. They barely wanted to raise you."

"All that is true," she agrees as she leans forward, her eyes shining with intensity. "But it's literally impossible. I am going to tell you a secret I have told no one else." She takes a deep breath and continues, "I was adopted. My mother was unable to have children, but they needed an heir. I found out when I was five. That's why I'm not too bothered with them not being around. I get it. They only meant for me to carry on the family line."

I feel like I've been doused in cold water and the silence around the room means everyone else is also piecing it together. Adri's parents got her from Talia, and most likely, that connection was made through my father.

"Why are you guys so quiet?" Adri asks as worry lines her face.

"We told you about Talia and why we were in Spain," Vin

explains quietly.

The second she figures it out, shock registers on her face. "My mother's cousin's daughter was also adopted."

"Or sold to them," E murmurs, her eyes shining with sympathy.

"Oh, God." Adri covers her mouth. "This town is so fucking corrupt."

"I'm going to rectify that," E swears, then winces as she moves on the bed. "Do you want to stay here tonight?"

"No." Adri shakes her head as her features harden. "I want to go home and search their office. I'll get more information for you."

She looks determined, and I can't help but be really proud of how tough she's become.

"I'll drop you off at home," Vin offers as he stands. "I'll be back later. I'm just going to make sure my mom gets to sleep."

E nods at him, and we all say goodbye to Adri. I hug her, then watch as Emmett gives her a soft kiss. One day I'll be able to do that too.

"Good night, guys," Adri mutters with a wave, her eyes landing on me. "I'll see you tomorrow."

"I'll pick you up!" Emmett calls out to her.

After hugging E good night, I nod to Emmett, finding his hooded eyes staring at me. I'm deadass tired and just want to get some sleep, despite Emmett's hungry look. I don't know how many more revelations I can take because I'm at my fucking end with the surprises. I take a quick shower, and when I step out of the bathroom, I find Emmett lying across my bed. He's in a pair of boxers and his mahogany hair is damp from the shower as well. He turns his ocean eyes on me and smirks.

"You owe me an apology," he sneers playfully, his plush lip curling upward.

"Emmett…" I raise a brow as I grip the towel tied around my waist. "I already said I was sorry."

"I know." He pulls his bottom lip into his mouth and bites down, his eyes turning molten as he slowly slips them over my body. "This time, I want you to show it."

"Okay," I start, rolling my eyes at his antics. "What do you want?"

"I want you to finish what we started in that bathroom at the bar." His voice is husky and his eyelids become heavy as he stares at me.

Just the thought of that night at the bar makes me nervous. I've been with guys, but this is different. I have real fucking feelings for him, and I don't want to fuck it up. He's never been with a guy. What if he decides he doesn't like it? What if I'm not good enough and fuck up all chances of being happy?

"Okay." He gets up with a huff and stalks over to me. "You've convinced me. I'll finish what we started in that bathroom."

He rips off my towel and throws it to the side, finding me hard and throbbing, then drops to his knees in front of me and grins as he looks up. "Your dick is fucking huge."

Before I can say anything, he has me in his hand and my tip in his mouth. I can't hold back the moan that escapes me, and I can only hope E doesn't hear. Looking down, I watch as he lavishes my cock with his mouth and tongue. My fingers slip into his hair, gripping the strands tightly and pulling him in closer. Then he fucking sucks me in so deep and gags, his throat constricting around me. When he pulls back, he releases me with a pop and continues licking the head and massaging my balls.

"I've been wondering what you would taste like for weeks now," he murmurs as he strokes his hand over me. "I never imagined it'd be this good."

"I want to taste you too," I state, my voice deep and husky, and pull him up from the floor.

His mouth slams into mine and our tongues tangle together in a mess of saliva and moans. The kiss is downright sloppy and unrestrained, but I don't care. We've been building up to this for weeks now.

I fall to my knees in front of him and yank down his boxers. His cock springs free and stands thick and firm in front of my face. The drop of pre-cum on the tip is tempting as I lean forward and lick it off. His taste is so intoxicating, and I'm sure I'll never have enough of Emmett. I want him so badly, I'm fucking shaking. As his taste floods my tongue, I groan and pull him into my mouth. How can one person be this fucking delicious?

I suck him and lick him in sequence and revel in the noises he's making. This has to be good for him. I want to be good to him. He pulls himself out of my mouth and I whimper with the loss, his chest rising and falling as he fights to calm his breathing.

"I want to go all the way," he breathes out. That's a huge step, and I want that too. So fucking bad. "How do you like it?" he asks me, clearly looking nervous. "Top or bottom?"

"You've done your research." I grin at him. He shrugs, but the blush that gathers on his cheeks is fucking adorable. "I like both."

"I want to try both then," he states, the blush spreading down his neck and over his chest.

"Tonight? Are you sure?" The last thing I want is to rush. We have all the time in the world to prepare for this moment.

"Yes, Travis. I don't know how much longer I can wait. I've wanted you since the first day I saw you at that fucking diner." The gravelly tone of his voice has my cock jerking and my heart beating faster. I remember that day because I wanted him from the very first moment too.

We stand chest to chest as his blue-green eyes darken. I put my hand on his cheek and spread my fingers into his hair, running my thumb over his plush mouth just begging to be ravished, and I do just that. He opens immediately under my assault and lets out a loud moan as I walk him back toward my bed. When his thighs hit my mattress, I break the kiss and push him down, grinning as he bounces.

"Hurry," he whines as I part his legs and run my fingers over his asshole. "I want you so bad."

Opening my side table, I grab the small tube of lube I brought with me from home. I smear it over his hole and insert a finger, nearly spilling my load when he groans at the intrusion and moves to bring himself closer. I ease one, then two more fingers to spread him and prepare him for my cock. Once he's panting and the noises are becoming louder, I pull my fingers out and grab a condom from the side table. I roll it on and then smear more lube over it as Emmett's eyes eat up every movement. Positioning myself between his legs, I push his knees up close to his chest before lining myself up with his rear hole. Slowly, I ease myself inside him, stretching his asshole over the head of my cock.

"Fuck," he groans as his hands fist into my blanket. "You're so big."

I continue to push in until I bottom out inside him, the tight hold he has on my cock making it hard to keep myself together. "How are you?" I husk out as I press my mouth against his neck, his pulse vibrating quickly against my lips.

"I'm good. Keep going," he pants. There's no way he's not feeling some pain, and I only harden further when I realize my boy likes it when it hurts.

I pull out slowly and ease back in, his tight asshole clenching around me. Grinding my teeth together, I try my best to keep it slow, but when he leans up on his elbows to gaze at the spot we're connected, I lose all restraint. I slam back into him, forcing him to fall back down as his moans echo around the room and his legs fall open farther. Grabbing onto his thighs, I really fuck him, his mouth dropping open on a silent scream. I bet it hurts but I couldn't stop now, even if he begged me to.

"I'm coming," I tell him a few moments later and slam in to the hilt. Stars explode behind my eyelids I'm coming so fucking hard.

Then I pull out of him and roll off the condom, tossing it in the bin by my desk. His cock is still hard and angry looking, nearly begging for release.

"How do you want me?" He gets up off the bed with my question, coming to stand in front of me, his chest brushing mine.

"On your hands and knees."

I do as he requests and crawl onto the bed on all fours as he grabs the tube of lube and slicks it against my puckered hole. When he eases two fingers inside me, I hang my head and moan softly.

"It's tight." He sounds curious as his other hand trails down my back.

"Mm-hmm," I say as I push back against his fingers.

The foil ripping from the condom wrapper sounds over my head, and I turn to watch as he rolls it down his cock. Then he liberally applies the lube and lines himself up.

"I want to be gentle, but I don't know if I can," he whispers, his body practically vibrating as he pushes himself inside me.

"It's okay." Relief loosens his shoulders as he exhales with my assurance, then he grabs my hips, and in one rough thrust, he's in balls deep.

"I'm sorry," he groans as he does shallow pumps. "I can't."

"I'm good. I'm really good," I promise him even though a painful burn radiates through me. It's a good pain, one I welcome.

He fucks me at a punishing rhythm, and I grow hard once again. As he's fucking my asshole, I jack off my cock, trying to match his thrusts.

"I'm going to…" He curses under his breath as he slams in one last time, his cock jerking with each spurt of cum. The feel of him finding his release drives me over that edge again, and I'm shooting my load all over my bedsheets.

He pulls out and stumbles over to my bathroom, muttering my praises as he turns on the water. Then he comes back out, picking his boxers up off the floor and shrugging them on.

"Why'd we wait so long to do that?" he breathes out as he stares at me, his eyes rounded.

"Not sure." I grin at him while moving to sit at the edge of the bed.

"I'm going to sleep like a baby," he states and leans down to kiss me softly.

"I'm going to change these sheets."

He chuckles at me as he leaves my room and heads to his own. I wait for his door to shut, then I walk over to my dresser and pull on a pair of pajama pants. Now that we've finally come together in the most intimate way, my connection to Emmett is strengthening and I'm becoming excited for what our future could be. I go out to the hallway and open the linen closet. After I grab the sheet, I close the door and find Vin leaning against the wall behind it. I muffle my yelp by putting the sheet over my mouth before glaring at him.

"Why are you being so creepy?" I whisper harshly as I drop the sheet from my face.

"It's a good thing Ember is on pain meds and can sleep through a hurricane right now." He smirks at me. "The sounds that came from your room were intense. I'm not gonna lie,"—he pushes himself off the wall and walks toward E's room—"I got a chub from that."

"You're gross." I shake my head at him as my stomach flips with nerves. What if he decides to tell Ember what Emmett and I are doing under her roof?

"Night," he says over his shoulder, his voice laced with laughter.

351

Chapter Seventeen

Adri walks down her driveway toward my car wearing her Precious Blood uniform and looking like a supermodel. Her hair is bone straight and flowing over her shoulders and her face has that sparkling, dewy look. When she gets into the car, I lean over and kiss her softly on her glossy lips.

"Morning." I smile at her.

"Morning, you're in a good mood." She raises her brow, making me wince with how my mood has been these last few days.

"I feel like things are starting to finally come together." I shrug and back out of her driveway. "Did you find anything last night?"

"Yeah, I found a file with some documents in it, but I can't tell what the fuck it means." She sounds irritated as she huffs and crosses her arms over her chest.

"Hey." I reach out and curl my hand around her bare thigh.

"We'll figure it out together."

She grabs my hand and pulls it up higher between her legs. I'm instantly hard and finding it difficult to concentrate on driving as my fingers brush against the silk of her panties, and I groan when I find her damp.

"I need to fuck out my irritation," she growls as she reaches over and palms my cock through my pants. "Pull over."

"Whoa… what?" I don't even realize I'm already pulling over to the side of the road. Not that I mind.

"Good thing these windows are tinted," she states as she reaches under her skirt and pulls off her underwear. "Pull your dick out."

I snap out of my shocked state and undo my uniform slacks with lightning speed. "Yes, ma'am." Having both a boyfriend and girlfriend means my dick will be constantly sore. A delicious fucking ache.

Before I'm fully released from my pants, she's climbing onto my lap and straddling my waist. She swats my hand away and lines me up, sinking down slowly. I don't fight her impatience because I'm feeling the same way.

"Yes," she rasps out and gyrates her hips, grinding against me.

This is her show so I let her have full rein. Leaning my seat back, I cross my arms behind my head. Might as well relax and watch the show. Her teeth are nipping into her bottom lip as she tips her head back, her throat fluttering with her rapid pulse. She places her hands on my chest and rides me, her pussy gripping me and soaking my balls. Fuck, she feels so good, and before long, I'm reaching out to grab her hips as I help her pick up the pace.

"I'm coming!" she exclaims, letting her head fall forward as she sinks all the way down and grinds into me once more.

As soon as I feel her contract, I'm not too far behind, spilling myself deep inside her. Just like that, I'm fucking tired and the thought of going to school makes me want to bash my head against the window. I'd even consider it if I didn't already worry about how hard school is. Every brain cell matters at this point.

"Thanks," Adri huffs out as she flops back over to her seat.

I watch as she puts her panties back on, my softening cock still hanging out of my slacks. "You're welcome?"

I feel thoroughly used… and I abso-fucking-lutely love it.

We make it to school, completely late and having to skip homeroom. Mrs. G is going to be remiss without my daily prayers. I'll have to make up for it tomorrow with something spectacular about our souls and Heaven.

I hastily rushed to Chem after planting a wet one on Adri's mouth. Bet her panties were also full of my wet stuff too. Skipping into the class with a minute to spare, Travis looks up from his textbook and narrows his eyes on me. What did I do now? I saunter over to my desk and slump down into my seat.

"'Sup?" I ask him as his brows crush together, making that adorable little crinkle between them.

"You weren't here this morning," he states, his jaw ticcing as his brows come together in confusion.

"I was late." I avoid his eyes as I chew into my cheek, my fingers drumming on the desk as a small smile comes over my mouth.

"Doing?"

"Adri." I turn and smirk at him. "While she was in a kilt, bro."

He bites down on his lower lip and releases a soft moan. Fuck me, I'm hard again. He's so hot, especially when he bites down on those full, dick-sucking lips.

"I love fucking her in that kilt." He adjusts his hard cock in his pants, and I watch shamelessly as I do the same. "Did she find anything last night?"

I blink out of my thoughts, letting my eyes slowly slip back up to his face. "She says she did," I reply, my voice husky as he grins. "She's going to show us later."

The rest of class goes by with me mostly daydreaming about Travis and how good he felt the night before. I want to hit that again tonight. As I'm packing up my stuff, Travis slams his bag on the desk and releases an irritated huff.

"What?" I startle at his sudden change in mood.

"The police have no new leads on Sonja, and I still can't get a hold of her." He runs his fingers through his hair. "I think my mother did something to her."

"Maybe she did," I agree. "But it doesn't mean she's harmed. It could mean she's hiding out."

"True." He slightly relaxes and grabs his bag again. "I'll see you at lunch."

As he leaves, his shoulders are bent forward and his head is down. I noticed that's his usual demeanor in this building, as if he hates being here. It's not about hating school in general, it's because of that coach. I want to ask him about it more, try to help him through whatever the fucking perv did, but I don't want to push him before he's ready.

Heading to my locker, I see a familiar purple head standing beside it. She doesn't have her locker open, and it looks more like she's waiting for someone. I hope for her sake it's not me.

"Hey." She clears her throat as soon as I get to my locker. She's fucking brave. "Emmett? Right?" I don't answer her, and instead, give her a narrowed look. "Right. I'm not here to start shit. I don't want anything to do with Vin and Ember. I'm here for a friend." I raise my eyebrow and motion for her to continue. "It's Shay. She and Adrianna talk sometimes." Her mouth turns down into a disgusted frown as if she hates anyone talking to Adri. "I'm worried about her, and I think you might know something."

"Me?" I point a finger at my chest. "I don't even know her."

"I know. I just have some information, and I think you could help." She flutters her fake eyelashes as she bites her bottom lip. If she's trying to be seductive, it's not working. She looks like she may be constipated with an eye infection.

"Okay, let's hear it and make it quick. I'm fucking hungry."

"Wow." She chuckles sarcastically and shakes her head, her eyes rolling. "Not only do you look like her, but you sound like her too."

"If you're referring to my sister, I'm crazy like her too." I open my locker and begin throwing my books inside, hoping she realizes how little time she's got left to talk.

"Anyway, in grade nine, Shay was caught in a compromising position with a coach here."

"Caught by whom?" I still as I glare at her.

"Me. I walked into the locker room and found them in the middle of stuff." She brushes her hair over her shoulder as she looks up and down the hall.

"Like you found my sister and Vin?" I step in closer to her, my voice dropping low.

"Yes." She doesn't even fucking deny it as she steps back a little. I don't know if she's actually brave or fucking stupid. "Exactly like that. I'm not excusing myself. I was looking for blackmail in both cases. But recently, Shay told me he was raping her."

Her mouth curls downward as she bites her bottom lip, her eyes looking a little skeptical.

"What can I do about any of that?" I ask.

"He used to be Travis' coach for baseball. Then he died in a house fire not too long ago."

"Again, what am I supposed to do with that?" I snap as the last of my patience runs out.

"Could you talk to Travis? I see you guys are close. Maybe ask him if he knows anything?" She sounds desperate for me to bring Travis into it and I can't help the way my stomach tightens with unease.

Suddenly, the hair on the back of my neck stands up and I can see an angle she might be working here. "Are you suggesting Travis was involved?"

"No. I'm suggesting maybe that coach was a fucking pervert who preyed on kids!" she yells before turning on her stiletto heels to march away.

A group of people standing around turn their attention to her retreating back and then onto me. What a fucking bitch. She knew yelling that would attract attention. I'll talk to Travis about all this, but not here. There are too many listening ears.

Stepping into the cafeteria, I see Adri, Vin, and Travis sitting together. That shit is rare. Usually, Travis is with his jock buddies, and Vin is with his artsy people. I make my way to their table and sit beside Adri as they all look down at an open file in front of them, forgetting about grabbing lunch.

"What is this?" I peer around her to look at the paper they're reading.

"The adoption file I found," she answers absently. "There's some weird shit in here that I just don't understand."

"Like what?"

"I think we should wait and show this to E," Travis mutters as he bites into his chicken wrap.

"I want to look at it now," Adri stresses to him. "I'll show her later."

"What is weird about it?" I reach over and grab a fry off Travis' plate.

"The fact that Adri was adopted in July, but her birthday is September thirtieth," Vin states as he chews his bite of burger.

"Wait… September thirtieth? That's in like three days!" I exclaim. "Were you going to say anything?"

"Sorry, I just got caught up in everything, and to be honest, I just fucking forgot." She presses her fingers to her temples. "I just want something low-key. Don't fucking plan a party, Emmett."

"Well, if these papers are correct, we fucking missed your birthday. You're already seventeen." I clasp her on the shoulder and grin.

"Actually," Travis points out, "she'd be eighteen."

We all lean in, and sure enough, the year of birth is one more than mine. Adri is eighteen years old, if these documents are to be believed.

"Let's close this up and we'll figure it out with Ember," Vin says softly as Adri continues to shake her head.

"I'm leaving," Adri huffs and stands up from the chair.

I look at both Vin and Travis as they shrug their shoulders and get up as well. This is my first time skipping. What am I supposed to do?

"Guys." I hold my hands out to stop them. "Shouldn't we tell Anna?"

Vin cackles and Travis has a smirk on his face.

"No, silly." Adri snorts and grabs my hand to pull me out of the seat. "We're skipping."

"Adrianna," Ember says as she reads over the paper from the file. "You were born in New York on July 28th, 2001. Given up by your mother with no father present."

"New York." Travis hums. "Talia."

"Yeah." Ember nods at him from her spot at the end of the bed. "That's what I was thinking."

Adri is sitting in an armchair in Ember's room, and she's been pretty quiet this entire time. She has a nervous energy crackling around her as she leans forward, her head hanging between her shoulders. It's a lot to take in to know your life isn't what it seemed or what you thought.

Standing from the bed, I go over to her and kneel. "Babe, are you okay?"

"I want to know the full truth. Is it what's on those papers or what was always told to me?" Her voice breaks with desolation, and I grab her hand and bring it to my mouth.

"We'll figure it all out, Adri." Ember sounds resolute, as always.

"I just want to get home." Adri yawns into her hand, then brushes my hold on her with a sad smile.

"I'll drop you off on my way to check on my mom," Vin offers as he stands from his spot beside Ember and grabs his keys.

"I'm going to hold on to these and continue to look them over." Ember points to the papers spread across her bed.

"Sure." Adri waves it off as we both stand. "I'll see you guys tomorrow." I haul her in for a hug, and then she does the same with Travis, his eyes finding mine over her shoulder. They're filled with worry for our girl and my stomach clenches with anxiety.

She leaves the room with Vin, her sadness still lingering behind. These past few weeks have been a fucking whirlwind. To learn that your birthday is completely wrong and that maybe your parents are involved in some shady operation is rough.

"I'm gonna head to bed." Travis yawns and pushes off the wall near the door. "I need some fucking sleep."

"Me too." I follow behind him, ruffling my sister's head as I pass. "Night, sissy."

"Night, fool," Ember retorts, swatting my hand away. I chuckle on my way out of her room as love for her warms my chest.

"Travis," I call out.

"Yeah?" He turns to look at me, his eyes guarded. With

everything going on with Adri, it slipped my mind that he has a lot on his plate too.

"I need to talk to you."

"Okay." He shrugs and leads the way to his room.

Stepping inside behind him, I close the door as Travis takes his uniform shirt off and throws it into the hamper on the side. "What's up?"

"Uh…" He's fucking hot. His body is sculpted and his fucking abs look delectable. "Uh… fuck. Can you put clothes on?" I snap at him.

He chuckles and pulls on a black T-shirt. "Better?"

"No, but I can't concentrate otherwise," I grumble as I lean against the wall by the door.

"What's up? Or did you come for round two? I'll warn you though… I'm tired." He sits on the end of his bed, his elbows resting on his knees as he lifts a brow.

"No. That's not why I'm here, but now I wish it was." I run my fingers along the growth on my chin. "It's about something that was said to me today."

"What?" He straightens as tension coats his shoulders.

"Marlana was waiting for me at my locker before lunch. She told me to tell you she thinks Shay was raped by Coach Halbert." I release a breath and drop my hand from my face, watching as a myriad of emotions play out over his.

He's quiet and looking off over my shoulder, his eyes becoming vacant. There's no doubt in my mind that his coach did something to Travis, but I don't know the extent of it.

He exhales heavily and scrubs a hand down his face. "I guess I believe that could've happened. Although, I have known Coach Halbert's preferences to be more toward young boys." His voice is small and sounds like he's in pain.

Sitting down beside him, I place my hand on his knee. I love him and I want him to feel like he has me to lean on. No matter what.

"Coach began sexually abusing me when I was ten years old. It started out small at first. Touches over clothing, working on my need for love and attention. My house was a cesspool of hate, my mother was hateful to the core, and my father enjoyed dealing out punishments. Coach was a distraction from them, and to a ten-year-old, he was a savior. Who cares if I had to massage him in certain places? I was loved. I was favored." His voice breaks and he buries his face into his hands as I rub circles into his back. "It slowly escalated. Pants were removed and I was rubbing him over his underwear, then they were removed and I was massaging a sore muscle. He covered it up by telling me he was teaching me about my body. To an eleven or twelve-year-old, it sounded legit. I didn't have parents who took notice of me, who cared and wanted to teach me about the ways of life. Instead, I had a coach who took an interest in me, and I ate it up. I was so fucking desperate for love. It carried on for years. Then one day, I got home and my father told me I had a meeting to attend with him. Little did I know I would forcibly lose my virginity to my father's regular prostitute. I was fourteen years old."

My heart is lodged in my throat and my hands shake as I pull them into my lap from the anger coursing through my veins. If my sister hadn't already killed the cunt, I'd have Travis' father's throat in my hands.

"I was in love with Adri. I think I always have been. I wanted her to be my first, and I was destroyed when she could never be. After I fucked the prostitute, I cried and my father found me more of a disappointment. The next baseball practice, I tried to take back my life. I told Coach I didn't want to continue any further. I wouldn't be participating in his activities anymore. He ended up raping me in the locker room showers later that day. He overpowered me and he was bigger. When he was through, he gave me a cigarette and said I was brave. Then thirteen more times after that. Once a month, and one month twice, he fucked me, and I let him. I let him because he threatened to expose my evil family. Even though they hated me, I protected them in the only way I knew how. After a solid year, I found a gun in my father's desk drawer. I couldn't stand myself any longer and I knew if I didn't make him stop, I would turn the gun on myself."

Hearing Travis was ready to end his life scares the shit out of me. He saw no other way out after hitting his rock bottom.

"I got to his house and found him there with a woman. I wasn't surprised because Coach dated many women. A lot of them were my teammate's single mothers. It made it easier for him to get to the child. That night, I barged in and had no idea who the woman was, but she left in a hurry when I pulled out the gun. I told Coach that night we were done, he couldn't touch me or anyone else again because if he did, I would be back to finish the job. He was to quit his job as our coach and never come back to Precious Blood. I regret leaving that house and not taking his life. I should've been the one to do it. I later learned the woman he was with was Charles' mother. I have yet to tell him about that."

His shoulders heave as his voice hitches on a sob. I gather him up and hold him close, his body trembling and his breathing erratic as his arms encircle my waist.

"Travis," I soothe him. "I am so sorry that happened to you, but you have a family now. I will always be here, and I'll never let something like that happen to you again."

"I know. I finally have a family now." He sniffs as he buries his face in my neck. "I thank God for Ember every day. She brought me all of you."

My heart is about to explode, so heavy with sadness and love. I finally know what it feels like to take on the pains of the one you love. Travis' pain is extensive and it can crumble mountains. It scares me because I feel like he's walking along the edge, and at any moment he could slip and fall.

"The funny thing is, I found out my father knew. He gave me to Coach as an incentive to stay quiet. Like 'Hey, fuck my kid, but make sure you shut your mouth about anything else.' At every corner, he called me derogatory slurs and laughed in my face. I wanted to kill him as well, but I didn't have the courage."

"Most people don't," I whisper as he pulls back to look at me, his eyes filled with despair. "It's not a bad thing. It's hard to carry the souls of your victims," I reveal to him. "Some are so dark and heavy."

Then we crawl up his bed and I curl up around him. I wait until his breathing levels out and try to stay awake to make it back to my bed, but in the end, I lose the battle with my exhaustion.

Travis

I stayed home today. School just seems so mundane in reality to all the things happening right now. Emmett wanted to stay with me, but I told him I needed to just reflect and maybe work on the pool at my house. At the mention of the green slime, he hopped out of my bed and told me to enjoy my day. It was nice waking up to him. He didn't monopolize my bed and let me have the blankets. It was actually pretty close to perfect.

Last night, after letting everything out about Coach and my father, I feel freer, and I also have a new flame lit under my ass. I need to pull in Ember to talk to the police chief. They aren't doing enough to find Sonja, and the longer she is missing, the more I fear for her. I'm her son and I understand why she stayed in that environment. It's also why I'm worried she hasn't reached out.

There's a soft knock on my bedroom door before E opens it slowly. "A little bird said you were staying home today." She tips her head to the side with confusion.

"Yeah, I want to drain that pool so I can call in the cleaners, and I need to speak to Chief Moore about Sonja's case. There's been nothing." I sit up in bed and run my fingers through my messy hair.

"I'll come with." She throws up a thumb. "But that nasty-ass pool is all you. Leave the Chief to me."

"Cool." I chuckle, noticing she has a bit more color in her face today and she's standing straight. "Are you sure you're feeling well enough?"

"Don't join the group of idiots I call our family. You're the smart one." She shakes her head as she leaves my room.

I guess that's a yes.

"Are we going to do something for Adri's birthday?" I ask her as we're pulling out of our driveway in my car.

"She was pretty clear she wanted nothing extravagant, but I know Adri and how much she loves a delightful party. I'm a little worried about her... and you." She cuts her eyes to me.

"Me? Why?" My foot eases on the brake as I look at her.

"Because you're not speaking as much. I don't want you clamming up," she stresses. "We're all here for you."

"Emmett came to me last night and told me Marlana approached him about Coach and Shay," I inform her, her eyes flashing with anger as her fists clench in her lap.

"I know. He told me this morning." She shakes her head. "I'm not sure what to believe with Marlana, but it's definitely something we can ask Shay about."

"I also told him about what happened with me and Coach," I confess, deciding to ease her into how close her brother and I have grown.

"I'm glad. It's not something you should have to hold inside and deal with alone. We all love you... obviously, me the most." She waves her hand like it's no big deal.

"Yeah, I know." I chuckle. "You do love me the most."

We pull up to my house and I press the button on the visor to open the gates. I hate this house and I can't wait to finally be done with it. Maybe I'll rent it out or sell it to make back some compensation for what created my trauma so long ago. The latter may be more difficult considering two people committed suicide here. Finding realtors should be fun too.

Parking the car in front of the garage, I look toward the front door, hoping to see Sonja standing there waiting to greet me. Nope, the house is just as dead as the people that were found in it.

We enter through the front door and there's still a lingering smell of sour milk, but it's much better than it was before.

"Mm!" Ember exclaims as she claps her hands. "Pine-Sol with a pinch of sour milk... appetizing."

I snort and shake my head at her. "I'm heading out to deal with slime."

"Gross, I'll come watch," she says with her nose crinkled.

I pull out a lawn chair for her to sit as I set up the pumps to drain the pool. This process will take about a half hour, so I head inside and pull some beers out of the still slightly-smelling fridge. I bring them out and hand one to E.

"Are you still on pain meds?" My eyes widen as she gulps down half the beer.

"Yep." She nods and licks her lips.

"Is that a good idea?"

"Who fucking cares?" She throws out her arms. "We have one life, Travis!"

"I'd like it to be a long one for you." I roll my eyes at her antics.

She grins as she drains the bottle. "I'll take another."

"Ember... that's a bad—"

"One life, Travis!" she screams happily, cutting me off.

I head back inside and grab her another beer. This is her last one, even if she threatens me with that big-ass knife she always has on her. We have to hit up the police station after this, so keeping a limit on our alcohol intake would be smart.

About fifteen minutes later, the shallow end is completely drained, and Ember is grumbling from her spot on the lawn chair.

"I can't believe you cut me off. I just want to live," she groans as she throws her arm over her face. "The green slime in this pool reminds me of Vin's smoothies." She gags.

"Gross." I chuckle.

I look out to the deep end and try to judge how much longer this is going to take when I see something bobbing just under the surface. I can't really tell what it is because of the dark green goo surrounding it. I get up from the chair and walk around the pool to the deep end.

Ember comes up beside me and we both watch as the water slowly drops. The water parts around a round, hairy object and I think it might be a raccoon or a fox because we get those around here, but why wasn't it floating?

"Oh, fuck." E grabs my arm and pulls me back. "Travis, look at me."

"What?" I look at her with my brow raised. "Some animal—"

"No." She shakes her head and drags me by the arm into the house.

"E." I yank out of her hold once we get inside the kitchen. "What's wrong with you?"

She pulls out her phone and calls Vin on speakerphone, who picks up immediately.

"Hey, baby."

"Get everyone and come to Travis'."

"Why?" He sounds worried, and frankly, so am I. Is Ember afraid of animals? I turn to go back out to the pool, but she pulls me back.

"Now, Vin!" She hangs up and pushes me into a chair.

"Ember!" I yell at her as shock rips through me. "What the hell?"

"Listen to me," she says quietly as she bends forward to look me in the eyes. "There's something in that pool."

"I know!" I exclaim as I throw my hands up. "It's just an animal. Relax! I'll grab it out!"

"No." A tear rolls down her cheek as she straightens, her hands on her hips. Okay, so maybe she loves wildlife?

"E," I whisper as I stand and wipe the tear. "I'll go remove it and I don't know… we can bury it or something."

"Travis, that's not an animal." She shakes her head.

"What?" I try to walk toward the door but she places a hand on my shoulder to stop me.

"I think we found Sonja."

I understand her words, but it's just not commuting in my brain correctly. Sonja? I turn my head slowly and look out toward the pool. Maybe she's mistaken. There's no way it could be Sonja. She wasn't an excellent swimmer though. Could she have fallen in?

"Let's give the pool a few more minutes to drain—"

I don't let her finish as I push by her. I need to go see. If it is Sonja, it should be me who finds her. I'm the one who caused this to happen anyway. If I hadn't left her here, she'd be fine. I throw open the patio door, hearing E's screams behind me and not giving a fuck. It's my duty as her son to face her.

The smell is the first thing that hits me. It's a bit like the green slime smell, but now I can detect the underlying stench of decay. I reach the edge and look over just as E makes it to my side and grabs my arm. It's a body. I can see it clearly now that the water has moved down more. The blonde hair coated in green slime is matted, but the body is face down and I can't see any distinguishable features. I'm not stupid. Sonja has blonde hair and she's been missing for weeks. Only she's not really missing. She's been here all along.

The water continues to drain, and with it, revealing a large kitchen knife protruding from the neck of the body. She was murdered. She didn't fall in here. She was put in here. I fall to my knees at the edge of the pool as my healing heart breaks all over again. The bitch who I thought was my mother murdered Sonja in cold blood. She was hateful and took it out on the one person who stuck it through to help her, even though she helped Sonja be raped and mistreated by my father. No, that's wrong. Sonja stayed here for me, endured the pain and mistreatment for me, and I abandoned her too.

I see her white maid's outfit, which is now stained green, and what looks to be one of my father's belts around her waist. Why the fuck is one of his belts on her? Then it slowly clicks. She's attached to the eighty-pound weight belonging to the umbrella base we were looking for before. It's the only thing heavy enough to keep her down. How the fuck did that bitch I called Mother manage this? And where was Sonja stabbed? I look around the yard, but there's no evidence of blood anywhere. Honestly though, why would there be? It's been weeks and has rained many times. What evidence there was has surely washed away.

I stand up and shrug E's arms off me. She's been quiet and respectful, but I can't be around anyone right now. Especially since the entire gang will be here any minute. I head back inside the house, through the kitchen, and up the stairs. I stop at my parents' room and look inside from the doorway. It's eerie seeing it unoccupied and free of screaming and crying. I grew up petrified of this room, and I remember how I used to run by it to get to mine, hoping no one heard me. I step inside just as I hear the front door open and all their voices calling out. Closing the door softly behind me, I shut out the sounds. I don't want to talk to anyone right now.

I walk into the bathroom, and as always, my eyes lock on the door. I wish I could remember every detail of her hanging from there, but I can't. She deserved so much worse, just like my father, and just like Coach. They all got the easy way out, free of the prolonged torture they deserved. I open the cabinet on the wall and find all my mother's different pills. Uppers, downers, Oxy, and many sleeping aids. Then I grab my father's shaving bag off the vanity and dump the contents on the floor, only to fill it back up with all the pill bottles in the cabinet. After that, I take one last look back before letting my feet take me out of the house and to my car.

I just need to get away for a bit.

Chapter Eighteen

The beep of a car unlocking sounds from the driveway, then the open and shut of its door. "Do you hear that?" I ask everyone.

"Just let him go," Vin says as he stares into the pool, his face grim. "It's better he isn't here for this. It's going to be a fucking shit-show."

"I called Moore," Ember says, coming back out from the kitchen. "Did Travis leave?"

"I'm going to go after him," I move by Vin, who grabs my arm.

"I'll call him soon. He needs time to digest," he assures me, stopping me from chasing the man who owns half my heart.

That's when I hear more cars pull in and I get swept up into the torrent of cops and coroners. I remember Sonja. She was a beautiful woman, but what they pulled out of that swimming pool was bloated and indistinguishable. Something that was distinguishable? The large kitchen knife sticking out of her throat with the Greene insignia on it. Did Robert's arrogance know no bounds? Did he have to see his name on every-fucking-thing? I'm happy I never met the man.

We stood around as they covered the body, and the cops said they were confident about getting prints from the knife. Ember relayed the story to them about Travis' mom being off the rails and more than capable of killing and dumping Sonja before taking her own life. The chief listened intently and reiterated the prints would determine everything.

Two hours later, we all pile into Vin's Hummer and he sets off back home. I need to speak with Travis. He's probably feeling so alone, and I didn't have to be stuck at his house for two hours, but the cops weren't letting us leave because we found the body. Travis is needed for questioning as well. When we get home, his car isn't in the driveway. My stomach sours with worry and I immediately call his cell phone. It rings through to voicemail, and I leave him a message telling him to come home.

Ten minutes later, we are all in the family room trying to figure out where he would've gone. "I'm going to check the park I took him to once." Vin stands and heads for the front door.

"I'll come with you!" Adri calls out and hurries behind him.

The front door shuts and I resume my frantic pacing. My heart is crashing against my rib cage, and I just can't stop thinking he might have hurt himself.

"You care about him?" Ember asks quietly from her seat on the couch.

I stop pacing and look over at her, her eyes are clear and she also has worry etched on her face. "Yeah." I nod as tears cloud my vision. "Of course I do."

"Like more than a friend?" she presses.

I scratch my fingers into my hair and tug on the ends. "It's complicated," I growl and resume pacing.

Then it hits me. Where was the one place Travis always looked uncomfortable? Probably downright hated because of what happened to him there. The place he was forced to endure for years afterward.

"I know where he is," I tell Ember and rush to grab my keys from beside the door.

"Wait!" she yells as she runs to keep up with me. "We'll take Shelby!"

Her car is a beast on the road, so I don't argue. I jump over the window to land in the passenger seat. If there's one thing I can count on Ember for, it's that she's always crazy, no matter what she's doing, and that includes her driving. So I tell her where to go as I grab on to anything with both hands.

The parking lot is empty save for the cobalt blue Civic parked across three spots. Ember barely has the car in park before I jump out and run to the doors. Of course they're locked. It's well past the end of day.

"Around here." Ember points down the side of the building. "It leads to the field. I can't run with you. It hurts. Go get him. I'll be close behind."

I take off in a full sprint, and as the baseball diamond comes into view, I know he's not sitting out here. This isn't his primary source of pain though. This field relieved some of it. I rush to the locker room doors and pull them open.

"Trav!" I call out but hear no response. "Travis! Answer me!"

I run down the aisle of lockers, but he's not here. *Please, God,* I chant over and over in my head, just praying to find him. I stop my running, bending over trying to catch my breath when I hear water hitting tiles. I follow it and come to a line of showers. The one at the far end is on, and I run as fast as I can to it.

I approach the stall, and what I see has me screaming and rushing in. Travis is lying across the tiled floor, the water spraying out and onto his legs. His face is white—too white—and tinged with blue. I rush to get to him and slip on the water. My head hits against the tile wall, the sharp sting telling me it's cut open. I don't think of that though as I grab his shoulders and pull him up. His skin is cold, and my fingers keep slipping along his neck when I try to find a pulse. I pull him up more and hear something drop from his hand. I look down and see an orange pill bottle.

"Emmett!" Ember's frantic voice calls out. "Where are you?"

"Over here!" I scream. "Oh God! He took pills… Ember, hurry!"

"Where is he?" I hear Vin as he comes up behind me. "Move, Emmett, let me get to him."

I move out of the way, and Vin lays Travis on his side, then sticks two fingers down his throat. I stand up to turn off the water and slowly back up. Nothing is happening. Vin does it a few more times before cursing as he hoists Travis up and over his shoulder.

"We need to get to the hospital." He rushes to the front of the locker room.

Ember and Adri are standing there and both gasp as they see Vin running by them and out the door. Keeping close behind Vin, I follow him to the Hummer. We put Travis in the Hummer's backseat before Vin guns it to the hospital. I know Ember will get Adri there.

"What did he take?" Vin asks as he runs his second red light.

I lift the empty bottle I somehow have in my hand and read the label. "Vicodin. It was prescribed to his mother."

"Shit!" Vin hits the wheel, and we skid tires as he turns into the emergency.

After that, it's a mess of nurses and doctors. They quickly take him away, compressing his chest, as I stare after them helplessly. Vin and I stand there long after they disappear, just staring down the empty corridor.

A few hours later, a doctor comes into our waiting area and sits beside Vin. I don't like the look he has on his face and my stomach is tied so tight with knots.

"Travis has had a severe opioid overdose. We attempted a Naloxone treatment but…"

His voice fades and I rest my head back against the wall, letting my eyes shut. Adri's and Ember's cries are dim in the background, and I vaguely hear Vin cursing.

Why, Travis? Why did you decide to leave me?

Chapter Nineteen

Travis

There's always worse...

Chapter Twenty

I can't breathe.

My lungs burn as my eyes struggle to stay open. For three days, I've been lying in my bed, unable to move except to use the bathroom. Emmett drops by a few times a day to force me to eat, and Ember FaceTimes me every day. She talks and never forces me to say a word, her voice soothing the turmoil inside me.

I fear the times I succumb to exhaustion, when trying to keep my eyes open fails, and I see his face. It's as though my soul is being ripped from me all over again and I wake up feeling just as bereft as I did the first day in the hospital.

There's no color, there's no light, everything is monochrome and shrouded in darkness. Will I ever find the light again?

Nothing prepares someone for the day when they have to face their regrets, and I have so many. The time I wasted being angry at him burns through my chest with every waking moment. Years were flushed down the drain and all I want is to turn back time.

Love's threads held strong though, and even when I thought I would never be able to speak to him again, those threads only grew stronger.

Now they've snapped, the frayed edges floating somewhere in oblivion.

My front door opens and I turn my head toward my bedroom door, knowing who will appear in the next few moments. I'm supposed to be ready, wearing the black dress hanging on the back of my door, but my body refuses to cooperate.

The door swings open and when my eyes meet his ocean blues, I suck in my first full breath today. Emmett looks just as miserable as I do, but somehow he can function, and he finds the energy to make sure I do the same.

"Hey, baby," he whispers as he steps inside, the bags under his eyes growing darker every day. "You were supposed to be dressed."

I open my mouth to apologize, but no sound emerges.

"It's okay," he assures me as he comes toward the bed and pulls back the covers. "I'm here to help you."

Emmett

They say if it rains during a funeral the spirit is at peace. Well, I say, fuck that. I know for a fact anyone would rather be alive than dead, and if there are such things as spirits, why the fuck would they be at peace with death? Especially if they are young and have so much more life ahead of them. A life that would've been filled with love—so much fucking love—and family. I know there's no fucking peace to be found here in Whitsborough and there never will be.

The rain pounds down on top of my head, and I refuse the offer of Ember's umbrella. It's late autumn and the rain is so fucking cold it'll probably be snowing soon, but I don't care if I catch the flu, at least I'm alive.

The mud sucks around my polished dress shoes as we make our way to the mausoleum. Our family crypt is filling up quickly, and I clench my hands to my sides in anger. Why do good people die young? Why would any deity deem it right to take away the ones filled with light and good intentions while letting the festering rot of evil stay here? I know I will never get that answer.

When the time came to seal the crypt, we had a small service. We let it be just the four of us. We spoke about it and thought that's what he would've wanted, just us, his close family. That's all we've been doing, discussing and thinking about what he would want. I can't do it anymore though. I'm still too fucking angry with him. How dare he put me in this position? To think and do what I think he would want. He should be here to just say it!

I don't function much anymore. School has been a no go and I've neglected my family so much that I wouldn't be surprised if they sent me back to New York. Ember is trying to stay strong and keep us together, but I can see it wearing heavily on her soul. She doesn't sleep, and when she eats, it's not very much.

Vin is an empty shell. He gets by day to day, but his eyes look vacant and lost. Not too long after the incident, he admitted he knew about Travis and me. I felt relieved and immediately angry. We were meant to do that together. So fuck it, I told them all myself. I told them about our plans, how I fell in love with him and Adri both, and we somehow wanted it to work with the three of us. I even told Carm, who was mostly silent, but in the end, told me to do whatever it was to be happy.

Adri wasn't shocked. She said she could see what was between us and she was so happy to be loved by not just one—but two men. Ember was skeptical about it ever working but conceded she caught Travis and me kissing that one night. She was just worried we were denying ourselves and hurting Adri. It's fucking ironic the one thing we were scared about revealing was the easiest. Not that it makes a difference.

I also told Adri about the abuse Travis endured. I did it because I wanted her to understand why he fought against her love and how much he held deep inside. Especially how he felt unloved from the start. I told her about Ember killing his worthless father and mother, and then I explained Travis' love for her, but it wasn't enough because he felt like he wasn't enough. The hardest part was telling her about my plan and how I wanted all three of us to be together completely. Now everything is out in the open, and still, my chest is heavy with despair.

"He would've liked this," Ember murmurs into the cavernous crypt.

"Oh, yeah?" I turn to her, finally having enough. "Would he? And how do you know that? Do you have a direct link with him or something? Can you pass on a fucking message? Tell him I said 'Fuck you! Fuck you, Travis, for everything!'" I turn around and head for the entrance.

"Wait!" Ember calls out. "I'll take you home."

"No," I say. "I want to be alone."

"In the rain?" Adri exclaims.

"Yeah. I'll meet you at home." I leave them behind me.

If they want to stay in there with the dead, then so be it.

I've somehow ended up at the baseball field. The rain is now a torrential downpour, and my suit and hair are plastered to me like a second skin. I'm shaking from the cold air and my teeth have been chattering for a while, but I just couldn't stop until I got here.

I climb the bleachers and sit dead center, the best possible spot to watch someone play on this field. Then, I let it out. Everything that's been held inside for the past ten days.

I cry for the little boy who looked up to these bleachers every game and failed to see anyone who loved him.

I cry for the boy who needed this team so badly that he endured abuse to have it.

I cry for the child who lost his innocence because he craved any form of affection.

And lastly, I cry for the teenager who pushed through all of that and more to find something worth living for. I cry for him the most because he just never found it in the end. He was so broken inside, and even knowing he finally had a family wasn't enough to make him want to stay here.

I cry for Adri, who lost her lifelong love.

I cry for Vin, who lost the chance to really experience having a brother.

I cry for Ember, who just keeps losing people around her.

And then I cry for me.

I cry for myself because I wasn't capable of making him stay. I wasn't the anchor that kept his soul perched here. In the end, he just wanted to fly.

My phone vibrates in my pocket, and I just don't want to hear Ember asking where I am, so I ignore it. I'm alive, right? That's really all that matters, right? I feel bad, but I can't deal with any of them right now. I can't deal with the fierce love and need to protect. I want to feel this anguish and the internal ripping pain.

The phone keeps buzzing incessantly, and I pull it out of my pocket. It's a miracle it still works with all the rain. Vin's name flashes a few more times, then disappears. My home screen tells me I have thirty-six missed calls. Really? Are they that worried? I'm not offing myself, I just want to be alone. They'll just have to deal. I tuck the phone back into my pocket as it starts buzzing again.

Whatever.

I bow my head and lean forward, my elbows on my knees. Maybe coming here to this fucked-up town was a terrible choice. Carm was right, I should be there and training to become head of security. If I had stayed there, I wouldn't be feeling this shit. I wouldn't be feeling so goddamned lost. I could always come back and visit Ember and I would never cut her out of my life. Trent was right. We are each other's balance.

"Emmett." I hear my name softly intertwined with the drops of rain hitting the metal bleachers. My tears fall harder as I realize I may hear his voice everywhere now. My mind might fucking be twisted forever.

"Emmett, you fucking asshole!" What the fuck?

I look up to find Vin standing at the bottom of the bleachers.

His grown-out curls on the top of his head are wet and the leather jacket he's wearing is covered in rivulets of rain.

"Get the fuck down here!" he screams. "We need to get to the hospital!"

Running down the hospital corridor, my dress shoes slip on the tile from how thoroughly soaked they are. Please, God, please. I can't take another disappointment. I see Ember standing at the end of the hallway and she turns when she hears my frantic steps.

"Hurry!" She glowers at me. "I'm fucking knocking you out later for worrying me." She smacks me hard on the back of the head as I run by her and skid into the hospital room.

Sharla is standing by the window with tears running down her cheeks and she's hugging a sobbing Adri. They don't keep my attention long as my gaze swings to the bed and the figure lying there.

"Hey, stranger," he croaks and grins at me.

I rush to his bedside and pull him up into my arms, his scent enveloping me and the warmth of his body combating the chill in mine.

"Ten days. You've been gone for ten days!" He rubs my back while I sob into his neck.

"I'm so sorry," he hiccups. "Everything was dark, and I couldn't focus on the things that brought me light."

I grab his face in my hands and look into his crystal-green eyes. "I love you, Travis Greene."

Travis

I woke up to Sharla's voice as she was telling me about the funeral they were having for Sonja today. I don't know if Vin told her that Sonja was my mother or not, but she spoke like she knew the woman was important to me. She told me how she wanted to be there but came here to me instead. She wanted to speak to me and try to convince me to come back to her son, who needed me terribly. I heard it all as my consciousness tunneled toward the rasp of her voice and back to the light. I was happy to hear my family put my mother in our mausoleum, and they cared enough to send her off with love.

When I opened my eyes and looked into hers, she nearly fell over. I don't remember much after that. It was a rotating circle of nurses, doctors, and vital checks. I was told I was out for ten days, and they were worried I might have never come back. But I did, and I will always be thankful for Sharla and her voice.

Not too long after that, Ember and Adri hovered over me. Adri's face and the love in her eyes helped soak warmth through my broken heart. A piece of the puzzle that made up my light locked into place with her embrace. I was just waiting for one more, the hardest piece to attain, and seemed to still be the most difficult.

"Travis, why?" Adri asks as tears flow down her face.

"I just lost myself in the dark," I say as my voice cracks, unable to explain it any more than that.

"I've been there." Ember reaches out to touch my face. "I'm sorry we didn't see it."

"I didn't let you." I shake my head.

Adri goes to stand with Sharla at the window and my heart

sinks as she continues to cry, hating that I caused it. Ember picks up her ringing phone and barks out Vin's name as she moves outside my hospital door.

Then I hear his footsteps. I know they're his because he's embedded so deep inside me. I know everything about him; his scent, how he sounds, the energy surrounding him, and the way my love coats him like a blanket. He's so ingrained inside me that I don't know where I end and where he begins. My heart pounds and the machines I'm hooked up to beep frantically. I keep my eyes on the door, anticipating the moment I see him.

He doesn't disappoint as he skids into the room. Emmett's wearing a suit—with a tie—and his hair is a mess and plastered to his head. He's completely soaked, like he ran through the rain to get here.

"Hey, stranger," I say to him. Did he run through the rain? I open my mouth to ask him, but he's quick as he wraps me up in his arms. He's freezing cold and the skin on his cheeks feels like ice.

"Ten days. You've been gone for ten days!" he cries into my neck. *He's crying.*

"I'm so sorry," I murmur. "Everything was so dark, and I couldn't focus on the things that brought me light."

His icy hands come up and press into my cheeks, his beautiful eyes looking into mine. "I love you, Travis Greene."

I don't think, I just say what I've known for a long time. "I love you, Emmett Torres."

We go back to hugging each other as a small sniff sounds to my left. I look and find Adri standing there watching us with a small smile on her face. It all hits me at once, and I'm not sure how to explain everything. Emmett must feel the tension in my hold because he looks up and at her. Then, to my shock, he extends his arm out and she comes down to snuggle into us both.

"I love you guys," she says through her tears.

"I told her," Emmett explains. "Everything."

When my eyes meet hers, the smile on her face widens. "Can we really just start our lives together now? All three of us?"

"I love you," I tell her, feeling tears run down my cheeks. "I always have."

"I know," she replies smugly and curls back into me.

The broken pieces of my soul meld together in their embrace, solidifying what was once broken.

"Bro?"

Both Emmett and Adri stand up and part, and I'm faced with an exhausted and very sad Vin. His eyes are boring into mine as sadness radiates from his body in thick waves.

"I'm so sorry." My chest caves in as my eyes begin to water. I'll be apologizing for the rest of my life if that's what it takes to make him trust me again.

"Everything is okay now," he croaks out as a single tear slips down his cheek.

I don't get a chance to continue speaking to him before my doctor comes in with a stern look on his face.

"Travis Greene, coma patient due to an overdose of Vicodin." He looks up from the paper in his hands. "We were almost ready to prepare for your funeral."

"Are you fucking serious?!" Ember exclaims as she rushes toward the doctor. "You watch your motherfucking mouth!" Vin grabs her before she can touch the doctor, but she's definitely putting the fear of God into him.

He clears his throat and takes a step back, his eyes wider and filled with apprehension as he looks from Ember then back to me. "You'll have to be placed in a mandatory thirty-day program." His eyes slide to Ember again as she glares at him from the circle of Vin's arms. "We have placed you on suicide watch and we can't release you before those thirty days are up."

"Like fuck you won't!" Ember screams.

"Wait,"—I hold my hand up—"I want to stay and take part in the program." Ember deflates in Vin's arms with a choked sob, her head hanging in defeat. This can't be easy on her because Ember takes every hardship this family endures personally.

"I'll go prepare a room in that ward." The doctor leaves in a hurry, giving a wide berth around Ember.

"Travis." Ember breaks away easily from Vin, just proving she let him stop her. "We can take care of you at home. We miss you and love you." Her voice cracks as she comes closer to the bed, her heart breaking further.

"I know. I'm sorry I did this to you guys, but my problems are deep, and I need help to heal. I can't do it by myself, and I need professional help." She crawls up in the bed beside me and I kiss her temple.

"I missed you," she mutters into my neck as her tears heat my skin. It's rare that Ember cries and it's breaking my heart that I did this to her, to them. I'm ashamed I tried to take the easy way out. I should've fought my demons and continued to want to live.

I pull her in against my chest and kiss the top of her head. "I need to be better for my family and for my... relationship."

"Your throuple," she whispers.

"My what?" I ask as she pulls back to look up into my face, her cheeks glistening with tears.

"Throuple. A three-person couple."

Emmett told everyone. It's a relief, another burden lifted from my shoulders, and I'm so thankful for him. It's relieving to know we'll be accepted and loved despite our unconventional relationship.

"Thanks for putting Sonja in the family's crypt." Her hand reaches up to stroke my cheek as she nods.

"She was family. It's where she belonged." Her answer is simple and straight from her heart, just like everything Ember ever says or does.

Chapter Twenty-One

9 Months Later…

"Is his speech long? Because it's as hot as a cougar looking for a good time out here," Emmett groans from his seat beside me.

"Just be happy you graduated, shit-for-brains, and listen to your boyfriend's valedictorian speech," I growl at him. I'm always a hair's breadth away from smacking him.

"It's long, by the way," Adri whispers between our heads from the row behind us.

"Ugh…" Emmett whines and drops lower in his seat. I'm going to smack her too.

"Drink this and shut the fuck up," Vin grits out from between his teeth, slapping a flask to Emmett's chest.

Yeah, the graduation ceremony is supposed to be seated alphabetically, but we do as we please with little resistance. So we decided to all sit together. Now I regret that decision as I watch my twin slugging back on what I know is potent whiskey. Fucking Vin.

This speech really is long though, and the fucking heat is messing with the curls I tamed earlier. As Travis drones on about being successful in life and all that jazz, I lean forward and snatch the flask from Vin just as Emmett hands it back. We put Emmett between us because he's like an unruly child sometimes.

Carm should be here somewhere with Trent, as well as Adri's driver and cook, and Travis has a cousin who came from Ukraine to watch him graduate. Emmett, Adri, and Travis took a trip about six months ago to find his family in Ukraine. He found out his grandmother had passed, but he gained a couple aunts and uncles and a whole slew of cousins. Once the results of the autopsy for Sonja came back, it was determined Christina had indeed murdered her. Not only did the knife have Christina's prints, but her blood was also under Sonja's nails. Travis felt he needed to find his family and confess everything. His fresh path in life is to live lighter and not hold everything inside.

"Did he have a fucking Red Bull for breakfast?" Vin mutters as Travis' speech carries on.

"No more Red Bull in the house," I retort and take a swig out of the flask.

"Ha!" Emmett slaps his knee. "You fuckers feel my pain now."

"Give me some of that." Adri snakes her hand between us, motioning for the flask.

Emmett grabs onto her hand before I can give her the flask and kisses her palm. They're cute, I'll admit it, and I'm so happy they've found love with each other. She smiles and it grows wider when she finally gets the flask.

Adri has permanently moved in with us when her parents decided not to come home at all this year, and we are all finally together under one roof. It feels right and exactly how it's supposed to be. Funny thing? Her parents haven't even checked in with her in almost a year. Not that she cares, but I do. They've been added to my list of people to look into. Something feels off, more than them buying a baby from Talia.

People clap and whistle, and the four of us look at each other before standing in unison to clap and cheer for Travis. Not that we heard much, but we love him anyway.

"He really thought of that much to say about the degenerates in this school?" Vin grumbles, and Emmett chokes on his mouthful of whiskey.

"I hope he doesn't ask us about it later," Adri replies.

I snort and push past Vin and Emmett to meet up with Travis in the center of the field. He looks handsome in his robe and the valedictorian stole hanging over his shoulders.

"Impressive speech!" I call out when he sees me.

"Fuck off." He chuckles as we all gather around him. "You guys didn't listen to shit."

"But judging by everyone else's faces, it was fucking bomb." Emmett nods like the fucking asshole he is.

"Guys!" Charles runs up and we each pull him in for a hug. "Everyone's gathering at General Grady's tonight. You in?"

"Fucking right we are!" Emmett exclaims as he wraps his arm around Travis' neck. "Husbands, lock up your wives!" He gyrates his hips.

"Fuck, you two are too similar," Adri says to me while shaking her head. "Sometimes it's like I'm dating you."

"Bet you like that, huh?" I wink at her.

"Tonight is going to be so dope." Charles fist pumps the air and runs back off to fuck knows where.

"I'm going to go see Katerina and drive her to the airport." Travis laughs as he kisses both Emmett and Adri. "I'll see you at home."

At first, their relationship was a hot topic, but eventually, everyone at school just accepted it and moved on. I may have violently threatened that consensus on a lot of the people but whatever, it worked.

"My twin little demons have graduated from high school." Carm's deep tenor cuts through the noise. "Whatever will they do with their lives now, Trent?"

"Oh, I don't know, cause destruction and mayhem?" Trent laughs.

"That's all Ember," Emmett retorts. "With my grades, I'm going to the stars!"

"He means to give tarot card readings and tell people about their zodiacs," I deadpan.

Everyone laughs except Emmett and me. He narrows his eyes on me and steps into my space. "Say that again, little sister."

"You don't know that you're older," I argue.

"Say it again," he grits out.

"You have shit for brains and barely graduated by the skin of your teeth. The only stars you'll see are the ones forming constellations when you give star readings." He bends down with a growl and throws me over his shoulder. I scream and slap his ass at the same time as he slaps mine.

"Emmett! Put me down!" I yell.

"No! Not until you tell me I can be an astronaut!"

"Fine!" I laugh. "You're a space cadet!"

Everyone laughs harder and Emmett twirls us quickly on the spot. My hair flies out and I close my eyes to keep the nausea at bay.

"I'll just make you puke!" he says with a laugh as he spins. He finally stops after a moment and we both tumble to the ground. "Ugh! Now I want to puke too," he groans, his skin looking a little green.

"See? Shit for brains." I laugh and kiss his cheek.

"All right, kids." Carm huffs at our antics but his eyes shine with adoration. "We gotta get going. We have somewhere to be tomorrow morning."

We give both Trent and him hugs before watching their very large retreating backs.

"You think those two…" I trail off.

"Nah." Emmett laughs, then shoves my shoulder. "They're manwhores."

"You question every set of dudes you see now." Adri laughs.

"I'm still forming my gaydar," I explain as I tap my temple.

"We should get going too," Vin says, coming up behind me and wrapping his arms around my waist. "We got to get something done."

Right, we do. We say our goodbyes and promise to be home in time to hit the bar. Vin takes my hand and interlaces our fingers.

His large hand encompassing mine always feels like I'm protected and loved. Adri asked me a few weeks ago how Vin and I manage not to fight because we both have strong alpha attitudes and clashing personalities. From the outside, we don't even act compatible. He's quiet, broody, and intense. I'm loud, opinionated, and downright crass. But we never butt heads, we move in sync and our energies mesh perfectly. I didn't have an answer for her because I don't fucking know. What I know is, I love him, every single thing about him; good, bad, perfect, and imperfect. I love every single thing.

Vin lets me breathe. He doesn't mind sitting on the sidelines and letting me run the show. He gets off on the power I exude and comes back looking for more. I love his quiet strength and knowing it would take next to nothing for him to pop off on anyone who even looked at me wrong, but why don't we fight? It could be all of these things, or it could be that our souls were made of the same dark material.

Adri and Travis bicker often, it's their thing, and Emmett sits back and watches. He's a creep about it sometimes, but whatever works for them.

We get to Hummy and Vin opens my door. *Chivalrous motherfucker.* I get in and toss my robe and hat into the backseat. I dressed in all black today for this very reason. My black skinny jeans—ripped at the knees—paired with a black lace tank and thigh-high boots. All black signature Ember killing clothes.

"So, we're just talking to him, right?" Vin asks as he gets into the vehicle, his green eyes roaming over my body as my skin heats.

"Let's see how it goes." I shrug.

"Em," he implores. "These aren't my blood-splatter clothes." I take in what he has on and suck my bottom lip into my mouth. He's wearing a pair of khaki slacks and a black dress top, rolled to his elbows. His top few buttons are undone to showcase his hard upper chest. Then, of course, in Vin style, he has on a pair of tanned Timberland boots.

"Vin." I widen my eyes at him. "Move this vehicle before I make you bleed on your clothes, then fuck you like I hate you."

"Baby girl…" He chuckles. "Was that meant to be a threat?" He grabs at his growing erection, and I grin. He's always loved my dark side.

"Can we get this over with?" I *tsk*. "I promise to let you fuck me in the ass later."

"Fine," he huffs and pulls out of the school parking lot.

These past nine months have been quiet, quiet for me anyway. Yes, I've fought in the cage a few times, but not to the death since the incident with the knife. Carm says he has it on good authority that Wade set it up. So I've already set a plan into motion to deal with that. I've continued to teach my MMA classes each Sunday and really enjoy looking like a normal, law-abiding citizen. *Looking* being the operative word.

I'm still the Head of Toronto and I've commissioned three times in the last nine months to make people disappear. A rogue gangbanger who was selling meth to kids, a Peeping Tom who upped his game to raping single women, and finally, a woman luring teenage girls into a black-market sex ring. Now, it is time to turn my sights back to Whitsborough, and I made tonight the beginning.

I've been doing my research between tutoring my brother, keeping an eye on Travis, fulfilling my commissions, and teaching classes. I need to peel back the glossy finish on Whitsborough and dig out the rot underneath. Everything is in place for tonight, just how I planned. Nothing can go wrong.

Vin pulls onto the street, and we slowly pass all the single-level bungalows with tire swings or children's bikes on the front lawn. They're middle-class income homes, still richer than what I was ever used to before moving here. We stop outside of number two eighty-four and see his car in the drive. A few lights are on, but mostly it looks quiet.

"The wife and kids?" Vin inquires.

"They won an all-expenses-paid trip to Disneyland. One adult, two kids." I snort.

"Good." He nods with a grin. "Let's get this shit done. I want to get shit-faced tonight."

We get out of the Hummer and walk up the path to the front door, hand in hand, looking like a well-dressed couple here for a visit, nothing out of the ordinary. I even ring the fucking doorbell and wait for the slow piece of shit to open his door. The door opens, and we are greeted by a friendly-looking man in his early to mid-forties. His temples are gray, giving him that George Clooney look.

"Yes?" He looks between Vin and me curiously.

"Andrew Cox?" I say in my sweet-as-sugar voice. "We finally meet. My name is Ember. I answered your ad for the live-in nanny?"

"Right." He smiles and then looks at Vin.

"He drove me here and would like to be present for the interview. Safety and all." I flutter my eyelashes like an innocent young lady coming for a first job interview.

"Sure." He shrugs and opens his door wider to let us in. *Big mistake, asshole.*

We stand in his foyer as he shuts the door. Then he gives me a slow perusal as Vin tenses up beside me. He may just want to make him bleed after all. Fuck the clothes.

He leads us to his dining table and offers us drinks. I decline and Vin just doesn't reply. He's feeling testy about the old man's pervy looks.

"I would like to have someone start right away—"

"That's nice," I cut him off. "But I'm not here for the fucking interview. My name is Ember Craven."

"Craven?" His eyes widen. "Related to Jack Craven?"

"Grandfather," Vin answers as a slow smile hits his sexy mouth, making his dimple pop.

"W—what are you d—doing here?" He flusters, fear in his eyes. Interesting.

"We're here to tell you you're resigning from your principal position, effective immediately," I state as I cross my arms on the table.

"That's not happening." He straightens in his seat and shakes his head, fear still lingering in his features. "It's this household's only source of income."

"The test has determined… that was a lie," I say in my best Maury Povich voice. Vin snorts from beside me and I grin. At least one person is enjoying my humor tonight. "Listen." I lean forward, placing my hands on the table. "We know about your preferences."

"Preferences?" His chin quakes with the effort to keep up his farce as his eyes widen. If they widen anymore, they're going to pop right out of his head. Something I wouldn't mind watching.

"Yes, you know, darker urges." I wave my hand in the air. "Here, I'll give you an example. Take me, for instance. I like blood, especially when it's pouring out of someone's dying body. What I like even more is when I've inflicted the wounds myself. Usually with this." I pull out my knife from my boot and point it toward him. Yep, his eyes are going to pop right out of his skull. "Nothing? Okay, how about this? Robert Greene had a similar look in his eyes right before I made him cut open his wrists. Or wait!" I press the tip of the knife to my bottom lip. "Coach Halbert lost a certain appendage because of this knife." I grin, then lick the blade. "Mmm-mm."

"You're the Black Slaughter." He shudders as his body begins to tremble.

"Oh!" I slap my hand on the table, making him jump as my chest fills with warmth. I've been named. "I like that!"

"Fuck, they've given her a name," Vin mutters, the groan in his tone clear.

"Who calls me this?" I ask Andrew curiously.

"Others in this… group." He looks back and forth between Vin and me. "We knew someone was slowly killing us."

"Probably helps that Moore is your bestie, huh?" I smile at him, showing all my sharp white teeth.

"He has let us know about a few details, yes." He nods as he links his hands together to try and hide the quaking. "I will do anything. You want me to quit? Done. You want me to stop my other activities? Done. Just don't hurt me. I have a family."

"Probably would be better off without you, considering you like watching kids their ages," Vin interjects, his voice rough and dark. Sexy as fuck.

"No!" he loudly refuses. "I don't hurt my kids."

I get up and stand next to him. His trembling increases until he's a shaking mess.

"Let's take a finger," I say to Vin as I bite down on my bottom lip. "Just one."

"Em," Vin warns.

"Wait." Andrew moves his clasped hands to his lap, his eyes shining with terror as he looks up at me. "Give me a chance to change."

"Fine." I twirl around and go to stand by Vin. "But only because you weren't harming the children at your school. Watching and distributing naked kids in videos is just as bad. You will resign and you will cease that activity. If you don't, I will know and, Andrew, I really want to come back here and finish this. So, please fuck up."

"You won't be back." He shakes his head. "I promise."

"He won't stop," Vin states as we're walking back to the Hummer.

"I'm counting on it." I grin.

They filled the bar to capacity tonight, jam-packed with the graduating class of Precious Blood Academy. The music is a deep thrum of hip-hop and the alcohol looks to be flowing smoothly.

"If another motherfucker checks out your legs, I'm going postal," Vin growls and pulls me back into his chest.

I'm showcasing them tonight in a pair of short leather shorts and strappy heels. My top is white lace and shows off my tan spectacularly. I straightened my hair and pulled it up into a high ponytail, the ends reaching to my mid-back. Vin has on a black sleeveless top and a dark blue pair of baggy jeans. He has a tied black bandana around his head and his permanent scruff on his cheeks make him look dark and scary. Just my type.

"Ember!" Adri slams into me, her arms wrapping around both Vin and me. "Everyone is here, including the dogs."

That's what she began calling Marlana and her crew at the

beginning of the school year.

"Oh, yeah?" I smile.

"Yep." She nods her head drunkenly. "Shay said hi though."

Shay.

She's another one I'll have to deal with soon. She's been carrying around a dark secret and it'll soon be her time to spill, but I'm not thinking about that tonight. Tonight I'm having fun.

"Come to our table!" She grabs my hand. "Travis has the beer on refill all night."

Vin and I follow her to a table near the back of the bar. The karaoke stage is empty tonight and a few girls from school are up there trying to look sexy as they sloppily dance around.

Looks like the guys pushed together a few tables so we could all sit together, and they're easily the loudest in here.

"Sister!" Emmett yells and jumps up out of his chair, knocking it to the floor. "Let's get fucked!"

"Done and done," Vin says and laughs.

"Gross." Emmett's face screws up. "We're already so far ahead of you two. What took so long?"

"Business," I say with a shrug of my shoulders.

"Ember!" Charles whistles before handing Vin and me a beer. "You are fucking smoking!"

"Watch it, Chuck," Vin warns.

"What have I missed?" Travis says as he comes up behind us.

"You just getting here?" I ask him.

"Yeah, I went to see Sharla." Travis has been spending a lot of time with Sharla since she was the first one he saw when he came out of his coma. Their closeness is something he needed, a true mother figure. "She says you need to mow the lawn tomorrow." He claps Vin on the back.

"Great," Vin moans.

A few hours later and multiple shots of tequila—thanks to Adri—I'm feeling fucking fine. Adri jumps up and runs over to the DJ.

"What is she planning?" Travis asks while checking out her bent-over ass.

"Some type of debauchery." I wave my hand.

Brra, ta, ta, tat…

Nicki Minaj's "Megatron" fills the bar's interior.

"Come on, bitch!" Adri screams and grabs my hand. "It's our turn on stage."

"Fuck yes!" I yell and jump to my feet.

Before Vin or Travis can grab us, we jump up on the stage and dance on each other. The guys cheer and Vin looks murderous, but both Adri and I tip our heads back and laugh.

I will hold all these good memories close to my heart because I know things are going to get dark and murky soon. *I'm* going to get dark soon, and after everything I've done and everything I am about to do, the road to redemption seems long and endless.

Epilogue

"You know the rules," Travis snaps at Adri as he pins her to the wall with his hand around her throat. "Nobody is allowed to see this ass but Emmett and me."

Adri's eyes roll to the back of her head and her tongue licks at her bottom lip in arousal. Fuck, I'm aroused too. I love when Travis becomes all possessive and rough, so does Adri.

"You can't tell me what to do, Travis," she pants. "If I want to shake my ass on stage, I will."

"Wrong answer," he growls and throws her over his shoulder. Adri screams and giggles when she's suddenly thrown on top of the mattress beside me. "Emmett," Travis says. "Let's teach our girl a lesson."

I flip her over and prop her ass in the air, in perfect view for Travis, then I flip her skirt up and around her waist. Her G-string is soaked through, and both Travis and I groan with approval.

"Take that off," he orders, pointing at the G-string.

"Yes, sir." I grin and pull it down to her knees.

Adri moans and the scent of her arousal makes me breathe in deep. I can never get enough of her. As he bends to take off his pants, I watch the muscles in his arms flex. Then he tears off his shirt as a breath gets trapped in my throat. I get caught up in watching him and Adri wiggles, stealing my attention back to her.

"Stop that." I slap her ass.

She moans again and Travis looks at me with a wink. "I don't think she's learning anything."

"Nothing," I agree.

Travis reaches out with both hands and grabs her ass cheeks, then he spreads them open. We both take in a good eyeful of her juices and groan. Travis lets go, lowers his boxers, and I watch as his thick cock springs out. I wrap my hand around him and pump slowly as he reaches out and gives Adri a good spank on her ass. She whimpers and then wiggles, looking for more. Insatiable.

I lean forward and lick him from tip to base, and Travis moans before laying another smack to Adri's ass. This time, she squeals and then moans into the bed. The noises drive me on, and I suck him into the back of my throat.

"Fuck," he groans as Adri tries to watch from over her shoulder.

Travis slaps her ass again. "Keep your head down," he demands.

She growls in response, and he slaps her again, her ass turning a nice red as her juices leak down her thigh.

"I think I'm done teaching her a lesson," I mumble and turn my attention to her glistening pussy.

"Weak." Travis snickers, but I really don't give a shit. For this pussy, I am completely weak.

I smother my face into her folds and listen to her mewls of pleasure. When I fasten my lips around her clit and suck, she screams my name. Travis gives her another whack on the ass and tells her to shush as I laugh with my tongue shoved as far as it can go inside her.

When I come up for air, Travis pulls Adri up and frees her from the rest of her clothing. Then he lies on the bed and pulls her on top of him as I remove my pants, watching as she slowly sinks down over him.

My cock is throbbing, begging to be inside of her.

"Hurry, Emmett," she pants while grinding over Travis. "I don't want to wait any longer."

I open up the bedside table drawer and pull out our bottle of lube, smearing it over my cock and then all over her rear hole. Adri drops forward with her hands on Travis' chest, giving me easier access. Lining myself up, I slowly sink into her tight asshole, feeling Travis through the thin membrane. The three of us moan in unison, and Travis and I pick up our usual rhythm. One in, the other out. He's the first to detonate, so I lift her off him quickly and pull out of her asshole. Then I quickly ram into her pussy just so I can feel him and her together. It's one of my favorite things. The sounds of both their cum mixed and sucking around my cock reverberates around our room. Suddenly, I feel Travis' fingers at my ass, and he inserts two inside me quick and rough. Within seconds, I'm coming as stars dance along my vision.

Sex with the three of us is always like this. Downright filthy and raw.

Instead of cleaning off, Travis fills the bath as I pick up a languid Adri.

"Don't let me drown," she murmurs on our way into the

bathroom, already half asleep.

"You got it." I chuckle and kiss her forehead.

"I was so fucked last night," Travis moans from the counter as he pours his coffee.

"I got fucked last night." Ember smirks.

"Yeah, you did." Vin nods.

"I was double fucked last night," Adri mutters as she sips her coffee.

Ember gets this far-off look in her eyes and I narrow my gaze on her. "Don't imagine it." She shrugs at me. "Don't imagine it!" I yell at her as I panic.

"What?" She throws her hands up. "I remove your heads when I do."

"It's still weird," I tell her as I roll my eyes.

"Actually,"—she waves between me and Travis—"you both just morph into Vin. Then I have two of him."

"You couldn't handle two of my dicks." Vin chuckles.

"That's true." Her eyes widen in fear. "I'd die. Death by double massive dicks."

Adri chokes on her coffee and laughs while Travis and I laugh along.

"Looks like Gerald is giving me a year to sort out what I want to do with my father's company," Travis informs us. "It'll give us time to investigate what Robert was into."

"That's good news." Ember hums as she sips her coffee. "We need the extra time."

"Your mom is pulling up the driveway." Adri lets Vin know as she looks down at the footage on her phone.

"What? Really?" He gets up and starts for the front door. Sharla doesn't usually show up unannounced.

I hear her come in and follow Vin back into the kitchen. Sharla looks very professional today in a black pinstripe pantsuit and her hair coiffed to the side.

"Hey, kiddos." She smiles as she comes into the kitchen.

Travis comes around and gives her a hug and kisses her cheek. "Hey, Ma."

She pats his cheek and smiles. "Hi, baby boy. I'm here because I had a lengthy conversation with Travis last week, and I remembered something that may be of importance."

"What's up?" Ember asks her.

"Debra and Scott started renting out your grandparents' home about fifteen years ago."

"Yeah, I know. I met the people." Ember sips her coffee again, her eyes on Sharla over the rim. They've been working on their relationship, but it's clear they're still not completely accepting of one another.

"Your grandparents had a lot of junk in that house that Deb just didn't want to go through. So they packed it up and put it in storage."

"Yeah," Ember replies, placing the cup on the table. "I pay the bill each month."

"Your mother's stuff is in there from when she ran away abruptly. She had journals and pictures." Her eyes widen on Ember. "I think you may find a lot of answers in there."

"I didn't think of that." Ember looks shocked. "Thank you, Sharla."

"No problem. You kids need to bathe. You smell and look like a brewery." She shakes her head and leaves the house.

"Road trip?" Ember looks at me.

"Yeah."

"Be back in time for this afternoon!" Travis calls out as Ember and I get up to leave, eager to learn more about our family.

"Okay!" we call out in unison.

Travis is going to have his house demolished today. He says maybe one day we'll build our house for the three of us and our family there. For now though, we're good living with Ember, and the thought of that house standing just pisses him off.

I don't know why Ember said it was a road trip, because we arrived at the storage unit in less than twenty minutes. Although, Ember driving Shelby means we get anywhere in half the time.

The storage units are just rows and rows of garages with padlocks sealing them shut.

"What number is it?" I ask her.

"Four forty-five."

We walk the aisles until we find the one we're looking for, then stop just outside of it and stare at the door. I'm feeling trepidation, and from her hesitation, I think Ember is as well.

"Let's do this." She stalks forward and unlocks the padlock with a key before throwing open the door, and we both gasp at the amount of stuff in here. There's some old-looking furniture, totes of what look to be dishes, and piles of books. They have my interest. I fucking love books and so does Travis.

"We'll look through those after," she says, following where my eyes have landed. "Let's find Mom's stuff first."

We pick through everything and climb over plastic-covered couches and antique-looking tables. Finally, in the far right back corner, we see boxes labeled 'Rebecca.'

"Grab a few and let's bring them out into the light."

We both pull out the six boxes and three totes to the front of the unit and then sit down to go through it all.

"This is a bunch of girls' crap," I mutter as I go through her stuffed unicorns and Barbie dolls.

"Here!" Ember exclaims as she opens a tote. I hurry over to her and look inside. "These are notebooks and diaries."

We each grab a few and begin skimming through it. I somehow ended up with her elementary ones and it's a bunch of nonsense about hating her sister and the girls at school. When I get to the last one though, I read a few things that sound disturbing.

'Today Daddy watched me while I had a bath.'

'Today Daddy made me brush my hair repeatedly without a top on.'

"Ember…" I mutter. "I found some weird shit."

"Me too." She sounds pissed as I continue to read over the diary. "I have a full account of what Robert and Halbert did to our mother," she growls. "Apparently, there is a VHS somewhere they used to blackmail her father."

"Let me guess," I mumble, "he didn't care."

"He didn't believe her!" she exclaims. "Called her a—"

"—slut," I finish.

'Today Daddy slapped me really hard on my bum and called me a slut.'

Ember gets up and pulls out two totes that say 'Dad's office' on them, but I just can't put down the diary as shit gets more and more depraved.

'Daddy says one day he and I will run away together.'

I'm feeling nauseous and throw the book back into the box. I can't believe the amount of evil that has been inside Whitsborough throughout the generations.

"Emmett." Ember's voice cuts through my thoughts. "I found something."

I get up and move to her side. She's looking through a large, leather-bound book, the inside filled with documents and notes. "What is it?"

"Our father didn't come here to check on his investment." She sounds like she's far-off. "Our grandfather hired him to come here and help him fake his death so he could go somewhere else."

"You think…" I begin.

"Raph didn't do it then." She shakes her head. "Something must have happened. But our father admitted to killing them after… but what if he didn't?"

"Where was our grandfather going to go?" I ask, but deep down, I think I already know the answer.

"New York."

For all book updates and social platforms, check out
my website

C.A. Rene lives in Toronto, Canada with her family, where most of the year varies from chilly to frigid. Most days you'll find her wrapped in her many blankets in bed while reading or writing her next dark, twisted story.
Her stories boast of inclusivity and refusal to be conformed in any small box. Writing across genres is a hobby and drinking wine is a must... Or coffee ... with a splash of Baileys.

Also by C.A. Rene

The Whitsborough Chronicles

Through the Pain

Into Darkness

Finding the Light

To Redemption

The Whitsborough Progenies

Ivy's Venom

Carmelo's Malice

Saxon's Distortion

Gabriel's Deception

Desecrated Duet

Desecrated Flesh

Desecrated Essence

The Reaped Series

The Reaper Incarnate

Hunting the Reaper

Claiming the Reaper

Hail Mary Duet

Blue 42

Red Zone

Fusion Core

Tension

Release

Steel Dragons MC

Dragon Slayer

Dragon Strife

Dragon Scorch

Hell's March MC Duet

Hell's Viper

TBA

Second Chance Standalones

Fighting the Tide